Lewis Alfred Henry

The boss, and how he
came to rule New York

The Boss

"You are to give me the Million at once." Page 178.

The Boss.

The Boss

And How He Came To Rule New York

By ALFRED HENRY LEWIS

Author of "PEGGY O'NEAL," "THE PRESIDENT,"
"WOLFVILLE DAYS," Etc.

THE GREGG PRESS / RIDGEWOOD, N.J.

First published in 1903 by A.L. Burt Company
Republished in 1967 by
The Gregg Press Incorporated
171 East Ridgewood Avenue
Ridgewood, New Jersey, U.S.A.
Copyright© 1967 by
The Gregg Press, Inc.

Library of Congress Catalog Card Number: 67-29272

Printed in United States of America

AMERICANS
IN
FICTION

INTRODUCTION BY PROFESSOR CLARENCE GOHDES
Editor of *American Literature* Magazine

In the domain of literature the play may once have been the chief abstract and chronicle of the times, but during the nineteenth and twentieth centuries the novel has usurped the chief place in holding the mirror up to the homely face of society. On this account, if for no other, the Gregg Press series of reprints of American fiction merits the attention of all students of Americana and of librarians interested in building up adequate collections dealing with the social and literary history of the United States. Most of the three score and ten novels or volumes of short stories included in the series enjoyed considerable fame in their day but have been so long out of print as to be virtually unobtainable in the original editions.

Included in the list are works by writers not presently fashionable in critical circles — but nevertheless well known to literary historians — among them Joel Chandler Harris, Harriet Beecher Stowe, Thomas Bailey Aldrich, and William Gilmore Simms. A substantial element in the list consists of authors who are known especially for their graphic portrayal of a particular American setting, such as Gertrude Atherton (California), Arlo Bates (Boston), Alice Brown (New England), Edward Eggleston (Indiana), Mary Wilkins Freeman (New England), Henry B. Fuller (Chicago), Richard M. Johnston (Georgia), James Lane Allen (Kentucky), Mary N. Murfree (Tennessee), and Thomas Nelson Page (Virginia). There is even a novel by Frederic Remington, one of the most popular painters of the Western cowboy and Indian — and another, an impressive minor classic on the early mining region of Colorado, from the pen of Mary Hallock Foote. The professional student of American literature will rejoice in the opportunity afforded by the collection to extend his reading of fiction belonging to what is called the "local-color movement" — a major current in the development of the national belles-lettres.

Among the titles in the series are also a number of famous historical novels. Silas Weir Mitchell's *Hugh Wynne* is one of the best fictional treatments of the American Revolution. John Esten Cooke is the foremost Southern writer of his day who dealt with the Civil War. The two books by Thomas Dixon are among the most famous novels on the Reconstruction Era, with sensational disclosures of the original Ku Klux Klan in action. They supplied the grist for the first great movie "spectacular" — *"The Birth of a Nation* (1915).

Paul Leicester Ford's *The Honorable Peter Stirling* is justly ranked among the top American novels which portray American politics in action — a subject illuminated by other novelists in the Gregg list — A. H. Lewis, Frances H. Burnett, and Alice Brown, for example. Economic problems are forcefully put before the reader in works by Aldrich, Mrs. Freeman, and John Hay, whose novels illustrate the ominous concern over the early battles between labor and capital. From the sweatshops of Eastern cities in which newly arrived immigrants toiled for pittances, to the Western mining camps where the laborers packed revolvers, the working class of the times enters into various other stories in the Gregg list. The capitalist class, also, comes in for attention, with an account of a struggle for the ownership of a railroad in Samuel Merwin's *The Short-Line War* and with the devastating documentation of the foibles of the newly rich and their wives in the narratives of David Graham Phillips. It was Phillips whose annoying talent for the exposure of abuses led Theodore Roosevelt to put the term "muck-raker" into currency.

While it is apparent that local-color stories, the historical novel, and the economic novel have all been borne in mind in choosing the titles for this important series of reprints, it is evident that careful consideration has also been given to treatments of various minority elements in the American population. The Negro, especially, but also the Indian, the half-breed, Creoles, Cajuns — and even the West Coast Japanese — appear as characters in various of these novels or volumes of short stories and sketches. Joel Chandler Harris's *Free Joe* will open the eyes of readers who know that author solely as the creator of humorous old Uncle Remus. And there is a revelatory volume of dialect tales, written by a Negro author, *The Conjure Woman* by Charles W. Chesnutt.

In literary conventions and the dominating attitudes toward life, the works in the Gregg series range from the adventurous romance illustrated so well by Mayne Reid or the polite urbanity of Owen Wister to the mordant irony of Kate Chopin and the grimmer realism of Joseph Kirkland's own experiences on bloody Civil War battlefields or the depressing display of New York farm life by Harold Frederic. In short, the series admirably illustrates the general qualities of the fiction produced in the United States during the era covered, just as it generously mirrors the geographical regions, the people, and the problems of the times.

TO
GEORGE HORACE LORIMER

THE WORD OF PREFACE

It should be said in the beginning that these memoirs will not be written by my own hand. I have no skill of pen and ink, and any relation of length would be beyond my genius. The phrasing would fall to be disreputable, and the story itself turn involved and to step on its own toes, and mayhap with the last of it to fall flat on its face, unable to proceed at all. Wherefore, as much for folk who are to read as for my own credit, I shall have one who makes print his trade to write these pages for me.

Nor shall I advance apology in this. If I plan for the construction of a house, I call to my aid architects and artisans in wood and stone and iron. I am not disgraced for that out of my own hands and head I do not throw up the walls and lay on the roof of the edifice. Why, then, when now I am about the paper-telling of my life, should I blush because I am driven to seek the aid of him who makes an inkpot his profession? I am like a lumber-yard or a stone-quarry, and full of the raw material for this work; but I require one drilled of saw and chisel to carry off the business of my house-building.

It would be the thing natural, should you who open these leaves put the question of motive and ask why, when now I am retired, and should be cautious with my threescore years, I come forth with confidences which, aside from the mere sorrow of them, are like to prove less for my honor than I might wish. Why is it that I who have removed my loneliness and my millions to scenes of peace at least, may not leave well enough alone? Why should I return with disclosures touching Tammany and the inner history of that organization, when the dullest must apprehend only trouble and pain as the foolish fruits of such garrulity?

To the cheer of ones still on the firing lines of Tammany effort, let me promise to say no more of them than belongs of necessity to the story of my own career. I aim towards the painting of no man's picture save my own. Also from first to last I will hold before the face of each old friend the shield of an alias and never for a moment in name or feature uncover him to the general eye.

As to why it pleases me to give the public my Tammany evolution, and whether I hope for good or ill therefrom, I am not able to set forth. There is that within my bosom to urge me to this work, that much I know; the thing uncertain being—is it vanity, or is it remorse or a hunger for sympathy to so ride me and force my frankness to top-speed? There comes one thought: how-

ever black that robe of reputation which the truth weaves
for me, it will seem milk-white when laid side by side with
what Mendacity has invented and Malice sworn to as the
story of my career.

Before I lift the latch of narration, I would have you
pardon me a first defensive word. Conceiving that, in
the theory of politics, whatever the practice may discover, there is such a commodity as morals and such
a ware as truth, and, remembering how much as the
Chief of Tammany Hall I have been condemned by pur-
ists and folk voluble for reform as a fashion of
City Satan, striving for all that was ebon in local conditions and control, I would remind the reader—hoping his
mind to be unbiased and that he will hold fairly the scales
for me—that both morals and truth as questions will ever
depend for their answer on environment and point of
view. The morality of one man is the sin of another,
and the truth in this mouth is the serpent lie in that.
Having said this much, let me now go forward without
more of flourish or time to be eaten up with words.

CONTENTS

THE BOSS

CHAPTER I

MY father was a blacksmith, and he and my mother came out of Clonmel, where I myself was born. There were four to our family, for besides my father and mother, I owned a sister named Anne, she being my better in age by a couple of years. Anne is dead now, with all those others I have loved, and under the grass roots; but while she lived —and she did not pass until after I had reached the size and manners of a man—she abode a sort of second mother to me, and the littlest of my interests was her chief concern.

That Anne was thus tenderly about my destinies, worked doubtless a deal of fortunate good to me. By nature, while nothing vicious, I was as lawless as a savage; and being resentful of boundaries and as set for liberty as water down hill, I needed her influence to hold me in some quiet order. That I have the least of letters is due wholly to Anne, for school stood to me, child and boy, as hateful as a rainy day, and it was only by her going with me to sit by my side and show me my blurred way across the page that I would mind my book at all.

It was upon a day rearward more than fifty years when my father, gathering together our slight belongings, took us aboard ship for America. We were six weeks between Queenstown and New York; the ship my father chose used sails, and there arose unfriendly seas and winds to baffle us and set us back. For myself, I hold no clear memory of that voyage, since I was but seven at the time. Nor could I have been called good company; I wept every foot of the way, being sick from shore to shore, having no more stomach to put to sea with then than I have now.

It was eight of the clock on a certain July night that my father, having about him my mother and Anne and myself, came ashore at Castle Garden. It being dark, and none to meet us nor place for us to seek, we slept that night, with our coats to be a bed to us, on the Castle Garden flags. If there were hardship to lurk in thus making a couch of the stone floors, I missed the notice of it; I was as sound asleep as a tree at midnight when we came out of the ship and for eight hours thereafter, never once opening my eyes to that new world till the sun was up.

Indeed, one may call it in all candor a new world! The more since, by the grace of accident, that first day fell upon the fourth of the month, and it was the near, persistent roar of cannon all about us, beginning with the break of day, to frighten away our sleep. My father and mother were as simple as was I, myself, on questions of Western story, and the fact of the Fourth of July told no news to them. Guns boomed; flags flaunted; bands of music brayed; gay troops went marching hither and yon; crackers sputtered and snapped; orators with iron throats swept down on spellbound crowds in gales of red-faced eloquence; flaming rockets when the sun went down streaked the night with fire! To these manifestations my father and the balance of us gave admiring ear and eye; although we were a trifle awed by the vehemence of an existence in which we planned to have our part, for we took what we heard and witnessed to be the everyday life of the place.

My father was by trade a blacksmith, and one fair of his craft. Neither he nor my mother had much learning; but they were peaceful, sober folk with a bent for work; and being sure, rain or shine, to go to church, and strict in all their duties, they were ones to have a standing with the clergy and the neighbors. It tells well for my father that within the forty-eight hours to follow our landing at Castle Garden, he had a roof above our heads, and an anvil to hammer upon; this latter at a wage double the best that Clonmel might offer even in a dream. And so we began to settle to our sur-

roundings, and to match with them, and fit them to ourselves; with each day Clonmel to gather a dimness, and
we to seem less strange and more at home, and in the last
to feel as naturally of America as though we had been
born upon the soil.

It has found prior intimation that my earlier years
ran as wild as a colt, with no strong power save Anne's
to tempt me in a right direction. My father, so far as
his mood might promise, would have led me in paths I
should go; but he was never sharp to a condition, and
with nothing to him alert or quick he was one easily
fooled, and I dealt with him as I would. Moreover, he
had his hands filled with the task of the family's support;
for while he took more in wage for his day's work than
had ever come to him before, the cost to live had equal
promotion, and it is to be doubted if any New York
Monday discovered him with riches in his pocket beyond
what would have dwelt there had he stayed in Clonmel.
But whether he lacked temper or time, and whatever
the argument, he cracked no thong of authority over
me; I worked out my days by patterns to please myself,
with never a word from him to check or guide me.

And my mother was the same. She had her house to
care for; and in a wash-tub day, and one when sewing
machines were yet to find their birth, a woman with a
family to be a cook to, and she of a taste besides to see
them clothed and clean, would find her every waking

hour engaged. She was a housekeeper of celebration, was my mother, and a star for neighboring wives to steer by; with floor and walls and everything about her as spick and span as scouring soap and lye might make them. Pale, work-worn, I still carry her on the skyline of my memory; and I recall how her eye would light and her gray cheek show a flush when the priest did us the credit of supper at our board, my father pulling down his sleeves over his great hairy arms in deference to the exalted station of the guest. It comes to this, however, that both my father and my mother, in their narrow simplicities and time taken up with the merest arts of living, had neither care nor commands for me. I came and I went by my own clock, and if I gave the business thought, it was a thought of gratitude to find myself so free.

To be sure I went now and then to my lessons. Anne had been brisk to seek forth a school; for she refused to grow up in ignorance, and even cherished a plan to one day teach classes from a book herself. Being established, she drew me after her, using both persuasion and force to that end, and to keep me in a way of enlightenment, invented a system of rewards and punishments, mainly the former, by which according to my merit I was to suffer or gain.

This temple of learning to which Anne lured me was nothing vast, being no bigger than one room. In lieu of a blackboard there was a box of clean white sand wherewith to teach dullards of my age and sort their alphabet. That feat of education the pedagogue in charge—a somber personage, he, and full of bitter muscularities—accomplished by tracing the letter in the sand. This he did with the point of a hickory ruler, which weapon was never out of his hand, and served in moments of thickness as a wand of inspiration, being laid across the dull one's back by way of brightening his wits. More than once I was made wiser in this fashion; and I found such stimulus to go much against the grain and to grievously rub wrong-wise the fur of my fancy.

These hickory drubbings to make me quicker, falling as thickly as October's leaves, went short of their purpose. On the heels of one of them I would run from my lessons for a week on end. To be brief with these matters of schools and books and alphabets and hickory beatings, I went to my classes for a day, only to hide from them for a week; as might be guessed, the system collected but a scanty erudition.

It is a pity, too: that question of education cannot too much invite an emphasis. It is only when one is young that one may be book-taught, just as the time of spring is the time for seed. There goes a byword of an old dog and a new trick, and I should say it meant a man when he is thirty or forty with a book; for, though driven by all the power of shame, I in vain strove with what was utmost in me to repair in middle years the loss of those schooldays wasted away. I could come by no advance; the currents of habitual ignorance were too strong and I made no head against them. You think I pause a deal over my want of letters? I tell you it is the thing I have most mourned in all my life.

When a fugitive from lessons, I would stay away from my home. This was because I must manage an escape from Anne; should she find me I was lost, and nothing for it save to be dragged again to school. The look of grief in her brown eyes meant ever defeat for me. My only safety was to turn myself out of doors and play the exile.

This vagabondage was pleasant enough, since it served to feed my native vagrancy of temper. And I fared well, too; for I grew into a kind of cateran, and was out of my sleeping lair with the sun to follow the milk-man and baker on their rounds. Coming betimes to the doors of customers who still snored between their sheets, these merchants left their wares in areas. That was all my worst need asked; by what time they doubled the nearest corner I had made my swoop and was fed for the whole of a day.

Moreover, I knew a way to pick up coppers. On a nearby corner in the Bowery a great auction of horses was going. Being light and little, and having besides a lively inclination for horses, I was thrown upon the

backs of ones put up for sale to show their paces. For
each of these mounts I came the better off by five cents,
and on lucky days have made as much as the half of a dollar at that trade. As for a bed, if it were summer time,
what should be finer than the docks? Or if winter, then
the fire-rooms of the tugs, with the engineers and stokers
whereof I made it my care to be friendly? I was always ready to throw off a line, or polish a lantern, or,
when a tug was at the wharf, run to the nearest tap-room
and fetch a pail of beer; for which good deeds the East
River went thickly dotted of my allies before ever I
touched the age of ten.

These meager etchings give some picture of what was
my earlier life, the major share of which I ran wild about
the streets. Neither my father nor my mother lived in
any command of me, and the parish priest failed as dismally as did they when he sought to confine my conduct
to a rule. That hickory-wielding dominie, with his sand-
box and alphabet, was a priest; and he gave me such a
distaste of the clergy that I rolled away from their touch
like quicksilver. Anne's tears and the soft voice of her
were what I feared, and so I kept as much as possible
beyond their spell.

Coming now to a day when I began first to consider
existence as a problem serious, I must tell you how my
lone sole claim to eminence abode in the fact that, lung
and limb, I was as strong and tireless as any bison or

any bear. It was my capital, my one virtue, the mark
that set me above my fellows. This story of vast
strength sounds the more strange, since I was under
rather than above the common height, and never, until
when in later life I took on a thickness of fat, scaled
heavier than one hundred and forty pounds. Thus
it stood, however, that my muscle strength, even as a
youth, went so far beyond what might be called legiti-
mate that it became as a proverb in the mouths of people. The gift was a kind of genius; I tell of it particularly because it turned to be the ladder whereby I climbed
into the first of my fortunes. Without it, sure, I never
would have lifted myself above the gutter levels of my
mates, nor fingered a splinter of those millions that now
lie banked and waiting to my name and hand.

CHAPTER II

IT was when I was in my fifteenth year that face to face I first met politics. Or to fit the phrase more nearly with the fact, I should say it was then when politics met me. Nor was that meeting in its incident one soon to slip from memory. It carried for a darkling element the locking of me in a graceless cell, and that is an adventure sure to leave its impress. The more if one be young, since the trail of events is ever deepest where the ground is soft. It is no wonder the business lies in my mind like a black cameo. It was my first captivity, and there will come on one no greater horror than seizes him when for the earliest time he hears bars and bolts grate home behind him.

On that day, had one found and measured me he would not have called me a child of thoughts or books or alcoves. My nature was as unkempt as the streets. Still, in a turbid way and to broadest banks, the currents of my sentiment were running for honesty and truth. Also, while I wasted no space over the question, I took it as I took the skies above me that law was for folk guilty of wrong, while justice even against odds of

10

power would never fail the weak and right.   My eyes
were to be opened; I was to be shown the lesson of Tammany, and how law would bend and judges bow before
the mighty breath of the machine.

It was in the long shadows of an August afternoon
when the Southhampton boat was docked—a clipper of
the Black Ball line.   I stood looking on; my leisure was
spent about the river front, for I was as fond of the
water as a petrel.   The passengers came throng-
ing down the gang-plank; once ashore, many of the
poorer steerage sort stood about in misty bewil-
derment, not knowing the way to turn or where
to go.

In that far day a special trade had grown up among
the piers; the men to follow it were called hotel runners.
These birds of prey met the ships to swoop on new-
comers with lie and cheat, and carry them away to
hostelries whose mean interests they served.   These latter were the poorest in town, besides being often
dens of wickedness.

As I moved boy-like in and out among the waiting
groups of immigrants, a girl called to me.   This girl
was English, with yellow hair, and cheeks red as apples.
I remember I thought her beautiful, and was the more to
notice it since she seemed no older than myself.   She
was stark alone and a trifle frightened.

" Boy," said Apple Cheek, " boy, where can I go for

to-night? I have money, though not much, so it must
not be a dear place."

Before I could set my tongue to a reply, a runner
known as Sheeny Joe had Apple Cheek by the arm and
was for leading her away.

" Come with me," said Sheeny Joe to Apple Cheek; " I
will show you to a house, as neat as pins, and quiet as a
church; kept it is by a Christian lady as wears out her
eyes with searching of the scriptures. You can stay
there as long as ever you likes for two shillin' a day."

This was reeled off by Sheeny Joe with a suave softness like the flow of treacle. He was cunning enough
to give the charge in shillings so as to match the British
ear and education of poor Apple Cheek.

" Where is this place? " asked Apple Cheek. I could
see how she shrunk from Sheeny Joe, with his eyes
greedy and black, and small and shiny like the eyes of a
rat.

" You wouldn't know the place, young lady," returned Sheeny Joe; " but it's all right, with prayers
and that sort of thing, both night and mornin'. It's
in Water Street, the place is. Number blank, Water
Street," repeated Sheeny Joe, giving a resort known as
the Dead Rabbit. " Come; which ones is your bundles?
I'll help you carry them."

Now by general word, the Dead Rabbit was not unknown to me. It was neither tavern nor boarding house,

but a mill of vice, with blood on its doorstep and worse inside. If ever prayers were said there they must have been parcel of some Black Sanctus; and if ever a Christian went there it was to be robbed and beaten, and then mayhap to have his throat cut for a lesson in silence.

"You don't want to go to that house," said I, finding my voice and turning to Apple Cheek. "You come to my mother's; my sister will find you a place to stay. The house he's talkin' about "—here I indicated Sheeny Joe—" aint no tavern. It's a boozin' ken for crimps and thieves."

Without a word, Sheeny Joe aimed a swinging blow at my head: Apple Cheek gave a low scream. While somewhat unprepared for Sheeny Joe's attack, it falling so sharply sudden, I was not to be found asleep; nor would I prove a simple conquest even to a grown man. My sinister strength, almost the strength of a gorilla, would stand my friend.

Quick as a goat on my feet, and as soon to see a storm coming up as any sailor, I leaped backward from the blow; and next, before Sheeny Joe recovered himself, I was upon him with a wrestler's twitch and trip that tossed him high in the air like a rag. He struck on his head and shoulders, the chimb of a cask against which he rolled cutting a fine gash in his scalp.

With a whirl of oaths, Sheeny Joe tried to scramble

to his feet; he was shaken with rage and wonder to be thus outfaced and worsted by a boy. As he gained his knees, and before he might straighten to his ignoble feet, I dealt him a crashing blow between the eyes, or rather, on the bridge of the nose, which latter feature for Sheeny Joe grew curved and beaky. The blow was of the sort that boxers style a "hook," and one nothing good to stop. Over Sheeny Joe went with the kicking force of it, and lay against the tier of casks, bleeding like tragedy, beaten, and yelling "murder!"

Sheeny Joe, bleeding and roaring, and I by no means glutted, but still hungry for his harm, were instantly the center of a gaping crowd that came about us like a whirlpool. With the others arrived an officer of the police.

"W'at's the row here?" demanded the officer.

"Take him to the station!" cried Sheeny Joe, picking himself up, a dripping picture of blood; "he struck me with a knuckle duster."

"Not so fast, officer," put in a reputable old gentleman. "Hear the lad's story first. The fellow was saying something to this girl. Nor does he look as though it could have been for her benefit."

"Tell me about it, youngster," said the officer, not unkindly. My age and weight, as against those of Sheeny Joe, told with this agent of the peace, who at heart was a fair man. "Tell me what there is to this shindy."

" Why don't you take him in? " screamed Sheeny Joe.   " W'at have you to do with his story? "

" Well, there's two ends to an alley," retorted the officer warmly.   " I'll hear what the boy has to say. Do you think you're goin' to do all the talkin'? "

" The first thing you'll know," cried Sheeny Joe fiercely, " I'll have them pewter buttons off your coat."

" Oh, you will! " retorted the officer with a scowl. " Now just for that I'll take you in.   A night in the jug will put the soft pedal on that mouth of yours." With that, the bluecoat seized Sheeny Joe, and there we were, one in each of his hands.

For myself, I had not uttered a syllable.   I was ever slow of speech, and far better with my hands than my tongue.   Apple Cheek, the cause of the war, stood weeping not a yard away; perhaps she was thinking, if her confusion allowed her thought, of the savageries of this new land to which she was come.   Apple Cheek might have taken herself from out the hubbub by merely merging with the crowd; I think she had the coolness to do this, but was too loyal.   She owned the spirit, as it stood, to come forward when I would not say a word to tell the officer the story.   Apple Cheek was encouraged to this steadiness by the reputable old gentleman.

Before, however, Apple Cheek could win to the end of the first sentence, a burly figure of a man, red of face and broad as a door across the shoulders, pushed his way through the crowd.

" What is it? " he asked, coming in front of the officer. " Turn that man loose," he continued, pointing to Sheeny Joe.

The red-faced man spoke in a low tone, but one of cool command. The officer, however, was not to be readily driven from his ground; he was new to the place and by nature an honest soul. Still, he felt an atmosphere of power about the red-faced personage; wherefore, while he kept strictest hold on both Sheeny Joe and myself, he was not wanting of respect in his response.

" These two coves are under arrest," said the officer, shaking Sheeny Joe and myself like rugs by way of identification.

" I know," said the other, still in the low cool tone. " All the same, you turn this one loose."

The officer still hesitated with a look of half-defiance. With that the red-faced man lost temper.

" Take your hands off him, I tell you! " cried the red-faced man, a spark of anger showing in his small gray eyes. " Do you know me? I'm Big Kennedy. Did you never hear of Big John Kennedy of Tammany Hall? You do what I say, or I'll have you out in Harlem with the goats before to-morrow night."

With that, he of the red face took Sheeny Joe from

between the officer's fingers; nor did the latter seek to detain him. The frown of authority left his brow, and his whole face became overcast with a look of surly submission.

"You should have said so at the jump," remarked the officer sullenly. "How was I to know who you are?"

"You're all right," returned the red-faced one, lapsing into an easy smile. "You're new to this stroll; you'll be wiser by an' by."

"What 'll I do with the boy?" asked the officer.

"Officer," broke in the reputable old gentleman, who was purple to the point apoplectic; "officer, do you mean that you will take your orders from this man?"

"Come, my old codger," interrupted the red-faced one loftily, "stow that. You had better sherry for Fift' Avenue where you belong. If you don't, th' gang down here may get tired, d'ye see, an' put you in the river." Then to the officer: "Take the boy in; I'll look him over later."

"An' the girl!" screamed Sheeny Joe. "I want her lagged too."

"An' the girl, officer," commanded the red-faced one. "Take her along with the boy."

Thus was the procession made up; the officer led Apple Cheek and myself to the station, with Sheeny Joe, still

bleeding, and the red-faced man to be his backer, bringing up the rear.

At the station it was like the whirl and roar of some
storm to me. It was my first captivity—my first collision with the police, and my wits were upside down.
I recall that a crowd of people followed us, and were
made to stand outside the door.

The reputable old gentleman came also, and tried to
interefere in behalf of Apple Cheek and myself. At a
sign from the red-faced man, who stood leaning on the
captain's desk with all the confidence of life, that po-
tentate gave his sharp command.

" Screw out! " cried he, to the reputable old gentleman. " We don't want any of your talk! " Then to
an officer in the station: " Put him out! "

" I'm a taxpayer! " shouted the reputable old gentleman furiously.

" You'll pay a fine," responded the captain with a
laugh, " if you kick up a row 'round my station. Now
screw out, or I'll put you the wrong side of the grate."

The reputable old gentleman was thrust into the
street with about as much ceremony as might attend
the delivery of a bale of goods at one's door. He disappeared, declaring he would have justice; at which a
smile widened the faces of the sophisticated officers,
several of whom were lounging about the room.

" He'll have justice! " repeated the captain with a

chuckle. " Say! he aought to put that in the Joe Miller Joke-book." Then to the red-faced man, who still leaned against the desk, the image of autocracy sure of itself : " What is it to be, Mr. Kennedy? "

" Why," quoth the red-faced one, " you must lock this boy up. Yes, an' the girl, too; she had better go in for the night. I'll take a look into th' business, an' let the judge know in the mornin'."

" I don't think, captain," interposed the officer who brought us from the docks, " there's any use locking up these people. It was nothin' but a cheap muss on the pier."

" Say! I don't stand that!" broke in Sheeny Joe. " This party smashed me with a bar of iron. The girl was in the play ; an' I say they're both to go in."

" You ' say,' " mocked the captain, in high scorn. " An' who are you? Who is this fellow? " he demanded, looking about him.

" He's one of my people," said the red-faced man, still coolly by the desk.

" No more out of you!" snarled the captain to the kindly officer, as the latter again tried to speak; " you get back to your beat!"

" An' say!" cried the red-faced man, slowly rousing from his position by the desk; " before you go, let me give you a word. You're a sight too gabby; you had better think more and say less, or you won't last long

enough as a copper to wear out that new uniform. An'
if anybody asks, tell him it was Big Kennedy that told
you."

They led me to a cell, while poor Apple Cheek, almost fainting, was carried to another. As I was being
taken away, Anne came rushing in. Bad news is a
creature of wings, and Anne had been told my ad-
ventures by a small urchin who ran himself nearly to
death in defeating two fellow urchins for the privilege
before I had reached the station.

Anne did not observe me as she came in, for I stood
somewhat to the rear, with several turnkeys and officers
between. I could see the white face of her, and how the
lamps of a great alarm were lighted in her eyes. Her
voice was so low with terror I could not hear her words.
Evidently she was pleading, girl-fashion, for my liberty.
The tones of the captain, however, rose clear and high.

"That 'll do ye now," said he in a manner of lordly
insolence, looking up from the desk to which he had returned. "If we put a prisoner on the pavement every
time a good-looking girl rushed in with a yarn about
bein' his sister, we wouldn't need no cells at all. This
boy stays till the judge takes a look at him in the
mornin'. Meanwhile, you had better get back to your
window, or all the men will have left the street."

At this, a mighty anger flamed up in my heart. I
tore away from the officer who had me by the shoulders,

and, save that three others as practiced in the sleight of it as football players instantly seized me, I should have gone straight at the captain's neck like a bulldog.

" I'll have his life! " I foamed.

The next moment I was thrown into a cell. The door slammed; the lock shot home; with that, my heart seemed to turn to water in my bosom and I sank upon the stone floor of my cage.

CHAPTER III

THE BOSS SEES THE POWER OF TAMMANY

THAT night under lock and key was a night of long delirium. Drunken men babbled and cursed and shouted; while a lunatic creature laughed and screamed like bedlam. Once I heard the low click of sobs, and thought it might be poor unhappy Apple Cheek. The surmise went wide, for she was held in another part of the prison.

It was in the first streaks of the morning before I slept. My slumbers did not last long; it seemed as though I had but shut my eyes when a loud rap of iron on iron brought me up, and there stood one armed of a key so large it might have done for the gate of a giant's castle. It was this man hammering with his weapon on the grate of my cell that roused me.

"Now then, young gallows-bird," said the functionary, "be you ready for court?"

The man, while rough, gave me no hard impression, for he wore a tolerant grin and had eyes of friendly brown. These amiable signs endowed me with courage to ask a question.

"What will they do with me?" I queried. I was

anxious, for I had no experience to be my guide. "What will they do? Will they let me go?"

"Sure! they'll let you go." My hopes gained their feet. "To Blackwell's." My hopes lay prone again.

The turnkey, for such was the man's station, had but humored me with one of the stock jokes of the place. On seeing my distress, and perhaps remembering that I should be something tender if years were to count, and no frequent tenant of the cells with sensibilities trained to the safe consistency of leather, he made me further reply.

"No, I'll tell you the truth, youngster. If you plead guilty, an' there's no one there but the cop, it 'll be about ten dollars or twenty days on the Island. But if Sheeny Joe comes 'round to exhibit his nose, or Big Kennedy shows up to stall ag'inst you, why I should say you might take six months and call yourself in luck."

There was nothing to brighten the eye in the story, and my ribs seemed to inclose a heart of wood.

With a vile dozen to be my companions, frowsy, bleary creatures, some shaking with the dumb ague of drink whose fires had died out, I was driven along a narrow corridor, up a pair of stairs, and into a room of respectable size! Its dimensions, however, would be its only claim to respectability, for the walls and ceiling were smoke-blackened, while the floor might have come the better off for a pailful of soap and water.

Once within the room I found myself in a railed pen. Against the wall, with a desk before him and raised above the herd by a platform, sat the magistrate. There was a fence which divided the big room, and beyond and leaning on it lolled the public, leering and listening, as hard an array as one might wish to see. One might have sentenced the entire roomful to the workhouse and made few mistakes.

Inside this fence, and gathered for the most part about the magistrate, were those who had business with the court; officers, witnesses, friends and enemies of the accused, with last although not least a collection of the talent of the bar. Many of these latter were brisk Jews, and all of them were marked by soiled linen, frayed elbows, greasy collars, and an evident carelessness as to the state of their hands and faces. There were boys to wait on these folk of law, a boy to each I should say. None of these urchins was older than was I, and some no more than twelve. They carried baize bags, chatted gravely while waiting the call of their masters, and gave themselves strutting airs and brows of consequence. These engaging children, in a spirit of loyalty, doubtless, showed themselves as untainted of water as were their betters.

While I rehearse these sordid appearances as developed in the dim lights which through the grimy windows fell across the scene, you are not to suppose the

notice of them preyed upon me. I was, in that hour,
neither so squeamish nor so observant as to make particular note of them, nor was I to that degree the slave
of soap in my own roving person, as to justify the risk
of strictures which might provoke retort. Besides, I
was thinking dolefully on that trip to Blackwell's Island
whereof the future seemed so full, and my eyes scanned
the judge on the bench rather than lesser folk who were
not so important in my affairs.

While in the mills of great misery, still I was steady
enough. I turned my gaze upon the magistrate, and
sought in his looks and words, as he went about the
sorry destinies of other delinquents, some slant of what
I might look forward to for myself. The dignitary in
question showed lean and sallow and bald, with a sly
face and an eye whereof the great expression was one
of sleepless self-interest. He did not come upon you
as either brave or good, but he had nothing brutal or
vindictive, and his timid mealy voice was shaken by a
quaver that seemed a perpetual apology for what
judgments he from time to time would pass. His
sentences were invariably light, except in instances
where some strong influence from the outside, generally
a politician or the agent of a big company, arose to
demand severity.

While within the railed pen with those other unfortu-
nates whom the dragnets of the police had brought to

these mean shores, and in an interval when my fascinated eyes were off the magistrate, I caught sight of Anne and my father. They had seats inside the fence. The latter's face was clouded with simple trouble; he wore his Sunday coat, and his hands, hard and showing the stains of his forge, roved in uneasy alternation from his pockets to his lapels and back again. Anne's young eyes were worn and tired, for she had slept as little as had I and wept much more the night before. I could not discover Apple Cheek, although I looked about the room for her more than once. I had it in my hopes that they had given Apple Cheek her freedom, and the thought was a half-relief. Nothing of such decent sort had come to pass, however; Apple Cheek was waiting with two or three harridans, her comrades of the cells, in an adjoining room.

When my name was called, an officer of the court opened a gate in the prisoner's pen and motioned me to come forth.

" Hurry up! " said the officer, who was for expedition. " W'at's the trouble with your heels? You aint got no ball an' chain on yet, you know."

Then he gave me a chair in front of the magistrate, where the man of power might run me up and down with his shifty deprecatory eye.

" There was a girl brought in with him, your honor," remarked the officer at the gate.

"Have her out, then," said the magistrate; whereupon Apple Cheek, a bit disheveled and cheeks redder than ever with the tears she had shed, was produced and given a seat by my side.

"Who complains of these defendants?" asked the magistrate in a mild non-committal voice, glancing about the room.

"I do, your honor."

It was Sheeny Joe who came pushing to the fore from a far corner. His head had received the benefit of several bandages, and it gave me a dullish joy to think it was I to furnish the reason of them.

The magistrate appeared to know Sheeny Joe, and to hold him in regard at that. The moment my enemy declared himself as the complainant, and no one springing up to take my part, the magistrate bent upon me a stony glance that spoke plainly of those six months concerning which the turnkey told. I gave up everything, myself and Apple Cheek, as surely lost.

"Tell your story," said the magistrate to Sheeny Joe. His manner was full of commiseration for that unworthy. "What did he assault you with?"

"With a blackjack, your honor, or a piece of lead pipe," replied Sheeny Joe. "He struck me when I wasn't lookin'. I'm busy trying to tell the girl there w'at hotel she wants. He gives it to me over the head from behind; then as I wheels, he smashes me across the

nose. I couldn't see with w'at, but it was a bar of some
kind, mebby iron, mebby lead. As I goes down, I hears
the sketch—the girl, I mean—sing out, ' Kill him!'
The girl was eggin' him on, your honor."

Sheeny Joe unwound this string of lies without hitch
or pause, and withal so rapidly it fair stole my breath
away. I felt the eyes of the magistrate upon me; I
knew my danger and yet could come by no words for my
own defense. I make no doubt, had it not been for a
diversion as unlooked-for as it was welcome, I would
have been marked for prison where I stood.

" I demand to be heard," came suddenly, in a high
angry voice. " What that rogue has just uttered is all
a pack of lies together! "

It was the reputable old gentleman of the evening before who thus threw himself in the way of events. Being
escorted through the press of onlookers by an officer, the
reputable old gentleman stood squarely in front of the
magistrate.

" I demand justice for that boy," fumed the reputable
old gentleman, glaring at the magistrate, and growing
crimson in the face; " I demand a jury. As for the
girl, she wasn't ten minutes off the boat; her only part
in the offense would seem to be that this scoundrel,"
pointing to Sheeny Joe, " was striving to lure her to a
low resort."

" The Dead Rabbit a low resort! " cried Sheeny

Joe indignantly. " The place is as straight as a gun."

" Will you please tell me who you are? " asked the magistrate of the reputable old gentleman. He had resumed his non-committal look. The confident vigor of the reputable old gentleman disconcerted him and made him wary.

" I am a taxpayer," said the reputable old gentleman; " yes," donning an air as though the thunders and lightnings of politics dwelt in the word, " yes, your honor, a taxpayer. I do not know this boy, but here are his father and sister to speak for him." Then, as he caught sight of the captain who had ordered him out of the station: " There is a man, your honor, who by the hands of his minions drove me from a public police office—me, a taxpayer! "

The captain grinned easily to find himself thus distinguished. The grin irritated the reputable old gentleman, who was even more peppery than reputable.

" Smile, sir! " cried the reputable old gentleman, shaking his wrathful finger at the captain. " I shall have you before your superiors on charges before I'm done! "

" That's what they all say," remarked the captain, stifling a yawn.

" One thing at a time, sir," said the magistrate to the reputable old gentleman. His attitude was wheedling and propitiatory. " Did I understand you to say that the gentleman and the lady at your back are the father and sister of this boy? "

My father and Anne had taken their stations to the rear of the reputable old gentleman. The latter, looking around as if to identify them, replied:

" If the court please, I'm told so."

" Your honor," broke in Sheeny Joe with a front of injury, " w'at's that got to do with his sandbaggin' me? Am I to be murdered w'en peacefully about me business, just 'cause a guy's got a father? "

" What were you saying to this girl? " asked the magistrate mildly of Sheeny Joe, and indicating Apple Cheek with his eye where she sat tearful and frightened by my side. " This gentleman "—the reputable old gentleman snorted fiercely—" declares that you were about to lure her to a low resort."

" Your honor, it was the Dead Rabbit," said Sheeny Joe.

" Is the Dead Rabbit," observed the magistrate, to the captain, who was still lounging about, " is the Dead Rabbit a place of good repute? "

" It aint no Astor House," replied the captain, " but no one expects an Astor House in Water Street."

" Is it a resort for thieves? "

The magistrate still advanced his queries in a fashion apologetic and subdued. The reputable old gentleman impressed him as one he would not like to offend. Then, too, there was my father—an honest working-man by plain testimony of his face. On the other hand stood Sheeny Joe, broken of nose, bandaged, implacable. Here were three forces of politics, according to our magistrate, who was thinking on a re-election; he would prefer to please them all. Obviously, he in no sort delighted in his present position, since whichever way he turned it might be a turn toward future disaster for himself.

"Is the Dead Rabbit a resort for thieves?" again asked the magistrate.

"Well," replied the captain judgmatically, "even a crook has got to go somewhere. That is," he added, "when he aint in hock."

Where this criss-cross colloquy of justice or injustice might have left me, and whether free or captive, I may only guess. The proceedings were to gain another and a final interruption. This time it was the red-faced man, he who had called himself "Big Kennedy," to come panting into the presence of the court. The red-faced man had hurried up the stairs, three steps at a time, and it told upon his breathing.

The magistrate made a most profound bow to the red-faced man. Remembering the somber prophecy of him with the big key, should "Big Kennedy show up to stall ag'inst me," my hope, which had revived with the stand taken by the reputable old gentleman, sunk now to lowest marks.

" What will you have, Mr. Kennedy? " purred the magistrate obsequiously.

" Is the court going to dispose of the cases of this boy and this girl? " interrupted the reputable old gentleman warmly. " I demand a jury trial for both of them. I am a taxpayer and propose to have justice."

" Hold up, old sport, hold up! " exclaimed the red-faced man in cheerful tones. He was addressing the reputable old gentleman. " Let me get to work. I'll settle this thing like throwin' dice."

" What do you mean, sir, by calling me an old sport? " demanded the reputable old gentleman.

The red-faced man did not heed the question, but wheeled briskly on the magistrate.

" Your honor," said the red-faced man, " there's nothin' to this. Sheeny Joe there has made a misdeal, that's all. I've looked the case over, your honor; there's nothin' in it; you can let the girl an' the boy go."

" But he said the Dead Rabbit was a drum for crooks! " protested Sheeny Joe, speaking to the red-faced man.

" S'ppose he did," retorted the other, " that don't take a dollar out of the drawer."

" An' he's to break my nose an' get away? " complained Sheeny Joe.

" Well, you oughter to take care of your nose," said the red-faced man, " an' not go leavin' it lyin' around where a kid can break it."

Sheeny Joe was not to be shaken off; he engaged in violent argument with the red-faced man. Their tones, however, were now more guarded, and no one might hear their words beyond themselves. While this went forward, the magistrate, to save his dignity, perhaps, and not to have it look as though he were waiting for orders, pretended to be writing in his book of cases which lay open on his desk.

It was Sheeny Joe to bring the discussion between himself and the red-faced man to an end. Throughout the whispered differences between them, differences as to what should be my fate, Sheeny Joe showed hot with fury, while the red-faced man was cool and conciliatory; his voice when one caught some sound of it was coaxing.

" There's been enough said!" cried Sheeny Joe, suddenly walking away from the red-faced man. " No duck is goin' to break my nose for fun."

" The boy's goin' loose," observed the red-faced man in placid contradiction. " An' the girl goes to her friends, wherever they be, an' they aint at the Dead Rabbit." Then in a blink the countenance of the red-faced man went from calm to rage. He whirled Sheeny Joe by the shoulder. " See here!" he growled, " one more roar out of you, an' I'll stand you up right now, an'

it's you who will take sixty days, or my name aint Big
John Kennedy. If you think that's a bluff, call it.
Another yeep, an' the boat's waitin' for you! You've
been due at the Island for some time."

"That's all right, Mr. Kennedy!" replied Sheeny
Joe, his crest falling, and the sharpest terror in his face,
"that's all right! You know me? Of course it goes as
you say! Did you ever know me to buck ag'inst you?"

The red-faced man smiled ferociously. The anger
faded from his brow, and leaving Sheeny Joe without
further word, he again spoke to the magistrate.

"The charges ag'inst these two children, your honor,
are withdrawn." He spoke in his old cool tones.
"Captain," he continued, addressing that dignitary,
"send one of your plain-clothes people with this girl
to find her friends for her. Tell him he mustn't make
any mistakes."

"The cases are dismissed," said the magistrate, making an entry in his book. He appeared relieved with
the change in the situation; almost as much, if that
were possible, as myself. "The cases are dismissed; no
costs to be taxed. I think that is what you desire, Mr.
Kennedy?"

"Yes, your honor." Then coming over to where I
sat, the red-faced man continued: "You hunt me up
to-morrow—Big John Kennedy—that's my name.
Any cop can tell you where to find me."

" Yes, sir," I answered faintly.

" There's two things about you," said the red-faced man, rubbing my stubble of hair with his big paw, " that's great in a boy. You can hit like the kick of a pony; an' you can keep your mouth shut. I aint heard a yelp out of you, mor'n if you was a Boston terrier." This, admiringly.

As we left the magistrate's office—the red-faced man, the reputable old gentleman, my father, Apple Cheek, and myself, with Anne holding my hand as though I were some treasure lost and regained—the reputable old gentleman spoke up pompously to the red-faced man.

" I commend what you have done, sir; but in that connection, and as a taxpayer, let me tell you that I resent your attitude towards the magistrate. You issued your orders, sir, and conducted yourself toward that officer of justice as though you owned him."

" Well, what of it? " returned the red-faced man composedly. " I put him there. What do you think I put him there for? To give me the worst of it? "

" Sir, I do not understand your expressions! " said the reputable old gentleman. " And I resent them! Yes, sir, I resent them as a taxpayer of this town! "

" Say," observed the red-faced man benignantly, " there's nothin' wrong about you but your head. You had better take a term or two at night school an' get it put on straight. You say you're a taxpayer; you've already fired the fact at me about five times.   An' now I ask you: Suppose you be?"

"Taxpayer; yes, sir, taxpayer!" repeated the reputable old gentleman, in a mighty fume.   "Do you intend to tell me there's no meaning to the word?"

"It means," said the red-faced man in the slow manner of one who gives instruction; "it means that if you're nothin' but a taxpayer—an' I don't think you be or you'd have told us—you might as well sit down. You're a taxpayer, eh?   All right; I'm a ward-leader of Tammany Hall. You're a taxpayer; good! I'm the man that settles how much you pay, d'ye see!"   Then, as though sympathy and disgust were blended: "Old man, you go home and take a hard look at the map, and locate yourself. You don't know it, but all the same you're in New York."

CHAPTER IV

PERHAPS you will say I waste space and lay too much of foolish stress upon my quarrel with Sheeny Joe and its police-cell consequences. And yet you should be mindful of the incident's importance to me as the starting point of my career. For I read in what took place the power of the machine as you will read this printed page. I went behind the bars by the word of Big John Kennedy; and it was by his word that I emerged and took my liberty again. And yet who was Big John Kennedy? He was the machine; the fragment of its power which molded history in the little region where I lived. As mere John Kennedy he would be nothing. Or at the most no more than other men about him. But as " Big John Kennedy," an underchief of Tammany Hall, I myself stood witness while a captain of police accepted his commands without a question, and a magistrate found folk guilty or innocent at the lifting of his finger. Also, that sweat of terror to sprinkle the forehead of Sheeny Joe, when in his moment of rebellion he found himself beneath the wrathful shadow of the machine, was not the least im-

pressive element of my experience; and the tolerant
smile, that was half pity, half amusement, as Big Kennedy set forth to the reputable old gentleman—who
was only "a taxpayer"—the little limits of his in-
significance, deepened the effect upon my mind of what
had gone before.

True, I indulged in no such analysis as the above, and
made no study of the picture in its detail; but I could
receive an impression just as I might receive a blow,
and in the innocence of my ignorance began instantly to
model myself upon the proven fact of a power that was
above law, above justice, and which must be consulted
and agreed with, even in its caprice, before existence
could be profitable or even safe. From that moment the
machine to me was as obviously and indomitably abroad
as the pavement under foot, and must have its account in
every equation of life to the solution whereof I was set.
To hold otherwise, and particularly to act otherwise,
would be to play the fool, with failure or something
worse for a reward.

Big Kennedy owned a drinking place. His barroom
was his headquarters; although he himself never served
among his casks and bottles, having barmen for that
work. He poured no whisky, tapped no beer, donned no
apron, but sat at tables with his customers and laid
out his campaigns of politics or jubilated over victory,
and seemed rather the visitor than the proprietor in his

own saloon. He owned shrewdness, force, courage, enterprise, and was one of those who carry a pleasant atmosphere that is like hypnotism, and which makes men like them. His manner was one of rude frankness, and folk held him for a bluff, blunt, genial soul, who made up in generosity what he lacked of truth.

And yet I have thought folk mistaken in Big Kennedy. For all his loud openness and friendly roar, which would seem to tell his every thought, the man could be the soul of cunning and turn secret as a mole. He was for his own interest; he came and went a cold calculating trader of politics; he never wasted his favors, but must get as much as he gave, and indulged in no revenges except when revenge was needed for a lesson. He did what men call good, too, and spent money and lost sleep in its accomplishment. To the ill he sent doctors and drugs; he found work and wages for idle men; he paid landlords and kept the roofs above the heads of the penniless; where folk were hungry he sent food, and where they were cold came fuel.

For all that, it was neither humanity nor any milk of kindness which put him to these labors of grace; it was but his method of politics and meant to bind men to him. They must do his word; they must carry out his will; then it was he took them beneath the wing of his power and would spare neither time nor money to protect and prosper them.

And on the other side, he who raised his head in opposition to Big Kennedy was crushed; not in anger, but in caution. He weeded out rebellion, and the very seed of it, with as little scruple and for the same reason a farmer weeds a field.

It took me years to collect these truths of Big Kennedy. Nor was their arrival when they did come one by one, to make a shade of change in my regard for him. I liked him in the beginning; I liked him in the end; he became that headland on the coasts of politics by which I steered my course. I studied Big Kennedy as one might study a science; by the lines of his conduct I laid down lines for my own; in all things I was his disciple and his imitator.

Big Kennedy is dead now; and I will say no worse nor better of him than this: He was a natural captain of men. Had he been born to a higher station, he might have lighted a wick in history that would require those ten thicknesses of darkness which belong with ten centuries, to obscure. But no such thing could come in the instance of Big Kennedy; his possibilities of eminence, like my own, were confined to Tammany and its politics, since he had no more of education than have I. The time has gone by in the world at large, and had in Big Kennedy's day, when the ignorant man can be the first man.

Upon the day following my release, as he had bid me,

I sought Big Kennedy. He was in his barroom, and the hour being mid-morning I was so far lucky as to find him quite alone. He was quick to see me, too, and seemed as full of a pleasant interest in me as though my simple looks were of themselves good news. He did most of the talking, for I sat backward and bashful, the more since I could feel his sharp eyes upon me, taking my measure. Never was I so looked over and so questioned, and not many minutes had come and gone before Big Kennedy knew as much of me and my belongings as did I myself. Mayhap more; for he weighed me in the scales of his experience with all the care of gold, considering meanwhile to what uses I should be put, and how far I might be expected to advance his ends.

One of his words I recall, for it gave me a glow of relief at the time; at that it was no true word. It was when he heard how slightly I had been taught of books.

"Never mind," said he, "books as often as not get between a party's legs and trip him up. Better know men than books. There's my library." Here he pointed to a group about a beer table. "I can learn more by studyin' them than was ever found between the covers of a book, and make more out of it."

Big Kennedy told me I must go to work.

"You've got to work, d'ye see," said he, "if it's only to have an excuse for livin'."

Then he asked me what I could do. On making nothing clear by my replies—for I knew of nothing—he descended to particulars.

"What do you know of horses? Can you drive one?"

My eye brightened; I might be trusted to handle a horse.

"An' I'll gamble you know your way about the East Side," said he confidently; "I'll answer for that." Then getting up he started for the door, for no grass grew between decision and action with Big Kennedy. "Come with me," he said.

We had made no mighty journey when we stopped before a grocery. It was a two-store front, and of a prosperous look, with a wealth of vegetables and fruits in crates, and baskets, and barrels, covering half the sidewalk. The proprietor was a rubicund German, who bustled forth at sight of my companion.

"How is Mr. Kennedy?" This with exuberance. "It makes me prout that you pay me a wisit."

"Yes?" said the other dryly. Then, going directly to the point: "Here's a boy I've brought you, Nick. Let him drive one of your wagons. Give him six dollars a week."

"But, Mr. Kennedy," replied the grocer dubiously, looking me over with the tail of his eye, "I haf yet no wacancy. My wagons is all full."

"I'm goin' to get him new duds," said Big Kennedy, "if that's what you're thinkin' about."

Still, the grocer, though not without some show of respectful alarm, insisted on a first position.

"If he was so well dressed even as you, Mr. Kennedy, yet I haf no wacancy," said he.

"Then make one," responded Big Kennedy coolly. "Dismiss one of the boys you have, d'ye see? At least two who work for you don't belong in my ward." As the other continued doubtful Big Kennedy became sharp. "Come, come, come!" he cried in a manner peremptory rather than fierce; "I can't wait all day. Don't you feed your horses in the street? Don't you obstruct the sidewalks with your stuff? Don't you sell liquor in your rear room without a license? Don't you violate a dozen ordinances? Don't the police stand it an' pass you up? An' yet you hold me here fiddlin' and foolin' away time!"

"Yes, yes, Mr. Kennedy," cried the grocer, who from the first had sought to stem the torrent of the other's eloquence, "I was only tryin' to think up w'ich horse I will let him drive alreatty. That's honest! sure as my name is Nick Fogel!"

Clothed in what was to me the splendors of a king, being indeed a full new suit bought with Big Kennedy's money, I began rattling about the streets with a delivery wagon the very next day. As well as I could, I tried to tell my thanks for the clothes.

" That's all right," said Big Kennedy. " I owe you
that much for havin' you chucked into a cell."

While Grocer Fogel might have been a trifle slow in
hiring me, once I was engaged he proved amiable enough.
I did my work well too, missing few of the customers
and losing none of the baskets and sacks. Grocer Fogel
was free with his praise and conceded my value. Still,
since he instantly built a platform in the street on
the strength of my being employed, and so violated a
new and further ordinance upon which he for long had
had an eye, I have sometimes thought that in forming
his opinion of my worth he included this misdemeanor
in his calculations. However, I worked with my worthy
German four years; laying down the reins of that delivery wagon of my own will at the age of nineteen.

Nor was I without a profit in this trade of delivering
potatoes and cabbages and kindred grocery forage.
It broadened the frontiers of my acquaintance, and made
known to me many of a solvent middle class, and of
rather a higher respectability than I might otherwise
have met. It served to clean up my manners, if nothing
more, and before I was done, that acquaintance became
with me an asset of politics.

While I drove wagon for Grocer Fogel, my work of
the day was over with six o'clock. I had nothing to do
with the care of the horses; I threw the reins to a stable
hand when at evening I went to the barn, and left for my

home without pausing to see the animals out of the straps or their noses into the corn. Now, had I been formed with a genius for it, I might have put in a deal of time at study. But nothing could have been more distant from my taste or habit; neither then nor later did I engage myself in any traffic with books, and throughout my life never opened a half-dozen.

Still, considering those plans I had laid down for myself, and that future of politics to which my ambition began to consider, I cannot say I threw away my leisure. If my nose were not between the pages of a book, my hands were within a pair of boxing gloves, and I, engaged against this or that opponent, was leading or guarding, hitting or stopping, rushing or getting away, and fitting to an utmost hand and foot and eye and muscle for the task of beating a foeman black and blue should the accidents or duties of life place one before me.

And I prospered with my boxing. I think I owned much native stomach for the business, since in my sullen fashion I was as near the touch of true happiness when in the midst of a mill as ever I hope to stand. My heart, and with that word I mean courage, was of fighting sort. While I was exceedingly cautious, my caution was based on courage. Men of this stamp stay until the last and either conquer or fall. There be ones who have courage, but their construction is the other way about. Their courage is based on caution; such if hard bested run away. Should you seek the man who will stand to the work of battle to the dour end, pick him whose caution, coming first in the procession of his nature, is followed by his courage, rather than that one whose caution follows his courage to tap it on the shoulder, preach to it of peril, and counsel flight.

You are not to assume that I went about these boxing gymnastics because of any savageries or blood-hunger dominant in my breast, or was moved solely of that instinct by which the game-cock fights. I went to my fist-studies as the result of thought and calculation. In my slow way I had noted how those henchmen of the inner circle who surrounded Big Kennedy—those who were near to him, and upon whom he most relied, were wholly valued by him for the two matters of force of fist and that fidelity which asks no question. Even a thicker intellect than mine would have seen that to succeed as I proposed, I must be the gladiator. Wherefore, I boxed and wrestled and perfected my muscles; also as corollary I avoided drink and tobacco as I would two poisons.

And Big Kennedy, who had a little of his eye on me most of the time, was so good as to approve. He applauded my refusal of alcohol and tobacco. And he indorsed my determination to be a boxer.

" A man who can take care of himself with his hands," said he, " an' who never lets whisky fool him or steal his head, can go far in this game of politics. An' it's a pretty good game at that, is politics, and can be brought to pay like a bank."

It chanced that I met with an adventure which added to my celebration in a way I could have wished. I was set upon by a drunken fellow—a stranger. He was an invader, bent upon mischief and came from an adjacent and a rival ward. I had offered no provocation; why he selected me to be his victim and whether it were accident or design I cannot say. Possibly I was pointed out to this drinking Hotspur as one from whose conquest honor would flow; perhaps some enemy of the pattern of Sheeny Joe had set him to it. All I know is that without challenge given, or the least offer of warning, the creature bore down upon me, whirling his fists like flails.

"You're the party I'm lookin' for!" was all he said.

In the mix-up to follow, and which I had neither time to consider nor avoid, the visitor from that other ward was fully and indubitably beaten. This was so evident that he himself admitted it when at the finish of hostilities certain Samaritans gave him strong drink as a restorative. It developed also that my assailant, in a shadowy subdued way, was a kind of prizefighter, and by his own tribe deemed invincible. My victory, therefore, made a noise in immediate circles; and I should say it saved me from a deal of trouble and later strife, since it served to place me in a class above the common. There came few so drunk or so bold as to ask for trouble with me, and I found that this casual battle—safe, too, because my prizefighter was too drunk to be dangerous—had brought me a wealth of peace.

There dawned a day when Big Kennedy gave me a decisive mark of his esteem. He presented me to his father. The elder Kennedy, white-haired and furrowed of age, was known as " Old Mike." He was a personage of gravity and power, since his was the only voice in that region to which Big Kennedy would yield. Wherefore to be of " Old Mike's " acquaintance shone in one's favor like a title of knighthood.

Big Kennedy's presentation speech, when he led me before his father, was characteristic and peculiar. Old Mike was in the shadow of his front porch, while three or four oldsters of the neighborhood, like a council or a little court about a monarch, and all smoking short clay pipes, were sitting about him.

" Here's a pup," cried Big Kennedy, with his hand on my shoulder, " I want you to look over. He's a great pup and ought to make a great dog."

Old Mike glanced at me out of his twinkling gray eyes. After a moment he said, addressing me:

" Come ag'in."

That was all I had from Old Mike that journey.

Big Kennedy it should be said was a model for all sons. He kept his father in ease and comfort in a house of his own. He was prone to have Old Mike's advice, par-

ticularly if what he proposed were a step novel or one
dangerous in its policy, and he never went to anything
in the face of Old Mike's word. It wasn't deference, it
was faith; Big Kennedy believed in the wisdom of Old
Mike and relied upon it with a confidence that was implicit. I shall have more to tell of Old Mike as my story
unrolls to the eye. If Big Kennedy were my example,
Old Mike should be called my mentor. Taking the cue
from Big Kennedy, I came to own for Old Mike that
veneration which the youths of Ancient Greece felt for
their oracles, and as utterly accepted either his argument
or conclusion. It stood no wonder that I was impressed
and played upon by this honor of an introduction to Old
Mike. To bring you before Old Mike and name you for
his consideration was the extremest proof of Big Kennedy's regard. As I've said, it glittered on one like the
chain and spurs of knighthood, and the fact of it
gave me a pedestal among my fellows.

After my bout with that erring one who came out of
his own ward to sup grief at my hands, there began to
collect about me a coterie of halfway bruisers. This
circle—and our enemies were quick to bestow upon it the
epithet of " gang "—never had formal organization.
And while the members were of the rougher sort,
and each a man of his hands, the argument of its coming
together was not so much aggression as protection.

The town forty years ago was not a theater of peace

and lambs'-wool safety. One's hand must keep one's head, and a stout arm, backed by a stout heart, traveled far. To leave one's own ward, or even the neighborhood where one lived, was to invite attack. In an alien ward, one would be set upon and beaten to rags before one traveled a mile. If one of the enemy were not equal to the business, others would lend a hand. Whether it required one or two or three or twenty, the interloper was fated to heir a drubbing. If his bones were not broken, he was looked upon as fortunate, while those who had undertaken to correct his wanderings went despised as bunglers who had slighted a task.

Now and then a war-party would make a sortie from their own region to break windows and heads in the country of an emeny. Such hands often descended upon the domain of Big Kennedy, and it was a notion of defense against these Goths which brought the militant spirits I have mentioned to my shoulder. It was we who must meet them, when they would make desolate our territory. The police were of no use; they either walked the other way in a spirit of cautious neutrality, or were driven into hiding with a shower of stones.

By the common tongue, this coterie to collect at my back was named the "Tin Whistle Gang." Each member carried a whistle as part of his pocket furniture. These were made of uniform pattern, and the same keen note, like the screech of a hawk, was common to all.

The screaming fife-like song would bring out the Tin Whistles as hotly bent for action as a colony of wasps. In those days, when might was right, the sound of these whistles was a storm signal. Quiet people shut their doors and drew their bolts, while apothecaries made ready to sell lint and plasters.

It is required that I speak of the Tin Whistles in this place. I was now for the first time to be called into political activity by Big Kennedy. I was eighteen, and of a sober, steady, confident cast, and trustworthy in a wordless way. Because I was sober of face and one not given to talk or to laughter, men looked on me as five years better than my age; I think these characteristics even imposed on Big Kennedy himself, for he dealt with me as though I were a man full grown.

It was in the height of a campaign. Two days before the balloting, Big Kennedy sent for me. There was a room to the rear of his bar. This room was a holy of holies; no one entered there who was not established in the confidence of Big Kennedy. It was a greater distinction even than the acquaintance of Old Mike. Knowing these things, my brow flushed when Big Kennedy led me into this sanctum of his policies.

" Now, if I didn't trust you," said Big Kennedy, looking me hard in the eye, " if I didn't trust you, you'd be t'other side of that door." I said nothing; I had found that silence pleased Big

Kennedy, and I learned early to keep my tongue between my teeth. Big Kennedy went on: " On election day the polls will close at six o'clock. Half an hour before they close, take that Bible Class of yours, the Tin Whistles, and drive every one of the opposition workers an' ticket peddlers away from the polling place. You'll know them by their badges. I don't want anyone hurt mor'n you have to. The less blood, the better. Blood's news; it gets into the papers. Now remember: half an hour before six, blow your whistle an' sail in. When you've got the other fellows on the run, keep 'em goin'. And don't let 'em come back, d'ye see."

CHAPTER V

BIG KENNEDY'S commands concerning the Tin Whistles taught me that lurking somewhere in the election situation he smelled peril to himself. Commonly, while his methods might be a wide shot to the left of the lawful, they were never violent. He must feel himself hard pressed to call for fist and club. He lived at present cross-purposes with sundry high spirits of the general organization; perhaps a word was abroad for his disaster and he had heard some sigh of it. This would be nothing wonderful; coarse as he seemed fibered, Big Kennedy had spun his web throughout the ward as close-meshed as any spider, and any fluttering proof of treason was certain to be caught in it.

The election, while the office at local bay came to be no weightier than that of Alderman, was of moment to Big Kennedy. Defeat would mean his eclipse, and might even spell his death of politics. To lose the Alderman was to let fall the reins of ward direction. The Alderman and his turtle-devouring fellows cracked the whip over the police whom they appointed or dismissed,

53

and the police were a ballot-engine not to be resisted. He who held the Alderman, held the police; and he who had the police, carried victory between his hands.

Doubtless it was some inner-circle treachery which Big Kennedy apprehended. The regular opposition, while numerous and carrying on its muster rolls the best respectability of the ward, lacked of that organization which was the ridgepole of Big Kennedy's supremacies. It straggled, and was mob-like in its movements; and while, as I've written, it showed strong in numbers, it was no more to be collected or fashioned into any telling force for political effort than a flock of grazing sheep. If there were to come nothing before him more formidable than the regular opposition, Big Kennedy would go over it like a train of cars and ask no aid of shoulder-hitters. Such innocent ones might stand three deep about a ballot-box, and yet Big Kennedy would take from it what count of votes he chose and they be none the wiser. It would come to no more than cheating a child at cards.

The open opposition to Big Kennedy was made up of divers misfit elements. At its head, as a sort of captain by courtesy, flourished that reputable peppery old gentleman who aforetime took my part against Sheeny Joe. A bit in love with his own eloquence, and eager for a forum wherein to exercise it, the reputable old gentleman had named himself for Alderman against Big Kennedy's candidate. As a campaign scheme of vote-getting—for he believed he had but to be heard to convince a listener —the reputable old gentleman engaged himself upon what he termed a house-to-house canvass.

It was the evening of that day whereon Big Kennedy gave me those orders touching the Tin Whistles when the reputable old gentleman paid a visit to Old Mike, that Nestor being as usual on his porch and comforting himself with a pipe.   I chanced to be present at the conversation, although I had no word therein; I was much at Old Mike's knee during those callow days, having an appetite for his counsel.

"Good-evening, sir," said the reputable old gentleman, taking a chair which Old Mike's politeness provided, "good-evening, sir.   My name is Morton—Mr. Morton of the Morton Bank.   I live in Lafayette Place. Incidentally, I am a candidate for the office of Alderman, and I thought I'd take the freedom of a neighbor and a taxpayer and talk with you on that topic of general interest."

"Why then," returned Old Mike, with a cynical grin, " I'm th' daddy of Big Jawn Kennedy, an' for ye to talk to me would be loike throwin' away your toime."

The reputable old gentleman was set aback by the news.   Next he took heart of grace.

"For," he said, turning upon Old Mike a pleasant eye, although just a dash of the patronizing showed in the curve of his brow, " if I should be so fortunate as to explain to you your whole duty of politics, it might influence your son. Your son, I understand, listens greatly to your word."

" He would be a ba-ad son who didn't moind his own father," returned Old Mike. " As to me jooty av politics—it's th' same as every other man's. It's the jooty av lookin' out for meself."

This open-air selfishness as declared by Old Mike rather served to shock the reputable old gentleman.

" And in politics do you think first of yourself? " he asked.

" Not only first, but lasht," replied Old Mike. " An' so do you; an' so does every man."

" I cannot understand the narrowness of your view," retorted the reputable old gentleman, somewhat austere and distant. " You are a respectable man; you call yourself a good citizen? "

" Why," responded Old Mike, for the other's remark concluded with a rising inflection like a question, " I get along with th' p'lice; an' I get along with th' priests— what more should a man say ! "

" Are you a taxpayer? "

" I have th' house," responded Old Mike, with a smile.

The reputable old gentleman considered the other dubiously. Evidently he didn't regard Old Mike's one-story cottage as all that might be desired in the way of credentials. Still he pushed on.

"Have you given much attention to political economy?" This with an erudite cough. "Have you made politics a study?"

"From me cradle," returned Old Mike. "Every Irishman does. I knew so much about politics before I was twenty-one, th' British Government would have transhported me av I'd stayed in Dublin."

"I should think," said the reputable old gentleman, with a look of one who had found something to stand on, "that if you ran from tyranny in Ireland, you would refuse here to submit to the tyranny of Tammany Hall. If you couldn't abide a Queen, how can you now put up with a Boss?"

"I didn't run from th' Queen, I ran from th' laws," said Old Mike. "As for the Boss—everything that succeeds has a Boss. The President's a boss; the Pope's a boss; Stewart's a boss in his store down in City Hall Park. That's right; everything that succeeds has a boss. Nothing is strong enough to stand the mishtakes av more than one man. Ireland would have been free th' long cinturies ago if she'd only had a boss."

"But do you call it good citizenship," demanded the reputable old gentleman, not a trifle nettled by Old Mike's hard-shell philosophy of state; "do you call it good citizenship to take your orders from a boss? You are loyal to Tammany before you are loyal to the City?"

"Shure!" returned Old Mike, puffing the puffs of him

who is undisturbed. "Do ye ever pick up a hand in a
game av ca-ards?" The reputable old gentleman
seemed properly disgusted. "There you be then!
City Government is but a game; so's all government.
Shure, it's as if you an' me were playin' a game av
ca-ards, this politics; your party is your hand, an'
Tammany is my hand. In a game of ca-ards, which are
ye loyal to, is it your hand or the game? Man, it's
your hand av coorse! By the same token! I am loyal to
Tammany Hall."

That closed the discussion; the reputable old gentleman went his way, and one might tell by his face that
the question to assail him was whether he had been in a
verbal encounter with a Bedlamite or an Anarchist. He
did not recognize me, nor was I sorry. I liked the
reputable old gentleman because of that other day, and
would not have had him discover me in what he so plainly
felt to be dangerous company.

"He's a mighty ignorant man," said Old Mike, pointing after the reputable old gentleman with the stem of
his pipe. "What this country has mosht to fear is th'
ignorance av th' rich."

It stood perhaps ten of the clock on the morning of
election day when, on word sent me, I waited on Big
Kennedy in his barroom. When he had drawn me into
his sanctum at the rear, he, as was his custom, came
pointedly to the purpose.

" There's a fight bein' made on me," he said. " They've put out a lot of money on the quiet among my own people, an' think to sneak th' play on me." While Big Kennedy talked, his eyes never left mine, and I could feel he was searching me for any flickering sign that the enemy had been tampering with my fealty. I stared back at him like a statue. " An'," went on Big Kennedy, " not to put a feather-edge on it, I thought I'd run you over, an' see if they'd been fixin' you. I guess you're all right; you look on the level." Then swinging abruptly to the business of the day: " Have you got your gang ready? "

" Yes," I nodded.

" Remember my orders. Five-thirty is the time. Go for the blokes with badges—th' ticket peddlers. An' mind! don't pound 'em, chase 'em. Unless they stop to slug with you, don't put a hand on 'em."

Being thus re-instructed and about to depart, I made bold to ask Big Kennedy if there were any danger of his man's defeat. He shook his head.

" Not a glimmer," he replied. " But we've got to keep movin'. They've put out stacks of money. They've settled it to help elect the opposition candidate—this old gent, Morton. They don't care to win; they're only out to make me lose. If they could take the Alderman an' the police away from me, they would go in next trip an' kill me too dead to skin. But

it's no go; they can't make th' dock. They've put in
their money; but I'll show 'em a trick that beats money
to a standstill."

It was as I had surmised; Big Kennedy feared treachery and the underhand support of the enemy by men
whom he called his friends. For myself, I would stand
by him. Beg Kennedy was the only captain I knew.

To the commands of Big Kennedy, and their execution, I turned with as ready a heart as ever sent duck
to drink. No impulse to disobey or desert so much as
crossed my slope of thought. Tammany Hall has ever
been military in its spirit. Big Kennedy was my superior officer, I but a subaltern; it was my province to accept his commands and carry them forward without argument or pause.

In full and proper season, I had my Tin Whistles in
hand. I did not march them to the polling place in a
body, since I was not one to obstreperously vaunt or
flaunt an enterprise in advance. Also, I was too much
the instinctive soldier to disclose either my force or my
purpose, and I knew the value of surprise.

There were a round twenty of my Tin Whistles, each
a shoulder-hitter and warm to shine in the graces of
Big Kennedy. I might have recruited a double strength,
but there was no need. I had counted the foe; the poll-
tenders of the opposition numbered but ten; my twenty,
and each a berserk of his fists, ought to scatter them like

a flock of sparrows. My instructions given to my fellows were precisely Big Kennedy's orders as given to
me; no blows, no blood unless made necessary by resistance.

As the time drew down for action, my Tin Whistles
were scattered about, sticking close to the elbows of the
enemy, and waiting the signal. The polling booth was
a small frame construction, not much larger than a
Saratoga trunk. On other occasions it served as the
office of a wood and coal concern. The table, with the
ballot-box thereon, stood squarely in the door; behind
it were the five or six officers—judges and tally clerks—
of election. There was a crush and crowd of Big Kennedy's clansmen to entirely surround the little building,
and they so choked up the path that ones who had still
to vote couldn't push through. There arose, too, a
deal of shoving and jostling, and all to a running uproar of profanity; affairs appeared to be drifting towards the disorderly.

The reputable old gentleman, his face red with indignation, was moving to and fro on the outskirts of the
crowd, looking for a police officer. He would have him
cut a way through the press for those who still owned
votes. No officer was visible; the reputable old gentleman, even though he searched with that zeal common of
candidates anxious for success, would have no aid from
the constabulary.

"And this is the protection," cried the reputable old gentleman, striding up to Big Kennedy, and shaking a wrathful finger in his face, "that citizens and taxpayers receive from the authorities! Here are scores of voters who are being blocked from the polls and robbed of their franchise. It's an outrage!"

Big Kennedy smiled upon the reputable old gentleman, but made no other reply.

"It's an outrage!" repeated the reputable old gentleman in a towering fury. "Do you hear? It's an outrage on the taxpaying citizens of this town!"

"Look out, old man!" observed a young fellow who stood at Big Kennedy's side, and who from his blackened hands and greasy blue shirt seemed to be the engineer of some tug. "Don't get too hot. You'll blow a cylinder head."

"How dare you!" fumed the reputable old gentleman; "you, a mere boy by comparison! how dare you address me in such terms! I'm old enough, sir, to be your father! You should understand, sir, that I've voted for a president eight times in my life."

"That's nothin'," returned the other gayly; "I have voted for a president eighty times before ten o'clock."

In the midst of the laugh that followed this piece of characteristic wit, Big Kennedy crossed to where I stood.

"Send your boys along!" said he. "Let's see how good you are."

My whistle screamed the signal. At the first sharp note, a cry went up:

" The Tin Whistles! The Tin Whistles! "

It was done in a moment; a pair to a man, my Tin Whistles were sending their quarry down the streets as fast as feet might follow. And they obeyed directions; not a blow was struck, no blood was drawn; there was a hustling flurry, and the others took to their heels. The hard repute of the Tin Whistles was such that no ten were wild enough to face them or meet their charge.

As the Tin Whistles fell upon their victims, the press of men that surged about the polling place began to shout, and strain, and tug. Suddenly, the small building commenced to heave and lift suspiciously. It was as though an earthquake were busy at its base. The mob about the structure seemed to be rolling it over on its side. That would be no feat, with men enough to set hand upon it and carry it off like a parcel.

With the first heave there came shouts and oaths from those within. Then arose a crashing of glass, and the table was cast aside, as the threatened clerks and judges fought to escape through door and window. In the rush and scamper of it, a sharp hand seized the ballot-box.

Ten minutes the riot raged. It was calmed by Big Kennedy, who forced himself into the middle of the tumult, hurling men right and left with his powerful hands as though they were sacks of bran, while he commanded the peace in a voice like the roar of a lion.

Peace fell; the little building, which had not been overthrown, but only rocked and tipped, settled again to a decorous safe solidity; the judges and the clerks returned; the restored ballot-box again occupied the table.

As that active one, who had saved the ballot-box when the downfall of the building seemed threatened came edgewise through the throng, he passed close to Big Kennedy. The latter gave him a sharp glance of inquiry.

" I stuffed it full to the cover," whispered the active one. " We win four to one, an' you can put down your money on that!"

Big Kennedy nodded, and the zealot who saved the ballot-box passed on and disappeared.

When the Tin Whistles fell upon their prey, I started to go with them. But in a moment I saw there was no call; the foe went off at top flight, and my twenty would keep them moving. Thus reasoning, I turned again to see what was going forward about the booth.

My interest was immediately engaged by the words and actions of the reputable old gentleman, who, driven to frenzy, was denouncing Big Kennedy and all who wore his colors as scoundrels without measure or mate.

" I defy both you and your plug-uglies," he was shouting, flourishing his fist in the face of Big Kennedy, who, busy with his own plans, did not heed him. " This is a plot to stuff the ballot-box."

The reputable old gentleman had gone thus far, when a hulking creature of a rough struck him from behind with a sandbag. I sprang forward, and fended away a second blow with my left arm. As I did so, I struck the rough on the jaw with such vengeful force that, not only did he drop like some pole-axed ox, but my right hand was fairly wrecked thereby. Without pausing to discover my own condition or that of the sandbag-wielding ruffian, I picked up the reputable old gentleman and bore him out of the crowd.

The reputable old gentleman had come by no serious harm; he was stunned a trifle, and his hat broken. With me to hold him up, he could stand on his feet, though still dazed and addled from the dull power of the blow. I beckoned a carriage which Big Kennedy had employed to bring the old and infirm to the polling place. It came at my signal, and I placed the reputable old gentleman inside, and told the driver to take him to his home. The reputable old gentleman was murmuring and shaking his head as he drove away. As I closed the carriage door, he muttered: " This is barbarous! That citizens and taxpayers should receive such treatment——" The balance was lost in the gride of the wheels.

The hurly-burly had now ceased; all was as calm and equal as a goose pond.

" So you saved the old gentleman," said Big Kennedy,
as he came towards me. " Gratitude, I s'pose, because he
stood pal to you ag'inst Sheeny Joe that time. Gratitude! You'll get over that in time," and Big Kennedy
wore a pitying look as one who dwells upon another's
weakness. " That was Jimmy the Blacksmith you
smashed. You'd better look out for him after this."

My dander was still on end, and I intimated a readi-
ness to look out for Jimmy the Blacksmith at once.

" Mind your back now!" cautioned Big Kennedy,
" and don't take to gettin' it up. Let things go as they
lay. Never fight till you have to, d'ye see! an' never
fight for fun. Don't go lookin' for th' Blacksmith
until you hear he's out lookin' for you." Then, as
shifting the subject: " It's been a great day, an' everything to run off as smooth an' true as sayin' mass.
Now let's go back and watch 'em count the votes."

" Did we beat them? " I asked.

" Snowed 'em under! " said Big Kennedy.

CHAPTER VI

BIG KENNEDY'S success at the election served to tighten the rivets of his rule. It was now I looked to see him ferret forth and punish those renegades who had wrought against him in the dark. To my amazement he engaged himself in no such retaliatory labor. On the contrary he smiled on all about him like the sun at noon. Was it folly or want of heart that tied his hands? Assuredly it was error, and this I submitted to Old Mike. That veteran of policy disagreed with this, meanwhile beaming upon me in a way of fatherly cunning.

" Jawn knows his business," said Old Mike. " Thim people didn't rebel, they sold out. That's over with an' gone by. Everybody 'll sell ye out if he gets enough; that's a rishk ye have to take. There's that Limerick man, Gaffney, however; ye'll see something happen to Gaffney. He's one of thim patent-leather Micks an' puts on airs. He's schemin' to tur-rn Jawn down an' take th' wa-ard. Ye'll see something happen to that Limerick man, Gaffney."

Gaffney made his money with flour and horse feed and

hay and similar goods. Also, as Old Mike said, Gaffney was ambitious. It was within the week, when a midnight shower of stones smashed sash and glass and laid waste that offensive merchant's place of business. Gaffney restored his sash and glass only to invite a second midnight storm of stones. Three times were Gaffney's windows smashed by hands unknown; and no police officer would go within two blocks of Gaffney's. In the end, Gaffney came to Big Kennedy. The latter met him with a hectoring laugh.

"Why do you come to me?" asked Big Kennedy. "Somebody's been trying to smash the windows of my leadership for over a year, but I never went howling about it to you."

Gaffney showed not a little shaken. He asked, in a manner sullen yet beaten, what he should do.

"I'd get out of th' ward," replied Big Kennedy as cool as ice. "Somebody's got it in for you. Now a man that 'll throw a brick will light a match, d'ye see, an' a feed store would burn like a tar barrel."

"If I could sell out, I'd quit," said Gaffney.

"Well," responded Big Kennedy, "I always like to help a friend."

Grocer Fogel bought Gaffney's store, making a bargain.

This iron-bound lesson in practical politics I dwell on in full. I drew from it some notion of the stern character of that science. Old Mike, from the pinnacles of his hard experience, looked down to justify it.

"Gaffney would do th' same," said Old Mike, " if his ar-rm was long enough. Politics is a game where losers lose all; it's like war, shure, only no one's kilt—at any rate, not so many."

As the days drew on, I grew in favor with Big Kennedy, and the blossom thereof took this color.

"Why don't you start a club?" he asked one afternoon, as we sat in his sanctum. "You could bring two hundred young fellows together, couldn't you?"

"Yes," I replied. I spoke doubtfully; the suggestion was of the sharpest, and gave me no space to think. It was one, too, which asked questions of the kind that don't answer themselves. "But where would they meet?" I put this after a pause.

"There's the big lodgeroom over my saloon," and Big Kennedy tossed his stubby thumb towards the ceiling. "You could meet there. There's a dumb waiter from the bar to send up beer and smokes."

"How about the Tin Whistles?" I hinted. "Would they do to build on?"

"Leave the Tin Whistles out. They're all right as shoulder-hitters, an' a swifter gang to help at the polls, or break up the opposition's meetin's, never walked the streets. But for a play of this kind, they're a little off color. Your Tin Whistles can join, man by

man, but if they do they must sing low.   They mustn't
try to give the show; it's the back seat for them.   What
you're out for now is the respectable young workin'-
man racket; that's the lay."

"But where's the money?" said I.   "These people I
have in mind haven't much money."

"Of course not," retorted Big Kennedy confidently,
"an' what little they have they want for beer.   But
listen: You get the room free.   Then once a year your
club gives an excursion on the river; it ought to sell
hundreds of tickets because there'll be hundreds of office-
holders, an' breweries, an' saloon keepers, an' that sort
who'll be crazy to buy 'em.   If they aint crazy to start
with, you ought to be able to make 'em crazy th' first
election that comes 'round.   The excursion should bring
three thousand dollars over an' above expenses, d'ye see.
Then you can give balls in the winter an' sell tickets.
Then there's subscriptions an' hon'ry memberships.
You'll ketch on; there's lots of ways to skin th' cat.
You can keep th' club in clover an' have some of the long
green left.   That's settled then; you organize a young
men's club.   You be president an' treasurer; see to that.
An' now," here Big Kennedy took me by the shoulder
and looked me instructively in the eye, "it's time for you
to be clinchin' onto some stuff for yourself.   This club's
goin' to take a lot of your time.   It 'll make you do
plenty of work.   You're no treetoad; you can't live on

air an' scenery." Big Kennedy's look deepened, and he
shook me as one who demands attention. " You'll be
president and treasurer, particularly treasurer; and I'll
chip you in this piece of advice. A good cook always
licks his fingers." Here he winked deeply.

This long speech was not thrown away. Big Kennedy, having delivered himself, lapsed into silence, while
I sat ruminating ways and means and what initiatory
steps I should take.

" What shall we call it? " I asked, as I arose to go.

" Give it an Indian name," said Big Kennedy. " S'p-
pose you call it the Red Jacket Association."

Within the fortnight the Red Jackets held their
maiden meeting. It was an hour rife of jubilation, fel-
lowship, and cheer. While abstinence from drink was
my guiding phrase, I made no point of that kind in the
conduct of others, and a nearby brewery having contributed unlimited beer those whom it pleased lacked no
reason for a light heart.

As Big Kennedy had advised, I was chosen for the
double responsibilities of president and treasurer. I may
say in my own compliment, however, that these honors
came drifting to my feet. There were reasons for this
aside from any stiffness of heart or fist-virtues which
might be mine. I have said that I was by disposition
as taciturn as a tree, and this wondrous gift of silence
earned me the name of wisdom. I was looked upon as one

whose depth was rival to the ocean's.   Stronger still, as
the argument by which I rose, was my sobriety.   The man
who drinks, and whether it be little or much, never
fails to save his great respect for him who sets whisky
aside.

"An' now," remarked Big Kennedy, when the club
had found fortunate birth, "with these Red Jackets to
make the decent front, th' Tin Whistles to fall back on
for the rough work, and Gaffney out of th' way, I call
th' ward cleaned up.   I'll tell you this, my son: after
th' next election you shall have an office, or there's no
such man as Big John Kennedy."   He smote the table
with his heavy hand until the glasses danced.

"But I won't be of age," I suggested.

"What's the difference?" said Big Kennedy.
"We'll play that you are, d'ye see.   There'll be no one
fool enough to talk about your age if I'm at your side.
We'll make it a place in the dock department; that 'll be
about your size.   S'ppose we say a perch where there's
twelve hundred dollars a year, an' nothin' to do but
draw th' scads an' help your friends."

Jimmy the Blacksmith was an under-captain of Big
Kennedy's and prevailed as vote-master in the northern
end of the ward.   Within certain fixed frontiers, which
ran on one side within a block of my home, it was the
business of Jimmy the Blacksmith to have watch and
ward.   He had charge of what meetings were held,

and under the thumb of Big Kennedy carried forward
the campaign, and on election day got out the
vote.

Having given the question its share of thought, I
determined for myself on a forward, upward step. My
determination—heart and soul—became agate-hard to
drive Jimmy the Blacksmith from his place, and set up
my own rule over that slender kingdom.

Nor would I say aught to Big Kennedy of this private
war which I meditated. Not that he would have inter-
fered either to thwart or aid me, but by the ethics of the
situation, to give him such notice was neither proper nor
expected. To fight Jimmy the Blacksmith for his crown
was not only right by every rule of ward justice, but it
was the thing encouraged as a plan best likely to bring
the strongest to the fore. Take what you may, keep
what you can! was a Tammany statute; I would be right
enough in that overthrow of Jimmy the Blacksmith, I
was bent upon, if only I proved strong enough to bring
it about. No, I was not to give word of my campaign
to Big Kennedy, it was none of his affair, and he would
prefer to be ignorant since he was bound to stand neutral. It is policy thus to let the younger cocks try
beak and spur among themselves; it develops leadership,
and is the one sure way of safety in picking out your
captains.

There was one drawback; I didn't live within the

region of which I would make prize.   However, ambition edged my wits and I bethought me of a plan whereby I might plow around that stump.

It was my own good fortune that I had no love, but only hate, for Jimmy the Blacksmith.   I was yet so softened of a want of years, that had we been friends I would have withheld myself from attacking him.   Youth is generous, wherefore youth is weak.   It is not until age has stopped these leaks in one's nature, and one ceases to give and only lives to take and keep, that one's estate begins to take on fat.   Have the word, therefore, of him whose scars speak for his experience: that one will be wise who regards generosity as a malady, a mere disease, and sets to cure it with every sullen, cruel drug the case demands.   I say it was my good luck to hate Jimmy the Blacksmith.   He had never condoned that election-day blow, and I must confess there was reason for this hardness.   His jaw had been broken, and, though mended, it was still all of one side and made of him a most forbidding spectacle.   And he nursed a thought of revenge in his breast; there came a light to his eye when we met that belongs with none save him whose merest wish is murder.   I would have had more than black looks, but his heart was of a pale and treacherous family that can strike no blow in front, and thus far the pathway of chance had not opened for him to come upon me unaware.   For all of which, not alone my ambition, but my safety and my pleasure urged me about the destruction of Jimmy the Blacksmith.

That epithet of the Blacksmith was born of no labors of the forge. Jimmy the Blacksmith was no more a blacksmith than a bishop. If he ever did a day's work, then the fact was already so far astern upon the tides of time that no eye of memory might discern it. The title was won in a brawl wherein he slew a man. True to his nature, Jimmy slunk away from his adversary and would not face him. He returned, carrying a blacksmith's fore-hammer. Creeping behind the other, Jimmy suddenly cried, with an oath:

" I'll clink your anvil for you! "

With that word, the hammer descended and the victim fell, skull crushed like an eggshell. It required a deal of perjury to save the murderer from noose and trap. I should not say he was set backward by this bloodshed, since most men feared him for it and stepped out of his way, giving him what he asked for in the name of their own safety. It was for this work he was called the Blacksmith, and he carried the word as though it were a decoration.

Such was the man on whose downfall I stood resolved and whose place I meant to make my own. The thing was simple of performance too; all it asked were secrecy and a little wit. There was a Tammany club, one of regular sort and not like my Red Jacket Association,

which was volunteer in its character. It met in that
kingdom of the Blacksmith's as a little parliament of
politics. This club was privileged each year to name for
Big Kennedy's approval a man for that post of under-
captain. The annual selection was at hand. For four
years the club had named Jimmy the Blacksmith; there
came never the hint for believing he would not be pitched
upon again.

Now be it known that scores of my Red Jackets were
residents of the district over which Jimmy the Blacksmith held sway. Some there were who already belonged
to his club. I gave those others word to join at once.
Also I told them, as they regarded their standing as
Red Jackets, to be present at that annual meeting.

The night arrived; the room was small and the at-
tendance—except for my Red Jackets—being sparse, my
people counted for three-quarters of those present. With
the earliest move I took possession of the meeting, and
selected its chairman. Then, by resolution, I added the
block in which I resided to the public domain of the club.
That question of residence replied to, instead of Jimmy
the Blacksmith, I was named ballot-captain for the year.
It was no more complex as a transaction than counting
ten. The fact was accomplished like scratching a match;
I had set the foot of my climbing on Jimmy the
Blacksmith's neck.

That unworthy was present; and to say he was made

mad with the fury of it would be to write with snow the
color of his feelings.

"It's a steal!" he cried, springing to his feet. The
little bandbox of a hall rang with his roarings. Then,
to me: "I'll fight you for it! You don't dare meet
me in the Peach Orchard to-morrow at three!"

"Bring your sledge, Jimmy," shouted some humorist;
"you'll need it."

The Peach Orchard might have been a peach orchard
in the days of Peter Stuyvesant. All formal battles
took place in the Peach Orchard. Wherefore, and because the challenge for its propriety was not without
precedent, to the Peach Orchard at the hour named I
repaired.

Jimmy the Blacksmith, however, came not. Someone
brought the word that he was sick; whereat those present,
being fifty gentlemen with a curiosity to look on
carnage, and ones whose own robust health led them to
regard the term "sickness" as a synonym for the preposterous, jeered the name of Jimmy the Blacksmith
from their hearts.

"Jimmy the Cur! it ought to be," growled one, whose
disappointment over a fight deferred was sore in the
extreme.

Perhaps you will argue that it smacked of the underhand to thus steal upon Jimmy the Blacksmith and take
his place from him without due warning given. I con-

fess it would have been more like chivalry if I had sent
him, so to say, a glove and told my intentions against
him.   Also it would have augmented labor and multiplied risk.   The great thing is to win and win cheaply;
a victory that costs more than it comes to is nothing
but a mask for defeat.

"You're down and out," said Big Kennedy, when
Jimmy the Blacksmith brought his injuries to that chieftain.   "Your reputation is gone too; you were a fool
to say 'Peach Orchard' when you lacked the nerve to
make it good.   You'll never hold up your head ag'in in
th' ward, an' if I was you I'd line out after Gaffney.
This is a bad ward for a mongrel, Jimmy, an' I'd skin
out."

Jimmy the Blacksmith followed Gaffney and disappeared from the country of Big Kennedy.   He was to
occur again in my career, however, as he who reads on
shall see, and under conditions which struck the color
from my cheek and set my heart to a trot with the terrors
they loosed at its heels.

CHAPTER VII

HOW THE BOSS WAS NAMED FOR ALDERMAN

NOW it was that in secret my ambition took a hearty start and would vine-like creep and clamber. My triumph over Jimmy the Blacksmith added vastly to my stature of politics. Moreover, the sly intrigue by which I conquered began to found for me a fame. I had been locally illustrious, if I may so set the term to work, for a granite fist and a courage as rooted as a tree. For these traits the roughs revered me, and I may say I found my uses and rewards. Following my conquest of that under-captaincy, however, certain upper circles began to take account of me; circles which, if no purer than those others of ruder feather, were wont to produce more bulging profits in the pockets of their membership. In brief, I came to be known for one capable and cunning of a plot, and who was not without a genius for the executive.

With Big Kennedy I took high position. His relations with Jimmy the Blacksmith never had been close; he had never unbuckled in any friendship and felt for him nothing nearer than distrust. But for me he held another pose. Big Kennedy, upon my elevation, fair made me his partner in the ward, a partnership wherein, to speak commercially, I might be said to have had an interest of one-fourth. This promotion brought me pleasure; and being only a boy when all was said, while I went outwardly quiet, my spirit in the privacy of my own bosom would on occasion spread moderately its tail and strut.

Now, as time passed, I became like the shadow of Big Kennedy's authority throughout the ward; my voice was listened to and my word obeyed. I should say, too, that I made it a first concern to carry the interest of Big Kennedy ever on the crest of my thought. This should be called the offspring neither of loyalty nor gratitude; I did it because it was demanded of my safety and to curry advantage for myself. For all that attitude of confident friendship, I was not put off my guard. Big Kennedy never let my conduct roam beyond his ken. A first sign of an interest outside his own would have meant my instant disappearance. He would have plucked me of my last plume. With a breath he could reduce me to be a beggarman where now I gave alms. Having, therefore, the measure of his fell abilities, I was not so blind as to draw their horns my way.

Still, while I went tamely to heel at a word from Big Kennedy, I had also resolved to advance. I meant before all was over to mount the last summit of Tammany

Hall. I laid out my life as architects lay out a building; it would call for years, but I had years to give.

My work with Grocer Fogel had ended long ago. I now gave myself entirely to the party, and to deepen the foundations of its power. Inside our lines a mighty harmony prevailed. Big Kennedy and those headquarters enemies who once schemed for his defeat had healed their differences and the surface of events showed as serene as summer seas. About this time a great star was rising in the Tammany sky; a new chief was gaining evolution. Already, his name was first, and although he cloaked his dictatorship with prudence, the sophisticated knew how his will was even then as law and through his convenient glove of velvet felt his grip of steel.

For myself, I closely observed the unfolding of his genius. His methods as well as those of Big Kennedy were now my daily lesson. I had ever before me in that formative, plastic hour the examples of these past-masters of the art of domination.

It was well for me. A dictator is so much unlike a poet that he is made, not born. He must build himself; and when completed he must save himself from being torn to pieces. No one blunders into a dictatorship; one might as well look to blunder upon some mountain peak. Even blunders are amenable to natural law, and it can be taken as a truism that no one blunders up hill.

Wherefore, he who would be dictator and with his touch determine the day for pushing, struggling, rebelling thousands and mold their times for them, must study. And study hard I did.

My Red Jackets received my most jealous care. They deserved that much from me, since their existence offered measurably for my support. When the day arrived, I was given that twelve-hundred-dollar place with the docks, whereof Big Kennedy had spoken, and under his suggestion and to the limits of my strength made what employ of it I might for my own and my friends' behoof. But those twelve hundred dollars would not go far in the affairs of one who must for their franchises lead hither and yon divers scores of folk, all of whom had but the one notion of politics, that it was founded of free beer. There came, too, a procession of borrowers, and it was a dull day when, in sums from a dime to a dollar, I did not to these clients part with an aggregate that would have supported any family for any decent week. There existed no door of escape; these charges, and others of similar kidney, must be met and borne; it was the only way to keep one's hold of politics; and so Old Mike would tell me.

" But it's better," said that deep one, " to lind people money than give it to 'em. You kape thim bechune your finger longer by lindin'."

It was on the Red Jackets I leaned most for per-

sonal revenue. They were my bread-winners. No
Tammany organization, great or small, keeps books.
No man may say what is received, or what is disbursed,
or name him who gave or got; and that is as it should be.
If it were otherwise, one's troubles would never earn an
end. For the Red Jackets I was—to steal a title from
the general organization—not alone the treasurer, but
the wiskinskie. In this latter rôle I collected the money
that came in. Thus the interests, financial, of the Red
Jackets were wholly within my hands, and recalling
what Big Kennedy had said anent a good cook, I failed
not to lick my fingers.

Money was in no wise difficult to get. The Red
Jackets were formidable both for numbers and influence,
and their favor or resentment meant a round one thousand votes. Besides, there stood the memorable Tin
Whistles, reckless, militant, ready for any midnight
thing, and their dim outlines, like a challenge or a threat,
filled up the cloudy background. Those with hopes or
fears of office, and others who as merchants or saloon-
keepers, or who gambled, or did worse, to say naught of
builders who found the streets and pavements a convenient
even though an illegal resting place for their materials
of bricks and lime and lumber, never failed of response
to a suggestion that the good Red Jackets stood in need
of help. Every man of these contributing gentry, at
their trades of dollar-getting, was violating law or ordi-

nance, and I who had the police at my beck could instantly contract their liberties to a point that pinched.
When such were the conditions, anyone with an imagination above a shoemaker's will see that to produce what
funds my wants demanded would be the lightest of tasks.
It was like grinding sugar canes, and as easily sure of
steady sweet returns.

True, as an exception to a rule, one met now and again
with him who for some native bull-necked obstinacy
would refuse a contribution. In such event the secret
of his frugality was certain to leak forth and spread
itself among my followers. It would not be required
that one offer even a hint. Soon as ever the tale of
that parsimony reached the ear of a Tin Whistle, disasters like a flock of buzzards collected about the saving
man. His windows were darkly broken like Gaffney's.
Or if he were a grocer his wares would upset themselves
about the pavements, his carts of delivery break down,
his harnesses part and fall in pieces, and he be set to dine
off sorrow in many a different dish.

And then and always there were the police to call his
violative eye to this ordinance, or hale him before a
magistrate for that one. And there were Health
Boards, and Street Departments, who at a wink of Red
Jacket disfavor would descend upon a recalcitrant and
provide burdens for his life. With twenty methods of
compulsion against him, and each according to law, there

arose no man strong enough to refuse those duties of donation. He must support the fortunes of my Red Jackets or see his own decline, and no one with a heart for commerce was long to learn the lesson.

The great credit, however, in such coils was due the police. With them to be his allies, one might not only finance his policies, but control and count a vote; and no such name as failure.

" They're the foot-stones of politics," said Old Mike. " Kape th' p'lice, an' you kape yourself on top."

Nor was this the task complex. It was but to threaten them with the powers above on the one hand, or on the other toss them individually an occasional small bone of profit to gnaw, and they would stand to you like dogs. I soon had these ins and outs of money-getting at the tips of my tongue and my fingers, for I went to school to Big Kennedy and Old Mike in the accomplishment, and I may tell you it was a branch of learning they were qualified to teach.

Blackmail! cry you? Now there goes a word to that. These folk were violating the law. What would you have?—their arrest? Let me inform you that were the laws of the State and the town enforced to syllable and letter, it would drive into banishment one-half the population. They would do business at a loss; it would put up the shutters for over half the town. Wherefore, it would be against the common interest to arrest them.

And still you would have the law enforced? And if it were, what, let me ask, would be the immediate response? These delinquents would be fined. You would then be satisfied. What should be the corrective difference between a fine paid to a court, and a donation paid to my Red Jackets? The corrective influence in both should be the same, since in either instance it is but a taking of dollars from the purses of the lawless. And yet, you clamor, " One is blackmail and the other is justice! " The separation I should say was academic rather than practical; and as for a name: why then, I care nothing for a name.

I will, however, go this farther journey for my own defense. I have not been for over twoscore years with Tammany and sixteen years its head, without being driven to some intimate knowledge of my times, and those principles of individual as well as communal action which underlie them to make a motive. And now I say, that I have yet to meet that man, or that corporation, and though the latter were a church, who wouldn't follow interest across a prostrate law, and in the chase of dollars break through ordinance and statute as a cow walks through a cobweb. And each and all they come most willingly to pay the prices of their outlawry, and receivers are as bad as thieves—your price-payer as black as your price-taker. Practically, the New York definition of an honest man has ever gone that he is one who denounces any robbery in the proceeds whereof he is not personally interested, and with that definition my life has never failed to comply. If Tammany and Tammany men have been guilty of receiving money from violators of law, they had among their accomplices the town's most reputable names and influences. Why then should you pursue the one while you excuse the other? And are you not, when you do so, quite as much the criminal as either?

When I was in the first year of my majority we went into a campaign for the ownership of the town. Standing on the threshold of my earliest vote, I was strung like a bow to win. My fervor might have gained a more than common heat, because by decision of Big Kennedy I, myself, was put down to make the run for alderman. There was a world of money against us, since we had the respectable clement, which means ever the rich, to be our enemies.

Big Kennedy and I, after a session in his sanctum, resolved that not one meeting should be held by our opponents within our boundaries. It was not that we feared for the vote; rather it swung on a point of pride; and then it would hearten our tribesmen should we suppress the least signal of the enemy's campaign.

Having limitless money, the foe decided for sundry gatherings. They also outlined processions, hired music by the band, and bought beer by the barrel. They would have their speakers to address the commons in halls and from trucks.

On each attempt they were encountered and dispersed. More than once the Red Jackets, backed by the faithful Tin Whistles, took possession of a meeting, put up their own orators and adopted their own resolutions. If the police were called, they invariably arrested our enemies, being sapient of their own safety and equal to the work of locating the butter on their personal bread. If the enemy through their henchmen or managers made physical resistance, the Tin Whistles put them outside the hall, and whether through door or window came to be no mighty matter.

At times the Red Jackets and their reserves of Tin Whistles would permit the opposition to open a meeting. When the first orator had been eloquent for perhaps five minutes, a phalanx of Tin Whistles would arise in their places, and a hailstorm of sponges, soaking wet and each the size of one's head, would descend upon the rostrum. It was a never-failing remedy; there lived never chairman nor orator who would face that fusillade. Sometimes the lights were turned out; and again when it was an open-air meeting and the speakers to talk from a truck, a bunch of crackers would be exploded under the horses and a runaway occur. That simple device was sure to cut the meeting short by carrying off the orators. The foe arranged but one procession; that was disposed of on the fringe of our territory by an unerring, even if improper, volley of eggs and vegetables and similar trumpery. The artillery used would have beaten back a charge by cavalry.

Still the enemy had the money, and on that important point could overpower us like ten for one, and did. Here and there went their agents, sowing sly riches in the hope of a harvest of votes. To counteract this still-hunt where the argument was cash, I sent the word abroad that our people were to take the money and promise votes. Then they were to break the promise.

"Bunco the foe!" was the watchword; "take their money and ' con ' them!"

This instruction was deemed necessary for our safety. I educated our men to the thought that the more money they got by these methods, the higher they would stand with Big Kennedy and me. If it were not for this, hundreds would have taken a price, and then, afraid to come back to us, might have gone with the banners of the enemy for that campaign at least. Now they would get what they could, and wear it for a feather in their caps. They exulted in such enterprise; it was spoiling the Egyptian; having filled their pockets they would return and make a brag of the fact. By these schemes we kept our strength. The enemy parted with money by the thousands, yet never the vote did they obtain. The goods failed of delivery.

Sheeny Joe was a handy man to Big Kennedy. He owned no rank; but voluble, active, well dressed, and ready with his money across a barroom counter, he grew to have a value. Not once in those years which fell in between our encounter on the dock and this time I have in memory, did Sheeny Joe express aught save friendship for me. His nose was queer of contour as the result of my handiwork, but he met the blemish in a spirit of philosophy and displayed no rancors against me as the author thereof. On the contrary, he was friendly to the verge of fulsome.

Sheeny Joe sold himself to the opposition, hoof and hide and horn. Nor was this a mock disposal of himself, although he gave Big Kennedy and myself to suppose he still held by us in his heart. No, it wasn't the money that changed him; rather I should say that for all his pretenses, his hankerings of revenge against me had never slept. It was now he believed his day to compass it had come. The business was no more no less than a sheer bald plot to take my life, with Sheeny Joe to lie behind it—the bug of evil under the dark chip.

It was in the early evening at my own home. Sheeny Joe came and called me to the door, and all in a hustle of hurry.

" Big Kennedy wants you to come at once to the Tub of Blood," said Sheeny Joe.

The Tub of Blood was a hang-out for certain bludgeon-wielding thugs who lived by the coarser crimes of burglary and highway robbery.   It was suspected by Big Kennedy and myself as a camping spot for " repeaters " whom the enemy had been at pains to import against us.   We had it then in plan to set the Tin Whistles to the sacking of it three days before the vote.

On this word from Sheeny Joe, and thinking that some new programme was afoot, I set forth for the Tub of Blood.   As I came through the door, a murderous creature known as Strong-Arm Dan was busy polishing glasses behind the bar.   He looked up, and giving a nod toward a door in the rear, said:

" They want you inside."

The moment I set foot within that rear door, I saw how it was a trap.   There were a round dozen waiting, and each the flower of a desperate flock.

In the first surprise of it I did not speak, but instinctively got the wall to my back.   As I faced them they moved uneasily, half rising from their chairs, growling, but speaking no word.   Their purpose was to attack me; yet they hung upon the edge of the enterprise, apparently in want of a leader.   I was not a yard from the door, and having advantage of their slowness began making my way in that direction.   They saw that I would escape, and yet they couldn't spur their courage to the leap.   It was my perilous repute as a hitter from the shoulder that stood my friend that night.

At last I reached the door.   Opening it with my hand behind me, my eyes still on the glaring hesitating roughs, I stepped backward into the main room.

"Good-night, gentlemen," was all I said.

"You'll set up the gin, won't you?" cried one, finding his voice.

"Sure!" I returned, and I tossed Strong-Arm Dan a gold piece as I passed the bar.   "Give 'em what they want while it lasts," said I.

That demand for gin mashed into the teeth of my thoughts like the cogs of a wheel.   It would hold that precious coterie for twenty minutes.   When I got into the street, I caught the shadow of Sheeny Joe as he twisted around the corner.

It was a half-dozen blocks from the Tub of Blood that I blew the gathering call of the Tin Whistles. They came running like hounds to huntsman.   Ten minutes later the Tub of Blood lay a pile of ruins, while Strong-Arm Dan and those others, surprised in the midst of that guzzling I had paid for, with heads and faces a hash of wounds and blood and the fear of death upon them, were running or staggering or crawling for shelter, according to what strength remained with them.

"It's plain," said Big Kennedy, when I told of the net that Sheeny Joe had spread for me, "it's plain that you haven't shed your milk-teeth yet.   However, you'll be older by an' by, an' then you won't follow off every band of music that comes playin' down the street. No, I don't blame Sheeny Joe; politics is like draw-poker, an' everybody's got a right to fill his hand if he can. Still, while I don't blame him, it's up to us to get hunk an' even on th' play." Here Big Kennedy pondered for the space of a minute. Then he continued: " I think we'd better make it up-the-river—better railroad the duffer. Discipline's been gettin' slack of late, an' an example will work in hot an' handy. The next crook won't pass us out the double-cross when he sees what comes off in th' case of Sheeny Joe."

CHAPTER VIII

THE FATE OF SHEENY JOE

BIG KENNEDY'S suggestion of Sing Sing for Sheeny Joe did not fit with my fancy. Not that a cropped head and a suit of stripes would have been misplaced in the instance of Sheeny Joe, but I had my reputation to consider. It would never do for a first bruiser of his day to fall back on the law for protection. Such coward courses would shake my standing beyond recovery. It would have disgraced the Tin Whistles; thereafter, in that vigorous brotherhood, my commands would have earned naught save laughter. To arrest Sheeny Joe would be to fly in the face of the Tin Whistles and their dearest ethics. When to this I called Big Kennedy's attention, he laughed as one amused.

"You don't twig!" said he, recovering a partial gravity. "I'm goin' to send him over th' road for robbery."

"But he hasn't robbed anybody!"

Big Kennedy made a gesture of impatience, mixed with despair.

"Here!" said he at last, "I'll give you a flash of what

I'm out to do an' why I'm out to do it. I'm goin' to put Sheeny Joe away to stiffen discipline. He's sold himself, an' th' whole ward knows it. Now I'm goin' to show 'em what happens to a turncoat, as a hunch to keep their coats on right side out, d'ye see."

"But you spoke of a robbery!" I interjected; "Sheeny Joe has robbed no one."

"I'm gettin' to that," returned Big Kennedy, with a repressive wave of his broad palm, "an' I can see that you yourself have a lot to learn. Listen: If I knew of any robbery Sheeny Joe had pulled off, I wouldn't have him lagged for that; no, not if he'd taken a jimmy an' cracked a dozen bins. There'd be no lesson in sendin' a duck over th' road in that. Any old woman could have him pinched for a crime he's really pulled off. To leave an impression on these people, you must send a party up for what he hasn't done. Then they understand."

For all Big Kennedy's explanation, I still lived in the dark. I made no return, however, either of comment or question; I considered that I had only to look on, and Big Kennedy's purpose would elucidate itself. Big Kennedy and I were in the sanctum that opened off his barroom. He called one of his barmen.

"Billy, you know where to find the Rat?" Then, when the other nodded: "Go an' tell the Rat I want him."

" Who is the Rat? " I queried.   I had never heard of
the Rat.

" He's a pickpocket," responded Big Kennedy, " an'
as fly a dip as ever nipped a watch or copped a leather."

The Rat belonged on the west side of the town, which
accounted for my having failed of his acquaintance.
Big Kennedy was sure his man would find him.

" For he grafts nights," said Big Kennedy, " an' at
this time of day it's a cinch he's takin' a snooze.   A
pickpocket has to have plenty of sleep to keep his hooks
from shakin'."

While we were waiting the coming of the Rat, one of
the barmen entered to announce a caller.   He whispered
a word in Big Kennedy's ear.

" Sure! " said he.   " Tell him to come along."

The gentleman whom the barman had announced, and
who was a young clergyman, came into the room.   Big
Kennedy gave him a hearty handshake, while his red face
radiated a welcome.

" What is it, Mr. Bronson? " asked Big Kennedy
pleasantly ; " what can I do for you? "

The young clergyman's purpose was to ask assistance
for a mission which he proposed to start near the Five
Points.

" Certainly," said Big Kennedy, " an' not a moment
to wait! "   With that he gave the young clergyman one
hundred dollars.

When that gentleman, after expressing his thanks, had departed, Big Kennedy sighed.

"I've got no great use for a church," he said. "I never bought a gold brick yet that wasn't wrapped in a tract. But it's no fun to get a preacher down on you. One of 'em can throw stones enough to smash every window in Tammany Hall. Your only show with the preachers is to flatter 'em;—pass 'em out the flowers. Most of 'em 's as pleased with flattery as a girl. Yes indeed," he concluded, "I can paste bills on 'em so long as I do it with soft soap."

The Rat was a slight, quiet individual and looked the young physician rather than the pickpocket. His hands were delicate, and he wore gloves the better to keep them in condition. His step and air were as quiet as those of a cat.

"I want a favor," said Big Kennedy, addressing the Rat, "an' I've got to go to one of the swell mob to get it. That's why I sent for you, d'ye see! It takes someone finer than a bricklayer to do th' work."

The Rat was uneasily questioning my presence with his eye. Big Kennedy paused to reassure him.

"He's th' straight goods," said Big Kennedy, speaking in a tone wherein were mingled resentment and reproach. "You don't s'ppose I'd steer you ag'inst a brace?"

The Rat said never a word, but his glance left me and he gave entire heed to Big Kennedy.

" This is the proposition," resumed Big Kennedy. " You know Sheeny Joe.   Shadow him ; swing and rattle with him no matter where he goes.   The moment you see a chance, get a pocketbook an' put it away in his clothes.   When th' roar goes up, tell th' loser where to look.   Are you on?   Sheeny Joe must get th' collar, an' I want him caught with th' goods, d'ye see."

" I don't have to go to court ag'inst him? " said the Rat interrogatively.

" No," retorted Big Kennedy, a bit explosively. " You'd look about as well in th' witness box as I would in a pulpit.   No, you shift th' leather.   Then give th' party who's been touched th' office to go after Sheeny Joe.   After that you can screw out; that's as far as you go."

It was the next evening at the ferry.   Suddenly a cry went up.

" Thief !   Thief !   My pocketbook is gone ! "

The shouts found source in a broad man.   He was top-heavy with too much beer, but clear enough to realize that his money had disappeared.   The Rat, sly, small, clean, inconspicuous, was at his shoulder.

" There's your man ! " whispered the Rat, pointing to Sheeny Joe, whose footsteps he had been dogging the livelong day; " there's your man ! "

In a moment the broad man had thrown himself upon Sheeny Joe.

"Call the police!" he yelled. "He's got my pocket-book!"

The officer pulled him off Sheeny Joe, whom he had thrown to the ground and now clung to with the desperation of the robbed.

"Give me a look in!" said the officer, thrusting the broad man aside. "If he's got your leather we'll find it."

Sheeny Joe was breathless with the surprise and fury of the broad man's descent upon him. The officer ran his hand over the outside of Sheeny Joe's coat, holding him meanwhile fast by the collar. Then he slipped his hand inside, and drew forth a chubby pocketbook.

"That's it!" screamed the broad man, "that's my wallet with over six hundred dollars in it! The fellow stole it!"

"It's a plant!" gasped Sheeny Joe, his face like ashes. Then to the crowd: "Will somebody go fetch Big John Kennedy? He knows me; he'll say I'm square!"

Big Kennedy arrived at the station as the officer, whose journey was slow because of the throng, came in with Sheeny Joe. Big Kennedy heard the stories of the officer and the broad man with all imaginable patience. Then a deep frown began to knot his brow. He waved

Sheeny Joe aside with a gesture that told of virtuous
indignation.

"Lock him up!" cried Big Kennedy. "If he'd
slugged somebody, even if he'd croaked him, I'd
have stuck to him till th' pen'tentiary doors pinched
my fingers. But I've no use for a crook. Sing Sing's th'
place for him! It's just such fine workers as him who
disgrace th' name of Tammany Hall. They lift a
leather, an' they make Tammany a cover for th'
play."

"Are you goin' back on me?" wailed Sheeny Joe.

"Put him inside!" said Big Kennedy to the officer
in charge of the station. Then, to Sheeny Joe, with the
flicker of a leer: "Why don't you send to the Tub of
Blood?"

"Shall I take bail for him, Mr. Kennedy, if any shows
up?" asked the officer in charge.

"No; no bail!" replied Big Kennedy. "If anyone
offers, tell him I don't want it done."

It was three weeks later when Sheeny Joe was found
guilty, and sentenced to prison for four years. The
broad man, the police officer, and divers who at the time
of his arrest were looking on, come forward as witnesses
against Sheeny Joe, and twelve honest dullards who
called themselves a jury, despite his protestations that
he was "being jobbed," instantly declared him guilty.
Sheeny Joe, following his sentence, was dragged from

the courtroom, crying and cursing the judge, the jury, the witnesses, but most of all Big Kennedy.

Nor do I think Big Kennedy's agency in drawing down this fate upon Sheeny Joe was misunderstood by ones with whom it was meant to pass for warning. I argue this from what was overheard by me as we left the courtroom where Sheeny Joe was sentenced. The two in conversation were walking a pace in advance of me.

" He got four spaces! " said one in an awed whisper.

" He's dead lucky not to go for life! " exclaimed the other. " How much of the double-cross do you guess now Big Kennedy will stand? I've seen a bloke take a slab in th' morgue for less. It was Benny the Bite; he gets a knife between his slats."

" What's it all about, Jawn? " asked Old Mike, who later sat in private review of the case of Sheeny Joe. " Why are you puttin' a four-year smother on that la-ad? "

" It's gettin' so," explained Big Kennedy, " that these people of ours look on politics as a kind of Virginny reel. It's first dance on one side an' then cross to th' other. There's a bundle of money ag'inst us, big enough to trip a dog, an' discipline was givin' way. Our men could smell th' burnin' money an' it made 'em crazy. Somethin' had to come off to sober 'em, an' teach 'em discipline, an' make 'em sing ' Home, Sweet Home'!"

"It's all right, then!" declared Old Mike decisively. "The main thing is to kape up th' organization! Better twinty like that Sheeny Joe should learn th' lockstep than weaken Tammany Hall. Besides, I'm not like th' law. I belave in sindin' folks to prison, not for what they do, but for what they are. An' this la-ad was a har-rd crackther."

The day upon which Sheeny Joe went to his prison was election day. Tammany Hall took possession of the town; and for myself, I was made an alderman by a majority that counted into the skies.

CHAPTER IX

HOW BIG KENNEDY BOLTED

BEFORE I abandon the late election in its history to the keeping of time past, there is an episode, or, if you will, an accident, which should find relation. Of itself it would have come and gone, and been of brief importance, save for an incident to make one of its elements, which in a later pinch to come of politics brought me within the shadow of a gibbet.

Busy with my vote-getting, I had gone to the docks to confer with the head of a certain gang of stevedores. These latter were hustling up and down the gangplanks, taking the cargo out of a West India coffee boat. The one I had come seeking was aboard the vessel.

I pushed towards the after gangplank, and as I reached it I stepped aside to avoid one coming ashore with a huge sack of coffee on his shoulders. Not having my eyes about me, I caught my toe in a ringbolt and stumbled with a mighty bump against a sailor who was standing on the string-piece of the wharf. With nothing to save him, and a six-foot space opening between the wharf and the ship, the man fell into the river with a cry and a splash. He went to the bottom like so much pig-iron, for he could not swim.

It was the work of a moment to throw off my coat and go after him. I was as much at ease in the water as a spaniel, and there would be nothing more dangerous than a ducking in the experiment. I dived and came up with the drowning man in my grip. For all his peril, he took it coolly enough, and beyond spluttering, and puffing, and cracking off a jargon of oaths, added no difficulties to the task of saving his life. We gained help from the dock, and it wasn't five minutes before we found the safe planks beneath our feet again.

The man who had gone overboard so unexpectedly was a keen small dark creature of a Sicilian, and to be noticed for his black eyes, a red handkerchief over his head, and ears looped with golden earrings.

" No harm done, I think? " said I, when we were both ashore again.

" I lose-a my knife," said he with a grin, the water dripping from his hair. He was pointing to the empty scabbard at his belt where he had carried a sheath-knife.

" It was my blunder," said I, " and if you'll hunt me up at Big Kennedy's this evening I'll have another for you."

That afternoon, at a pawnshop in the Bowery, I bought a strange-looking weapon, that was more like a

single-edged dagger than anything else. It had a buck-
horn haft, and was heavy and long, with a blade of full
nine inches.

My Sicilian came, as I had told him, and I gave him
the knife. He was extravagant in his gratitude.

"You owe me nothing!" he cried. "It is I who owe
for my life that you save. But I shall take-a the knife
to remember how you pull me out. You good-a man;
some day I pull you out—mebby so! who knows?"

With that he was off for the docks again, leaving me
neither to hear nor to think of him thereafter for a
stirring handful of years.

It occurred to me as strange, even in a day when I
gave less time to thought than I do now, that my
first impulse as an alderman should be one of revenge.
There was that police captain, who, in the long ago,
offered insult to Anne, when she came to beg for my
liberty. "Better get back to your window," said he,
"or all the men will have left the street!" The
memory of that evil gibe had never ceased to burn me
with the hot anger of a coal of fire, and now I resolved
for his destruction.

When I told Big Kennedy, he turned the idea on his
wheel of thought for full two minutes.

"It's your right," said he at last. "You've got the
ax; you're entitled to his head. But say! pick him up on
proper charges; get him dead to rights! That aint

hard, d'ye see, for he's as crooked as a dog's hind leg. To throw him for some trick he's really turned will bunco these reform guys into thinkin' that we're on th' level."

The enterprise offered no complexities. A man paid that captain money to save from suppression a resort of flagrant immorality. The bribery was laid bare; he was overtaken in this plain corruption; and next, my combinations being perfect, I broke him as I might break a stick across my knee. He came to me in private the following day.

"What have I done?" said he. "Can I square it?"

"Never!" I retorted; "there's some things one can't square." Then I told him of Anne, and his insult.

"That's enough," he replied, tossing his hand resignedly. "I can take my medicine when it's come my turn."

For all that captain's stoicism, despair rang in his tones, and as he left me, the look in his eye was one to warm the cockles of my heart and feed my soul with comfort.

"Speakin' for myself," said Big Kennedy, in the course of comment, "I don't go much on revenge. Still when it costs nothin', I s'ppose you might as well take it in. Besides, it shows folks that there's a dead-line in th' game. The wise ones will figger that this captain held out on us, or handed us th' worst of it on th' quiet. The example of him gettin' done up will make others run true."

Several years slipped by wherein as alderman I took my part in the town's affairs. I was never a talking member, and gained no glory for my eloquence. But what I lacked of rhetoric, I made up in stubborn loyalty to Tammany, and I never failed to dispose of my vote according to its mandates.

It was not alone my right, but my duty to do this. I had gone to the polls the avowed candidate of the machine. There was none to vote for me who did not know that my public courses would be shaped and guided by the organization. I was free to assume, therefore, being thus elected as a Tammany member by folk informed to a last expression of all that the phrase implied, that I was bound to carry out the Tammany programmes and execute the Tammany orders. Where a machine and its laws are known, the people when they lift to office one proposed of that machine, thereby direct such officer to submit himself to its direction and conform to its demands.

There will be ones to deny this. And these gentry of denials will be plausible, and furnish the thought of an invincible purity for their assumptions. They should not, however, be too sure for their theories. They themselves may be the ones in error. They should reflect that wherever there dwells a Yes there lives also a No. These contradictionists should emulate my own forbearance. I no more claim to be wholly right for my attitude of implicit obedience to the machine, than I condemn as wholly wrong their own position of boundless denunciation. There is no man so bad he may not be defended; there lives none so good he does not need defense; and what I say of a man might with equal justice be said of any dogma of politics. As I set forth in my preface, the true and the false, the black and the white in politics will rest ever with the point of view.

During my years as an alderman I might have made myself a wealthy man. And that I did not do so, was not because I had no profit of the place. As the partner, unnamed, in sundry city contracts, riches came often within my clutch. But I could not keep them; I was born with both hands open and had the hold of money that a riddle has of water.

This want of a money wit is a defect of my nature. A great merchant late in my life once said to me:

"Commerce—money-getting—is like a sea, and every man, in large or little sort, is a mariner. Some are buccaneers, while others are sober merchantmen. One lives by taking prizes, the other by the proper gains of trade. You belong to the buccaneers by your birth. You are not a business man, but a business wolf. Being a wolf, you will waste and never save. Your instinct is to pull

down each day's beef each day. You should never buy
nor sell nor seek to make money with money. Your
knowledge of money is too narrow. Up to fifty dollars
you are wise. Beyond that point you are the greatest
dunce I ever met."

Thus lectured the man of markets, measuring sticks,
and scales; and while I do not think him altogether
exact, there has been much in my story to bear out
what he said. It was not that I wasted my money in
riot, or in vicious courses. My morals were good, and I
had no vices. This was not much to my credit; my
morals were instinctive, like the morals of an animal. My
one passion was for politics, and my one ambition the
ambition to lead men. Nor was I eager to hold office;
my hope went rather to a day when I should rule Tammany as its Chief. My genius was not for the show-
ring; I cared nothing for a gilded place. That dream
of my heart's wish was to be the power behind the
screen, and to put men up and take men down, place
them and move them about, and play at government as
one might play at chess. Still, while I dreamed of an un-
bridled day to come, I was for that the more sedulous
to execute the orders of Big Kennedy. I had not then
to learn that the art of command is best studied in the
art of obedience.

To be entirely frank, I ought to name the one weakness that beset me, and which more than any spend-

thrift tendency lost me my fortune as fast as it flowed in. I came never to be a gambler in the card or gaming table sense, but I was inveterate to wager money on a horse. While money lasted, I would bet on the issue of every race that was run, and I was made frequently bankrupt thereby. However, I have said enough of my want of capacity to hoard. I was young and careless; moreover, with my place as alderman, and that sovereignty I still held among the Red Jackets, when my hand was empty I had but to stretch it forth to have it filled again.

In my boyhood I went garbed of rags and patches. Now when money came, I sought the first tailor of the town. I went to him drawn of his high prices; for I argued, and I think sagaciously, that where one pays the most one gets the best.

Nor, when I found that tailor, did I seek to direct him in his labors. I put myself in his hands, and was guided to quiet blacks and grays, and at his hint gave up thoughts of those plaids and glaring checks to which my tastes went hungering. That tailor dressed me like a gentleman and did me a deal of good. I am not one to say that raiment makes the man, and yet I hold that it has much to do with the man's behavior. I can say in my own case that when I was thus garbed like a gentleman, my conduct was at once controlled in favor of the moderate. I was instantly ironed of those rougher wrinkles of my nature, which last, while neither noisy nor gratuitously violent, was never one of peace.

The important thing was that these clothes of gentility gave me multiplied vogue with ones who were peculiarly my personal followers. They earned me emphasis with my Red Jackets, who still bore me aloft as their leader, and whose favor I must not let drift. The Tin Whistles, too, drew an awe from this rich yet civil uniform which strengthened my authority in that muscular quarter. I had grown, as an alderman and that one next in ward power to Big Kennedy, to a place which exempted me from those harsher labors of fist and bludgeon in which, whenever the exigencies of a campaign demanded, the Tin Whistles were still employed. But I claimed my old mastery over them. I would not permit so hardy a force to go to another's hands, and while I no longer led their war parties, I was always in the background, giving them direction and stopping them when they went too far.

It was demanded of my safety that I retain my hold upon both the Tin Whistles and the Red Jackets. However eminent I might be, I was by no means out of the ruck, and my situation was to be sustained only by the strong hand. The Tin Whistles and the Red Jackets were the sources of my importance, and if my voice were heeded or my word owned weight it was because they stood ever ready to my call. Wherefore, I cultivated their favor, secured my place among them, while at the same time I forced them to obey to the end that they as well as I be preserved.

Those clothes of a gentleman not only augmented, but declared my strength. In that time a fine coat was an offense to ones more coarsely clothed. A well-dressed stranger could not have walked three blocks on the East Side without being driven to do battle for his life. Fine linen was esteemed a challenge, and that I should be so arrayed and go unscathed, proved not alone my popularity, but my dangerous repute. Secretly, it pleased my shoulder-hitters to see their captain so garbed; and since I could defend my ·feathers, they made of themselves another reason of leadership. I was growing adept of men, and I counted on this effect when I spent my money with that tailor.

While I thus lay aside for the moment the running history of events that were as the stepping stones by which I crossed from obscurity and poverty to power and wealth, to have a glance at myself in my more personal attitudes, I should also relate my marriage and how I took a wife. It was Anne who had charge of the business, and brought me this soft victory. Had it not been for Anne, I more than half believe I would have had no wife at all; for I was eaten of an uneasy awkwardness whenever my fate delivered me into the presence of a girl. However earnestly Anne might counsel, I had no more of parlor wisdom than a savage. Anne, while sighing over my crudities and the hopeless thickness of my wits, established herself as a bearward to supervise my conduct. She picked out my wife for me, and in days when I should have been a lover, but was a graven image and as stolid, carried forward the courting in my stead.

It was none other than Apple Cheek upon whom Anne pitched—Apple Cheek, grown rounder and more fair, with locks like cornsilk, and eyes of even a deeper blue than on that day of the docks. Anne had struck out a friendship for Apple Cheek from the beginning, and the two were much in one another's company. And so one day, by ways and means I was too much confused to understand, Anne had us before the priest. We were made husband and wife; Apple Cheek brave and sweet, I looking like a fool in need of keepers.

Anne, the architect of this bliss, was in tears; and yet she must have kept her head, for I remember how she recalled me to the proprieties of my new station.

" Why don't you kiss your bride! " cried Anne, at the heel of the ceremony.

Anne snapped out the words, and they rang in my delinquent ears like a storm bell. Apple Cheek, eyes wet to be a match for Anne's, put up her lips with all the courage in the world. I kissed her, much as one might salute a hot flatiron. Still I kissed her; and I think to the satisfaction of a church-full looking on; but **I** knew what men condemned have felt on that journey to block and ax.

Apple Cheek and her choice of me made up the sweetest fortune of my life, and now when I think of her it is as if I stood in a flood of sunshine. So far as I was able, I housed her and robed her as though she were the daughter of a king, and while I have met treason in others and desertion where I looked for loyalty, **I** held her heart-fast, love-fast, faith-fast, ever my own. She was my treasure, and when she died it was as though my own end had come.

Big Kennedy and the then Chief of Tammany, during my earlier years as alderman, were as Jonathan and David. They were ever together, and their plans and their interests ran side by side. At last they began to fall apart. Big Kennedy saw a peril in this too-close a partnership, and was for putting distance between them. It was Old Mike who thus counseled him. The aged one became alarmed by the raw and insolent extravagance of the Chief's methods.

" Th' public," said Old Mike, " is a sheep, while ye do no more than just rob it. But if ye insult it, it's a wolf. Now this man insults th' people. Better cut loose from him, Jawn; he'll get ye all tor-rn to pieces."

The split came when, by suggestion of Old Mike and **Big Kennedy, I** refused to give my vote as alderman **to a**

railway company asking a terminal. There were millions of dollars in the balance, and without my vote the
machine and the railway company were powerless. The
stress was such that the mighty Chief himself came down
to Big Kennedy's saloon—a sight to make men stare!

The two, for a full hour, were locked in Big Kennedy's
sanctum; when they appeared I could read in the black
anger that rode on the brow of the Chief how Big Kennedy had declined his orders, and now stood ready to
abide the worst. Big Kennedy, for his side, wore an air
of confident serenity, and as I looked at the pair and
compared them, one black, the other beaming, I was surprised into the conviction that Big Kennedy of the two
was the superior natural force. As the Chief reached
the curb he said:

"You know the meaning of this. I shall tear you in
two in the middle an' leave you on both sides of the
street!"

"If you do, I'll never squeal," returned Big Kennedy carelessly. "But you can't; I've got you counted.
I can hold the ward ag'inst all you'll send. An' you look
out for yourself! I'll throw a switch on you yet that 'll
send you to th' scrapheap."

"I s'ppose you think you know what you're doin'?"
said the other angrily.

"You can put a bet on it that I do," retorted Big
Kennedy. "I wasn't born last week."

That evening as we sat silent and thoughtful, **Big Kennedy** broke forth with a word.

" I've got it! You're on speakin' terms with that old duffer, Morton, who's forever talkin' about bein' a tax-payer. He likes you, since you laid out Jimmy the Blacksmith that time. See him, an' fill him up with th' notion that he ought to go to Congress. It won't be hard ; he's sure he ought to go somewhere, an' Congress will fit him to a finish. In two days he'll think he's on his way to be a second Marcy. Tell him that if his people will put him up, we'll join dogs with 'em an' pull down th' place. You can say that we can't stand th' dishonesty an' corruption at th' head of Tammany Hall, an' are goin' to make a bolt for better government. We'll send the old sport to Congress. He'll give us a bundle big enough to fight the machine, an' plank dollar for dollar with it.   An' it 'll put us in line for a hook-up with th' reform bunch in th' fight for th' town next year. It's the play to make ; we're goin' to see stormy weather, you an' me, an' it's our turn to make for cover. We'll put up this old party, Morton, an' give th' machine a jolt. Th' Chief 'll leave me on both sides of th' street, will he? I'll make him think, before he's through, that he's run ag'inst th' pole of a dray."

CHAPTER X

BIG KENNEDY was right; the reputable old gentleman rose to that lure of Congress like any bass to any fly. It was over in a trice, those preliminaries; he was proud to be thus called upon to serve the people. Incidentally, it restored his hope in the country's future to hear that such tried war-dogs of politics as Big Kennedy and myself were making a line of battle against dishonesty in place. These and more were said to me by the reputable old gentleman when I bore him that word how Big Kennedy and I were ready to be his allies. The reputable old gentleman puffed and glowed with the sheer glory of my proposal, and seemed already to regard his election as a thing secured.

In due course, his own tribe placed him in nomina-ton. That done, Big Kennedy called a meeting of his people and declared for the reputable old gentleman's support. Big Kennedy did not wait to be attacked by the Tammany machine; he took the initiative and went to open rebellion, giving as his reason the machine's corruption.

"Tammany Hall has fallen into the hands of

thieves!" shouted Big Kennedy, in a short but pointed address which he made to his clansmen. "As an honest member of Tammany, I am fighting to rescue the organization."

In its way, the move was a master-stroke. It gave us the high ground, since it left us still in the party, still in Tammany Hall. It gave us a position and a battle-cry, and sent us into the conflict with a cleaner fame than it had been our wont to wear.

In the beginning, the reputable old gentleman paid a pompous visit to Big Kennedy. Like all who saw that leader, the reputable old gentleman came to Big Kennedy's saloon. This last was a point upon which Big Kennedy never failed to insist.

"Th' man," said Big Kennedy, "who's too good to go into a saloon, is too good to go into politics; if he's goin' to dodge th' one, he'd better duck the' other."

The reputable old gentleman met this test of the barrooms, and qualified for politics without a quaver. Had a barroom been the shelter of his infancy, he could not have worn a steadier assurance. As he entered, he laid a bill on the bar for the benefit of the public then and there athirst. Next he intimated a desire to talk privately with Big Kennedy, and set his course for the sanctum as though by inspiration. Big Kennedy called me to the confab; closing the door behind us, we drew together about the table.

" Let's cut out th' polite prelim'naries," said Big Kennedy, " an' come down to tacks. How much stuff do you feel like blowin' in? "

" How much should it take? " asked the reputable old gentleman.

" Say twenty thousand! " returned Big Kennedy, as cool as New Year's Day.

" Twenty thousand dollars! " repeated the reputable old gentleman, with wide eyes. " Will it call for so much as that? "

" If you're goin' to put in money, put in enough to win. There's no sense puttin' in just enough to lose. Th' other fellows will come into th' district with money enough to burn a wet dog. We've got to break even with 'em, or they'll have us faded from th' jump."

" But what can you do with so much? " asked the reputable old gentleman dismally. " It seems a fortune! What would you do with it? "

" Mass meetin's, bands, beer, torches, fireworks, halls; but most of all, buy votes."

" Buy votes! " exclaimed the reputable old gentleman, his cheek paling.

" Buy 'em by th' bunch, like a market girl sells radishes." Then, seeing the reputable old gentleman's horror: " How do you s'ppose you're goin' to get votes? You don't think that these dock-wallopers an' river pirates are stuck on you personally, do you? "

" But their interest as citizens! I should think they'd look at that!"

" Their first interest as citizens," observed Big Kennedy, with a cynical smile, " is a five-dollar bill."

" But do you think it right to purchase votes? " asked the reputable old gentleman, with a gasp.

" Is it right to shoot a man? No. Is it right to shoot a man if he's shootin' at you? Yes. Well, these mugs are goin' to buy votes, an' keep at it early an' late. Which is why I say it's dead right to buy votes to save yourself. Besides, you're th' best man; it's th' country's welfare we're protectin', d'ye see!"

The reputable old gentleman remained for a moment in deep thought. Then he got upon his feet to go.

" I'll send my son to talk with you," he said. Then faintly: " I guess this will be all right."

" There's somethin' you've forgot," said Big Kennedy with a chuckle, as he shook hands with the reputable old gentleman when the latter was about to depart; " there's a bet you've overlooked." Then, as the other seemed puzzled: " You aint got off your bluff about bein' a taxpayer. But, I understand! This is exec'-tive session, an' that crack about bein' a taxpayer is more of a public utterance. You're keepin' it for th' stump, most likely."

" I'll send my son to you to-night," repeated the reputable old gentleman, too much in the fog of Big

Kennedy's generous figures to heed his jests about tax-payers. " He'll be here about eight o'clock."

" That's right!" said Big Kennedy. " The sooner we get th' oil, th' sooner we'll begin to light up."

The reputable old gentleman kept his word concerning his son and that young gentleman's advent. The latter was with us at eight, sharp, and brought two others of hard appearance to bear him company as a kind of bodyguard. The young gentleman was slight and superfine, with eyeglass, mustache, and lisp. He accosted Big Kennedy, swinging a dainty cane the while in an affected way.

" I'm Mr. Morton—Mr. James Morton," he drawled. " You know my father."

Once in the sanctum, and none save Big Kennedy and myself for company, young Morton came to the question.

" My father's running for Congress. But he's old-fashioned; he doesn't understand these things." The tones were confident and sophisticated. I began to see how the eyeglass, the cane, and the lisp belied our caller. Under his affectations, he was as keen and cool a hand as Big Kennedy himself. " No," he repeated, taking meanwhile a thick envelope from his frock-coat, " he doesn't understand. The idea of money shocks him, don't y' know."

" That's it!" returned Big Kennedy, sympatheti-

cally. " He's old-fashioned ; he thinks this thing is like
runnin' to be superintendent of a Sunday school. He
aint down to date."

" Here," observed our visitor, tapping the table with
the envelope, and smiling to find himself and Big Kennedy a unit as to the lamentable innocence of his father,
" here are twenty one-thousand-dollar bills. I didn't draw
a check for reasons you appreciate. I shall trust you to
make the best use of this money. Also, I shall work with
you through the campaign."

With that, the young gentleman went his way, hum-
ming a tune; and all as though leaving twenty thousand dollars in the hands of some chance-sown politician
was the common employment of his evenings. When he
was gone, Big Kennedy opened the envelope. There
they were; twenty one-thousand-dollar bills. Big Kennedy pointed to them as they lay on the table.

" There's the reformer for you! " he said. " He'll go
talkin' about Tammany Hall; but once he himself goes
out for an office, he's ready to buy a vote or burn a
church! But say! that young Morton's all right!"
Here Big Kennedy's manner betrayed the most profound admiration. " He's as flossy a proposition as
ever came down th' pike." Then his glance recurred
doubtfully to the treasure. " I wish he'd brought it
'round by daylight. I'll have to set up with this bundle
till th' bank opens. Some fly guy might cop a sneak

on it else. There's a dozen of my best customers, any of whom would croak a man for one of them bills."

The campaign went forward rough and tumble. Big Kennedy spent money like water, the Red Jackets never slept, while the Tin Whistles met the plug-uglies of the enemy on twenty hard-fought fields.

The only move unusual, however, was one made by that energetic exquisite, young Morton. Young Morton, in the thick from the first, went shoulder to shoulder with Big Kennedy and myself. One day he asked us over to his personal headquarters.

"You know," said he, with his exasperating lisp, and daintily adjusting his glasses, "how there's a lot of negroes to live over this way—quite a settlement of them."

"Yes," returned Big Kennedy, "there's about three hundred votes among 'em. I've never tried to cut in on 'em, because there's no gettin' a nigger to vote th' Tammany ticket."

"Three hundred votes, did you say?" lisped the youthful manager. "I shall get six hundred." Then, to a black who was hovering about: "Call in those new recruits."

Six young blacks, each with a pleasant grin, marched into the room.

"There," said young Morton, inspecting them with

the close air of a critic, " they look like the real thing, don't they? Don't you think they'll pass muster? "

" An' why not? " said Big Kennedy. " I take it they're game to swear to their age, an' have got sense enough to give a house number that's in th' district? "

" It's not that," returned young Morton languidly. " But these fellows aren't men, old chap, they're women, don't y' know! It's the clothes does it. I'm going to dress up the wenches in overalls and jumpers; it's my own little idea."

" Say! " said Big Kennedy solemnly, as we were on our return; " that young Morton beats four kings an' an ace. He's a bird! I never felt so much like takin' off my hat to a man in my life. An' to think he's a Republican! " Here Big Kennedy groaned over genius misplaced. " There's no use talkin'; he ought to be in Tammany Hall."

The district which was to determine the destinies of the reputable old gentleman included two city wards besides the one over which Big Kennedy held sway. The campaign was not two weeks old before it stood patent to a dullest eye that Big Kennedy, while crowded hard, would hold his place as leader in spite of the Tammany Chief and the best efforts he could put forth. When this was made apparent, while the strife went forward as fiercely as before, the Chief sent overtures to Big Kennedy. If that rebellionist would return to the fold of the machine, bygones would be bygones, and a feast of love and profit would be spread before him. Big Kennedy, when the olive branch was proffered, sent word that he would meet the Chief next day. He would be at a secret place he named.

" An' tell him to come alone," said Big Kennedy to the messenger. " That's th' way I'll come; an' if he goes to ringin' in two or three for this powwow, you can say to him in advance it's all off."

Following the going of the messenger, Big Kennedy fell into a brown study.

" Do you think you'll deal in again with the Chief and the machine? " I asked.

" It depends on what's offered. A song an' dance won't get me."

" But how about the Mortons? Would you abandon them? "

Big Kennedy looked me over with an eye of pity. Then he placed his hand on my head, as on that far-off day in court.

" You're learnin' politics," said Big Kennedy slowly, " an' you're showin' speed. But let me tell you: You must chuck sentiment. Quit th' Mortons? I'll quit 'em in a holy minute if th' bid comes strong enough."

" Would you quit your friends? "

" That's different," he returned. " No man ought to quit his friends. But you must be careful an' never

have more'n two or three, d'ye see. Now these Mortons
aint friends, they're confed'rates. It's as though we
happened to be members of the same band of porch-
climbers, that's all. Take it this way: How long do
you guess it would take the Mortons to sell us out if it
matched their little game? How long do you think we'd
last? Well, we'd last about as long as a drink of whisky."

Big Kennedy met the Chief, and came back shaking
his head in decisive negative.

" There's nothin' in it," he said; " he's all for playin'
th' hog. It's that railway company's deal. Your vote
as Alderman, mind you, wins or loses it! What do you
think now he offers to do? I know what he gets. He
gets stock, say two hundred thousand dollars, an' one
hundred thousand dollars in cold cash. An' yet he talks
of only splittin' out fifteen thousand for you an' me!
Enough said; we fight him!"

Jimmy the Blacksmith, when, in response to Big Kennedy's hint, he " followed Gaffney," pitched his tent in
the ward next north of our own. He made himself useful to the leader of that region, and called together a
somber bevy which was known as the Alley Gang. With
that care for himself which had ever marked his conduct,
Jimmy the Blacksmith, and his Alley Gang, while they
went to and fro as shoulder-hitters of the machine, were
zealous to avoid the Tin Whistles, and never put themselves within their reach. On the one or two occasions

when the Tin Whistles, lusting for collision, went hunting them, the astute Alleyites were no more to be discovered than a needle in the hay.

"You couldn't find 'em with a search warrant!" reported my disgusted lieutenant. "I never saw such
people! They're a disgrace to th' East Side."

However, they were to be found with the last of it, and
it would have been a happier fortune for me had the
event fallen the other way.

It was the day of the balloting, and Big Kennedy and
I had taken measures to render the result secure. Not
only would we hold our ward, but the district and the
reputable old gentleman were safe. Throughout the
morning the word that came to us from time to time was
ever a white one. It was not until the afternoon that
information arrived of sudden clouds to fill the sky.
The news came in the guise of a note from young
Morton:

"Jimmy the Blacksmith and his heelers are driving
our people from the polls."

"You know what to do!" said Big Kennedy, tossing
me the scrap of paper.

With the Tin Whistles at my heels, I made my way to
the scene of trouble. It was full time; for a riot was
on, and our men were winning the worst of the fray.
Clubs were going and stones were being thrown.

In the heart of it, I had a glimpse of Jimmy the

Blacksmith, a slungshot to his wrist, smiting right and left, and cheering his cohorts. The sight gladdened me. There was my man, and I pushed through the crowd to reach him. This last was no stubborn matter, for the press parted before me like water.

Jimmy the Blacksmith saw me while yet I was a dozen feet from him. He understood that he could not escape, and with that he desperately faced me. As I drew within reach, he leveled a savage blow with the slungshot. It would have put a period to my story if I had met it. The shot miscarried, however, and the next moment I had rushed him and pinned him against the walls of the warehouse in which the precinct's polls were being held.

" I've got you!" I cried, and then wrenched myself free to give me distance.

I was to strike no blow, however; my purpose was to find an interruption in midswing. While the words were between my teeth, something like a sunbeam came flickering by my head, and a long knife buried itself vengefully in Jimmy the Blacksmith's throat. There was a choking gurgle; the man fell forward upon me while the red torrent from his mouth covered my hands. Then he crumpled to the ground in a weltering heap; dead on the instant, too, for the point had pierced the spine. In a dumb chill of horror, I stooped and drew forth the knife. It was that weapon of the Bowery pawnshop which I had given the Sicilian.

CHAPTER XI

WHEN I gave that knife to the Sicilian, I had not thought how on the next occasion that I encountered it I should draw it from the throat of a dead and fallen enemy. With the sight of it there arose a vision of the dark brisk face, the red kerchief, and the golden earrings of him to whom it had been presented. In a blurred way I swept the throng for his discovery. The Sicilian was not there; my gaze met only the faces of the common crowd—ghastly, silent, questioning, staring, as I stood with knife dripping blood and the dead man on the ground at my feet. A police officer was pushing slowly towards me, his face cloudy with apology.

"You mustn't hold this ag'inst me," said he, "but you can see yourself, I can't turn my blind side to a job like this. They'd have me pegged out an' spread-eagled in every paper of th' town."

"Yes!" I replied vaguely, not knowing what I said.

"An' there's th' big Tammany Chief you're fightin'," went on the officer; "he'd just about have my scalp, sure. I don't see why you did it! Your heart must be turnin'

129

weak, when you take to carryin' a shave, an' stickin' people like pigs!"

"You don't think I killed him!" I exclaimed.

"Who else?" he asked.

The officer shrugged his shoulders and turned his hands palm upwards with a gesture of deprecation. To the question and the gesture I made no answer. It came to me that I must give my Sicilian time to escape. I could have wished his friendship had taken a less tropical form; still he had thrown that knife for me, and I would not name him until he had found his ship and was safe beyond the fingers of the law. Even now I think my course a proper one. The man innocent has ever that innocence to be his shield; he should be ready to suffer a little in favor of ones who own no such strong advantage.

It was nine of that evening's clock before Big Kennedy visited me in the Tombs. Young Morton came with him, clothed of evening dress and wearing white gloves. He twisted his mustache between his kid-gloved finger and thumb, meanwhile surveying the grimy interior—a fretwork of steel bars and freestone—with looks of ineffable objection. The warden was with them in his own high person when they came to my cell. That functionary was in a mood of sullen uncertainty; he could not make out a zone of safety for himself, when now Big Kennedy and the Tammany Chief were at daggers drawn. He feared he might go too far in pleasuring the former, and so bring upon him the dangerous resentment of his rival.

" We can't talk here, Dave," said Big Kennedy, addressing the warden, after greeting me through the cell grate. " Bring him to your private office."

" But, Mr. Kennedy," remonstrated the warden, " I don't know about that. It's after lockin'-up hours now."

" You don't know! " repeated Big Kennedy, the specter of a threat peeping from his gray eyes. " An' you're to hand me out a line of guff about lockin'-up hours, too! Come, come, Dave; it won't do to get chesty! The Chief an' I may be pals to-morrow. Or I may have him done for an' on th' run in a month. Where would you be then, Dave? No more words, I say: bring him to your private office."

There was no gainsaying the masterful manner of Big Kennedy. The warden, weakened with years of fear of him and his power, grumblingly undid the bolts and led the way to his room.

" Deuced wretched quarters, I should say! " murmured young Morton, glancing for a moment inside the cell. " Not at all worth cutting a throat for."

When we were in the warden's room, that master of the keys took up a position by the door. This was not to Big Kennedy's taste.

" Dave, s'ppose you step outside," said Big Kennedy.

" It's no use you hearin' what we say; it might get you
into trouble, d'ye see!"   The last, insinuatingly.

" Mr. Kennedy, I'm afraid!" replied the warden, with
the voice of one worried.   " You know the charge is
murder.   He's here for killin' Jimmy the Blacksmith.
I've no right to let him out of my sight."

" To be sure, I know it's murder," responded Big
Kennedy.   " I'd be plankin' down bail for him if it was
anything else.   But what's that got to do with you skip-
pin' into th' hall?   You don't think I'm goin' to pass
him any files or saws, do you?"

" Really, Mr. Warden," said young Morton, crossing
over to where the warden lingered irresolutely, " really,
you don't expect to stay and overhear our conversation!
Why, it would be not only impolite, but perposterous!
Besides, it's not my way, don't y' know!"   And here
young Morton put on his double eyeglass and ran the
warden up and down with an intolerant stare.

" But he's charged, I tell you," objected the warden,
" with killin' Jimmy th' Blacksmith.   I can't go to
givin' him privileges an' takin' chances; I'd get done
up if I did."

" You'll get done up if you don't!" growled Big
Kennedy.

" It is as you say," went on young Morton, still holding the warden in the thrall of that wonderful eyeglass,
" it is quite true that this person, James the Horse-

shoer as you call him, has been slain and will never shoe a horse again. But our friend had no hand in it, as we stand ready to spend one hundred thousand dollars to establish. And by the way, speaking of money,"—here young Morton turned to Big Kennedy—" didn't you say as we came along that it would be proper to remunerate this officer for our encroachments upon his time? "

" Why, yes," replied Big Kennedy, with an ugly glare at the warden, " I said that it might be a good idea to sweeten him."

" Sweeten! Ah, yes; I recall now that sweeten was the term you employed. A most extraordinary word for paying money. However," and here young Morton again addressed the warden, tendering him at the same time a one-hundred-dollar bill, " here is a small present. Now let us have no more words, my good man."

The warden, softened by the bill, went out and closed the door. I could see that he looked on young Morton in wonder and smelled upon him a mysterious authority. As one disposed to cement a friendship just begun, the warden, as he left, held out his hand to young Morton.

" You're th' proper caper! " he exclaimed, in a gush of encomium; " you're a gent of th' right real sort! "

Young Morton gazed upon the warden's outstretched hand as though it were one of the curious things of nature. At last he extended two fingers, which the warden grasped.

" 'This weakness for shaking hands," said young Morton, dusting his gloved fingers fastidiously, " this weakness for shaking hands on the part of these common people is inexcusable.　Still, on the whole, I did not think it a best occasion for administering a rebuke, don't y' know, and so allowed that low fellow his way."

" Dave's all right," returned Big Kennedy.　Then coming around to me: " Now let's get down to business. You understand how the charge is murder, an' that no bail goes.　But keep a stiff upper lip.　The Chief is out to put a crimp in you, but we'll beat him just th' same. For every witness he brings, we'll bring two.　Do you know who it was croaked th' Blacksmith? "

I told him of the Sicilian; and how I had recognized the knife as I drew it from the throat of the dead man.

" It's a cinch he threw it," said Big Kennedy; " he was in the crowd an' saw you mixin' it up with th' Blacksmith, an' let him have it.　Them Dagoes are great knife throwers.　Did you get a flash of him in the crowd? "

" No," I said, " there was no sign of him.　I haven't told this story to anybody.　We ought to give him time to take care of himself."

" Right you are," said Big Kennedy approvingly. " He probably jumped aboard his boat; it's even money he's outside the Hook, out'ard bound, by now."

Then Big Kennedy discussed the case.　I would be

indicted and tried; there was no doubt of that. The Chief, our enemy, had possession of the court machinery; so far as indictment and trial were concerned he would not fail of his will.

"An' it's th' judge in partic'lar, I'm leary of," said Big Kennedy thoughtfully. "The Chief has got that jurist in hock to him, d'ye see! But there's another end to it; I've got a pull with the party who selects the jury, an' it 'll be funny if we don't have half of 'em our way. That's right; th' worst they can hand us is a hung jury. If it takes money, now," and here Big Kennedy rolled a tentative eye on young Morton, "if it should take money, I s'ppose we know where to look for it?"

Young Morton had been listening to every word, and for the moment, nothing about him of his usual languor. Beyond tapping his white teeth with the handle of his dress cane, he retained no trace of those affectations. I had much hope from the alert earnestness of young Morton, for I could tell that he would stay by my fortunes to the end.

"What was that?" he asked, when Big Kennedy spoke of money.

"I said that if we have to buy any little thing like a juror or a witness, we know where to go for the money."

"Certainly!" he lisped, relapsing into the exquisite; "we shall buy the courthouse should the purchase of that edifice become necessary to our friend's security."

"Aint he a dandy!" exclaimed Big Kennedy, surveying young Morton in a rapt way. Then coming back to me: "I've got some news for you that you want to keep under your waistcoat. You know Billy Cassidy —Foxy Billy—him that studied to be a priest? You remember how I got him a post in th' Comptroller's office. Well, I sent for him not an hour ago; he's goin' to take copies of th' accounts that show what th' Chief an' them other highbinders at the top o' Tammany have been doin'. I'll have the papers on 'em in less'n a week. If we get our hooks on what I'm after, an' Foxy Billy says we shall, we'll wipe that gang off th' earth."

"Given those documents, we shall, as you say, obliterate them," chimed in young Morton. "But speaking of your agent: Is this Foxy Billy as astute as his name would imply?"

"He could go down to Coney Island an' beat th' shells," said Big Kennedy confidently.

"About the knife which gave James the Horseshoer his death wound," said young Morton. His tones were vapid, but his glance was bright enough. "They've sent it to the Central Office. The detectives are sure to discover the pawnbroker who sold it. I think it would be wise, therefore, to carry the detectives the word ourselves. It will draw the sting out of that wasp; it would, really. It wouldn't look well to a jury, should we let them track down this information, while it will destroy its effect if we ourselves tell them. I think with the start he has, we can trust that Sicilian individual to take care of himself."

This suggestion appealed to Big Kennedy as good. He thought, too, that he and young Morton might better set about the matter without delay.

"Don't lose your nerve," said he, shaking me by the hand. "You are as safe as though you were in church. I'll crowd 'em, too, an' get this trial over inside of six weeks. By that time, if Foxy Billy is any good, we'll be ready to give the Chief some law business of his own."

"One thing," I said at parting; "my wife must not come here. I wouldn't have her see me in a cell to save my life."

From the moment of my arrival at the Tombs, I had not ceased to think of Apple Cheek and her distress. Anne would do her best to comfort her; and for the rest —why! it must be borne. But I could not abide her seeing me a prisoner; not for her sake, but for my own.

"Well, good-by!" said young Morton, as he and Big Kennedy were taking themselves away. "You need give yourself no uneasiness. Remember, you are not only right, but rich; and when, pray, was the right, on being backed by riches, ever beaten down?"

"Or for that matter, the wrong either?" put in Big

Kennedy sagely. "I've never seen money lose a fight."

"Our friend," said young Morton, addressing the warden, who had now returned, and speaking in a high superior vein, " is to have everything he wants. Here is my card. Remember, now, this gentleman is my friend; and it is not to my fancy, don't y' know, that a friend of mine should lack for anything; it isn't, really!"

As Big Kennedy and young Morton reached the door, I bethought me for the first time to ask the result of the election.

"Was your father successful?" I queried. "These other matters quite drove the election from my head."

"Oh, yes," drawled young Morton, "my father triumphed. I forget the phrase in which Mr. Kennedy described the method of his success, but it was highly epigrammatic and appropriate. How was it you said the old gentleman won?"

"I said that he won in a walk," returned Big Kennedy. Then, suspiciously: "Say you aint guying me, be you?"

"Me guy you?" repeated young Morton, elevating his brows. "I'd as soon think of deriding a king with crown and scepter!"

My trial came on within a month. Big Kennedy had a genius for expedition, and could hurry both men and events whenever it suited his inclinations. When I

went to the bar I was accompanied by two of the leaders
of the local guild of lawyers. These were my counsel,
and they would leave no stone unturned to see me free.
Big Kennedy sat by my side when the jury was em-
paneled.

" We've got eight of 'em painted," he whispered. " I'd
have had all twelve," he continued regretfully, " but
what with the challengin', an' what with some of 'em not
knowin' enough, an' some of 'em knowin' too much, I
lose four. However, eight ought to land us on our
feet."

There were no Irishmen in the panel, and I com-
mented on the fact as strange.

" No, I barred th' Irish," said Big Kennedy. " Th'
Irish are all right; I'm second-crop Irish—bein' born in
this country—myself. But you don't never want one on a
jury, especially on a charge of murder. There's this
thing about a Mick: he'll cry an' sympathize with you
an' shake your hand, an' send you flowers; but just th'
same he always wants you hanged."

As Big Kennedy had apprehended, the Judge on the
bench was set hard and chill as Arctic ice against me; I
could read it in his jadestone eye. He would do his utmost
to put a halter about my neck, and the look he bestowed
upon me, menacing and full of doom, made me feel lost
and gallows-ripe indeed. Suppose they should hang me!
I had seen Sheeny Joe dispatched for Sing Sing from

that very room! The memory of it, with the Judge lowering from the bench like a death-threat, sent a cold thought to creep and coil about my heart and crush it as in the folds of a snake.

There came the pawnbroker to swear how he sold me the knife those years ago. The prosecution insisted as an inference drawn from this, that the knife was mine. Then a round dozen stood up to tell of my rush upon Jimmy the Blacksmith; and how he fell; and how, a moment later, I fronted them with the red knife in my clutch and the dead man weltering where he went down. Some there were who tried to say they saw me strike the blow.

While this evidence was piling up, ever and again some timid juryman would glance towards Big Kennedy inquiringly. The latter would send back an ocular volley of threats that meant death or exile should that juror flinch or fail him.

When the State ended, a score of witnesses took the stand in my behalf. One and all, having been tutored by Big Kennedy, they told of the thrown knife which came singing through the air like a huge hornet from the far outskirts of the crowd. Many had not seen the hand that hurled the knife; a few had been more fortunate, and described him faithfully as a small lean man, dark, a red silk cloth over his head, and earrings dangling from his ears.

"He was a sailorman, too," said one, more graphic than the rest; "as I could tell by the tar on his hands an' a ship tattooed on th' back of one of 'em. He stood right by me when he flung the knife."

"Why didn't you seize him?" questioned the State's Attorney, with a half-sneer.

"Not on your life!" said the witness. "I aint collarin' nobody; I don't get policeman's wages."

The Judge gave his instructions to the jury, and I may say he did his best, or worst, to drag me to the scaffold. The jurors listened; but they owned eyes as well as ears, and for every word spoken by the Judge's tongue, Big Kennedy's eyes spoke two. Also, there was that faultless exquisite, young Morton, close and familiar to my side. The dullest ox-wit of that panel might tell how I was belted about by strong influences, and ones that could work a vengeance. Wherefore, when the jury at last retired, there went not one whose mind was not made up, and no more than twenty minutes ran by before the foreman's rap on the door announced them as prepared to give decision. They filed soberly in. The clerk read the verdict.

"Not guilty!"

The Judge's face was like thunder: he gulped and glared, and then demanded:

"Is this your verdict?"

"It is," returned the foreman, standing in his place;

and his eleven fellow jurors, two of whom belonged to my Red Jackets, nodded assent.

Home I went on wings. Anne met me in the hallway and welcomed me with a kiss. She wore a strange look, but in my hurry for Apple Cheek I took no particular heed of that.

"Where is she—where is my wife?" said I.

Then a blackcoat man came from the rear room; he looked the doctor and had the smell of drugs about him. Anne glanced at him questioningly.

"I think he may come in," he said. "But make no noise! Don't excite her!"

Apple Cheek, who was Apple Cheek no longer with her face hollowed and white, was lying in the bed. Her eyes were big and bright, and the ghost of a smile parted her wan lips.

"I'm so happy!" she whispered, voice hardly above a breath. Then with weak hands she drew me down to her. "I've prayed and prayed, and I knew it would come right," she murmured.

Then Anne, who had followed me to the bedside, drew away the coverings. It was like a revelation, for I had been told no word of it, nor so much as dreamed of such sweet chances. The dear surprise of it was in one sense like a blow, and I staggered on my feet as that day's threats had owned no power to make me. There, with little face upturned and sleeping, was a babe!—our babe!

—Apple Cheek's and mine!—our baby girl that had been born to us while its father lay in jail on a charge of murder! While I looked, it opened its eyes; and then a wailing, quivering cry went up that swept across my soul like a tune of music.

CHAPTER XII

DARBY THE GOPHER

FOXY BILLY CASSIDY made but slow work of obtaining those papers asked for to overthrow our enemy, the Chief. He copied reams upon reams of contracts and vouchers and accounts, but those to wholly match the crushing purposes of Big Kennedy were not within his touch. The documents which would set the public ablaze were held in a safe, of which none save one most trusted by the Chief, and deep in both his plans and their perils, possessed the secret.

"That's how the game stands," explained Big Kennedy. "Foxy Billy's up ag'inst it. The cards we need are in th' safe, an' Billy aint got th' combination, d'ye see."

"Can anything be done with the one who has?"

"Nothin'," replied Big Kennedy. "No, there's no gettin' next to th' party with th' combination. Billy did try to stand in with this duck; an' say! he turned sore in a second."

"Then you've no hope?"

"Not exactly that," returned Big Kennedy, as though

144

revolving some proposal in his mind. " I'll hit on a way. When it comes to a finish, I don't think there's a safe in New York I couldn't turn inside out. But I've got to have time to think."

There existed strong argument for exertion on Big Kennedy's part. Both he and I were fighting literally for liberty and for life. Our sole hope of safety lay in the overthrow of the Chief; we must destroy or be destroyed.

Big Kennedy was alive to the situation. He said as much when, following that verdict of " Not guilty! " I thanked him as one who had worked most for my defense.

" There's no thanks comin'," said Big Kennedy, in his bluff way. " I had to break th' Chief of that judge-an'-jury habit at th' go-off. He'd have nailed me next."

Big Kennedy and I, so to phrase it, were as prisoners of politics. Our feud with the Chief, as the days went by, widened to open war. Its political effect was to confine us to our own territory, and we undertook no enterprise which ran beyond our proper boundaries. It was as though our ward were a walled town. Outside all was peril; inside we were secure. Against the Chief and the utmost of his power, we could keep our own, and did. His word lost force when once it crossed our frontiers; his mandates fell to the ground.

Still, while I have described ourselves as ones in a kind of captivity, we lived sumptuously enough on our small domain. Big Kennedy went about the farming of his narrow acres with an agriculture deeper than ever. No enterprise that either invaded or found root in our region was permitted to go free, but one and all paid tribute. From street railways to push carts, from wholesale stores to hand-organs, they must meet our levy or see their interests pine. And thus we thrived.

However, for all the rich fatness of our fortunes, Big Kennedy's designs against the Chief never cooled. On our enemy's side, we had daily proof that he, in his planning, was equally sleepless. If it had not been for my seat in the Board of Aldermen, and our local rule of the police which was its corollary, the machine might have broken us down. As it was, we sustained ourselves, and the sun shone for our ward haymaking, if good weather went with us no farther.

One afternoon Big Kennedy of the suddenest broke upon me with an exclamation of triumph.

"I have it!" he cried; "I know the party who will show us every paper in that safe."

"Who is he?" said I.

"I'll bring him to you to-morrow night. He's got a country place up th' river, an' never leaves it. He hasn't been out of th' house for almost five years, but I think I can get him to come." Big Kennedy looked as though the situation concealed a jest. " But I can't stand here talkin'; I've got to scatter for th' Grand Central."

Who should this gifted individual be? Who was he who could come in from a country house, which he had not quitted for five years, and hand us those private papers now locked, and fast asleep, within the Comptroller's safe? The situation was becoming mysterious, and my patience would be on a stretch until the mystery was laid bare. The sure enthusiasm of Big Kennedy gave an impression of comfort. Big Kennedy was no hare-brained optimist, nor one to count his chickens before they were hatched.

When Big Kennedy came into the sanctum on the following evening, the grasp he gave me was the grasp of victory.

" It's all over but th' yellin'!" said he; "we've got them papers in a corner."

Big Kennedy presented me to a shy, retiring person, who bore him company, and who took my hand reluctantly. He was not ill-looking, this stranger; but he had a furtive roving eye—the eye of a trapped animal. His skin, too, was of a yellow, pasty color, like bad pie-crust, and there abode a damp, chill atmosphere about him that smelled of caves and caverns.

After I greeted him, he walked away in a manner strangely unsocial, and, finding a chair, sate himself down in a corner. He acted as might one detained against his will and who was not the master of himself. Also, there was something professional in it all, as though the purpose of his presence were one of business. I mentioned in a whisper. the queer sallowness of the stranger.

" Sure ! " said Big Kennedy. " It's th' prison pallor on him. I've got to let him lay dead for a week or ten days to give him time to cover it with a beard, as well as show a better haircut."

" Who is he? " I demanded, my amazement beginning to sit up.

" He's a gopher," returned Big Kennedy, surveying the stranger with victorious complacency. " Yes, indeed; he can go through a safe like th' grace of heaven through a prayer meetin'."

" Is he a burglar? "

" Burglar? No ! " retorted Big Kennedy disgustedly; " he's an artist. Any hobo could go in with drills an' spreaders an' pullers an' wedges, an' crack a box. But this party does it by ear; just sits down before a safe, an' fumbles an' fools with it ten minutes, an' swings her open. I tell you he's a wonder ! He knows th' insides of a safe like a priest knows th' insides of a prayer-book."

" Where was he? " I asked. " Where did you pick him up? " and here I took a second survey of the talented stranger, who dropped his eyes on the floor.

"The Pen," said Big Kennedy. "The warden an' me are old side-partners, an' I borrowed him. I knew where he was, d'ye see! He's doin' a stretch of five years for a drop-trick he turned in an Albany bank. That's what comes of goin' outside your specialty; he'd ought to have stuck to safes."

"Aren't you afraid he'll run?" I said. "You can't watch him night and day, and he'll give you the slip."

"No fear of his side-steppin'," replied Big Kennedy confidently. "He's only got six weeks more to go, an' it wouldn't pay to slip his collar for a little pinch of time like that. Besides, I've promised him five hundred dollars for this job, an' left it in th' warden's hands."

"What's his name?" I inquired.

"Darby the Goph."

Big Kennedy now unfolded his plan for making Darby the Goph useful in our affairs. Foxy Billy would allow himself to get behind in his labors over the City books. In a spasm of industry he would arrange with his superiors to work nights until he was again abreast of his duties. Foxy Billy, night after night, would thus be left alone in the Comptroller's office. The safe that baffled us for those priceless documents would be unguarded. Nothing would be thought by janitors and night watchmen of the presence of Darby the Goph. He would be with Foxy Billy in the rôle of a friend, who meant no more than to kindly cheer his lonely labors.

Darby the Goph would lounge and kill time while Foxy
Billy moiled.

"There's the scheme to put Darby inside," said Big
Kennedy in conclusion. "Once they're alone, he'll tear
th' packin' out o' that safe. When Billy has copied the
papers, th' game's as simple as suckin' eggs. We'll
spring 'em, an' make th' Chief look like a dress suit at a
gasfitters' ball."

Big Kennedy's programme was worked from beginning
to end by Foxy Billy and Darby the Goph, and never
jar nor jolt nor any least of friction. It ran out as
smoothly as two and two make four. In the end, Big
Kennedy held in his fingers every evidence required to
uproot the Chief. The ear and the hand of Darby the
Goph had in no sort lost their cunning.

"An' now," said Big Kennedy, when dismissing Darby
the Goph, "you go back where you belong. I've wired
the warden, an' he'll give you that bit of dough. I've
sent for a copper to put you on th' train. I don't want
to take chances on you stayin' over a day. You might
get to lushin', an' disgrace yourself with th' warden."

The police officer arrived, and Big Kennedy told him
to see Darby the Goph aboard the train.

"Don't make no mistake," said Big Kennedy, by way
of warning. "He belongs in Sing Sing, an' must get
back without fail to-night. Stay by th' train till it pulls
out."

" How about th' bristles? " said the officer, pointing
to the two-weeks' growth of beard that stubbled the chin
of the visitor. " Shall I have him scraped? "

" No, they'll fix his face up there," said Big Kennedy.
" The warden don't care what he looks like, only so he
gets his clamps on him ag'in."

" Here's the documents," said Big Kennedy, when
Darby the Goph and his escort had departed. " The
question now is, how to give th' Chief th' gaff, an' gaff
him deep an' good. He's th' party who was goin' to
leave me on both sides of th' street." This last with an
exultant sneer.

It was on my thoughts that the hand to hurl the
thunderbolt we had been forging was that of the reputable old gentleman. The blow would fall more smit-
ingly if dealt by him; his was a name superior for this
duty to either Big Kennedy's or my own. With this
argument, Big Kennedy declared himself in full accord.

" It 'll look more like th' real thing," said he, " to have
th' kick come from th' outside. Besides, if I went to th'
fore it might get in my way hereafter."

The reputable old gentleman moved with becoming
conservatism, not to say dignity. He took the documents furnished by the ingenuity of Darby the Goph,
and the oil-burning industry of Foxy Billy, and pored
over them for a day. Then he sent for Big Kennedy.

" The evidence you furnish me," said he, " seems absolutely conclusive. It betrays a corruption not paralleled in modern times, with the head of Tammany as the hub of the villainy. The town has been plundered of millions," concluded the reputable old gentleman, with a fine oratorical flourish, " and it is my duty to lay bare this crime in all its enormity, as one of the people's Representatives."

" An' a taxpayer," added Big Kennedy.

" Sir, my duty as a Representative," returned the reputable old gentleman severely, " has precedence over my privileges as a taxpayer." Then, as though the question offered difficulties: " The first step should be the publication of these documents in a paper of repute."

The reputable old gentleman had grounds for hesitation. Our enemy, the Chief, was not without his allies among the dailies of that hour. The Chief was popular in certain glutton circles. He still held to those characteristics of a ready, laughing, generous recklessness that marked him in a younger day when, as head of a fire company, with trousers tucked in boots, red shirt, fire helmet, and white coat thrown over arm, he led the ropes and cheered his men. But what were excellent as traits in a fireman, became fatal under conditions where secrecy and a policy of no noise were required for his safety. He was headlong, careless; and, indifferent to discovery since he believed himself secure, the trail of his wrongdoing was as widely obvious, not to say as unclean, as was Broadway.

"Yes," said the reputable old gentleman, "the great thing is to pitch upon a proper paper."

"There's the *Daily Tory?*" suggested Big Kennedy.

"It's a very honest sheet," said the reputable old gentleman approvingly.

"Also," said Big Kennedy, "the Chief has just cut it out of th' City advertisin', d'ye see, an' it's as warm as a wolf."

For these double reasons of probity and wrath, the *Daily Tory* was agreed to. The reputable old gentleman would put himself in touch with the *Daily Tory* without delay.

"Who is this Chief of Tammany?" asked the reputable old gentleman, towards the close of the conference. "Personally, I know but little about him."

"He'd be all right," said Big Kennedy, "but he was spoiled in the bringin' up. He was raised with th' fire companies, an' he made th' mistake of luggin' his speakin' trumpet into politics."

"But is he a deep, forceful man?"

"No," returned Big Kennedy, with a contemptuous toss of the hand. "If he was, you wouldn't have been elected to Congress. He makes a brash appearance, but there's nothin' behind. You open his front door an' you're in his back yard."

The reputable old gentleman was bowing us out of his library, when Big Kennedy gave him a parting word.

"Now remember: my name aint to show at all."

"But the honor!" exclaimed the reputable old gentleman. "The honor of this mighty reform will be rightfully yours. You ought to have it."

"I'd rather have Tammany Hall," responded Big Kennedy with a laugh, "an' if I get to be too much of a reformer it might queer me. No, you go in an' do up th' Chief. When he's rubbed out, I intend to be Chief in his place. I'd rather be Chief than have th' honor you tell of. There's more money in it."

"Do you prefer money to honor?" returned the reputable old gentleman, somewhat scandalized.

"I'll take th' money for mine, every time," responded Big Kennedy. "Honor ought to have a bank account. The man who hasn't anything but honor gets pitied when he doesn't get laughed at, an' for my part I'm out for th' dust."

Four days later the *Daily Tory* published the first of its articles; it fell upon our enemy with the force of a trip-hammer. From that hour the assaults on the Chief gained never let or stay. The battle staggered on for months. The public, hating him for his insolence, joined in hunting him. One by one those papers, so lately his adorers, showed him their backs.

" Papers sail only with the wind," said Big Kennedy sagely, in commenting on these ink-desertions of the Chief.

In the midst of the trouble, Old Mike began to sicken for his end. He was dying of old age, and the stream of his life went sinking into his years like water into sand. Big Kennedy gave up politics to sit by the bedside of the dying old man. One day Old Mike seemed greatly to revive.

" Jawn," he said, " you'll be th' Chief of Tammany. The Chief, now fightin' for his life, will lose. The mish-take he made was in robbin' honest people. Jawn, he should have robbed th' crim'nals an' th' law breakers. The rogues can't fight back, an' th' honest people can. An' remember this: the public don't care for what it hears, only for what it sees. Never interfere with people's beer; give 'em clean streets; double the number of lamp-posts—th' public's like a fly, it's crazy over lamps—an' have bands playin' in every par-rk. Then kape th' streets free of ba-ad people, tinhorn min, an' such. You don't have to drive 'em out o' town, only off th' streets; th' public don't object to dirt, but it wants it kept in the back alleys. Jawn, if you'll follow what I tell you, you can do what else ye plaze. The public will go with ye loike a drunkard to th' openin' of a new s'loon."

" What you must do, father," said Big Kennedy

cheerfully, " is get well, an' see that I run things
straight."

" Jawn," returned Old Mike, smiling faintly, " this
is Choosday ; by Saturday night I'll be dead an' under th'
daisies."

Old Mike's funeral was a creeping, snail-like, reluc-
tant thing of miles, with woe-breathing bands to mark
the sorrowful march. Big Kennedy never forgot ; and to
the last of his power, the question uppermost in his mind,
though never in his mouth, was whether or not that one
who sought his favor had followed Old Mike to the
grave.

The day of Old Mike's funeral saw the destruction
of our enemy, the Chief. He fell with the crash of a tree.
He fled, a hunted thing, and was brought back to perish
in a prison. And so came the end of him, by the wit of
Big Kennedy and the furtive sleighty genius of Darby
the Goph.

CHAPTER XIII

BIG KENNEDY AND THE MUGWUMPS

WHEN the old Chief was gone, Big Kennedy succeeded to his place as the ruling spirit of the organization. For myself, I moved upward to become a figure of power only a whit less imposing; for I stepped forth as a leader of the ward, while in the general councils of Tammany I was recognized as Big Kennedy's adviser and lieutenant.

To the outside eye, unskilled of politics in practice, everything of Tammany sort would have seemed in the plight desperate. The efforts required for the overthrow of the old Chief, and Big Kennedy's bolt in favor of the forces of reform—ever the blood enemy of Tammany—had torn the organization to fragments. A first result of this dismemberment was the formation of a rival organization meant to dominate the local Democracy. This rival coterie was not without its reasons of strength, since it was upheld as much as might be by the State machine. The situation was one which for a time would compel Big Kennedy to tolerate the company of his reform friends, and affect, even though he privately opposed them, some appearance of sympathy with their plans for the purification of the town.

" But," observed Big Kennedy, when we considered the business between ourselves, " I think I can set these guys by the ears. There aint a man in New York who, directly or round th' corner, aint makin' money through a broken law, an' these mugwumps aint any exception. I've invited three members of the main squeeze to see me, an' I'll make a side bet they get tired before I do."

In deference to the invitation of Big Kennedy, there came to call upon him a trio of civic excellence, each a personage of place. Leading the three was our long-time friend, the reputable old gentleman. Of the others, one was a personage whose many millions were invested in real estate, the rentals whereof ran into the hundreds of thousands, while his companion throve as a wholesale grocer, a feature of whose business was a rich trade in strong drink.

Big Kennedy met the triumvirate with brows of sanctimony, and was a moral match for the purest. When mutual congratulations over virtue's late successes at the ballot box, and the consequent dawn of whiter days for the town, were ended, Big Kennedy, whose statecraft was of the blunt, positive kind, brought to the discussional center the purpose of the meeting.

" We're not only goin' to clean up th' town, gents," said Big Kennedy unctuously, " but Tammany Hall as well. There's to be no more corruption; no more black-mail; every man an' every act must show as clean as a dog's tooth. I s'ppose, now, since we've got th' mayor, th' alderman, an' th' police, our first duty is to jump in an' straighten up th' village?" Here Big Kennedy scanned the others with a virtuous eye.

"Precisely," observed the reputable old gentleman. "And since the most glaring evils ought to claim our earliest attention, we should compel the police, without delay, to go about the elimination of the disorderly elements—the gambling dens, and other vice sinks. What do you say, Goldnose?" and the reputable old gentleman turned with a quick air to him of the giant rent-rolls.

"Now on those points," responded the personage of real estate dubiously, "I should say that we ought to proceed slowly. You can't rid the community of vice; history shows it to be impossible." Then, with a look of cunning meaning: "There exist, however, evils not morally bad, perhaps, that after all are violations of law, and get much more in the way of citizens than gambling or any of its sister iniquities." Then, wheeling spitefully on the reputable old gentleman: "There's the sidewalk and street ordinances: You know the European Express Company, Morton? I understand that you are a heaviest stockholder in it. I went by that corner the other day and I couldn't get through for the jam of horses and trucks that choked the street. There they

stood, sixty horses, thirty trucks, and the side street
fairly impassable. I scratched one side of my brougham
to the point of ruin—scratched off my coat-of-arms, in
fact, on the pole of one of the trucks. I think that to
enforce the laws meant to keep the street free of obstruc-
tions is more important, as a civic reform, than driving
out gamblers. These latter people, after all, get in nobody's way, and if one would find them one must hunt
for them. They are prompt with their rents, too, and
ready to pay a highest figure; they may be reckoned
among the best tenants to be found."

The real estate personage was red in the face when he
had finished this harangue. He wiped his brow and
looked resentfully at the reputable old gentleman.
That latter purist was now in a state of great personal heat.

"Those sixty horses were being fed, sir," said he with
spirit. "The barn is more than a mile distant; there's
no time to go there and back during the noon hour. You
can't have the barn on Broadway, you know. That
would be against the law, even if the value of Broadway
property didn't put it out of reach."

"Still, it's against the law to obstruct the streets,"
declared the real-estate personage savagely, "just as
much as it is against the law to gamble. And the trucks
and teams are more of a public nuisance, sir!"

"I suppose," responded the reputable old gentleman,

with a sneer, " that if my express horses paid somebody
a double rent, paid it to you, Goldnose, for instance, they
wouldn't be so much in the way." Then, as one exas-
perated to frankness: " Why don't you come squarely
out like a man, and say that to drive the disorderly
characters from the town would drive a cipher or two
off your rents? "

" If I, or any other real-estate owner," responded the
baited one indignantly, " rent certain tenements, not
otherwise to be let, to disorderly characters, whose fault
is it? I can't control the town for either its morals or
its business. The town grows up about my property,
and conditions are made to occur that practically condemn it. Good people won't live there, and the property
is unfit for stores or warehouses. What is an owner to
do? The neighborhood becomes such that best people
won't make of it a spot of residence. It's either no rent,
or a tenant who lives somewhat in the shade. Real-
estate owners, I suppose, are to be left with millions of
unrentable property on their hands; but you, on your
side, are not to lose half an hour in taking your horses to
a place where they might lawfully be fed? What do
you say, Casebottle? " and the outraged real-estate prince
turned to the wholesale grocer, as though seeking an
ally.

" I'm inclined, friend Goldnose," returned the wholesale grocer suavely, " I'm inclined to think with you that

it will be difficult to deal with the town as though it were
a camp meeting. Puritanism is offensive to the urban
taste." Here the wholesale grocer cleared his throat
impressively.

" And so," cried the reputable old gentleman, " you
call the suppression of gamblers and base women, puritanism? Casebottle, I'm surprised!"

The wholesale grocer looked nettled, but held his
peace. There came a moment of silence. Big Kennedy,
who had listened without interference, maintaining the
while an inflexible morality, took advantage of the pause.

" One thing," said he, " about which I think you will
all agree, is that every ginmill open after hours, or on
Sunday, should be pinched, and no side-doors or speak-
easy racket stood for. We can seal th' town up as tight
as sardines."

Big Kennedy glanced shrewdly at Casebottle. Here
was a move that would injure wholesale whisky. Casebottle, however, did not immediately respond; it was the
reputable old gentleman who spoke.

" That's my notion," said he, pursing his lips.
" Every ginmill ought to be closed as tight as a drum.
The Sabbath should be kept free of that disorder which
rum-drinking is certain to breed."

" Well, then," broke in Casebottle, whose face began to
color as his interests began to throb, " I say that a saloon
is a poor man's club. If you're going to close the

saloons, I shall be in favor of shutting up the clubs. I don't believe in one law for the poor and another for the rich."

This should offer some impression of how the visitors agreed upon a civil policy. Big Kennedy was good enough to offer for the others, each of whom felt himself somewhat caught in a trap, a loophole of escape.

"For," explained Big Kennedy, "while I believe in rigidly enforcin' every law until it is repealed, I have always held that a law can be tacitly repealed by th' people, without waitin' for th' action of some skate legislature, who, comin' for th' most part from th' corn-fields, has got it in for us lucky ducks who live in th' town. To put it this way: If there's a Sunday closin' law, or a law ag'inst gamblers, or a law ag'inst obstructin' th' streets, an' th' public don't want it enforced, then I hold it's repealed by th' highest authority in th' land, which is th' people, d'ye see!"

"Now, I think that very well put," replied the real-estate personage, with a sigh of relief, while the whole-sale grocer nodded approval. "I think that very well put," he went on, "and as it's getting late, I suggest that we adjourn for the nonce, to meet with our friend, Mr. Kennedy, on some further occasion. For myself, I can see that he and the great organization of which he is now, happily, the head, are heartily with us for reforming the shocking conditions that have heretofore persisted in this community. We have won the election; as a corollary, peculation and blackmail and extortion will of necessity cease. I think, with the utmost safety to the public interest, we can leave matters to take their natural course, without pushing to extremes. Don't you think so, Mr. Kennedy?"

"Sure!" returned that chieftain. "There's always more danger in too much steam than in too little."

The reputable old gentleman was by no means in accord with the real-estate personage; but since the wholesale grocer cast in his voice for moderation and no extremes, he found himself in a hopeless minority of no one save himself. With an eye of high contempt, therefore, for what he described as "The reform that needs reform," he went away with the others, and the weighty convention for pure days was over.

"An' that's th' last we'll see of 'em," said Big Kennedy, with a laugh. "No cat enjoys havin' his own tail shut in th' door; no man likes th' reform that pulls a gun on his partic'lar interest. This whole reform racket," continued Big Kennedy, who was in a temper to moralize, "is, to my thinkin', a kind of pouter-pigeon play. Most of 'em who go in for it simply want to swell 'round. Besides the pouter-pigeon, who's in th' game because he's stuck on himself, there's only two breeds of reformers. One is a Republican who's got ashamed of himself; an' th' other is some crook who's been kicked out o' Tammany for graftin' without a license."

"Would your last include you and me?" I asked. I thought I might hazard a small jest, since we were now alone.

"It might," returned Big Kennedy, with an iron grin. Then, twisting the subject: "Now let's talk serious for two words. I've been doin' th' bunco act so long with our three friends that my face begins to ache with lookin' pious. Now listen: You an' me have got a long road ahead of us, an' money to be picked up on both sides. But let me break this off to you, an' don't let a word get away. When you do get th' stuff, don't go to buildin' brownstone fronts, an' buyin' trottin' horses, an' givin' yourself away with any Coal-Oil Johnny capers. If we were Republicans or mugwumps it might do. But let a Democrat get a dollar, an' there's a warrant out for him before night. When you get a wad, bury it like a dog does a bone. An' speakin' of money; I've sent for th' Chief of Police. Come to think of it, we'd better talk over to my house. I'll go there now, an' you stay an' lay for him. When he shows up, bring him to me. There won't be so many pipin' us off over to my house."

Big Kennedy left the Tammany headquarters, where he and the good government trio had conferred, and sauntered away in the direction of his habitat. The

Chief of Police did not keep me in suspense. Big Kennedy was not four blocks away when that blue functionary appeared.

"I'm to go with you to his house," said I.

The head of the police was a bloated porpoise-body of a man, oily, plausible, masking his cunning with an appearance of frankness. As for scruple; why then the sharks go more freighted of a conscience.

Big Kennedy met the Chief of Police with the freedom that belongs with an acquaintance, boy and man, of forty years. In a moment they had gotten to the marrow of what was between them.

"Of course," said Big Kennedy, "Tammany's crippled just now with not havin' complete swing in th' town; an' I've got to bunk in more or less with the mugwumps. Still, we've th' upper hand in th' Board of Aldermen, an' are stronger everywhere than any other single party. Now you understand;" and here Big Kennedy bent a keen eye on the other. "Th' organization's in need of steady, monthly contributions. We'll want 'em in th' work I'm layin' out. I think you know where to get 'em, an' I leave it to you to organize th' graft. You get your bit, d'ye see! I'm goin' to name a party, however, to act as your wardman an' make th' collections. What sort is that McCue who was made Inspector about a week ago?"

"McCue!" returned the Chief of Police in tones of

surprise. " That man would never do! He's as honest
as a clock!"

" Honest!" exclaimed Big Kennedy, and his amazement was a picture. " Well, what does he think he's
doin' on th' force, then? "

" That's too many for me," replied the other. Then,
apologetically: " But you can see yourself, that
when you rake together six thousand men, no matter
how you pick 'em out, some of 'em's goin' to be honest."

" Yes," assented Big Kennedy thoughtfully, " I
s'ppose that's so, too. It would be askin' too much
to expect that a force, as you say, of six thousand
could be brought together, an' have 'em all crooked. It
was Father Considine who mentioned this McCue; he said
he was his cousin an' asked me to give him a shove along.
It shows what I've claimed a dozen times, that th' Church
ought to keep its nose out o' politics. However, I'll look
over th' list, an' give you some good name to-morrow."

" But how about th' town? " asked the Chief of
Police anxiously. " I want to know what I'm doin'.
Tell me plain, just what goes an' what don't."

" This for a pointer, then," responded Big Kennedy.
" Whatever goes has got to go on th' quiet. I've got
to keep things smooth between me an' th' mugwumps.
The gamblers can run; an' I don't find any fault with
even th' green-goods people. None of 'em can beat a
man who don't put himself within his reach, an' I don't

protect suckers. But knucks, dips, sneaks, second-story people, an' strong-arm men have got to quit. That's straight; let a trick come off on th' street cars, or at th' theater, or in the dark, or let a crib get cracked, an' there'll be trouble between you an' me, d'ye see! An' if anything as big as a bank should get done up, why then, you send in your resignation. An' at that, you'll be dead lucky if you don't do time."

" There's th' stations an' th' ferries," said the other, with an insinuating leer. " You know a mob of them Western fine-workers are likely to blow in on us, an' we not wise to 'em—not havin' their mugs in th' gallery. That sort of knuck might do business at th' depots or ferries, an' we couldn't help ourselves. Anyway," he concluded hopefully, " they seldom touch up our own citizens; it's mostly th' farmers they go through."

" All right," said Big Kennedy cheerfully, " I'm not worryin' about what comes off with th' farmers. But you tell them fine-workers, whose mugs you haven't got, that if anyone who can vote or raise a row in New York City goes shy his watch or leather, th' artist who gets it can't come here ag'in. Now mind: You've got to keep this town so I can hang my watch on any lamp-post in it, an' go back in a week an' find it hasn't been touched. There'll be plenty of ways for me an' you to get rich without standin' for sneaks an' hold-ups."

Big Kennedy, so soon as he got possession of Tammany, began divers improvements of a political sort, and each looking to our safety and perpetuation. One of his moves was to break up the ward gangs, and this included the Tin Whistles.

" For one thing, we don't need 'em—you an' me," said he. " They could only help us while we stayed in our ward an' kept in touch with 'em. The gangs strengthen th' ward leaders, but they don't strengthen th' Chief. So we're goin' to abolish 'em. The weaker we make th' ward leaders, the stronger we make ourselves. Do you ketch on?" and Big Kennedy nudged me significantly.

" You've got to disband, boys," said I, when I had called the Tin Whistles together. " Throw away your whistles. Big Kennedy told me that the first toot on one of 'em would get the musician thirty days on the Island. It's an order; so don't bark your shins against it."

After Big Kennedy was installed as Chief, affairs in their currents for either Big Kennedy or myself went flowing never more prosperously. The town settled to its lines; and the Chief of Police, with a wardman whom Big Kennedy selected, and who was bitten by no defect of integrity like the dangerous McCue, was making monthly returns of funds collected for " campaign purposes " with which the most exacting could have found no fault. We were rich, Big Kennedy and I; and acting on that suggestion of concealment, neither was blowing a bugle over his good luck.

I could have been happy, being now successful beyond any dream that my memory could lay hands on, had it not been for Apple Cheek and her waning health. She, poor girl, had never been the same after my trial for the death of Jimmy the Blacksmith; the shock of that trouble bore her down beyond recall. The doctors called it a nervous prostration, but I think, what with the fright and the grief of it, that the poor child broke her heart. She was like something broken; and although years went by she never once held up her head. Apple Cheek faded slowly away, and at last died in my arms.

When she passed, and it fell upon me like a pall that Apple Cheek had gone from me forever, my very heart withered and perished within me. There was but one thing to live for: Blossom, my baby girl. Anne came to dwell with us to be a mother to her, and it was good for me what Anne did, and better still for little Blossom. I was no one to have Blossom's upbringing, being ignorant and rude, and unable to look upon her without my eyes filling up for thoughts of my lost Apple Cheek. That was a sharpest of griefs—the going of Apple Cheek! My one hope lay in forgetfulness, and I courted it by working at politics, daylight and dark.

It would seem, too, that the blow that sped death to Apple Cheek had left its nervous marks on little Blossom. She was timid, hysterical, terror-whipped of fears that had no form. She would shriek out in the night as though a fiend frighted her, and yet could tell no story of it. She lived the victim of a vast formless fear that was to her as a demon without outlines or members or face. One blessing: I could give the trembling Blossom rest by holding her close in my arms, and thus she has slept the whole night through. The " frights," she said, fled when I was by.

In that hour, Anne was my sunshine and support; I think I should have followed Apple Cheek had it not been for Blossom, and Anne's gentle courage to hold me up. For all that, my home was a home of clouds and gloom; waking or sleeping, sorrow pressed upon me like a great stone. I took no joy, growing grim and silent, and far older than my years.

One evening when Big Kennedy and I were closeted over some enterprise of politics, that memorable exquisite, young Morton, was announced. He greeted us with his old-time vacuity of lisp and glance, and after mounting that double eyeglass, so potent with the herd, he said: " Gentlemen, I've come to make some money."

CHAPTER XIV

THE MULBERRY FRANCHISE

THAT'S my purpose in a nutshell," lisped young Morton; " I've decided to make some money; and I've come for millions." Here he waved a delicate hand, and bestowed upon Big Kennedy and myself his look of amiable inanity.

"Millions, eh?" returned Big Kennedy, with his metallic grin. " I've seen whole fam'lies taken the same way. However, I'm glad you're no piker."

" If by ' piker,' " drawled young Morton, " you mean one of those cheap persons who play for minimum stakes, I assure you that I should scorn to be so described; I should, really! No, indeed; it requires no more of thought or effort to play for millions than for ten-dollar bills."

" An' dead right you are!" observed Big Kennedy with hearty emphasis. " A sport can buck faro bank for a million as easily as for a white chip. That is, if he can find a game that 'll turn for such a bundle, an' has th' money to back his nerve. What's true of faro is true of business. So you're out for millions! I thought your old gent, who's into fifty enterprises an' has been for as

172

many years, had long ago shaken down mankind for a whole mountain of dough. The papers call him a multi-millionaire."

Young Morton, still with the empty smile, brought forth a cigarette case. The case, gold, was adorned with a ruby whereon to press when one would open it, and wore besides the owner's monogram in diamonds. Having lighted a cigarette, he polished his eyeglass with a filmy handkerchief. Re-establishing the eyeglass on his high patrician nose, he again shone vacuously upon Big Kennedy.

That personage had watched these manifestations of fastidious culture in a spirit of high delight. Big Kennedy liked young Morton; he had long ago made out how those dandyisms were no more than a cover for what fund of force and cunning dwelt beneath. In truth, Big Kennedy regarded young Morton's imbecilities as a most fortunate disguise. His remark would show as much. As young Morton—cigarette just clinging between his lips, eye of shallow good humor—bent towards him, he said, addressing me:

"Say! get onto that front! That look of not knowin' nothin' ought by itself to cash in for half a million! Did you ever see such a throw-off?" and here Big Kennedy quite lost himself in a maze of admiration. Recovering, however, and again facing our caller, he repeated: "Yes, I thought your old gent had millions."

"Both he and the press," responded young Morton, "concede that he has; they do, really! Moreover, he possesses, I think, the evidence of it in a cord or two of bonds and stocks, don't y' know! But in what fashion, pray, does that bear upon my present intentions as I've briefly laid them bare?"

"No fashion," said Big Kennedy, "only I'd naturally s'ppose that when you went shy on th' long green, you'd touch th' old gentleman."

"Undoubtedly," returned young Morton, "I could approach my father with a request for money—that is if my proposal were framed in a spirit of moderation, don't y' know!—say one hundred thousand dollars. But such a sum, in my present temper, would be but the shadow of a trifle. I owe five times the amount; I do, really! I've no doubt I'm on Tiffany's books for more than one hundred thousand, while my bill at the florist's should be at least ten thousand dollars, if the pen of that brigand of nosegays has kept half pace with his rapacity. However," concluded young Morton, breaking into a soft, engaging laugh, "since I intend, with your aid, to become the master of millions, such bagatelles are unimportant, don't y' know."

"Certainly!" observed Big Kennedy in a consolatory tone; "they don't amount to a deuce in a bum deck. Still, I must say you went in up to your neck on sparks an' voylets. I never saw such a plunger on gewgaws an' garlands since a yard of cloth made a coat for me."

" Those bills arose through my efforts to make grand opera beautiful. I set the prima donna ablaze with gems; and as for the stage, why, it was like singing in a conservatory; it was really! "

" Well, let that go! " said Big Kennedy, after a pause. " I shall be glad if through my help you make them millions. If you do, d'ye see, I'll make an armful just as big; it's ag'inst my religion to let anybody grab off a bigger piece of pie than I do when him an' me is pals. It would lower my opinion of myself. However, layin' guff aside, s'ppose you butt in now an' open up your little scheme. Let's see what button you think you're goin' to push."

" This is my thought," responded young Morton, and as he spoke the eyeglass dropped from its aquiline perch, and under the heat of a real animation those mists of affectation were dissipated; " this is my thought: I want a street railway franchise along Mulberry Avenue, the length of the Island."

" Go on," said Big Kennedy.

" It's my plan to form a corporation—Mulberry Traction. There'll be eight millions of preferred stock at eight per cent. I can build and equip the road with that. In addition, there'll be ten millions of common stock."

" Have you th' people ready to take th' preferred? "

" Ready and waiting. If I had the franchise, I could float those eight millions within ten days."

" What do you figger would be th' road's profits? "

" It would carry four hundred thousand passengers a day, and take in twenty thousand dollars. The operating expenses would not exceed an annual four millions and a half. That, after the eight per cent. on the preferred were paid, would leave over two millions a year on the common—a dividend of twenty per cent., or five per cent. every quarter. You can see where such returns would put the stock. You, for your ride, would go into the common on the ground floor."

" We'll get to how I go in, in a minute," responded Big Kennedy dryly. He was impressed by young Morton's proposal, and was threshing it out in his mind as they talked. " Now, see here," he went on, lowering his brows and fixing his keen gray glance on young Morton, " you mustn't get restless if I ask you questions. I like to tap every wheel an' try every rivet on a scheme or a man before I hook up with either."

" Ask what you please," said young Morton, as brisk as a terrier.

" I'll say this," observed Big Kennedy. " That traction notion shows that you're a hogshead of horse sense. But of course you understand that you're going to need money, an' plenty of it, before you get th' franchise. I can take care of th' Tammany push, perhaps; but there's highbinders up to your end of th' alley who'll want to be greased."

" How much do you argue that I'll require as a preliminary to the grant of the franchise? " asked young Morton, interrupting Big Kennedy.

" Every splinter of four hundred thousand."

" That was my estimate," said young Morton; " but I've arranged for twice that sum."

" Who is th' Rothschild you will get it from? "

" My father," replied young Morton, and now he lapsed anew into his manner of vapidity. " Really, he takes an eighth of the preferred at par—one million! I've got the money in the bank, don't y' know! "

" Good! " ejaculated Big Kennedy, with the gleam which never failed to sparkle in his eye at the mention of rotund riches.

" My father doesn't know my plans," continued young Morton, his indolence and his eyeglass both restored. " No; he wouldn't let me tell him; he wouldn't, really! I approached him in this wise:

" ' Father,' said I, ' you are aware of the New York alternative? '

" ' What is it? ' he asked.

" ' Get money or get out.'

" ' Well! ' said he.

" ' Father, I've decided not to move. Yes, father;

after a full consideration of the situation, I've resolved
to make, say twenty or thirty millions for myself; I
have, really! It's quite necessary, don't y' know; I am
absolutely bankrupt. And I don't like it; there's nothing
comfortable in being bankrupt, it so deucedly restricts a
man. Besides, it's not good form. I've evolved an idea,
however; there's a business I can go into.'

" ' Store? ' he inquired.

" ' No, no, father,' I replied, for the odious supposi-
tion quite upset me; ' it's nothing so horribly vulgar as
trade; it's a speculation, don't y' know. There'll be
eight millions of preferred stock; you are to take a million. Also, you are to give me the million at once.'

" ' What is this speculation? ' he asked. ' If I'm to
go in for a million, I take it you can entrust me with the
outlines.'

" ' Really, it was on my mind to do so,' I replied.
' My scheme is this: I shall make an alliance with Mr.
Kennedy.'

" ' Stop, stop! ' cried my father hastily. ' On the
whole, I don't care to hear your scheme. You shall have
the money; but I've decided that it will reflect more
glory upon you should you bring things to an issue
without advice from me. Therefore, you need tell me no
more; positively, I will not hear you.' "

" It was my name made him leary," observed Big
Kennedy, with the gratified face of one who has been

paid a compliment. " When you said ' Kennedy,' he just about figgered we were out to get a kit of tools an' pry a shutter off th' First National. It's th' mugwump notion of Tammany, d'ye see! You put him onto it some time, that now I'm Chief I've got center-bits an' jimmies skinned to death when it comes to makin' money."

" I don't think it was your name," observed young Morton. " He's beginning to learn, however, about my voting those three hundred wenches in overalls and jumpers, don't y' know, and it has taught him to distrust my methods as lacking that element of conservatism which he values so much. It was that which came uppermost in his memory, and it occurred to him that perhaps the less he knew about my enterprises the sounder he would sleep. Is it not remarkable, how fondly even an advanced man like my father will cling to the moss-grown and the obsolete? "

" That's no dream neither!" exclaimed Big Kennedy, in earnest coincidence with young Morton. " It's this old fogy business on th' parts of people who ought to be leadin' up th' dance for progress, that sends me to bed tired in th' middle of th' day!" And here Big Kennedy shook his head reproachfully at gray ones whose sluggishness had wounded him.

" My father drew his check," continued young Morton. " He couldn't let it come to me, however, without a chiding. Wonderful, how the aged like to lord it over younger folk with rebukes for following in their foot-steps—really!

" ' You speak of bankruptcy,' said my father, sucking in his cheeks. ' Would it violate confidence should you tell me how you come to be in such a disgraceful predicament?' This last was asked in a spirit of sarcasm, don't y' know.

" ' It was by following your advice, sir,' said I.

" ' Following my advice!' exclaimed my father. ' What do you mean, sir? Or are you mad?'

" ' Not at all,' I returned. ' Don't you recall how, when I came from college, you gave me a world of advice, and laid particular stress on my establishing a perfect credit? " Nothing is done without credit," you said on that occasion; " and it should be the care of a young man, as he enters upon life, to see to it that his credit is perfect in every quarter of trade. He should extend his credit with every opportunity." This counsel made a deep impression upon me, it did, really! and so I've extended my credit wherever I saw a chance until I owe a half-million. I must say, father, that I think it would have saved me money, don't y' know, had you told me to destroy my credit as hard as I could. In fostering my credit, I but warmed a viper,' "

Young Morton paused to fire another cigarette, while the pucker about the corner of his eye indicated that he felt as though he had turned the laugh upon his father. Following a puff or two, he returned gravely to Mulberry Traction.

"Do you approve my proposition?" he asked of Big Kennedy, "and will you give me your aid?"

"The proposition's all hunk," said Big Kennedy. "As to my aid: that depends on whether we come to terms."

"What share would you want?"

"Forty per cent. of th' common stock," responded Big Kennedy. "That's always th' Tammany end; forty per cent."

Young Morton drew in his lips. The figure seemed a surprise. "Do you mean that you receive four millions of the common stock, you paying nothing?" he asked at last.

"I don't pony for a sou markee. An' I get th' four millions, d'ye see! Who ever heard of Tammany payin' for anything!" and Big Kennedy glared about the room, and sniffed through his nose, as though in the presence of all that might be called preposterous.

"But if you put in no money," remonstrated young Morton, "why should you have the stock? I admit that you ought to be let in on lowest terms; but, after all, you should put in something."

"I put in my pull," retorted Big Kennedy grimly. "You get your franchise from me."

"From the City," corrected young Morton.

" I'm the City," replied Big Kennedy; " an' will be
while I'm on top of Tammany, an' Tammany's on top
of th' town." Then, with a friendliness of humor:
" Here, I like you, an' I'll go out o' my way to educate
you on this point. You're fly to some things, an' a
farmer on others. Now understand: The City's a come-
on—a sucker—an' it belongs to whoever picks it up.
That's me this trip, d'ye see! Now notice: I've got no
office; I'm a private citizen same as you, an' I don't owe
no duty to th' public. Every man has his pull—his influence. You've got your pull; I've got mine. When
a man wants anything from th' town, he gets his pull to
work. In this case, my pull is bigger than all th' other
pulls clubbed together. You get that franchise or you
don't get it, just as I say. In short, you get it from
me—get it by my pull, d'ye see! Now why shouldn't I
charge for th' use of my pull, just as a lawyer asks his
fee, or a bank demands interest when it lends? My pull's
my pull; it's my property as much as a bank's money is
th' bank's, or a lawyer's brains is the lawyer's. I worked
hard to get it, an' there's hundreds who'd take it from
me if they could. There's my doctrine: I'm a private
citizen; my pull is my capital, an' I'm as much entitled
to get action on it in favor of myself as a bank has to
shave a note. That's why I take forty per cent. It's
little enough: The franchise will be four-fifths of th'
whole value of th' road; an' all I have for it is two-fifths

of five-ninths, for you've got to take into account them eight millions of preferred."

Young Morton was either convinced of the propriety of what Big Kennedy urged, or saw—the latter is the more likely surmise--that he must agree if he would attain success for his enterprise. He made no more objection, and those forty per cent. in favor of Big Kennedy were looked upon as the thing adjusted.

"You spoke of four hundred thousand dollars as precedent to the franchise," said young Morton. "Where will that go?"

"There's as many as thirty hungry ones who, here an' there an' each in our way, must be met an' squared."

"How much will go to your fellows?"

"Most of th' Tammany crowd I can beat into line. But there's twelve who won't take orders. They were elected as 'Fusion' candidates, an' they think that entitles 'em to play a lone hand. Whenever Tammany gets th' town to itself, you can gamble! I'll knock their blocks off quick. You ask what it 'll take to hold down th' Tammany people? I should say two hundred thousand dollars. We'll make it this way: I'll take thirty per cent. instead of forty of th' common, an' two hundred thousand in coin. That 'll be enough to give us th' Tammany bunch as solid as a brick switch shanty."

"That should do," observed young Morton thoughtfully.

When young Morton was about to go, Big Kennedy detained him with a final query.

"This aint meant to stick pins into you," said Big Kennedy, "but, on th' dead! I'd like to learn how you moral an' social high-rollers reconcile yourselves to things. How do you agree with yourself to buy them votes needed to get th' franchise? Not th' ones I'll bring in, an' which you can pretend you don't know about; but them you'll have to deal with personally, d'ye see!"

"There'll be none I'll deal with personally, don't y' know," returned young Morton, getting behind his lisp and eyeglass, finding them a refuge in what was plainly an embarrassed moment, "no; I wouldn't do anything with the vulgar creatures in person. They talk such awful English, it gets upon my nerves —really! But I've retained Caucus & Club; they're lawyers, only they don't practice law, they practice politics. They'll attend to those low details of which you speak. For me to do so wouldn't be good form. It would shock my set to death, don't y' know!"

"That's a crawl-out," observed Big Kennedy reproachfully, "an' it aint worthy of you. Why don't you come to th' center? You're goin' to give up four hundred thousand dollars to get this franchise. You don't think it's funny—you don't do it because you like it, an' are swept down in a gust of generosity. An' you do think it's wrong."

"Really, now you're in error," replied young Morton earnestly, but still clinging to his lisp and his languors. "As you urge, one has scant pleasure in paying this money. On the contrary, I shall find it extremely dull, don't y' know! But I don't call it wrong. I'm entitled, under the law, and the town's practice—a highly idiotic one, this latter, I concede!—of giving these franchises away, to come forward with my proposition. Since I offer to build a perfect road, and to run it in a perfect manner, I ought, as a matter of right—always bearing in mind the town's witless practice aforesaid—to be granted this franchise. But those officers of the city who, acting for the city, should make the grant, refuse to do their duty by either the city or myself, unless I pay to each of them, say ten thousand dollars; they do, really! What am I to do? I didn't select those officers; the public picked them out. Must I suffer loss, and go defeated of my rights, because the public was so careless or so ignorant as to pitch upon those improper, or, if you will, dishonest officials? I say, No. The fault is not mine; surely the loss should not be mine. I come off badly enough when I submit to the extortion. No, it is no more bribery, so far as I am involved, than it is bribery when I surrender my watch to that footpad who has a pistol at my ear. In each instance, the public should

have saved me and has failed, don't y' know. The
public, thus derelict, must not denounce me when, under
conditions which its own neglect has created, I take
the one path left open to insure myself; it mustn't,
really!"

Young Morton wiped the drops from his brow, and I
could tell how he was deeply in earnest in what he thus
put forward. Big Kennedy clapped him lustily on the
back.

"Put it there!" he cried, extending his hand. "I
couldn't have said it better myself, an' I aint been doin'
nothin' but buy aldermen since I cut my wisdom teeth.
There's one last suggestion, however: I take it, you're
onto the' fact that Blackberry Traction will lock horns
with us over this franchise. We parallel their road, d'ye
see, an' they'll try to do us up." Then to me: "Who
are th' Blackberry's pets in th' Board?"

"McGinty and Doloran," I replied.

"Keep your peepers on them babies. You can tell
by th' way they go to bat, whether th' Blackberry has
signed up to them to kill our franchise."

"I can tell on the instant," I said.

"That has all been anticipated," observed young Morton. "The president of Blackberry Traction is a member of my club; we belong in the same social set. I
foresaw his opposition, and I've provided for it; I have,
really! McGinty and Doloran, you say? The names

sound like the enemy. Please post me if those interesting individuals move for our disfavor."

And now we went to work. Whatever was demanded of the situation as it unfolded found prompt reply, and in the course of time Mulberry Traction was given its franchise. The Blackberry at one crisis came forward to work an interruption; the sudden hot enmity of McGinty and Doloran was displayed. I gave notice of it to young Morton.

"I'll arrange the matter," he said. "At the next meeting of the Board I think they will be with us, don't y' know."

It was even so; and since Big Kennedy, with my aid, discharged every responsibility that was his, the ordinance granting the franchise went through, McGinty and Doloran voting loudly with the affirmative. They were stubborn caitiffs, capable of much destructive effort, and their final tameness won upon my surprise. I put the question of it to young Morton.

"This is the secret of that miracle," said he. "The president of Blackberry has been a Wall Street loser, don't y' know, for more than a year—has lost more than he could honestly pay. And yet he paid! Where did he get the money? At first I asked myself the question in a feeling of lazy curiosity. When I decided to organize our Mulberry Traction, I asked it in earnest; I did, really! I foresaw my friend's opposition, and was seek-

ing a weapon against him. Wherefore I looked him
over with care, trying to determine where he got his loans.
Now, he was the president, and incidentally a director, of
the Confidence Trust Company. I bought stock in the
Confidence. Then I drew into my interest that employee
who had charge of the company's loans. I discovered
that our Blackberry president had borrowed seven millions from the Trust Company, giving as security a collection of dogs and cats and chips and whetstones, don't
y' know! That was wrong; considering his position as
an officer of the company, it was criminal. I made myself master of every proof required to establish his guilt
in court. Then I waited. When you told me of those
evil symptoms manifested by McGinty and Doloran, I
took our president into the Fifth Avenue window of the
club and showed him those evidences of his sins. He
looked them over, lighted a cigar, and after musing for
a moment, asked if the help of McGinty and Doloran
for our franchise would make towards my gratification.
I told him I would be charmed—really! You know the
rest. Oh, no; I did not do so rude a thing as threaten
an arrest. It wasn't required. Our president is a highly
intellectual man. Besides, it wouldn't have been clubby;
and it would have been bad form. And," concluded
young Morton, twirling his little cane, and putting on
that look of radiant idiocy, " I've an absolute mania for
everything that's form, don't y' know."

CHAPTER XV

YOUNG MORTON was president of Mulberry Traction. When the franchise came sound and safe into the hands of Mulberry, young Morton evolved a construction company and caused himself to be made president and manager thereof. These affairs cleared up, he went upon the building of his road with all imaginable spirit. He was still that kid-gloved, eye-glassed exquisite of other hours, but those who dealt with him in his road-building knew in him a hawk to see and a lion to act in what he went about. Big Kennedy was never weary of his name, and glowed at its merest mention.

" He's no show-case proposition! " cried Big Kennedy exultantly. " To look at him, folks might take him for a fool. They'd bring him back, you bet! if they did. You've got to see a party in action before you can tell about him. A mudscow will drift as fast as an eight-oared shell; it's only when you set 'em to goin' endwise, an' give 'em a motive, you begin to get onto th' difference."

One day young Morton told me how the Gas Company had lodged suit against Mulberry.

189

"They've gotten a beastly injunction, they have, really!" said he. "They say we're digging, don't y' know, among their pipes and mains. The hearing is put down for one week from to-day."

"The Gas Company goes vastly out of its way in this!" observed the reputable old gentleman indignantly.

He had arrived in company with young Morton. When now the franchise was obtained, and those more devious steps for Mulberry advancement had been taken, the reputable old gentleman began to feel a vigorous interest in his son's enterprise. The reputable old gentleman had grown proud of his son, and it should be conceded that young Morton justified the paternal admiration.

"Let us go over to Tammany Hall," said I, "and talk with Big Kennedy."

We found Big Kennedy in cheerful converse with the Reverend Bronson, over the latter's Five Points Mission. He and the dominie were near Big Kennedy's desk; in a far corner lolled a drunken creature, tattered, unshorn, disreputable, asleep and snoring in his chair. As I entered the room, accompanied by the reputable old gentleman and young Morton, Big Kennedy was giving the Reverend Bronson certain hearty assurances of his good will.

"I'll see to it to-day," Big Kennedy was saying. "You go back an' deal your game. I'll have two cops detailed to every meetin', d'ye see, an' their orders will be to break their night-sticks over th' head of th' first duck that laughs or makes a row.   You always come to me for what you want; you can hock your socks I'll back you up. What this town needs is religious teachin' of an elevated kind, an' no bunch of Bowery bums is goin' to give them exercises th' smother.   An' that goes!"

" I'm sure I'm much obliged," murmured the Reverend Bronson, preparing to take himself away.   Then, turning curious: " May I ask who that lost and abandoned man is? " and he indicated the drunkard, snoring in his chair.

" You don't know him," returned Big Kennedy, in a tone of confident, friendly patronage.   " Just now he's steeped in bugjuice to th' eyes, an' has been for a week. But I'm goin' to need him; so I had him brought in."

" Of what earthly use can one who has fallen so low be put to? " asked the Reverend Bronson.   Then, with a shudder: " Look at him! "

" An' that's where you go wrong! " replied Big Kennedy, who was in one of his philosophical humors. " Now if it was about morals, or virtue, or th' hereafter, I wouldn't hand you out a word.   That's your game, d'ye see, an' when it's a question of heaven, you've got me beat.   But there's other games, like Tammany Hall for instance, where I could give you cards an' spades. Now take that sot there: I know what he can do, an'

what I want him for, an' inside of a week I'll be makin'
him as useful as a corkscrew in Kentucky."

"He seems a most unpromising foundation upon which
to build one's hope," said the Reverend Bronson dubiously.

"He aint much to look at, for fair!" responded Big
Kennedy, in his large tolerant way. "But you mustn't
bet your big stack on a party's looks. You can't tell
about a steamboat by th' coat of paint on her sides; you
must go aboard. Now that fellow "—here he pointed
to the sleeping drunkard—" once you get th' booze out
of him, has a brain like a buzzsaw. An' you should hear
him talk! He's got a tongue so acid it would eat
through iron. The fact is, th' difference between that
soak an' th' best lawyer at the New York bar is less'n
one hundred dollars. I'll have him packed off to a
Turkish bath, sweat th' whisky out of him, have him
shaved an' his hair cut, an' get him a new suit of clothes.
When I'm through, you won't know him. He'll run
sober for a month, which is as long as I'll need him this
trip."

"And will he then return to his drunkenness?" asked
the Reverend Bronson.

"Sure as you're alive!" said Big Kennedy. "The
moment I take my hooks off him, down he goes."

"What you say interests me! Why not send him to
my mission, and let me compass his reform."

" You might as well go down to th' morgue an' try an' revive th' dead.   No, no, Doctor; that duck is out of humanity's reach.   If you took him in hand at your mission, he'd show up loaded some night an' tip over your works.   Better pass him up."

" If his case is so hopeless, I marvel that you tolerate him."

The Reverend Bronson was a trifle piqued at Big Kennedy for thinking his influence would fall short of the drunkard's reform.

" You aint onto this business of bein' Chief of Tammany," responded Big Kennedy, with his customary grin.   " I always like to do my work through these incurables.   It's better to have men about you who are handicapped by some big weakness, d'ye see!   They're strong on th' day you need 'em, an' weak when you lay 'em down.   Which makes it all the better.   If these people were strong all th' year 'round, one of 'em, before we got through, would want my job, an' begin to lay pipes to get it.   Some time, when I wasn't watchin', he might land th' trick at that.   No, as hands to do my work, give me fellows who've got a loose screw in their machinery.   They're less chesty; an' then they work better, an' they're safer.   I've only one man near me who don't show a blemish.   That's him," and he pointed to where I sat waiting with young Morton and the reputable old gentleman.   " I'll trust him; because I'm goin'

to make him Boss when I get through; an' he knows
it. That leaves him without any reason for doin' me
up."

Big Kennedy called one of his underlings, and gave
him directions to have the sleeping drunkard conveyed
instantly to a bath-house.

"Get th' kinks out of him," said he; "an' bring him
back to me in four days. I want to see him as straight as
a string, an' dressed as though for a weddin'. I'm goin'
to need him to make a speech, d'ye see! at that mugwump
ratification meetin' in Cooper Union."

When the Reverend Bronson, and the drunken Cicero,
in care of his keeper, had gone their several ways, Big
Kennedy wheeled upon us. He was briefly informed of
the troubles of Mulberry Traction.

"If them gas crooks don't hold hard," said he, when
young Morton had finished, "we'll have an amendment to
th' city charter passed at Albany, puttin' their meters
under th' thumb an' th' eye of th' Board of Lightin' an'
Supplies. I wonder how they'd like that! It would cut
sixty per cent. off their gas bills. However, mebby th'
Gas Company's buttin' into this thing in th' dark.
What judge does the injunction come up before?"

"Judge Mole," said young Morton.

"Mole, eh?" returned Big Kennedy thoughtfully.
"We'll shift th' case to some other judge. Mole won't
do; he's th' Gas Company's judge, d'ye see."

" The Gas Company's judge!" exclaimed the reputable old gentleman, in horrified amazement.

Big Kennedy, at this, shone down upon the reputable
old gentleman like a benignant sun.

" Slowly but surely," said he, " you begin to tumble
to th' day an' th' town you're livin' in.   Don't you know
that every one of our giant companies has its own judge?
Why! one of them Captains of Industry, as th'
papers call 'em, would no more be without his judge than
without his stenographer."

" In what manner," snorted the reputable old gentleman, " does one of our great corporations become possessed of a judge? "

" Simple as sloppin' out champagne! " returned Big
Kennedy.   " It asks us to nominate him.   Then it comes
up with his assessment, d'ye see!—an' I've known that to
run as high as one hundred thousand—an' then every
year it contributes to our various campaigns, say fifty
thousand dollars a whirl.   Oh! it comes high to have
your own private judge; but if you're settin' into a game
of commerce where th' limit's higher than a cat's back,
it's worth a wise guy's while."

" Come, come! " interposed young Morton, " we've no
time for moral and political abstractions, don't y' know!
Let's get back to Mulberry Traction.   You say Judge
Mole won't do.   Can you have the case set down before
another judge? "

"Easy money!" said Big Kennedy. "I'll have Mole send it over to Judge Flyinfox. He'll knock it on th' head, when it comes up, an' that's th' last we'll ever hear of that injunction."

"You speak of Judge Flyinfox with confidence," observed the reputable old gentleman, breaking in. "Why are you so certain he will dismiss the application for an injunction?"

"Because," retorted Big Kennedy, in his hardy way, "he comes up for renomination within two months. He'd look well throwin' the harpoon into me right now, wouldn't he?" Then, as the double emotions of wrath and wonder began to make purple the visage of the reputable old gentleman: "Look here: you're more'n seven years old. Why should you think a judge was different from other men? Haven't you seen men crawl in th' sewer of politics on their hands an' knees, an' care for nothin' only so they crawled finally into th' Capitol at Albany? Is a judge any better than a governor? Or is either of 'em any better than other people? While Tammany makes th' judges, do you s'ppose they'll be too good for th' organization? That last would be a cunnin' play to make!"

"But these judges," said the reputable old gentleman. "Their terms are so long and their salaries so large, I should think they would defy you and your humiliating orders."

" Exactly," returned Big Kennedy, with the pleasant air of one aware of himself, " an' that long term an' big salary works square th' other way. There's so many of them judges that there's one or two to be re-elected each year. So we've always got a judge whose term is on th' blink, d'ye see! An' he's got to come to us—to me, if you want it plain—to get back. You spoke of th' big salary an' th' long term. Don't you see that you've only given them guys more to lose? Now th' more a party has to lose, th' more he'll bow and scrape to save himself. Between us, a judge within a year or so of re-nomination is th' softest mark on th' list."

The reputable old gentleman expressed unbounded indignation, while Big Kennedy laughed.

" What 're you kickin' about? " asked Big Kennedy, when he had somewhat recovered. " That's the ' Boss System.' Just now, d'ye see! it's water on your wheel, so you oughtn't to raise th' yell. But to come back to Mulberry Traction: We'll have Mole send th' case to Flyinfox; an' Flyinfox will put th' kybosh on it, if it comes up. But I'll let you into a secret. Th' case 'll never come up; th' Gas Company will go back to its corner."

" Explain," said young Morton eagerly.

" Because I'll tell 'em to."

" Do you mean that you'll go to the Gas Company," sneered the reputable old gentleman, " and give its

officers orders the same as you say you give them to the
State's and the City's officers?"

"Th' Gas Company 'll come to me, an' ask for
orders."

The reputable old gentleman drew a long breath, while
his brows worked up and down.

"And dare you tell me," he cried, "that men of millions—our leading men of business, will come to you and
ask your commands?"

"My friend," replied Big Kennedy gravely, "no
matter how puffed up an' big these leadin' men of business get to be, th' Chief of Tammany is a bigger toad
than any. Listen: th' bigger the target th' easier th'
shot. If you'll come down here with me for a month,
I'll gamble you'll meet an' make th' acquaintance of
every business king in th' country. An' you'll notice,
too, that they'll take off their hats, an' listen to what I
say; an' in th' end, they'll do what I tell 'em to do." Big
Kennedy glowered impressively upon the reputable old
gentleman. "That sounds like a song that is sung,
don't it?" Then turning to me: "Tell th' Street Department not to give th' Gas Company any more permits
to open streets until further orders. An' now"—coming back to the reputable old gentleman—"can't you see
what 'll come off?"

The reputable old gentleman looked mystified.
Young Morton, for his part, began to smile.

"He sees!" exclaimed Big Kennedy, pointing to young Morton. "Here's what 'll happen. Th' Gas Company has to have two hundred permits a day to tear open th' streets. After that order. reaches the Street Commissioner, it won't get any."

"'Better see the Boss,' the Street Commissioner will whisper, when the Gas Company asks what's wrong.

"The next day one of th' deck hands will come to see me. I'll turn him down; th' Chief of Tammany don't deal with deck hands. The next day th' Gas Company will send th' first mate. The mate 'll get turned down; th' Chief of Tammany deals with nobody less'n a captain, d'ye see! On th' third day, or to put it like a prophet, say next Friday—since this is Tuesday—th' president of th' Gas Company will drive here in his brougham. I'll let him wait ten minutes in the outer room to take the swell out of his head. Then I'll let him in, an', givin' him th' icy eye, I'll ask: 'What's th' row?' Th' Gas Company will have been three days without permits to open th' streets; —its business will be at a standstill;—th' Gas Company 'll be sweatin' blood. There'll be th' Gas Company's president, an' here'll be Big John Kennedy. I think that even you can furnish th' wind-up. As I tell you, now that I've had time to think it out, th' case will be withdrawn. Still, to make sure, we'll have Mole send th' papers over to Flyinfox, just as though we had nowhere except th' courts to look for justice."

On Monday, the day before the case was to have been called, the Gas Company, humbled and made penitent with a stern paucity of " permits," dismissed its petition for an injunction against Mulberry Traction, and young Morton returned to his career, unchecked of a court's decree.

" Father," said young Morton, as we came from our interview with Big Kennedy, " I'm not sure that the so-called Boss System for the Government of Cities is wholly without its advantages, don't y' know!" And here young Morton puffed a complacent, not to say superior, cigarette.

" Humph!" retorted the reputable old gentleman angrily. " Every Esau, selling his birthright for a mess of pottage, would speak the same."

" Esau with a cigarette—really!" murmured young Morton, giving a ruminative puff. " But I say, father, it isn't a mess of pottage, don't y' know, it's a street rail-way."

As Mulberry Traction approached completion, the common stock reached forty. At that point Big Kennedy closed out his interest. Snapping the catchlock behind us, to the end that we be alone, he tossed a dropsical gray envelope on the table.

" There's two hundred thousand dollars' worth of

Uncle Sam's bonds," said he. "That's your end of Mulberry Traction."

" You've sold out? "

" Sold out an' got one million two hundred thousand."

" The stock would have gone higher," said I. " You would have gotten more if you'd held on."

" Wall Street," returned Big Kennedy, with a cautious shake of the head, " is off my beat. I'm afraid of them stock sharps; I feel like a come-on th' minute I begin to talk with one, an' I wouldn't trust 'em as far as I could throw a dog by th' tail. I break away as fast as ever I can, an' chase back to Fourteenth Street, where I'm wise to th' game. I've seen suckers like me who took a million dollars into Wall Street, an' came out in a week with nothin' but a pocket full of canceled postage stamps."

" I've been told," said I with a laugh, and going with Big Kennedy's humor, " that two hundred years ago, Captain Kidd, the pirate, had his home on the site of the present Stock Exchange."

" Did he? " said Big Kennedy. " Well, I figger that his crew must have lived up an' down both sides of the street from him, an' their descendants are still holdin' down th' property. An' to think," mused Big Kennedy, " that Trinity Church stares down th' length of Wall Street, with th' graves in th' Trinity churchyard to remind them stock wolves of th' finish! I'm a hard man, an' I play a hard game, but on th' level! if I was as big a robber as them Wall Street sharps, I couldn't look Trinity Church in th' face!" Then, coming back to Mulberry Traction and to me: " I've put it in bonds, d'ye see! Now if I was you, I'd stand pat on 'em just as they are. Lay 'em away, an' think to yourself they're for that little Blossom of yours."

At the name of Blossom, Big Kennedy laid his heavy hand on mine as might one who asked a favor. It was the thing unusual. Big Kennedy's rough husk gave scanty promise of any softness of sentiment to lie beneath. Somehow, the word and the hand brought the water to my eyes.

" It is precisely what I mean to do," said I.   " Blossom is to have it, an' have it as it is—two hundred thousand dollars in bonds."

Big Kennedy, with that, gave my hand a Titan's grip in indorsement of my resolve.

Blossom was growing up a frail, slender child, and still with her frightened eyes.   Anne watched over her; and since Blossom lacked in sturdiness of health, she did not go to a school, but was taught by Anne at home.   Blossom's love was for me; she clung to me when I left the house, and was in my arms the moment the door opened upon my return.   She was the picture of my lost Apple Cheek, wanting her roundness, and my eyes went wet and weary with much looking upon her.

My home was quiet and, for me, gloomy.   Anne, I

think, was happy in a manner pensive and undemonstrative. As for Blossom, that terror she drew in from her mother when the latter was struck by the blow of my arrest for the death of Jimmy the Blacksmith, still held its black dominion over her fancy; and while with time she grew away from those agitations and hysterias which enthralled her babyhood, she lived ever in a twilight of melancholy that nothing could light up, and from which her spirit never emerged. In all her life I never heard her laugh, and her smile, when she did smile, was as the soul of a sigh. And so my house was a house of whispers and shadows and silences as sad as death—a house of sorrow for my lost Apple Cheek, and fear for Blossom whose life was stained with nameless mourning before ever she began to live at all.

Next door to me I had brought my father and mother to dwell. Anne, who abode with me, could oversee both houses. The attitude of Big Kennedy towards Old Mike had not been wanting in effect upon me. The moment my money was enough, I took my father from his forge, and set both him and my mother to a life of workless ease. I have feared more than once that this move was one not altogether wise. My people had been used to labor, and when it was taken out of their hands they knew not where to turn with their time. They were much looked up to by neighbors for the power and position I held in the town's affairs; and each Sunday they could give the

church a gold piece, and that proved a mighty boon to
their pride. But, on the whole, the leisure of their lives,
and they unable to employ it, carked and corroded them,
and it had not a little to do in breaking down their health.
They were in no sense fallen into the vale of years, when
one day they were seized by a pneumonia and—my
mother first, with her patient peasant face! and my father
within the week that followed—passed both to the other
life.

And now when I was left with only Blossom and Anne
to love, and to be dear and near to me, I went the more
among men, and filled still more my head and hands and
heart with politics. I must have action, motion. Grief
walked behind me; and, let me but halt, it was never long
in coming up.

Sundry years slipped by, and the common routine
work of the organization engaged utterly both Big Kennedy and myself. We struggled heartily, and had our
ups and our downs, our years of black and our years of
white. The storm that wrecked Big Kennedy's predeces-
sor had left Tammany in shallow, dangerous waters for
its sailing. Also Big Kennedy and I were not without
our personal enemies. We made fair weather of it, however, particularly when one considers the broken condition
of Tammany, and the days were not desolate of their
rewards.

Now ensues a great heave upward in my destinies.

One evening I came upon Big Kennedy, face gray and drawn, sitting as still as a church. Something in the look or the attitude went through me like a lance.

" What's wrong? " I asked.

" There was a saw-bones here," said he, " pawin' me over for a life-insurance game that I thought I'd buy chips in. He tells me my light's goin' to flicker out inside a year. That's a nice number to hand a man! Just as a sport finds himself on easy street, along comes a scientist an' tells him it's all off an' nothin' for it but the bone-yard! Well," concluded Big Kennedy, grimly lighting a cigar, " if it's up to me, I s'ppose I can hold down a hearse as good as th' next one. If it's th' best they can do, why, let her roll! "

CHAPTER XVI

BIG KENNEDY could not live a year; his doom was written. It was the word hard to hear, and harder to believe, of one who, broad, burly, ruddy with the full color of manhood at its prime, seemed in the very feather of his strength. And for all that, his hour was on its way. Death had gained a lodgment in his heart, and was only pausing to strengthen its foothold before striking the blow. I sought to cheer him with the probability of mistake on the side of ones who had given him this dark warning of his case.

" That's all right," responded Big Kennedy in a tone of dogged dejection; " I'm up ag'inst it just th' same. It didn't need th' doctor to put me on. More'n once I've felt my heart slip a cog. I shall clean up an' quit. They say if I pull out an' rest, I may hang on for a year. That's th' tip I've got, an' I'm goin' to take it. I'm two millions to th' good, an' when all is done, why, that's enough."

Big Kennedy declared for a vacation; the public announcement went for it that he would rest. I was to take control as a fashion of Boss by brevet.

" Of course," said Big Kennedy when we talked privately of the situation, " you understand. I'm down an' out, done for an' as good as dead right now. But it's better to frame th' play as I've proposed. Don't change th' sign over th' door for a month or two; it 'll give you time to stiffen your grip. There's dubs who would like th' job, d'ye see, an' if they found an openin' they'd spill you out of th' place like a pup out of a basket. It's for you to get your hooks on th' levers, an' be in control of th' machine before I die." Then, with a ghastly smile: " An' seein' it's you, I'll put off croakin' till th' last call of th' board."

Big Kennedy, seeking that quiet which had been the physician's prescription, went away. When, later by ten months, he came back, his appearance was a shock to me. The great, bluff man was gone, and he who feebly took me by the hand seemed no more than a weak shadow of that Big John Kennedy whom I had followed. The mere looks of him were like a knife-stab. He stayed but a day, and then returned to his retreat in the silent hills. Within a month Big Kennedy was dead.

" You've got things nailed," said he, on the last evening, " an' I'm glad it's so. Now let me give you a few points; they may help you to hold down your place as Boss. You're too hungry for revenge; there's your weakness. The revenge habit is worse than a taste for whisky. Th' best you can say for it is it's a waste of time. When

you've downed a man, stop. To go on beatin' him is
like throwin' water on a drowned rat.

"When it comes to handin' out th' offices an' th' contracts, don't play fav'rites. Hand every man what's
comin' to him by th' rules of th' game. It 'll give you
more power to have men say you'll do what's square, than
that you'll stick by your friends. Good men—dead-game
men, don't want favors; they want justice.

"Never give a man the wrong office; size every man
up, an' measure him for his place th' same as a tailor does
for a suit of clothes. If you give a big man a little office,
you make an enemy; if you give a little man a big office,
you make trouble.

"Flatter th' mugwumps. Of course, their belfry is
full of bats; but about half th' time they have to be your
pals, d'ye see, in order to be mugwumps. An' you
needn't be afraid of havin' 'em around; they'll never
ketch onto anything. A mugwump, as some wise guy
said, is like a man ridin' backward in a carriage; he never
sees a thing until it's by.

"Say 'No' nineteen times before you say 'Yes' once.
People respect th' man who says 'No,' an' his 'Yes' is
worth more where he passes it out. When you say 'No,'
you play your own game; when you say 'Yes,' you're
playin' some other duck's game. 'No,' keeps; 'Yes,'
gives; an' th' gent who says 'No' most will always be
th' biggest toad in his puddle.

" Don't be fooled by a cheer or by a crowd. Cheers are nothin' but a breeze; an' as for a crowd, no matter who you are, there would always be a bigger turn-out to see you hanged than to shake your mit.

" Always go with th' current; that's th' first rule of leadership. It's easier; an' there's more water down stream than up.

" Think first, last, an' all th' time of yourself. You may not be of account to others, but you're the whole box of tricks to yourself. Don't give a man more than he gives you. Folks who don't stick to that steer land either in bankruptcy or Bloomin'dale.

" An' remember: while you're Boss, you'll be forced into many things ag'inst your judgment. The head of Tammany is like th' head of a snake, an' gets shoved forward by the tail. Also, like th' head of a snake, th' Boss is th' target for every rock that is thrown.

" Have as many lieutenants as you can; twenty are safer than two. Two might fake up a deal with each other to throw you down; twenty might start, but before they got to you they'd fight among themselves.

" Have people about you who distrust each other an' trust you. Keep th' leaders fightin' among themselves. That prevents combinations ag'inst you; an' besides they'll do up each other whenever you say the word, where every man is hated by the rest.

"Always pay your political debts; but pay with a jolly as far as it 'll go. If you find one who won't take a jolly, throw a scare into him and pay him with that. If he's a strong, dangerous mug with whom a jolly or a bluff won't work, get him next to you as fast as you can. If you strike an obstinate party, it's th' old rule for drivin' pigs. If you want 'em to go forward, pull 'em back by th' tails. Never trust a man beyond his interest; an' never love the man, love what he does.

"The whole science of leadership lies in what I've told you, an' if you can clinch onto it, you'll stick at th' top till you go away, like I do now, to die. An' th' last of it is, don't get sentimental—don't take politics to heart. Politics is only worth while so long as it fills your pockets. Don't tie yourself to anything. A political party is like a street car; stay with it only while it goes your way. A great partisan can never be a great Boss."

When I found myself master of Tammany, my primary thought was to be cautious. I must strengthen myself; I must give myself time to take root. This was the more necessary, for not only were there a full score of the leaders, any one of whom would prefer himself for my place, but the political condition was far from reassuring. The workingman—whom as someone said we all respect and avoid—was through his unions moving to the town's conquest. It was as that movement of politics in the land of the ancient Nile. Having discovered a Moses, the

hand-workers would offer him for the mayoralty on the
issue of no more bricks without straw.

Skilled to the feel of sentiment, I could gauge both
the direction and the volume of the new movement. Nor
was I long in coming to the knowledge that behind it
marched a majority of the people. Unless checked, or
cheated, that labor uprising would succeed; Tammany
and its old-time enemies would alike go down.

This news, self-furnished as a grist ground of the mills
of my own judgment, stimulated me to utmost action.
It would serve neither my present nor my future should
that battle which followed my inauguration be given
against me. I was on my trial; defeat would be the
signal for my overthrow. And thus I faced my first
campaign as Boss.

That rebellion of the working folk stirred to terror
the conservatives, ever the element of wealth. Each man
with a share of stock to shrink in value, or with a dollar
loaned and therefore with security to shake, or with a
store through the plate-glass panes of which a mob might
hurl a stone, was prey to a vast alarm. The smug citizen of money, and of ease-softened hands, grew sick as
he reflected on the French Revolution; and he predicted
gutters red with blood as the near or far finale should the
town's peasantry gain the day. It was then those rich
ones, panic-bit, began to ask a succor of Tammany Hall.
There were other septs, but Tammany was the drilled,

traditional corps of political janissaries. Wherefore, the local nobility, being threatened, fled to it for refuge.

These gentry of white faces and frightened pocketbooks came to me by ones and twos and quartettes; my every day was filled with them; and their one prayer was for me to make a line of battle between them and that frowning peril of the mob. To our silken worried ones, I replied nothing. I heard; but I kept myself as mute for hope or for fear as any marble.

And yet it was sure from the beginning that I must make an alliance with my folk of purple. The movement they shuddered over was even more of a menace to Tammany than it was to them. It might mean dollars to them, but for Tammany it promised annihilation, since of every five who went with this crusade, four were recruited from the machine.

Fifth Avenue, in a fever, did not realize this truth. Nor was I one to enlighten my callers. Their terror made for the machine; it could be trained to fill the Tammany treasure chest with a fund to match those swelling fears, the reason of its contribution. I locked up my tongue; it was a best method to augment a mugwump horror which I meant should find my resources.

Young Morton, still with his lisp, his affectations, his scented gloves, and ineffable eyeglass, although now no longer " young," but like myself in the middle journey of his life, was among my patrician visitors. Like the others, he came to urge a peace-treaty between Tammany and the mugwumps, and he argued a future stored of fortune for both myself and the machine, should the latter turn to be a defense for timid deer from whom he came ambassador.

To Morton I gave particular ear. I was never to forget that loyalty wherewith he stood to me on a day of trial for the death of Jimmy the Blacksmith. If any word might move me it would be his. Adhering to a plan, however, I had as few answers for his questions as I had for those of his mates, and wrapped myself in silence like a mantle.

Morton was so much his old practical self that he bade me consider a candidate and a programme.

"Let us nominate my old gentleman for mayor," said he. "He's very old; but he's clean and he's strong, don't y' know. Really he would draw every vote to his name that should of right belong to us."

"That might be," I returned; "but I may tell you, and stay within the truth, that if your father got no more votes than should of right be his, defeat would over-take him to the tune of thousands. Add the machine to the mugwumps, and this movement of labor still has us beaten by twenty thousand men. That being the case, why should I march Tammany—and my own fortune, too—into such a trap?"

"What else can you do?" asked Morton.

"I can tell you what was in my mind," said I. "It was to go with this labor movement and control it."

"That labor fellow they've put up would make the worst of mayors. You and Tammany would forever be taunted with the errors of his administration. Besides, the creature's success would vulgarize the town; it would, really!"

"He is an honest man," said I.

"Honest, yes; but what of that? Honesty is the commonest trait of ignorance. There should be something more than honesty, don't y' know, to make a mayor. There be games like draw poker and government where to be merely honest is not a complete equipment. Besides, think of the shock of such a term of hobnails in the City Hall. If you, with your machine, would come in, we could elect my old gentleman over him or any other merely honest candidate whom those vulgarians could put up; we could, really!"

"Tell me how," said I.

"There would be millions of money," lisped Morton, pausing to select a cigarette; "since Money would be swimming for dear life. All our fellows at the club are scared to death—really! One can do anything with money, don't y' know."

"One can't stop a runaway horse with money," I retorted; "and this labor movement is a political runaway."

" With money we could build a wall across its course
and let those idiots of politics run against it. My dear
fellow, let us make a calculation. Really, how many
votes should those labor animals overrun us, on the situation's merits? "

" Say twenty-five thousand."

" This then should give so experienced a hand as yourself some shade of comfort. The Master of the Philadelphia Machine, don't y' know, is one of my railway
partners. ' Old chap,' said he, when I told him of the
doings of our New York vandals, ' I'll send over to you
ten thousand men, any one of whom would loot a convent.
These common beggars must be put down! The example might spread to Philadelphia.' So you see," concluded Morton, " we would not be wanting in election
material. What should ten thousand men mean? "

" At the least," said I, " they should count for forty
thousand. A man votes with a full beard; then he votes
with his chin shaved; then he shaves the sides of his face
and votes with a mustache; lastly he votes with a smooth
face and retires to re-grow a beard against the next campaign. Ten thousand men should tally forty thousand
votes. Registration and all, however, would run the cost
of such an enterprise to full five hundred thousand
dollars."

" Money is no object," returned Morton, covering a
yawn delicately with his slim hand, " to men who feel

that their fortunes, don't y' know, and perhaps their lives, are on the cast. Bring us Tammany for this one war, and I'll guarantee three millions in the till of the machine; I will, really! You would have to take those ten thousand recruits from Philadelphia into your own hands, however; we Silk Stockings don't own the finesse required to handle such a consignment of goods. Besides, if we did, think what wretched form it would be."

To hide what was in my thought, I made a pretense of considering the business in every one of its angles. There was a minute during which neither of us spoke.

"Why should I put the machine," I asked at last, "in unnecessary peril of the law? This should be a campaign of fire. Every stick of those three millions you speak of would go to stoke the furnaces. I will do as well, and win more surely, with the labor people."

"But do you want to put the mob in possession?" demanded Morton, emerging a bit from his dandyisms. "I'm no purist of politics; indeed, I think I'm rather practical than otherwise, don't y' know. I am free to say, however, that I fear a worst result should those savages of a dinner-can and a dollar-a-day, succeed— really! You should think once in a while, and particularly in a beastly squall like the present, of the City itself."

"Should I?" I returned. "Now I'll let you into an

organization tenet. Tammany, blow high, blow low,
thinks only of itself."

" You would be given half the offices, remember."

" And the Police? "

" And the Police."

" Tammany couldn't keep house without the police,"
said I, laughing. " You've seen enough of our house-
keeping to know that."

" You may have the police, and what else you
will."

" Well," said I, bringing the talk to a close, " I can't
give you an answer now. I must look the situation in
the eyes. To be frank, I don't think either the Tammany interest or my own runs with yours in this. I,
with my people, live at the other end of the lane."

While Morton and I were talking, I had come to a
decision. I would name the reputable old gentleman for
mayor. He was stricken of years; but I bethought me
how for that very reason he might be, when elected,
the easier to deal with. But I would keep my resolve
from Morton. There was no stress of hurry; the election was months away. I might see reason to change.
One should ever put off his contract-making until the
last. Besides, Morton would feel the better for a surprise.

Before I went to an open alliance with the mugwumps, I would weaken the labor people. This I might

do by pretending to be their friend. There was a strip of the labor candidate's support which was rabid anti-Tammany. Let me but seem to come to his comfort and aid, and every one of those would desert him.

Within the week after my talk with Morton, I sent a sly scrap of news to the captains of labor. They were told that I had given utterance to sentiments of friendship for them and their man. Their taste to cultivate my support was set on edge. These amateurs of politics came seeking an interview. I flattered their hopes, and spoke in high terms of their candidate, his worth and honesty. The city could not be in safer hands.

There were many interviews. It was as an experience, not without a side to amuse, since my visitors, while as pompous as turkey cocks, were as innocently shallow as so many sheep. Many times did we talk; and I gave them compliments and no promises.

My ends were attained. The papers filled up with the coming partnership between the labor movement and the machine, and those berserks of anti-Tammany, frothing with resentment against ones who would sell themselves into my power as the price of my support, abandoned the laborites in a body. There were no fewer than five thousand of these to shake the dust of labor from their feet. When I had driven the last of them from the labor champion, by the simple expedient of appearing to be his friend, I turned decisively my back on him. Also, I at once called Tammany Convention—being the first in the field—and issued those orders which named the reputable old gentleman.

There arose a roar and a cheer from my followers at this, for they read in that name a promise of money knee-deep; and what, than that word, should more brighten a Tammany eye! I was first, with the machine at my back, to walk upon the field with our reputable old gentleman. The mugwumps followed, adopting him with all dispatch; the Republicans, proper, made no ticket; two or three straggling cliques and split-offs of party accepted the reputable old gentleman's nomination; and so the lines were made. On the heels of the conventions, the mugwump leaders and I met and merged our tickets, I getting two-thirds and surrendering one-third of those names which followed that of the reputable old gentleman for the divers offices to be filled.

When all was accomplished, the new situation offered a broad foundation, and one of solvency and depth, whereon to base a future for both Tammany and myself. It crystallized my power, and my grip on the machine was set fast and hard by the sheer effect of it. The next thing was to win at the polls; that would ask for studied effort and a quickness that must not sleep, for the opposition, while clumsy, straggling, and unwieldly with no skill, overtopped us in strength by every one of those thousands of which I had given Morton the name.

"Really, you meant it should be a surprise," observed Morton, as he grasped my hand. It was the evening of the day on which the Tammany Convention named the reputable old gentleman. "I'll plead guilty; it was a surprise. And that's saying a great deal, don't y' know. To be surprised is bad form, and naturally I guard myself against such a vulgar calamity. But you had me, old chap! I was never more baffled and beaten than when I left you. I regarded the conquest of the City by those barbarians as the thing made sure. Now all is changed. We will go in and win; and not a word I said, don't y' know, shall be forgotten and every dollar I mentioned shall be laid down. It shall, 'pon honor!"

CHAPTER XVII

THE REPUTABLE OLD GENTLEMAN IS MAYOR

THE Philadelphia machine was a training school for repeaters. Those ten thousand sent to our cause by Morton's friend, went about their work like artillerymen about their guns. Each was good for four votes. As one of the squad captains said:

"There's got to be time between, for a party to change his face an' shift to another coat an' hat. Besides, it's as well to give th' judges an hour or two to get dim to your mug, see!"

Big Kennedy had set his foot upon the gang spirit, and stamped out of existence such coteries as the Tin Whistles and the Alley Gang, and I copied Big Kennedy in this. Such organizations would have been a threat to me, and put it more in reach of individual leaders to rebel against an order. What work had been done by the gangs was now, under a better discipline and with machine lines more tightly drawn, transacted by the police.

When those skillful gentry, meant to multiply a ballot-total, came in from the South, I called my Chief of Police into council. He was that same bluff girthy person-

age who, aforetime, had conferred with Big Kennedy.
I told him what was required, and how his men, should
occasion arise, must foster as far as lay with them the
voting purposes of our colonists.

"You can rely on me, Gov'nor," said the Chief. He
had invented this title for Big Kennedy, and now trans-
ferred it to me. "Yes, indeed, you can go to sleep on me
doin' my part. But I'm bothered to a standstill with my
captains. Durin' th' last four or five years, th' force
has become honeycombed with honesty; an', may I be
struck! if some of them square guys aint got to be
captains."

"Should any get in your way," said I, "he must be
sent to the outskirts. I shall hold you for everything
that goes wrong."

"I guess," said the Chief thoughtfully, "I'll put the
whole racket in charge of Gothecore. He'll keep your
emigrants from Philadelphia walkin' a crack. They'll
be right, while Gothecore's got his peeps on 'em."

"Has Gothecore had experience?"

"Is Bill Gothecore wise? Gov'nor, I don't want to
paint a promise so brilliant I can't make good, but Gothecore is th' most thorough workman on our list. Why,
they call him 'Clean Sweep Bill!' I put him in th'
Tenderloin for six months, an' he got away with everything but th' back fence."

"Very well," said I, "the care of these colonists is

in your hands. Here's a list of the places where they're berthed."

" You needn't give 'em another thought, Gov'nor," observed the Chief. Then, as he arose to depart: " Somethin's got to be done about them captains turnin' square. They act as a scare to th' others. I'll tell you what: Make the price of a captaincy twenty thousand dollars. That 'll be a hurdle no honest man can take. Whoever pays it, we can bet on as a member of our tribe. One honest captain queers a whole force; it's like a horse goin' lame." This last, moodily.

In the eleventh hour, by our suggestion and at our cost, the Republican managers put up a ticket. This was made necessary by certain inveterate ones who would unite with nothing in which Tammany owned a part. As between us and the labor forces, they would have offered themselves to the latter. They must be given a ticket of their own whereon to waste themselves.

The campaign itself was a whirlwind of money. That princely fund promised by Morton was paid down to me on the nail, and I did not stint or save it when a chance opened to advance our power by its employment. I say " I did not stint," because, in accord with Tammany custom, the fund was wholly in my hands.

As most men know, there is no such post as that of Chief of Tammany Hall. The office is by coinage, and the title by conference, of the public. There exists a finance committee of, commonly, a dozen names. It never meets, and the members in ordinary are to hear and know no more about the money of the organization than of sheep-washing among Ettrick's hills and vales. There is a chairman; into his hands all moneys come. These, in his care and name, and where and how and if he chooses, are put in bank. He keeps no books; he neither gives nor takes a scrap of paper, nor so much as writes a letter of thanks, in connection with such treasurership. He replies to no one for this money; he spends or keeps as he sees fit, and from beginning to end has the sole and only knowledge of either the intake or the outgo of the millions of the machine. The funds are wholly in his possession. To borrow a colloquialism, " He is the Man with the Money," and since money is the mainspring of practical politics, it follows as the tail the kite, and without the intervention of either rule or statute, that he is THE Boss. Being supreme with the money, he is supreme with the men of the machine, and it was the holding of this chairmanship which gave me my style and place as Chief.

The position is not wanting in its rewards. Tammany, for its own safety, should come forth from each campaign without a dollar. There is no argument to carry over a residue from one battle to the next. It is not required, since Tammany, from those great corporations whose taxes and liberties it may extend or shrink by a

word, may ever have what money it will; and it is not
wise, because the existence of a fund between campaigns
would excite dissension, as this leader or that one conceived some plan for its dissipation. It is better to up-
turn the till on the back of each election, and empty it
in favor of organization peace. And to do this is the
duty of the Chairman of the Finance Committee; and I
may add that it is one he was never known to overlook.

There was nothing notable in that struggle which sent
the reputable old gentleman to the city fore as Mayor,
beyond the energy wherewith the work required was
performed. Every move ran off as softly sure as could
be wished. The police did what they should. Those
visitors from below turned in for us full forty thousand
votes, and then quietly received their wages and as quietly
went their way. I saw to it that, one and all, they
were sharply aboard the ferryboats when their work
was done. No one would care for them, drunken and
mayhap garrulous, about the streets, until after the
last spark of election interest had expired. The polls
were closed: the count was made; the laborites and their
Moses was beaten down, and the reputable old gentleman was declared victor by fifteen thousand. Those rich
ones, late so pale, revived the color in their cheeks; and as
for Tammany and myself, we took deep breaths, and felt
as ones from whose shoulders a load had been lifted.

It was for me a fortunate upcome; following that

victory, my leadership could no more be shaken than
may the full-grown oaks. Feeling now my strength, I
made divers machine changes of the inner sort. I caused
my executive leaders to be taken from the assembly districts, rather than from the wards. There would be one
from each; and since there was a greater number of districts than wards, the executive array was increased. I
smelled safety for myself in numbers, feeling, as Big
Kennedy advised, the more secure with twenty than
with two. Also the new situation gave the leaders less
influence with the Aldermen, when now the frontiers of
the one no longer matched those of the other. I had
aimed at this; for it was my instant effort on becoming
Chief to collect within my own fingers every last thread
of possible authority. I wanted the voice of my leadership to be the voice of the storm; all others I would stifle
to a whisper.

While busy within the organization, deepening and
broadening the channels of my power, I did not neglect
conditions beyond the walls. I sent for the leaders of
those two or three bands of Democracy which professed
themselves opposed to Tammany Hall. I pitched upon
my men as lumber folk in their log-driving pitch upon
the key-logs in a " jam." I loosened them with office,
or the promise of it, and they instantly came riding
down to me on the currents of self-interest, and brought
with them those others over whom they held command.

Within the twelvemonth Tammany was left no rival within the lines of the regular party; I had, either by purring or by purchase, brought about the last one's disappearance. It was a fair work for the machine, and I could feel the gathering, swelling confidence of my followers uplifting me as the deep sea uplifts a ship.

There was a thorn with that rose of leadership, nor did my hand escape its sting. The papers in their attacks upon me were as incessant as they were vindictive, and as unsparing as they were unfair. With never a fact set forth, by the word of these unmuzzled and uncaring imprints I stood forth as everything that was thievish, vile, and swart.

While I made my skin as thick against these shafts as I could, since I might neither avoid nor return them, still they pierced me and kept me bleeding, and each new day saw ever a new wound to my sensibilities. It is a bad business—these storms of black abuse! You have but to fasten upon one, even an honest one, the name of horsethief and, behold you! he will steal a horse. Moreover, those vilifications of types become arrows to glance aside and bury themselves in the breasts of ones innocent.

Blossom was grown now to be a grave stripling girl of fifteen. Anne conceived that she should be taught in a school. She, herself, had carried Blossom to a considerable place in her books, but the finishing would be the better accomplished by teachers of a higher skill, and among children of Blossom's age. With this on her thought, Anne completed arrangements with a private academy for girls, one of superior rank; and to this shop of learning, on a certain morning, she conveyed Blossom. Blossom was to be fitted with a fashionable education by those modistes of the intellectual, just as a dressmaker might measure her, and baste her, and stitch her into a frock.

But insult and acrid grief were lying there in ambush for Blossom—Blossom, then as ever, with her fear-haunted eyes. She was home before night, tearful, hysterical—crying in Anne's arms. There had been a cartoon in the papers. It showed me as a hairy brutal ape, the city in the shape of a beautiful woman fainting in my arms, and a mighty rock labeled "Tammany" in one hand, ready to hurl at my pursuers. The whole was hideous; and when one of the girls of the school showed it to Blossom, and taunted her with this portrait of her father, it was more than heart might bear. She fled before the outrage of it, and would never hear the name of school again. This ape-picture was the thing fearful and new to Blossom, for to save her, both Anne and I had been at care to have no papers to the house. The harm was done, however; Blossom, hereafter, would shrink from all but Anne and me, and when she was eighteen, save for us, the priest, and an old Galway serving woman who had been her nurse, she knew no one in the whole wide world.

The reputable old gentleman made a most amazing Mayor. He was puffed with a vanity that kissed the sky. Honest, and by nature grateful, he was still so twisted as to believe that to be a good Mayor one must comport himself in an inhuman way.

"Public office is a public trust!" cried he, quoting some lunatic abstractionist.

The reputable old gentleman's notion of discharging this trust was to refuse admittance to his friends, while he sat in council with his enemies. To show that he was independent, he granted nothing to ones who had builded him; to prove himself magnanimous, he went truckling to former foes, preferring them into place. As for me, he declined every suggestion, refused every name, and while there came no open rupture between us, I was quickly taught to stay away.

"My luck with my father," said Morton, when one day we were considering that lofty spirit of the reputable old gentleman, "is no more flattering than your own, don't y' know. He waves me away with a flourish. I reminded him that while he might forget me as one who with trowel and mortar had aided to lay the walls of his career, he at least should remember that I was none the less his son; I did, really! He retorted with the story of the Roman father who in his rôle as judge sentenced his

son to death. Gad! he seemed to regret that no chance
offered for him to equal though he might not surpass that
noble example. Speaking seriously, when his term verges
to its close, what will be your course? You know the old
gentleman purposes to succeed himself. And, doubtless,
since such is mugwump thickness, he'll be renominated."

" Tammany," said I, " will fight him. We'll have a
candidate on a straight ticket of our own. His honor,
your father, will be beaten."

" On my soul! I hope so," exclaimed Morton.
" Don't you know, I expect every day to find him doing
something to Mulberry Traction—trying to invalidate
its franchise, or indulging in some similar piece of humor.
I shall breathe easier with my parent returned to private
life—really! "

" Never fear; I'll have the city in the hollow of my
hand within the year," said I.

" I will show you where to find a million or two in Wall
Street, if you do," he returned.

The downfall of the reputable old gentleman was already half accomplished. One by one, I had cut the
props from beneath him. While he would grant me no
contracts, and yield me no offices for my people, he was
quite willing to consider my advice on questions of political concern. Having advantage of this, I one day
pointed out that it was un-American to permit certain
Italian societies to march in celebration of their victories

over the Pope long ago. Why should good Catholic Irish-Americans be insulted with such exhibitions! These Italian festivals should be kept for Italy; they do not belong in America. The reputable old gentleman, who was by instinct more than half a Know Nothing, gave warm assent to my doctrines, and the festive Italians did not celebrate.

Next I argued that the reputable old gentleman should refuse his countenance to the Irish exercises on St. Patrick's Day. The Irish were no better than the Italians. He could not make flesh of one and fish of the other. The reputable old gentleman bore testimony to the lucid beauty of my argument by rebuffing the Irish in a flame of words in which he doubted both their intelligence and their loyalty to the land of their adoption. In another florid tirade he later sent the Orangemen to the political right-about. The one powerful tribe he omitted to insult were the Germans, and that only because they did not come within his reach. Had they done so, the reputable old gentleman would have heaped contumely upon them with all the pleasure in life.

It is not needed that I set forth how, while guiding the reputable old gentleman to these deeds of derring, I kept myself in the background. No one knew me as the architect of those wondrous policies. The reputable old gentleman stood alone; and in the inane fullness of his vanity took a deal of delight in the uproar he aroused.

There was an enemy of my own. He was one of those elegant personalities who, in the elevation of riches and a position to which they are born, find the name of Tammany a synonym for crime. That man hated me, and hated the machine. But he loved the reputable old gentleman; and, by his name and his money, he might become of utmost avail to that publicist in any effort he put forth to have his mayorship again.

One of the first offices of the city became vacant, that of chamberlain. I heard how the name of our eminent one would be presented for the place. That was my cue. I instantly asked that the eminent one be named for that vacant post of chamberlain. It was the earliest word which the reputable old gentleman had heard on the subject, for the friends of the eminent one as yet had not broached the business with him.

When I urged the name of the eminent one, the reputable old gentleman pursed up his lips and frowned. He paused for so long a period that I began to fear lest he accept my suggestion. To cure such chance, I broke violently in upon his cogitations with the commands of the machine.

" Mark you," I cried, in the tones wherewith I was wont in former and despotic days to rule my Tin Whistles, " mark you! there shall be no denial! I demand it in the name of Tammany Hall."

. The sequel was what I sought; the reputable old

gentleman elevated his crest. We straightway quarreled, and separated in hot dudgeon. When the select bevy who bore among them the name of the eminent one arrived upon the scene, the reputable old gentleman, metaphorically, shut the door in their faces. They departed in a rage, and the fires of their indignation were soon communicated to the eminent one.

As the result of these various sowings, a nodding harvest of enemies sprung up to hate and harass the reputable old gentleman. I could tell that he would be beaten; he, with the most formidable forces of politics against him solid to a man! To make assurance sure, however, I secretly called to me the Chief of Police. In a moment, the quiet order was abroad to close the gambling resorts, enforce the excise laws against saloons, arrest every contractor violating the ordinances regulating building material in the streets, and generally, as well as specifically, to tighten up the town to a point that left folk gasping.

No one can overrate the political effect of this. New York has no home. It sits in restaurants and barrooms day and night. It is a city of noisome tenements and narrow flats so small that people file themselves away therein like papers in a pigeonhole.

These are not homes: they grant no comfort; men do not seek them until driven by want of sleep. It is for the cramped reasons of flats and tenements that New

York is abroad all night. The town lives in the streets; or, rather, in those houses of refreshment which, open night and day, have thrown away their keys.

This harsh enforcement of the excise law, or as Old Mike put it, " Gettin' bechune th' people an' their beer," roused a wasps' nest of fifty thousand votes. The reputable old gentleman was to win the stinging benefit, since he, being chief magistrate, must stand the brunt as for an act of his administration.

Altogether, politically speaking, my reputable old gentleman tossed and bubbled in a steaming kettle of fish when he was given his renomination. For my own side, I put up against him a noble nonentity with a historic name. He was a mere jelly-fish of principle—one whose boneless convictions couldn't stand on their own legs. If the town had looked at my candidate, it would have repudiated him with a howl. But I knew my public. New York votes with its back to the future. Its sole thought is to throw somebody out of office—in the present instance, the offensive reputable old gentleman—and this it will do with never a glance at that one who by the effect of the eviction is to be raised to the place. No, I had no apprehensions; I named my jelly-fish, and with a straight machine-made ticket, mine from truck to keel, shoved **boldly forth**. This time **I** meant to own the town.

CHAPTER XVIII

HOW THE BOSS TOOK THE TOWN

THE reputable old gentleman was scandalized by what he called my defection, and told me so. That I should put up a ticket against him was grossest treason.

"And why should I not?" said I. "You follow the flag of your interest; I but profit by your example."

"Sir!" cried the reputable old gentleman haughtily, "I have no interest save the interest of the public."

"So you say," I retorted, "and doubtless so you think." I had a desire to quarrel finally and for all time with the reputable old gentleman, whose name I no longer needed, and whose fame as an excise purist would now be getting in my way. "You deceive yourself," I went on. "Your prime motive is to tickle your own vanity with a pretense of elevation. From the pedestal of your millions, and the safe shelter of a clean white shirt, you patronize mankind and play the prig. That is what folk say of you. As to what obligation in your favor rests personally upon myself, I have only to recall your treatment of my candidate for that place of chamberlain."

" Do you say men call me a prig? " demanded the reputable old gentleman with an indignant start. He ignored his refusal of the eminent one as chamberlain. " Sir, I deny the term ' prig.' If such were my celebration, I should not have waited to hear it from you."

" What should you hear or know of yourself? " said I. " The man looking from his window does not see his own house. He who marches with it, never sees the regiment of which he is a unit. No more can you, as mayor, see yourself, or estimate the common view concerning you. It is your vanity to seem independent and above control, and you have transacted that vanity at the expense of your friends. I've stood by while others went that road, and politically at least it ever led down hill."

That was my last conference with the reputable old gentleman. I went back to Fourteenth Street, and called on my people of Tammany to do their utmost. Nor should I complain of their response, for they went behind their batteries with the cool valor of buccaneers.

There was but one question which gave me doubt, and that was the question of the Australian ballot, then a novelty in our midst. Theretofore, a henchman of the machine went with that freeman to the ballot-box, and saw to it how he put no cheat upon his purchasers. Now our commissioners could approach a polls no nearer than two hundred feet; the freeman went in alone, took his

folded ticket from the judges, retired to privacy and a
pencil, and marked his ballot where none might behold
the work. Who then could know that your mercenary,
when thus removed from beneath one's eye and hand,
would fight for one's side? I may tell you the situation
was putting a wrinkle in my brow when Morton came
lounging in.

"You know I've nothing to do with the old gentleman's campaign," said he, following a mouthful or two
of commonplace, and puffing the while his usual cigarette. "Gad! I told him that I had withdrawn from
politics; I did, really! I said it was robbing me of all
fineness; and that I must defend my native purity of
sensibility, don't y' know, and preserve it from such
sordid contact.

"'Father,' said I, 'you surely would not, for the
small cheap glory of a second term, compel me into experiences that must leave me case-hardened in all that
is spiritual?'

"No, he made no reply; simply turned his back upon
me in merited contempt. Really, I think he was aware
of me for a hypocrite. It was beastly hard to go back
on the old boy, don't y' know! But for what I have
in mind it was the thing to do."

Now, when I had him to counsel with, I gave Morton
my troubles over the Australian law. The situation,
generally speaking, showed good; the more because there

were three tickets in the field. Still, nothing was sure.
We must work; and we must omit no usual means of
adding to our strength. And the Australian law was
in our way.

"Really, you're quite right," observed Morton, polishing his eyeglass meditatively. "To be sure, those
beasts of burden, the labor element, have politically gone
to pieces since our last campaign. But they are still
wandering about by twos and threes, like so many lost
sheep, and unless properly shepherded—and what a
shepherd's crook is money!—they may fall into the
mouths of opposition wolves, don't y' know. What exasperating dullards these working people are! I know
of but one greater fool than the working man, and that
is the fool he works for! And so you say this Australian
law breeds uncertainty for our side?"

"There is no way to tell how a man votes."

Morton behind that potent eyeglass narrowed his gaze
to the end of his nose, and gave a full minute to thought.
Then his eyes, released from contemplation of his nose,
began to brighten. I placed much reliance upon the fer-
tility of our exquisite, for all his trumpery affectations
of eyeglass and effeminate mannerisms, and I waited with
impatience for him to speak.

"Really, now," said he, at last, "how many under the
old plan would handle your money about each polling
place?"

" About four," I replied. " Then at each polling
booth there would be a dozen pullers-in, to bring up the
voters, and go with them to see that they put in the
right ballots. This last, you will notice, is by the
Australian system made impossible."

" It is the duty of artillery people," drawled Morton,
" whenever the armor people invent a plate that cannot be
perforated by guns in being, don't y' know, to at once invent a gun that shall pierce it. The same holds good in
politics. Gad! we must invent a gun that shall knock a
hole through this Australian armor; we must, really! A
beastly system, I should call it, which those beggarly
Australians have constructed! It's no wonder: they are
all convicts down there, and it would need a felon to de-
vise such an interference. However, this is what I suggest. You must get into your hands, we'll put it, five
thousand of the printed ballots in advance of election
day. This may be secretly done, don't y' know, by paying the printers where the tickets are being struck off.
A printer is such an avaricious dog; he is, really!
The tickets would be equally distributed among those
men with the money whom you send about the polling
places. A ballot in each instance should be marked with
the cross for Tammany Hall before it is given to the
recruit. He will then carry it into the booth in his
pocket. Having received the regular ticket from the
hands of the judges, he can go through the form of re-

tiring, don't y' know; then reappear and give in the
ticket which was marked by your man of the machine."

"And yet," said I breaking in, " I do not see how
you've helped the situation. The recruit might still vote
the ticket handed him by the judges, for all our wisdom.
Moreover, it would be no easy matter to get hold of
fifty thousand tickets, all of which we would require to
make sure. Five thousand we might manage, but that
would not be enough."

"You should let me finish; you should, really!" returned Morton. " One would not pay the recruit until he
returned to that gentleman of finance with whom he was
dealing, don't y' know, and put into his hands the un-
marked ballot with which the judges had endowed him.
That would prove his integrity; and it would also equip
your agent with a new fresh ballot against the next recruit. Thus you would never run out of ballots. Gad!
I flatter myself, I've hit upon an excellent idea, don't y'
know!" and with that, Morton began delicately to caress
his mustache, again taking on his masquerade of the in-
effably inane.

Morton's plan was good; I saw its merits in a flash.
He had proposed a sure system by which the machine
might operate in spite of that antipodean law. We
used it too, and it was half the reason of our victory.
Upon its proposal, I extended my compliments to
Morton.

" Really, it's nothing," said he, as though the business bored him. " Took the hint from football, don't y' know. It is a rule of that murderous amusement, when you can't buck the center, to go around the ends. But I must have a ride in the park to rest me; I must, really! I seldom permit myself to think—it's beastly bad form to think—and, therefore, when I do give my intelligence a canter, it fatigues me beyond expression. Well, good-by! I shall see you when I am recuperated. Meanwhile, you must not let that awful parent of mine succeed; it would be our ruin, don't y' know!" and Morton glared idiotically behind the eyeglass at the thought of the reputable old gentleman flourishing through a second term. " Yes, indeed," he concluded, " the old boy would become a perfect juggernaut!"

Morton's plan worked to admiration. The mercenary was given a ballot, ready marked; and later he returned with the one which the judges gave him, took his fee, and went his way.

In these days, when the ballot furnished by the judges is stamped on the back, each with its separate number in red ink, which number is set opposite a voter's name at the time he receives the ballot, and all to be verified when he brings it again to the judges for deposit in the box, the scheme would be valueless. There lies no open chance for the substitution of a ready-made ballot, because of the deterrent number in red ink.

Under these changed conditions, however, as Morton declared they must, the gunners of party have invented both the projectile and the rifle to pierce this new and stronger plate. The party emblems, the Eagle, the Star, the Ship, and other totems of partisanship, are printed across the head of the ticket in black accommodating ink. The recruit now makes his designating cross with a pencil that is as soft as fresh paint. Then he spreads over the head of the ticket, as he might a piece of blotting paper, a tissue sheet peculiarly prepared. A gentle rub of the fingers across the tissue, stains it plainly with the Eagle, the Star, the Ship, and the entire procession of totems; also, it takes with the rest an impression of that penciled cross. This tissue, our recruit brings to that particular paymaster of the forces with whom he is in barter, and a glance answers the query was the vote made right or wrong. If "right," the recruit has his reward; if "wrong," he is spurned from the presence as one too densely ignorant to be of use.

The reputable old gentleman, when the vote came on, was overpowered; he retired to private life, inveighing against republics for that they were ungrateful. My jelly-fish of historic blood took his place as mayor, and Tammany dominated every corner of the town. My word was absolute from the bench of the jurist to the beat of the policeman; the second greatest city in the world, with every dollar of its treasure, was in my hands to do with it as I would. I drew a swelling sense of comfort from the situation which my breast had never known.

And yet, I was not made mad by this sudden grant of power. I knew by the counsel of Big Kennedy, and the dungeon fate of that Boss who was destroyed, that I must light a lamp of caution for my journeyings. Neither the rôle of bully, nor the bluff method of the highwayman, would serve; in such rough event, the people, overhanging all, would be upon one like an avalanche. One must proceed by indirection and while the common back was turned; one, being careful, might bleed the public while it slept.

When the town in its threads was thus wholly in my hands, with every office, great or small, held by a man of the machine, Morton came to call upon me.

" And so you're the Czar! " said he.

" You have the enemy's word for it," I replied. " ' Czar ' is what they call me in their papers when they do not call me ' rogue.' "

" Mere compliments, all," returned Morton airily. " Really, I should feel proud to be thus distinguished. And yet I'm surprised! I was just telling an editor of one of our rampant dailies: ' Can't you see,' said I, ' that he who speaks ill of his master speaks ill of himself? To call a man a scoundrel or an ignoramus, is to call him weak, since neither is a mark of strength. And

when you term him scoundrel and ignoramus who has
beaten you, you but name yourself both viler, weaker still.
Really,' I concluded, ' if only to preserve one's own standing, one should ever speak well of one's conqueror, don't
y' know!' But it was of no use; that ink-fellow merely
scowled and went his way. However, to discuss a theory
of epithet was not my present purpose. Do you recall
how, on the edge of the campaign, I said that if you
would but win the town I'd lead you into millions?"

"Yes," said I, "you said something of the sort."

"You must trust me in this: I understand the market
better than you do, don't y' know. Perhaps you have
noticed that Blackberry Traction is very low—down to
ninety, I think?"

"No," I replied, "the thing is news to me. I know
nothing of stocks."

"It's as well. This, then, is my road to wealth for
both of us. As a first move, don't y' know, and as
rapidly as I can without sending it up, I shall load myself for our joint account with we'll say—since I'm sure
I can get that much—forty thousand shares of Blackberry. It will take me ten days. When I'm ready, the
president of Blackberry will call upon you; he will,
really! He will have an elaborate plan for extending
Blackberry to the northern limits of the town; and he
will ask, besides, for a half-dozen cross-town franchises
to act as feeders to the main line, and to connect it with

the ferries. Be slow and thoughtful with our Blackberry president, but encourage him. Gad! keep him coming to you for a month, and on each occasion seem nearer to his view. In the end, tell him he can have those franchises—cross-town and extensions—and, for your side, go about the preliminary orders to city officers. It will send Blackberry aloft like an elevator, don't y' know! Those forty thousand shares will go to one hundred and thirty-five—really!"

Two weeks later Morton gave me the quiet word that he held for us a trifle over forty thousand shares of Blackberry which he had taken at an average of ninety-one. Also, he had so intrigued that the Blackberry's president would seek a meeting with me to consider those extensions, and discover my temper concerning them.

The president of Blackberry and I came finally together in a parlor of the Hoffman House, as being neutral ground. I found him soft-voiced, plausible, with a Hebrew cast and clutch. He unfurled his blue-prints, which showed the proposed extensions, and what grants of franchises would be required.

At the beginning, I was cold, doubtful; I distrusted a public approval of the grants, and feared the public's resentment.

"Tammany must retain the people's confidence," said I. "It can only do so by protecting jealously the people's interests."

The president of Blackberry shrugged his shoulders. He looked at me hard, and as one who waited for my personal demands. He would not speak, but paused for me to begin. I could feel it in the air how a half-million might be mine for the work of asking. I never said the word, however; I had no mind to put my hand into that dog's mouth.

Thus we stood; he urging, I considering the advisability of those asked-for franchises. This was our attitude throughout a score of conferences, and little by little I went leaning the Blackberry way.

To be sure, the secret of our meetings was whispered in right quarters, and every day found fresh buyers for Blackberry. Meanwhile, the shares climbed high and ever higher, until one bland April morning they stood at one hundred and thirty-seven.

Throughout my series of meetings with the president of Blackberry, I had seen no trace of Morton. For that I cared nothing, but played my part slowly so as to give him time, having confidence in his loyalty, and knowing that my interest was his interest, and I in no sort to be worsted. On that day when Blackberry showed at one hundred and thirty-seven, Morton appeared. He laid down a check for an even million of dollars.

" I've been getting out of Blackberry for a week," said he, with his air of delicate lassitude. " I found that it was tiring me, don't y' know; I did really! Besides, we've done enough: No gentlemen ever makes more than one million on a single turn; it's not good form."

That check, drawn to my order, was the biggest of its kind I'd ever handled. I took it up, and I could feel a pringling to my finger-ends with the contact of so much wealth all mine. I envied my languid friend his genius for coolness and aplomb. He selected a cigarette, and lighted it as though a million here and there, on a twist of the market, was a commonest of affairs. When I could command my voice, I said:

"And now I suppose we may give Blackberry its franchises?"

"No, not yet," returned Morton. "Really, we're not half through. I've not only gotten rid of our holdings, but I've sold thirty-five thousand shares the other way. It was a deuced hard thing to do without sending the stock off—the market is always so beastly ready to tumble, don't y' know. But I managed it; we're now short about thirty-five thousand shares at one hundred and thirty-seven."

"What then?" said I.

"On the whole," continued Morton, with just a gleam of triumph behind his eyeglass, "on the whole, I think I should refuse Blackberry, don't y' know. The public interest would be thrown away; and gad! the people are prodigiously moved over it already, they are, really! It would be neither right nor safe. I'd come out in an interview declaring that a grant of what Blackberry asks for would be to pillage the town. Here, I've the interview prepared. What do you say? Shall we send it to the *Daily Tory?* "

The interview appeared; Blackberry fell with a crash. It slumped fifty points, and Morton and I were each the better by fairly another million. Blackberry grazed the reef of a receivership so closely that it rubbed the paint from its side.

CHAPTER XIX

THE SON OF THE WIDOW VAN FLANGE

WHEN now I was rich with double millions, I became harrowed of new thoughts and sown with new ambitions. It was Blossom to lie at the roots of it—Blossom, looking from her window of young womanhood upon a world she did not understand, and from which she drew away. The world was like a dark room to Blossom, with an imagined fiend to harbor in every corner of it. She must go forth among people of manners and station. The contact would mend her shyness; with time and usage she might find herself a pleasant place in life. Now she lived a morbid creature of sorrow which had no name—a twilight soul of loneliness—and the thought of curing this went with me day and night.

Nor was I unjustified of authority.

"Send your daughter into society," said that physician to whom I put the question. "It will be the true medicine for her case. It is her nerves that lack in strength; society, with its dinners and balls and fêtes and the cheerful hubbub of drawing rooms, should find them exercise, and restore them to a complexion of health."

249

Anne did not believe with that savant of nerves. She distrusted my society plans for Blossom.

"You think they will taunt her with the fact of me," I said, "like that one who showed her the ape cartoon as a portrait of her father. But Blossom is grown a woman now. Those whom I want her to meet would be made silent by politeness, even if nothing else might serve to stay their tongues from such allusions. And I think she would be loved among them, for she is good and beautiful, and you of all should know how she owns to fineness and elevation."

"But it is not her nature," pleaded Anne. "Blossom would be as much hurt among those men and women of the drawing rooms as though she walked, barefooted, over flints."

For all that Anne might say, I persisted in my resolve. Blossom must be saved against herself by an everyday encounter with ones of her own age. I had more faith than Anne. There must be kindness and sympathy in the world, and a countenance for so much goodness as Blossom's. Thus she should find it, and the discovery would let in the sun upon an existence now overcast with clouds. These were my reasonings. It would win her from her broodings and those terrors without cause, which to my mind were a kind of insanity that might deepen unless checked.

Full of my great design, I moved into a new home—

a little palace in its way, and one to cost me a penny. I cared nothing for the cost; the house was in the center of that region of the socially select. From this fine castle of gilt, Blossom should conquer those alliances which were to mean so much for her good happiness.

Being thus fortunately founded,· I took Morton into my confidence. He was a patrician by birth and present station; and I knew I might have both his hand and his wisdom for what was in my heart. When I laid open my thought to Morton, he stood at gaze like one planet-struck, while that inevitable eyeglass dropped from his amazed nose.

" You must pardon my staring," said he, at last. " It was a beastly rude thing to do. But, really, don't y' know, I was surprised that one of force and depth, and who was happily outside society, should find himself so badly guided as to seek to enter it."

" You, yourself, are in its midst."

" That should be charged," he returned, " to accident rather than design. I am in the midst of society, pre· cisely as some unfortunate tree might be found in the middle of its native swamp, and only because being born there I want of that original energy required for my transplantation. I will say this," continued Morton, getting up to walk the floor; " your introduction into what we'll style the Four Hundred, don't y' know, might easily be brought about. You

have now a deal of wealth; and that of itself should
be enough, as the annals of our Four Hundred offer
ample guaranty. But more than that, stands the argument of your power, and how you, in your peculiar
fashion, are unique. Gad, for the latter cause alone,
swelldom would welcome you with spread arms; it would,
really! But believe me, if it were happiness you came
seeking you would miss it mightily. There is more
laughter in Third Avenue than in Fifth."

"But it is of my Blossom I am thinking," I cried.
"For myself I am not so ambitious."

"And what should your daughter," said Morton,
"find worth her young while in society? She is, I hear
from you, a girl of sensibility. That true, she would
find nothing but disappointment in this region you think
so select. Do you know our smart set? Sir, it is com-
posed of savages in silk." Morton, I found, had much
the manner of his father, when stirred. "It is," he went
on, "that circle where discussion concerns itself with
nothing more onerous than golf or paper-chases or single-
stickers or polo or balls or scandals; where there is no
literature save the literature of the bankbook; where
snobs invent a pedigree and play at caste; where folk
give lawn parties to dogs and dinners to which monkeys
come as guests of honor; where quarrels occur over questions of precedence between a mosquito and a flea; where
pleasure is a trade, and idleness an occupation; in short,

it is that place where the race, bruised of riches, has turned cancerous and begun to rot."

"You draw a vivid picture," said I, not without a tincture of derision. "For all that, I stick by my determination, and ask your help. I tell you it is my daughter's life or death."

Morton, at this, relapsed into his customary attitude of moral, mental Lah-de-dah, and his lisp and his drawl and his eyeglass found their usual places. He shrugged his shoulders in his manner of the superfine.

"Why then," said he, "and seeing that you will have no other way for it, you may command my services. Really, I shall be proud to introduce you, don't y' know, as one who, missing being a monkey by birth, is now determined to become one by naturalization. Now I should say that a way to begin would be to discover a dinner and have you there as a guest. I know a society queen who will jump at the chance; she will have you at her chariot wheel like another Caractacus in another Rome, and parade you as a latest captive to her social bow and spear. I'll tell her; it will offer an excellent occasion for you to declare your intentions and take out your first papers in that Apeland whereof you seem so strenuous to become a citizen."

While the work put upon me by my place as Boss had never an end, but filled both my day and my night to overflowing, it brought with it compensation. If I were ground and worn away on the wheel of my position like a knife on a grindstone, still I was kept to keenest edge, and I felt that joy I've sometimes thought a good blade must taste in the sheer fact of its trenchant quality. Besides, there would now and then arrive a moment which taught me how roundly I had conquered, and touched me with that sense of power which offers the highest pleasure whereof the soul of man is capable.   Here would be an example of what I mean, although I cannot believe the thing could happen in any country save America or any city other than New York.

It was one evening at my own door, when that judge who once sought to fix upon me the murder of Jimmy the Blacksmith, came tapping for an interview.   His term was bending towards the evening of its close, and the mean purpose of him was none better than to just plead for his place again.   I will not say the man was abject; but then the thought of his mission, added to a memory of that relation to each other in which it was aforetime our one day's fate to have stood, choked me with contempt.   I shall let his conduct go by without further characterization; and yet for myself, had our fortunes been reversed and he the Boss and I the Judge, before I had been discovered in an attitude of office-begging from a hand I once plotted to kill, I would have died against the wall.   But so it was; my visitor would labor with me for a renomination.

My first impulse was one of destruction; I would put him beneath the wheel and crush out the breath of his hopes. And then came Big Kennedy's warning to avoid revenge when moved of nothing broader than a reason of revenge.

I sat and gazed mutely upon that judge for a space; he, having told his purpose, awaited my decision without more words. I grew cool, and cunning began to have the upper hand of violence in my breast. If I cast him down, the papers would tell of it for the workings of my vengeance. If, on the quiet other hand, he were to be returned, it would speak for my moderation, and prove me one who in the exercise of power lifted himself above the personal. I resolved to continue him; the more since the longer I considered, the clearer it grew that my revenge, instead of being starved thereby, would find in it a feast.

"You tried to put a rope about my neck," said I at last.

"I was misled as to the truth."

"Still you put a stain upon me. There be thousands who believe me guilty of bloodshed, and of that you shall clear me by printed word."

"I am ever ready to repair an error."

Within a week, with black ink and white paper, my judge in peril set forth how since my trial he had gone to the ends of that death of Jimmy the Blacksmith in its history.   I was, he said, an innocent man, having had neither part nor lot therein.

I remember that over the glow of triumph wherewith I read his words, there came stealing the chill shadow of a hopeless grief.   Those phrases of exoneration would not recall poor Apple Cheek; nor would they restore Blossom to that poise and even balance from which she had been shaken on a day before her birth.   For all the sorrow of it, however, I made good my word; and I have since thought that whether our judge deserved the place or no, to say the least he earned it.

Every man has his model, and mine was Big John Kennedy.   This was in a way of nature, for I had found Big Kennedy in my boyhood, and it is then, and then only, when one need look for his great men.   When once you have grown a beard, you will meet with few heroes, and make to yourself few friends; wherefore you should the more cherish those whom your fortunate youth has furnished.

Big Kennedy was my exemplar, and there arose few conditions to frown upon me with a problem to be solved, when I did not consider what Big Kennedy would have done in the face of a like contingency.   Nor was I to one side of the proprieties in such a course.   Now, when I glance backward down that steep aisle of endeavor up which I've come, I recall occasions, and some meant for my compliment, when I met presidents, governors, grave

jurists, reverend senators, and others of tallest honors in
the land.   They talked and they listened, did these
mighty ones; they gave me their views and their reasons
for them, and heard mine in return; and all as equal
might encounter equal in a commerce of level terms.
And yet, choose as I may, I have not the name of him
who in a pure integrity of force, or that wisdom which
makes men follow, was the master of Big John Kennedy.
My old chief won all his wars within the organization,
and that is the last best test of leadership.   He made no
backward steps, but climbed to a final supremacy and
sustained himself.   I was justified in steering by Big
Kennedy.   Respect aside, I would have been wrecked
had I not done so.   That man who essays to live
with no shining example to show his feet the path, is
as one who wanting a lantern, and upon a moonless
midnight, urges abroad into regions utterly unknown.

Not alone did I observe those statutes for domination
which Big Kennedy both by precept and example had
given me, but I picked up his alliances; and that one was
the better in my eyes, and came to be observed with wider
favor, who could tell of a day when he carried Big Kennedy's confidence.   It was a brevet I always honored with
my own.

One such was the Reverend Bronson, still working for
the regeneration of the Five Points,   He often came to

me for money or countenance in his labors, and I did ever as Big Kennedy would have done and heaped up the measure of his requests.

It would seem, also, that I had more of the acquaintance of this good man than had gone to my former leader. For one thing, we were more near in years, and then, too, I have pruned my language of those slangy rudenesses of speech which loaded the conversation of Big Kennedy, and cultivated in their stead softness and a verbal cleanliness which put the Reverend Bronson at more ease in my company. I remember with what satisfaction I heard him say that he took me for a person of education.

It was upon a time when I had told him of my little learning; for the gloom of it was upon me constantly, and now and then I would cry out against it, and speak of it as a burden hard to bear. I shall not soon forget the real surprise that showed in the Reverend Bronson's face, nor yet the good it did me.

"You amaze me!" he cried. "Now, from the English you employ I should not have guessed it. Either my observation is dulled, or you speak as much by grammar as do I, who have seen a college."

This was true by more than half, since like many who have no glint of letters, and burning with the shame of it, I was wont to listen closely to the talk of everyone learned of books; and in that manner, and by imitation, I taught

myself a decent speech just as a musician might catch
a tune by ear.

" Still I have no education," I said, when the Reverend
Bronson spoke of his surprise.

" But you have, though," returned he, " only you came
by that education not in the common way."

That good speech alone, and the comfort of it to curl
about my heart, more than repaid me for all I ever did or
gave by request of the Reverend Bronson ; and it pleases
me to think I told him so.   But I fear I set down these
things rather in vanity than to do a reader service, and
before patience turns fierce with me, I will get onward
with my story.

One afternoon the Reverend Bronson came leading a
queer bedraggled boy, whose years—for all he was
stunted and beneath a size—should have been four-
teen.

" Can't you find something which this lad may do? "
asked the Reverend Bronson.   " He has neither father
nor mother nor home—he seems utterly friendless.   He
has no capacity, so far as I have sounded him, and, while
he is possessed of a kind of animal sharpness, like the
sharpness of a hawk or a weasel, I can think of nothing
to set him about by which he could live.   Even the streets
seem closed to him, since the police for some reason pursue him and arrest him on sight.   It was in a magistrate's
court I found him.   He had been dragged there by an

officer, and would have been sent to a reformatory if I had not rescued him."

"And would not that have been the best place for him?" I asked, rather to hear the Reverend Bronson's reply, than because I believed in my own query. Aside from being a born friend of liberty in a largest sense, my own experience had not led me to believe that our reformatories reform. I've yet to hear of him who was not made worse by a term in any prison. "Why not send him to a reformatory?" said I again.

"No one should be locked up," contended the Reverend Bronson, "who has not shown himself unfit to be free. That is not this boy's case, I think; he has had no chance; the police, according to that magistrate who gave him into my hands, are relentless against him, and pick him up on sight."

"And are not the police good judges of these matters?"

"I would not trust their judgment," returned the Reverend Bronson. "There are many noble men upon the rolls of the police." Then, with a doubtful look: "For the most part, however, I should say they stand at the head of the criminal classes, and might best earn their salaries by arresting themselves."

At this, I was made to smile, for it showed how my reverend visitor's years along the Bowery had not come and gone without lending him some saltiness of wit.

" Leave the boy here," said I at last, " I'll find him work to live by, if it be no more than sitting outside my door, and playing the usher to those who call upon me."

" Melting Moses is the only name he has given me," said the Reverend Bronson, as he took his leave. " I suppose, if one might get to it, that he has another."

" Melting Moses, as a name, should do very well," said I.

Melting Moses looked wistfully after the Reverend Bronson when the latter departed, and I could tell by that how the urchin regretted the going of the dominie as one might regret the going of an only friend. Somehow, the lad's forlorn state grew upon me, and I made up my mind to serve as his protector for a time at least. He was a shrill child of the Bowery, was Melting Moses, and spoke a kind of gutter dialect, one-half slang and the other a patter of the thieves that was hard to understand. My first business was to send him out with the janitor of the building to have him thrown into a bathtub, and then buttoned into a new suit of clothes.

Melting Moses submitted dumbly to these improvements, being rather resigned than pleased, and later with the same docility went home to sleep at the janitor's house. Throughout the day he would take up his post on my door and act as herald to what visitors might come.

Being washed and combed and decently arrayed, Melting Moses, with black eyes and a dark elfin face, made no bad figure of a boy. For all his dwarfishness, I found him surprisingly strong, and as active as a monkey. He had all the love and loyalty of a collie for me, and within the first month of his keeping my door, he would have cast himself into the river if I had asked him for that favor.

Little by little, scrap by scrap, Melting Moses gave me his story. Put together in his words, it ran like this:

" Me fadder kept a joint in Kelly's Alley; d' name of d' joint was d' Door of Death, see! It was a hot number, an' lots of trouble got pulled off inside. He used to fence for d' guns an' dips, too, me fadder did; an' w'en one of 'em nipped a super or a rock, an' wanted d' quick dough, he brought it to me fadder, who chucked down d' stuff an' no questions asked. One day a big trick comes off— a jooeler's winder or somet'ing like dat. Me fadder is in d' play from d' outside, see! An' so w'en dere's a holler, he does a sneak an' gets away, 'cause d' cops is layin' to pinch him. Me fadder gets put wise to this be a mug who hangs out about d' Central Office. He sherries like I says.

" At dat, d' Captain who's out to nail me fadder toins sore all t'rough. W'en me fadder sidesteps into New Joisey or some'ers, d' Captain sends along a couple of his harness bulls from Mulberry Street, an' dey

pinches me mudder, who aint had nothin' to do wit' d'
play at all. Dey rings for d' hurry-up wagon, an' takes
me mudder to d' station. D' Captain he gives her d' eye,
an' asts where me fadder is. She says she can't put him
on, 'cause she aint on herself. Wit' dat, dis Captain
t'rows her d' big chest, see! an' says he'll give her d'
t'ree degrees if she don't cough up d' tip. But she
hands him out d' old gag: she aint on. So then, d' Captain has her put in a cell; an' nothin' to eat.

"After d' foist night he brings her up ag'in.

" 'Dat's d' number one d'gree,' says he.

"But still me mudder don't tell, 'cause she can't. Me
fadder aint such a farmer as to go leavin' his address
wit' no one.

"D' second night dey keeps me mudder in a cell, an'
toins d' hose on d' floor so she can't do nothin' but stan'
'round—no sleep! no chuck! no nothin'!

" 'Dat's d' number two d'gree,' says d' bloke of a
Captain to me mudder. 'Now where did dat husband of
yours skip to?'

"But me mudder couldn't tell.

" 'Give d' old goil d' dungeon,' says d' Captain; 'an'
t'row her in a brace of rats to play wit'.'

"An' now dey locks me mudder in a place like a
cellar, wit' two rats to squeak an' scrabble about all
night, an' t'row a scare into her.

"An' it would too, only she goes dotty.

"Next day, d' Captain puts her in d' street. But w'at's d' use? She's off her trolley. She toins sick; an' in a week she croaks. D' sawbones gets her for d' colleges."

Melting Moses shed tears at this.

"Dat's about all," he concluded. "W'en me mudder was gone, d' cops toined in to do me. D' Captain said he was goin' to clean up d' fam'ly; so he gives d' orders, an' every time I'd show up on d' line, I'd get d' collar. It was one of dem times, w'en d' w'itechoker, who passes me on to you, gets his lamps on me an' begs me off from d' judge, see!"

Melting Moses wept a deal during his relation, and I was not without being moved by it myself. I gave the boy what consolation I might, by assuring him that he was safe with me, and that no policeman should threaten him. A tale of trouble, and particularly if told by a child, ever had power to disturb me, and I did not question Melting Moses concerning his father and mother a second time.

My noble nonentity—for whom I will say that he allowed me to finger him for offices and contracts, as a musician fingers the keyboard of a piano, and play upon him what tunes of profit I saw fit—was mayor, and the town wholly in my hands, with a Tammany man in every office, when there occurred the first of a train of events which in their passage were to plow a furrow in my life so deep that all the years to come after have not served to smooth it away. I was engaged at my desk, when Melting Moses announced a caller.

" She's a dame in black," said Melting Moses; " an' she's of d' Fift' Avenoo squeeze all right."

Melting Moses, now he was fed and dressed, went through the days with uncommon spirit, and when not thinking on his mother would be gay enough. My visitors interested him even more than they did me, and he announced but few without hazarding his surmise as to both their origins and their errands.

" Show her in!" I said.

My visitor was a widow, as I could see by her mourning weeds. She was past middle life; gray, with hollow cheeks, and sad pleading eyes.

" My name is Van Flange," said she. " The Reverend Bronson asked me to call upon you. It's about my son; he's ruining us by his gambling."

Then the Widow Van Flange told of her son's infatuation; and how blacklegs in Barclay Street were fleecing him with roulette and faro bank.

I listened to her story with patience. While I would not find it on my programme to come to her relief, I aimed at respect for one whom the Reverend Bronson had endorsed. I was willing to please that good man, for I liked him much since he spoke in commendation of my English. Besides, if angered, the Reverend Bronson

would be capable of trouble. He was too deeply and too
practically in the heart of the East Side; he could not
fail to have a tale to tell that would do Tammany Hall
no good, but only harm. Wherefore, I in no wise cut
short the complaints of the Widow Van Flange. I heard
her to the end, training my face to sympathy the while,
and all as though her story were not one commonest of
the town.

"You may be sure, madam," said I, when the Widow
Van Flange had finished, "that not only for the Reverend Bronson's sake, but for your own, I shall do all I
may to serve you. I own no personal knowledge of that
gambling den of which you speak, nor of those sharpers
who conduct it. That knowledge belongs with the police.
The number you give, however, is in Captain Gothecore's precinct. We'll send for him if you'll wait."
With that I rang my desk bell for Melting Moses.
"Send for Captain Gothecore," said I. At the name,
the boy's black eyes flamed up in a way to puzzle.
"Send a messenger for Captain Gothecore; I want him
at once."

CHAPTER XX

WHILE the Widow Van Flange and I sat waiting the coming of Gothecore, the lady gave me further leaves of her story. The name of Van Flange was old. It had been honorable and high in the days of Wouter Van Twiller, and when the town was called New Amsterdam. The Van Flanges had found their source among the wooden shoes and spinning-wheels of the ancient Dutch, and were duly proud. They had been rich, but were now reduced, counting—she and her boy—no more than two hundred thousand dollars for their fortune.

This son over whom she wept was the last Van Flange; there was no one beyond him to wear the name. To the mother, this made his case the more desperate, for mindful of her caste, she was borne upon by pride of family almost as much as by maternal love. The son was a drunkard; his taste for alcohol was congenital, and held him in a grip that could not be unloosed. And he was wasting their substance; what small riches remained to them were running away at a rate that would soon leave nothing.

267

"But why do you furnish him money?" said I. "You should keep him without a penny."

"True!" responded the Widow Van Flange, "but those who pillage my son have found a way to make me powerless. There is a restaurant near this gambling den. The latter, refusing him credit and declining his checks, sends him always to this restaurant-keeper. He takes my son's check, and gives him the money for it. I know the whole process," concluded the Widow Van Flange, a sob catching in her throat, "for I've had my son watched, to see if aught might be done to save him."

"But those checks," I observed, "should be worthless, for you have told me how your son has no money of his own."

"And that is it," returned the Widow Van Flange. "I must pay them to keep him from prison. Once, when I refused, they were about to arrest him for giving a spurious check. My own attorney warned me they might do this. My son, himself, takes advantage of it. I would sooner be stripped of the last shilling, than suffer the name of Van Flange to be disgraced. Practicing upon my fears, he does not scruple to play into the hands of those who scheme his downfall. You may know what he is about, when I tell you that within the quarter I have been forced in this fashion to pay over twenty-seven thousand dollars. I see no way for it but to be ruined;" and her lips twitched with the despair she felt.

While the Widow Van Flange and I talked of her son and his down-hill courses, I will not pretend that I pondered any interference. The gamblers were a power in politics. The business of saving sons was none of mine; but, as I've said, I was willing, by hearing her story, to compliment the Reverend Bronson, who had suggested her visit. In the end, I would shift the burden to the police; they might be relied upon to find their way through the tangle to the advantage of themselves and the machine.

Indeed, this same Gothecore would easily dispose of the affair. Expert with practice, there was none who could so run with the hare while pretending to course with the hounds. Softly, sympathetically, he would talk with the Widow Van Flange; and she would depart in the belief that her cause had found a friend.

As the Widow Van Flange and I conversed, we were brought to sudden silence by a strange cry. It was a mad, screeching cry, such as might have come from some tigerish beast in a heat of fury. I was upon my feet in a moment, and flung open the door.

Gothecore was standing outside, having come to my message. Over from him by ten feet was Melting Moses, his shoulders narrowed in a feline way, crouching, with brows drawn down and features in a snarl of hate. He was slowly backing away from Gothecore; not in fear, but rather like some cat-creature, measuring for a spring.

On his side, Gothecore's face offered an equally forbidding picture. He was red with rage, and his bulldog jaws had closed like a trap. Altogether, I never beheld a more inveterate expression, like malice gone to seed.

I seized Melting Moses by the shoulder, and so held him back from flying at Gothecore with teeth and claws.

" He killed me mudder! " cried Melting Moses, struggling in my fingers like something wild.

When the janitor with whom Melting Moses lived had carried him off—and at that, the boy must be dragged away by force—I turned to Gothecore.

" What was the trouble? "

" Why do you stand for that young whelp? " he cried. " I won't have it! "

" The boy is doing you no harm."

" I won't have it! " he cried again. The man was like a maniac.

" Let me tell you one thing," I retorted, looking him between the eyes; " unless you walk with care and talk with care, you are no better than a lost man. One word, one look, and I'll snuff you out between my thumb and finger as I might a candle."

There must have been that which showed formidable in my manner, for Gothecore stood as though stunned. The vicious insolence of the scoundrel had exploded the

powder in my temper like a coal of fire. I pointed the
way to my room.

" Go in; I've business with you."

Gothecore seemed to recall himself to steadiness.
Without more words, he entered my door.

With as much dignity as I might summon in the track
of such a storm, I presented him to the Widow Van
Flange. She had heard the sound of our differences;
but, taken with her own troubles, she made no account
of them. The Widow Van Flange received the rather
boorish salutation of Gothecore in a way politely
finished. Upon my hint, she gave him her story. Gothecore assumed a look at once professional and deprecatory.

" An' now you're done, Madam," said Gothecore, giving that slight police cough by which he intimated for
himself a limitless wisdom, " an' now you're done,
Madam, let me chip in a word. I know your son; I've
knowed Billy Van Flange, now, goin' on three year—ever
since he comes out o' college. I don't want to discourage
you, Madam; but, to put it to you on th' square, Billy
Van Flange is a warm member. I leave it to you to say
if I aint right. Yes, indeed! he's as hot a proposition as
ever went down th' line."

Here the eye of Gothecore wandered towards the ceiling, recalling the mad pranks of young Van Flange.

" But these gamblers are destroying him!" moaned

the Widow Van Flange. "Is there no way to shield him? Surely, you should know how to punish them, and keep him out of their hands!"

"I know that gang of card sharps in Barclay Street," remarked Gothecore; "an' they're a bunch of butes at that! But let me go on: I'll tell you what we can do; and then I'll tell you why it won't be fly to do it. In th' finish, however, it will all be up to you, Madam. We'll act on any steer you hand us. If you say 'pinch,' pinch goes.

"But as I was tellin': I'm dead onto Billy Van Flange; I know him like a gambler knows an ace. He hits up th' bottle pretty stiff at that, an' any man who finds him sober has got to turn out hours earlier than I do. An' I'll tell you another thing, Madam: This Billy Van Flange is a tough mug to handle. More'n once, I've tried to point him for home, an' every time it was a case of nothin' doin'. Sometimes he shed tears, an' sometimes he wanted to scrap; sometimes he'd give me th' laugh, an' sometimes he'd throw a front an' talk about havin' me fired off th' force. He'd run all the way from th' sob or th' fiery eye, to th' gay face or th' swell front, accordin' as he was jagged."

While Gothecore thus descanted, the Widow Van Flange buried her face in her handkerchief. She heard his every word, however, and when Gothecore again consulted the ceiling, she signed for him to go on.

" Knowin' New York as I do," continued Gothecore,
" I may tell you, Madam, that every time I get my lamps
on that son of yours, I hold up my mits in wonder to
think he aint been killed."   The Widow Van Flange
started ; her anxious face was lifted from the handkerchief.   " That's on th' level! I've expected to hear of
him bein' croaked, any time this twelve months.   Th'
best I looked for was that th' trick wouldn't come off in
my precinct.   He carries a wad in his pocket ; an' he
sports a streak of gilt, with a thousand-dollar rock, on
one of his hooks ; an' I could put you next to a hundred
blokes, not half a mile from here, who'd do him up for
half th' price.   That's straight! Billy Van Flange, con-
siderin' th' indoocements he hangs out, an' th' way he lays
himself wide open to th' play, is lucky to be alive.

" Now why is he alive, Madam?   It is due to them
very gamblin' ducks in Barclay Street.   Not that they
love him ; but once them skin gamblers gets a sucker on
th' string, they protect him same as a farmer does his
sheep.   They look on him as money in th' bank ; an' so
they naturally see to it that no one puts his light out.

" That's how it stands, Madam!"   And now Gothecore made ready to bring his observations to a close.
" This Billy Van Flange, like every other rounder, has
his hangouts.   His is this deadfall on Barclay Street,
with that hash-house keeper to give him th' dough for
his checks.   Now I'll tell you what I think.   While he

sticks to th' Barclay Street mob, he's safe. You'll get
him back each time. They'll take his stuff; but they'll
leave him his life, an' that's more than many would do.

"Say th' word, however, an' I can put th' damper on.
I can fix it so Billy Van Flange can't gamble nor cash
checks in Barclay Street. They'll throw him out th'
minute he sticks his nut inside the door. But I'll put
you wise to it, Madam: If I do, inside of ninety days
you'll fish him out o' th' river; you will, as sure as I'm a
foot high!"

The face of the Widow Van Flange was pale as paper
now, and her bosom rose and fell with new terrors for her
son. The words of Gothecore seemed prophetic of the
passing of the last Van Flange.

"Madam," said Gothecore, following a pause, "I've
put it up to you. Give me your orders. Say th' word,
an' I'll have th' screws on that Barclay Street joint as
fast as I can get back to my station-house."

"But if we keep him from going there," said the
Widow Van Flange, with a sort of hectic eagerness,
"he'll find another place, won't he?" There was a
curious look in the eyes of the Widow Van Flange.
Her hand was pressed upon her bosom as if to smother a
pang; her handkerchief went constantly to her lips.
"He would seek worse resorts?"

"It's a cinch, Madam!"

"And he'd be murdered?"

" Madam, it's apples to ashes!"

The eyes of the Widow Van Flange seemed to light up with an unearthly sparkle, while a flush crept out in her cheek. I was gazing upon these signs with wonder regarding them as things sinister, threatening ill.

Suddenly, she stood on her feet; and then she tottered in a blind, stifled way toward the window as though feeling for light and air. The next moment, the red blood came trickling from her mouth; she fell forward and I caught her in my arms.

" It's a hemorrhage!" said Gothecore.

The awe of death lay upon the man, and his coarse voice was stricken to a whisper.

" Now Heaven have my soul!" murmured the dying woman. Then: " My son! oh, my son!"

There came another crimson cataract, and the Widow Van Flange was dead.

" This is your work!" said I, turning fiercely to Gothecore.

" Or is it yours?" cries he.

The words went over my soul like the teeth of a harrow. Was it my work?

" No, Chief!" continued Gothecore, more calmly, and as though in answer to both himself and me, " it's the work of neither of us. You think that what I said killed her. That may be as it may. Every word, however, was true. I but handed her th' straight goods."

The Widow Van Flange was dead; and the thought of her son was in her heart and on her lips as her soul passed. And the son, bleared and drunken, gambled on in the Barclay Street den, untouched. The counters did not shake in his hand, nor did the blood run chill in his veins, as he continued to stake her fortune and his own in sottish ignorance.

One morning, when the first snow of winter was beating in gusty swirls against the panes, Morton walked in upon me. I had not seen that middle-aged fop since the day when I laid out my social hopes and fears for Blossom. It being broad September at the time, Morton had pointed out how nothing might be done before the snows.

" For our society people," observed Morton, on that September occasion, " are migratory, like the wild geese they so much resemble. At this time they are leaving Newport for the country, don't y' know. They will not be found in town until the frost."

Now, when the snow and Morton appeared together, I recalled our conversation. I at once concluded that his visit had somewhat to do with our drawing-room designs. Nor was I in the wrong.

" But first," said he, when in response to my question he had confessed as much, " let us decide another matter. Business before pleasure; the getting of money should have precedence over its dissipation; it should, really! I am about to build a conduit, don't y' know, the whole length of Mulberry, and I desire you to ask your street department to take no invidious notice of the enterprise. You might tell your fellows that it wouldn't be good form."

"But your franchise does not call for a conduit."

"We will put it on the ground that Mulberry intends a change to the underground trolley—really! That will give us the argument; and I think, if needs press, your Corporation Counsel can read the law that way. He seems such a clever beggar, don't y' know!"

"But what do you want the conduit for?"

"There's nothing definite or sure as yet. My notion, however, is to inaugurate an electric-light company. The conduit, too, would do for telephone or telegraph wires. Really, it's a good thing to have; and my men, when this beastly weather softens a bit, might as well be about the digging. All that's wanted of you, old chap, is to issue your orders to the department people to stand aloof, and offer no interruptions. It will be a great asset in the hands of Mulberry, that conduit; I shall increase the capital stock by five millions, on the strength of it."

"Your charter isn't in the way?"

"The charter contemplates the right on the part of Mulberry to change its power, don't y' know. We shall declare in favor of shifting to the underground trolley;

although, really, we won't say When. The necessity of a conduit follows. Any chap can see that."

" Very well! " I replied, " there shall be no interference by the city. If the papers grumble, I leave you and them to fight it out."

" Now that's settled," said Morton, producing his infallible cigarette, " let us turn to those social victories we have in contemplation. I take it you remain firm in your frantic resolutions? "

" I do it for the good of my child," said I.

" As though society, as presently practiced," cried Morton, " could be for anybody's good! However, I was sure you would not change. You know the De Mudds? One of our best families, the De Mudds—really! They are on the brink of a tremendous function. They'll dine, and they'll dance, and all that sort of thing. They've sent you cards, the De Mudds have; and you and your daughter are to come. It's the thing to do; you can conquer society in the gross at the De Mudds."

" I'm deeply obliged," said I. " My daughter's peculiar nervous condition has preyed upon me more than I've admitted. The physician tells me that her best hope of health lies in the drawing-rooms."

" Let us trust so! " said Morton. " But, really, old chap, you ought to be deucedly proud of the distinction which the De Mudds confer upon you. Americans are quite out of their line, don't y' know! And who can

blame them?   Americans are such common beggars;
there's so many of them, they're vulgar.   Mamma De
Mudd's daughters—three of them—all married earls.
Mamma DeMudd made the deal herself; and taking them
by the lot, she had those noblemen at a bargain; she did,
really!   Five millions was the figure.   Just think of it!
five millions for three earls!   Why, it was like finding
them in the street!

"'But what is he?' asked Mamma DeMudd, when I
proposed you for her notice.

"'He's a despot,' said I, 'and rules New York.   Every
man in town is his serf.'

"When Mamma DeMudd got this magnificent idea
into her head, she was eager to see you; she was, really.

"However," concluded Morton, "let us change the
subject, if only to restore my wits.   The moment I speak
of society, I become quite idiotic, don't y' know!"

"Speaking of new topics, then," said I, "let me ask
of your father.   How does he fare these days?"

"Busy, exceeding busy!" returned Morton.   "He's
buying a home in New Jersey.   Oh, no, he won't live
there; but he requires it as a basis for declaring that he's
changed his residence, don't y' know!   You'd wonder,
gad! to see how frugal the old gentleman has grown in
his old age.   It's the personal property tax that bothers
him; two per cent. on twenty millions come to quite a
sum; it does, really!   The old gentleman doesn't like it;

so he's going to change his residence to New Jersey. To be sure, while he'll reside in New Jersey, he'll live here.

" ' It's a fribble, father,' said I, when he set forth his little game. ' Why don't you go down to the tax office, and commit perjury like a man? All your friends do.'

" But, really! he couldn't; and he said so. The old gentleman lacks in those rugged characteristics, required when one swears to a point-blank lie."

When Morton was gone, I gave myself to pleasant dreams concerning Blossom. I was sure that the near company and conversation of those men and women of the better world, whom she was so soon to find about her, would accomplish all for which I prayed. Her nerves would be cooled; she would be drawn from out that hypochondria into which, throughout her life, she had been sinking as in a quicksand.

I had not unfolded either my anxieties or my designs to Blossom. Now I would have Anne tell her of my plans. Time would be called for wherein to prepare the necessary wardrobe. She should have the best artistes; none must outshine my girl, of that I was resolved. These dress-labors, with their selections and fittings, would of themselves be excellent. They would employ her fancy, and save her from foolish fears of the De Mudds and an experience which she might think on as an ordeal. I never once considered myself—I, who was as ignorant of drawing-rooms as a cart-horse! Blossom

held my thoughts. My heart would be implacable until
it beheld her, placed and sure of herself, in the pleasant
midst of those most elevated circles, towards which not
alone my faith, but my admiration turned its eyes. I
should be proud of her station, as well as relieved on the
score of her health, when Blossom, serene and even and
contained, and mistress of her own house, mingled on
equal terms with ones who had credit as the nobility of
the land.

Was this the dream of a peasant grown rich? Was it
the doting vision of a father mad with fondness? Why
should I not so spread the nets of my money and my
power as to ensnare eminence and the world's respect for
this darling Blossom of mine? Wherein would lie the
wild extravagance of the conceit? Surely, there were
men in every sort my inferiors, and women, not one of
whom was fit to play the rôle of maid to Blossom, who
had rapped at this gate, and saw it open unto them.

Home I went elate, high, walking on air. Nor did I
consider how weak it showed, that I, the stern captain of
thousands, and with a great city in my hands to play or
labor with, should be thus feather-tickled with a toy! It
was amazing, yes; and yet it was no less sweet:—this
building of air-castles to house my Blossom in!

It stood well beyond the strike of midnight as I told
Anne the word that Morton had brought. Anne raised
her dove's eyes to mine when I was done, and they were

wet with tears. Anne's face was as the face of a nun, in
its self-sacrifice and the tender, steady disinterest that
looked from it.

Now, as I exulted in a new bright life to be unrolled to
the little tread of Blossom, I saw the shadows of a sorrow,
vast and hopeless, settle upon Anne. At this I halted.
As though to answer my silence, she put her hand ca-
ressingly upon my shoulder.

" Brother," said Anne, " you must set aside these
thoughts for Blossom of men and women she will never
meet, of ballrooms she will never enter, of brilliant costumes she will never wear. It is one and all impossible;
you do not understand."

With that, irritated of too much opposition and the
hateful mystery of it, I turned roughly practical.

" Well! " said I, in a hardest tone, " admitting that I
do not understand; and that I think on men and women
she will never meet, and ballrooms she will never enter.
Still, the costumes at least I can control, and it will
mightily please me if you and Blossom at once attend
to the frocks."

" You do not understand! " persisted Anne, with sober
gentleness. " Blossom would not wear an evening
dress."

" Anne, you grow daft! " I cried. " How should
there be aught immodest in dressing like every best
woman in town? The question of modesty is a ques-

tion of custom; it is in the exception one will find the
indelicate. I know of no one more immodest than a
prude."

"Blossom is asleep," said Anne, in her patient way.
Then taking a bed-candle that burned on a table, she
beckoned me. "Come; I will show you what I mean.
Make no noise; we must not wake Blossom. She must
never know that you have seen. She has held this a secret
from you; and I, for her poor sake, have done the same."

Anne opened the door of Blossom's room. My girl
was in a gentle slumber. With touch light as down,
Anne drew aside the covers from about her neck.

"There," whispered Anne, "there! Look on her
throat!"

Once, long before, a man had hanged himself, and I
was called. I had never forgotten the look of those
marks which belted the neck of that self-strangled man.
Encircling the lily throat of Blossom, I saw the fellows to
those marks—raw and red and livid!

There are no words to tell the horror that swallowed
me up. I turned ill; my reason stumbled on its feet.
Anne led me from the room.

"The mark of the rope!" I gasped. "It is the mark
of the rope!"

CHAPTER XXI

THE REVEREND BRONSON'S REBELLION

WHAT should it be?—this gallows-brand to show like a bruised ribbon of evil about the throat of Blossom! Anne gave me the story of it. It was a birthmark; that hangman fear which smote upon the mother when, for the death of Jimmy the Blacksmith, I was thrown into a murderer's cell, had left its hideous trace upon the child. In Blossom's infancy and in her earliest childhood, the mark had lain hidden beneath the skin as seeds lie buried and dormant in the ground. Slowly, yet no less surely, the inveterate years had quickened it and brought it to the surface; it had grown and never stopped—this mark! and with each year it took on added sullenness. The best word that Anne could give me was that it would so continue in its ugly multiplication until the day of Blossom's death. There could be no escape; no curing change, by any argument of medicine or surgery, was to be brought about; there it glared and there it would remain, a mark to shrink from! to the horrid last. And by that token, my plans of a drawing room for Blossom found annihilation. Anne had said the truth; those dreams that my girl should shine, starlike, in the firmament of high society, must be put away.

It will have a trivial sound, and perchance be scoffed at, when I say that for myself, personally, I remember no blacker disappointment than that which overtook me as I realized how there could come none of those triumphs of chandeliers and floors of wax. Now as I examine myself, I can tell that not a little of this was due to my own vanity, and a secret wish I cherished to see my child the equal of the first.

And if it were so, why should I be shamed? Might I not claim integrity for a pride which would have found its account in such advancement? I had been a ragged boy about the streets. I had grown up ignorant; I had climbed, if climbing be the word, unaided of any pedigree or any pocketbook, into a place of riches and autocratic sway. Wherefore, to have surrounded my daughter with the children of ones who had owned those advantages which I missed—folk of the purple, all!—and they to accept her, would have been a victory, and to do me honor. I shall not ask the pardon of men because I longed for it; nor do I scruple to confess the blow my hopes received when I learned how those ambitions would never find a crown.

Following my sight of that gallows mark, I sat for a long time collecting myself. It was a dreadful thing to think upon; the more, since it seemed to me that Blossom suffered in my stead. It was as if that halter, which I defeated, had taken my child for a revenge.

" What can we do? " said I, at last.

I spoke more from an instinct of conversation, and because I would have the company of Anne's sympathy, than with the thought of being answered to any purpose. I was set aback, therefore, by her reply.

" Let Blossom take the veil," said Anne. " A convent, and the good work of it, would give her peace."

At that, I started resentfully. To one of my activity, I, who needed the world about me every moment—struggling, contending, succeeding—there could have come no word more hateful. The cell of a nun! It was as though Anne advised a refuge in the grave. I said as much, and with no special choice of phrases.

" Because Heaven in its injustice," I cried, " has destroyed half her life, she is to make it a meek gift of the balance? Never, while I live! Blossom shall stay by me; I will make her happy in the teeth of Heaven!"

Thus did I hurl my impious challenge. What was to be the return, and the tempest it drew upon poor Blossom, I shall unfold before I am done. I have a worm of conscience whose slow mouth gnaws my nature, and you may name it superstition if you choose. And by that I know, when now I sit here, lonesome save for my gold, and with no converse better than the yellow mocking leer of it, that it was this, my blasphemy, which wrought in

Heaven's retort the whole of that misery which descended
to dog my girl and drag her down.   How else shall I
explain that double darkness which swallowed up her innocence?   It was the bolt of punishment, which those
skies I had outraged, aimed at me.

Back to my labors of politics I went, with a fiercer heat
than ever.   My life, begun in politics, must end in politics.   Still, there was a mighty change.   I was not to
look upon that strangling mark and escape the scar of it.
I settled to a savage melancholy; I saw no pleasant moment.   Constantly I ran before the hound-pack of my
own thoughts, a fugitive, flying from myself.

Also, there came the signs visible, and my hair was to
turn and lose its color, until within a year it went as
white as milk.   Men, in the idleness of their curiosity,
would notice this, and ask the cause.   They were not to
know; nor did Blossom ever learn how, led by Anne, I
had crept upon her secret.   It was a sorrow without a
door, that sorrow of the hangman's mark; and because
we may not remedy it, we will leave it, never again to be
referred to until it raps for notice of its own black will.

The death of the Widow Van Flange did not remove
from before me the question of young Van Flange and
his degenerate destinies.   The Reverend Bronson took
up the business where it fell from the nerveless fingers of
his mother on that day she died.

" Not that I believe he can be saved," observed the

Reverend Bronson; " for if I am to judge, the boy is already lost beyond recall. But there is such goods as a pious vengeance—an anger of righteousness!—and I find it in my heart to destroy with the law, those rogues who against the law destroy others. That Barclay Street nest of adders must be burned out; and I come to you for the fire."

In a sober, set-faced way, I was amused by the dominie's extravagance. And yet I felt a call to be on my guard with him. Suppose he were to dislodge a stone which in its rolling should crash into and crush the plans of the machine! The town had been lost before, and oftener than once, as the result of beginnings no more grave. Aside from my liking for the good man, I was warned by the perils of my place to speak him softly.

"Well," said I, trying for a humorous complexion, " if you are bound for a wrestle with those blacklegs, I will see that you have fair play."

"If that be true," returned the Reverend Bronson, promptly, " give me Inspector McCue."

"And why Inspector McCue?" I asked. The suggestion had its baffling side. Inspector McCue was that honest one urged long ago upon Big Kennedy by Father Considine. I did not know Inspector McCue; there might lurk danger in the man. "Why McCue?" I repeated. " The business of arresting gamblers belongs more with the uniformed police.   Gothecore is your proper officer."

" Gothecore is not an honest man," said the Reverend Bronson, with sententious frankness.   McCue, on the other hand, is an oasis in the Sahara of the police.   He can be trusted.   If you support him he will collect the facts and enforce the law."

" Very well," said I, " you shall take McCue.   I have no official control in the matter, being but a private man like yourself.   But I will speak to the Chief of Police, and doubtless he will grant my request."

" There is, at least, reason to think so," retorted the Reverend Bronson in a dry tone.

Before I went about an order to send Inspector McCue to the Reverend Bronson, I resolved to ask a question concerning him.   Gothecore should be a well-head of information on that point; I would send for Gothecore. Also it might be wise to let him hear what was afoot for his precinct.   He would need to be upon his defense, and to put others interested upon theirs.

Melting Moses, who still stood warder at my portals, I dispatched upon some errand.   The sight of Gothecore would set him mad.   I felt sorrow rather than affection for Melting Moses.   There was something unsettled and mentally askew with the boy.   He was queer of feature, with the twisted fantastic face one sees carved on the far end of a fiddle.   Commonly, he was light of heart,

and his laugh would have been comic had it not
been for a note of the weird which rang in it. I had
not asked him, on the day when he went backing for a
spring at the throat of Gothecore, the reason of his hate.
His exclamation, " He killed me mudder! " told the story.
Besides, I could have done no good. Melting Moses
would have given me no reply. The boy, true to his
faith of Cherry Hill, would fight out his feuds for himself; he would accept no one's help, and regarded the
term " squealer " as an epithet of measureless disgrace.

When Gothecore came in, I caught him at the first of
it glowering furtively about, as though seeking someone.

" Where is that Melting Moses? " he inquired, when he
saw how I observed him to be searching the place with his
eye.

" And why? " said I.

" I thought I'd look him over, if you didn't mind. I
can't move about my precinct of nights but he's behind
me, playin' th' shadow. I want to know why he pipes
me off, an' who sets him to it."

" Well then," said I, a bit impatiently, " I should
have thought a full-grown Captain of Police was above
fearing a boy."

Without giving Gothecore further opening, I told him
the story of the Reverend Bronson, and that campaign of
purity he would be about.

"And as to young Van Flange," said I. "Does he still lose his money in Barclay Street?"

"They've cleaned him up," returned Gothecore. "Billy Van Flange is gone, hook, line, and sinker. He's on his uppers, goin' about panhandlin' old chums for a five-dollar bill."

"They made quick work of him," was my comment.

"He would have it," said Gothecore. "When his mother died th' boy got his bridle off. Th' property— about two hundred thousand dollars—was in paper an' th' way he turned it into money didn't bother him a bit. He came into Barclay Street, simply padded with th' long green—one-thousand-dollar bills, an' all that—an' them gams took it off him so fast he caught cold. He's dead broke; th' only difference between him an' a hobo, right now, is a trunk full of clothes."

"The Reverend Bronson," said I, "has asked for Inspector McCue. What sort of a man is McCue?"

Gothecore wrinkled his face into an expression of profound disgust.

"Who's McCue?" he repeated. "He's one of them mugwump pets. He makes a bluff about bein' honest, too, does McCue. I think he'd join a church, if he took a notion it would stiffen his pull."

"But is he a man of strength? Can he make trouble?"

" Trouble? "   This with contempt.   " When it comes to makin' trouble, he's a false alarm."

" Well," said I, in conclusion, " McCue and the dominie are going into your precinct."

" I'll tell you one thing," returned Gothecore, his face clouding up, " I think it's that same Reverend Bronson who gives Melting Moses th' office to dog me.   I'll put Mr. Whitechoker onto my opinion of th' racket, one of these days."

" You'd better keep your muzzle on," I retorted. " Your mouth will get you into trouble yet."

Gothecore went away grumbling, and much disposed to call himself ill-used.

During the next few days I was to receive frequent visits from the Reverend Bronson.   His mission was to enlist me in his crusade against the gamblers.   I put him aside on that point.

" You should remember," said I, as pleasantly as I well could, " that I am a politician, not a policeman.   I shall think of my party, and engage in no unusual moral exploits of the sort you suggest.   The town doesn't want it done."

" The question," responded the Reverend Bronson warmly, " is one of law and morality, and not of the town's desires.   You say you are a politician, and not a policeman.   If it comes to that, I am a preacher, and not a policeman.   Still, I no less esteem it my duty to inter-

fere for right.   I see no difference between your position
and my own."

" But I do.   To raid gamblers, and to denounce them,
make for your success in your profession.   With me, it
would be all the other way.   It is quite easy for you to
adopt the path you do.   Now I am not so fortunately
placed."

" You are the head of Tammany Hall," said the Reverend Bronson solemnly.   " It is a position which loads
you with responsibility, since your power for good or bad
in the town is absolute.   You have but to point your
finger at those gambling dens, and they would wither
from the earth."

" Now you do me too much compliment," said I.
" The Chief of Tammany is a much weaker man than you
think.   Moreover, I shall not regard myself as respon-
sible for the morals of the town."

" Take young Van Flange," went on the Reverend
Bronson, disregarding my remark.   " They've ruined
the boy; and you might have saved him."

" And there you are mistaken," I replied.   " But if it
were so, why should I be held for his ruin?   ' I am not
my brother's keeper.' "

" And so Cain said," responded the Reverend Bronson.
Then, as he was departing: " I do not blame you too
much, for I can see that you are the slave of your position.   But do not shield yourself with the word that you

are not your brother's keeper. You may be made grievously to feel that your brother's welfare is your welfare,
and that in his destruction your own destruction is also
to be found."

Men have rallied me as superstitious, and it may be
that some grains of truth lie buried in that charge. Sure
it is, that this last from the Reverend Bronson was not
without its uncomfortable effect. It pressed upon me
in a manner vaguely dark, and when he was gone, I
caught myself regretting the "cleaning up," as
Gothecore expressed it, of the dissolute young Van
Flange.

And yet, why should one feel sympathy for him who,
by his resolute viciousness, struck down his own mother?
If ever rascal deserved ruin, it was he who had destroyed
the hopes of one who loved him before all! The more I
considered, the less tender for the young Van Flange I
grew. And as to his destruction carrying personal
scathe for me, it might indeed do, as a flourish of the
pulpit, to say so, but it was a thought too far fetched, as
either a warning or a prophecy, to justify one in trans-
acting by its light his own existence, or the affairs of a
great organization of politics. The end of it was that I
smiled over a weakness that permitted me to be disturbed
by mournful forebodes, born of those accusing preach-
ments of the Reverend Bronson.

For all that my reverend mentor was right; the sequel

proved how those flames which licked up young Van
Flange were to set consuming fire to my own last
hope.

It would seem that young Van Flange, as a topic, was
in everybody's mouth. Morton, having traction occasion
for calling on me, began to talk of him at once.

" Really! " observed Morton, discussing young Van
Flange, " while he's a deuced bad lot, don't y' know, and
not at all likely to do Mulberry credit, I couldn't see him
starve, if only for his family. So I set him to work, as
far from the company's money as I could put him, and
on the soberish stipend of nine hundred dollars a year.
I look for the best effects from those nine hundred dollars; a chap can't live a double life on that; he can't,
really! "

" And you call him a bad lot," said I.

" The worst in the world," returned Morton. " You
see young Van Flange is such a weakling; really, there's
nothing to tie to. All men are vicious; but there are
some who are strong enough to save themselves. This
fellow isn't."

" His family is one of the best," said I.

For myself, I've a sincere respect for blood, and some
glimpse of it must have found display in my face.

" My dear boy," cried Morton, " there's no more
empty claptrap than this claptrap of family." Here
Morton adorned his high nose with the eyeglass that

meant so much with him, and surveyed me as from a
height.   " There's nothing in a breed when it comes to a
man."

" Would you say the same of a horse or a dog? "

" By no means, old chap; but a dog or a horse is
prodigiously a different thing, don't y' know. The
dominant traits of either of those noble creatures are
honesty, courage, loyalty—they're the home of the virtues. Now a man is another matter. He's an evil beggar, is a man; and, like a monkey, he has virtues only so
far as you force him to adopt them. As Machiavelli
says : ' We're born evil, and become good only by compulsion.' Now to improve a breed, as the phrase is,
makes simply for the promotion of what are the dominant
traits of the creature one has in hand. Thus, to refine or
emphasize the horse and the dog, increases them in honesty, loyalty, and courage since such are top-traits with
those animals. With a monkey or a man, and by
similar argument, the more you refine him, the more
abandoned he becomes. Really," and here Morton restored himself with a cigarette, " I shouldn't want these
views to find their way to my club. It would cause the
greatest row ever in our set; it would, really! I am
made quite ill to only think of it."

" What would you call a gentleman, then? " I asked.

Morton's theories, while I in no manner subscribed to
them, entertained me.

" What should I call a gentleman?   Why I should call
him the caricature of a man, don't y' know."

The Reverend Bronson had been abroad in his campaign against those sharpers of Barclay Street for perhaps four weeks.   I understood, without paying much
heed to the subject, that he was seeking the evidence of
their crimes, with a final purpose of having them before
a court.   There had been no public stir; the papers had
said nothing.   What steps had been taken were taken
without noise.   I doubted not that the investigation would,
in the finish, die out.   The hunted ones of Barclay Street
were folk well used to the rôle of fugitive, and since
Gothecore kept them informed of the enemy's strategy,
I could not think they would offer the Reverend Bronson
and his ally, McCue, any too much margin.

As yet, I had never seen this McCue.   By that, I knew
him to be an honest man.   Not that one is to understand
how none save a rogue would come to me.   I need hardly
explain, however, that every policeman of dark-lantern
methods was eagerly prone to make my acquaintance.
It was a merest instinct of caution; the storm might
break and he require a friend.   Now this McCue had never
sought to know me, and so I argued that his record was
pure white.

This did not please me; I preferred men upon whom
one might have some hold.   These folk of a smooth honesty go through one's fingers like water, and no more of

a grip to be obtained upon one of them than upon the Hudson. I made up my mind that I would see this McCue.

Still I did not send for him; it was no part of my policy to exhibit concern in one with whom I was strange, and who later might open his mouth to quote it against me. McCue, however, was so much inclined to humor my desire, that one afternoon he walked into my presence of his own free will.

"My name is McCue," said he, "Inspector McCue." I motioned him to a chair. "I've been told to collect evidence against certain parties in Barclay Street," he added. Then he came to a full stop.

While I waited for him to proceed in his own way and time, I studied Inspector McCue. He was a square-shouldered man, cautious, keen, resolute; and yet practical, and not one to throw himself away in the jaws of the impossible. What he had come to say, presently proved my estimate of him. On the whole, I didn't like the looks of Inspector McCue.

"What is your purpose?" I asked at last. "I need not tell you that I have no official interest in what you may be about. Still less have I a personal concern."

Inspector McCue's only retort was a grimace that did not add to his popularity. Next he went boldly to the object of his call.

"What I want to say is this," said he. "I've col-

lected the evidence I was sent after; I can lay my hands
on the parties involved as keepers and dealers in that Barclay Street den.   But I'm old enough to know that all the
evidence in the world won't convict these crooks unless
the machine is willing.   I'm ready to go ahead and take
my chances.   But I'm not ready to run against a stone
wall in the dark.   I'd be crazy, where no good can come,
to throw myself away."

"Now this is doubtless of interest to you," I replied,
putting some impression of distance into my tones, "but
what have I to do with the matter?"

"Only this," returned McCue.   "I'd like to have you
tell me flat, whether or no you want these parties
pinched."

"Inspector McCue," said I, "if that be your name and
title, it sticks in my head that you are making a mistake.
You ask me a question which you might better put to
your chief."

"We won't dispute about it," returned my caller;
"and I'm not here to give offense.   I am willing to do
my duty; but, as I've tried to explain, I don't care to
sacrifice myself if the game's been settled against me in
advance.   You speak of my going to the chief.   If arrests are to be made, he's the last man I ought to get my
orders from."

"If you will be so good as to explain?" said I.

"Because, if I am to go on, I must begin by collaring

the chief. He's the principal owner of that Barclay Street joint."

This was indeed news, and I had no difficulty in looking grave.

"Captain Gothecore is in it, too; but his end is with the restaurant keeper. That check-cashing racket was a case of flam; there was a hold-out went with that play. The boy, Van Flange, was always drunk, and the best he ever got for, say a five-hundred-dollar check, was three hundred dollars. Gothecore was in on the difference. There's the lay-out. Not a pleasant outlook, certainly; and not worth attempting arrests about unless I know that the machine is at my back."

"You keep using the term ' machine,' " said I coldly. "If by that you mean Tammany Hall, I may tell you, sir, that the ' machine ' has no concern in the affair. You will do your duty as you see it."

Inspector McCue sat biting his lips. After a moment, he got upon his feet to go.

"I think it would have been better," said he, " if you had met me frankly. However, I've showed you my hand; now I'll tell you what my course will be. This is Wednesday. I must, as you've said yourself, do my duty. If—mark you, I say ' If '—if I am in charge of this case on Saturday, I shall make the arrests I've indicated."

"Did you ever see such gall!" exclaimed the Chief of

Police, when I recounted my conversation with Inspector McCue. Then, holding up his pudgy hands in a manner of pathetic remonstrance: " It shows what I told you long ago. One honest man will put th' whole force on th' bum!"

Inspector McCue, on the day after his visit, was removed from his place, and ordered to a precinct in the drear far regions of the Bronx. The order was hardly dry on the paper when there descended upon me the Reverend Bronson, his eyes glittering with indignation, and a protest against this Siberia for Inspector McCue apparent in his face.

" And this," cried the Reverend Bronson, as he came through the door, " and this is what comes to an officer who is willing to do his duty!"

" Sit down, Doctor," said I soothingly, at the same time placing a chair; " sit down."

CHAPTER XXII

THE MAN OF THE KNIFE

WHEN the first gust was over, the Reverend Bronson seemed sad rather than enraged. He reproached the machine for the failure of his effort against that gambling den.

"But why do you call yourself defeated?" I asked. It was no part of my purpose to concede, even by my silence, that either I or Tammany was opposed to the Reverend Bronson. "You should put the matter to the test of a trial before you say that."

"What can I do without Inspector McCue? and he has been removed from the affair. I talked with him concerning it; he told me himself there was no hope."

"Now, what were his words?" said I, for I was willing to discover how far Inspector McCue had used my name.

"Why, then," returned the Reverend Bronson, with a faint smile at the recollection, "if I am to give you the precise words, our talk ran somewhat like this:

"'Doctor, what's the use?' said Inspector McCue. 'We're up against it; we can't move a wheel.'

302

" ' There's such a word as law,' said I, advancing much the argument you have just now given me; ' and such a thing as justice.'

" ' Not in the face of the machine,' responded Inspector McCue. ' The will of the machine stands for all the law and all the justice that we're likely to get. The machine has the courts, the juries, the prosecuting officers, and the police. Every force we need is in its hands. Personally, of course, they couldn't touch you; but if I were to so much as lift a finger, I'd be destroyed. Some day I, myself, may be chief; and if I am, for once in a way, I'll guarantee the decent people of this town a run for their money.'

" ' And yet,' said I, ' we prate of liberty ! '

" ' Liberty ! ' cried he. ' Doctor, our liberties are in hock to the politicians, and we've lost the ticket.' "

It was in my mind to presently have the stripes and buttons off the loquacious, honest Inspector McCue. The Reverend Bronson must have caught some gleam of it in my eye; he remonstrated with a gentle hand upon my arm.

" Promise me that no more harm shall come to McCue," he said. " I ought not to have repeated his words. He has been banished to the Bronx; isn't that punishment enough for doing right? "

" Yes," I returned, after a pause; " I give you my word, your friend is in no further peril. You should tell him, however, to forget the name, 'machine.' Also, he has too many opinions for a policeman."

The longer I considered, the more it was clear that it would not be a cautious policy to cashier McCue. It would make an uproar which I did not care to court when so near hand to an election. It was not difficult, therefore, to give the Reverend Bronson that promise, and I did it with a good grace.

Encouraged by my compliance, the Reverend Bronson pushed into an argument, the object of which was to bring me to his side for the town's reform.

"Doctor," said I, when he had set forth what he conceived to be my duty to the premises, "even if I were disposed to go with you, I would have to go alone. I could no more take Tammany Hall in the direction you describe, than I could take the East River. As I told you once before, you should consider our positions. It is the old quarrel of theory and practice. You proceed upon a theory that men are what they should be; I must practice existence upon the fact of men as they are."

"There is a debt you owe Above!" returned the Reverend Bronson, the preacher within him beginning to struggle.

"And what debt should that be?" I cried, for my mind, on the moment, ran gloomily to Blossom. "What debt should I owe there?—I, who am the most unhappy man in the world!"

There came a look into the eyes of the Reverend Bronson that was at once sharp with interrogation and soft with sympathy. He saw that I had been hard wounded, although he could not know by what; and he owned the kindly tact to change the course of his remarks.

"There is one point, sure," resumed the Reverend Bronson, going backward in his trend of thought, " and of that I warn you. I shall not give up this fight. I began with an attack upon those robbers, and I've been withstood by ones who should have strengthened my hands. I shall now assail, not alone the lawbreakers, but their protectors. I shall attack the machine and the police. I shall take this story into every paper that will print it; I shall summon the pulpits to my aid; I shall arouse the people, if they be not deaf or dead, to wage war on those who protect such vultures in their rapine for a share of its returns. There shall be a moral awakening; and you may yet conclude, when you sit down in the midst of defeat, that honesty is after all the best policy, and that virtue has its reward."

The Reverend Bronson, in the heat of feeling, had risen from the chair, and declaimed rather than said this, while striding up and down. To him it was as though my floor were a rostrum, and the private office of Tammany's Chief, a lecture room. I am afraid I smiled a bit cynically at his ardor and optimism, for he took me in sharp hand.

"Oh! I shall not lack recruits," said he, "and some will come from corners you might least suspect. I met your great orator, Mr. Gutterglory, but a moment ago; he gave me his hand, and promised his eloquence to the cause of reform."

"Nor does that surprise me," said I. Then, with a flush of wrath: "You may say to orator Gutterglory that I shall have something to remind him of when he takes the stump in your support."

My anger over Gutterglory owned a certain propriety of foundation. He was that sodden Cicero who marred the scene when, long before, I called on Big Kennedy, with the reputable old gentleman and Morton, to consult over the Gas Company's injunction antics touching Mulberry Traction. By some wonderful chance, Gutterglory had turned into sober walks. Big Kennedy, while he lived, and afterward I, myself, had upheld him, and put him in the way of money. He paid us with eloquence in conventions and campaigns, and on show occasions when Tammany would celebrate a holiday or a victory. From low he soared to high, and surely none was more pleased thereby than I. On every chance I thrust him forward; and I was sedulous to see that always a stream of dollar-profit went running his way.

Morton, I remember, did not share my enthusiasm. It was when I suggested Gutterglory as counsel for Mulberry.

" But really now ! " objected Morton, with just a taint of his old-time lisp, " the creature doesn't know enough.   He's as shallow as a skimming dish, don't y' know."

" Gutterglory is the most eloquent of men," I protested.

" I grant you the beggar is quite a talker, and all that," retorted Morton, twirling that potential eyeglass, " but the trouble is, old chap, that when we've said that, we've said all.   Gutterglory is a mere rhetorical freak. He ought to take a rest, and give his brain a chance to grow up with his vocabulary."

What Morton said had no effect on me; I clung to Gutterglory, and made his life worth while.   I was given my return when I learned that for years he had gone about, unknown to me, extorting money from people with the use of my name.   Scores have paid peace-money to Gutterglory, and thought it was I who bled them.   So much are we at the mercy of rascals who win our confidence !

It was the fact of his learning that did it.   I could never be called a good judge of one who knew books.   I was over prone to think him of finest honor who wrote himself a man of letters, for it was my weakness to trust where I admired.   In the end, I discovered the villain duplicity of Gutterglory, and cast him out; at that, the scoundrel was rich with six figures to his fortune, and

every dime of it the harvest of some blackmail in my
name.

He became a great fop, did Gutterglory; and when
last I saw him—it being Easter Day, as I stepped from
the Cathedral, where I'd been with Blossom—he was
teetering along Fifth Avenue, face powdered and a glow
of rouge on each cheekbone, stayed in at the waist, top
hat, frock coat, checked trousers, snowy "spats" over
his patent leathers, a violet in his buttonhole, a cane
carried endwise in his hand, elbows crooked, shoulders
bowed, the body pitched forward on his toes, a perfect
picture of that most pitiful of things—an age-seamed
doddering old dandy! This was he whom the Reverend
Bronson vaunted as an ally!

"You are welcome to Gutterglory," said I to my reverend visitor on that time when he named him as one to become eloquent for reform. "It but proves the truth of
what Big John Kennedy so often said: Any rogue, kicked
out of Tammany Hall for his scoundrelisms, can always
be sure of a job as a 'reformer.'"

"Really!" observed Morton, when a few days later I
was telling him of the visit of the Reverend Bronson,
"I've a vast respect for Bronson. I can't say that I
understand him—working for nothing among the scum
and rubbish of humanity!—for personally I've no talent
for religion, don't y' know! And so he thinks that honesty is the best policy!"

" He seemed to think it not open to contradiction."

" Hallucination, positive hallucination, my boy! At least, if taken in a money sense; and 'pon my word! that's the only sense in which it's worth one's while to take anything—really! Honesty the best policy! Why, our dominie should look about him. Some of our most profound scoundrels are our richest men. Money is so much like water, don't y' know, that it seems always to seek the lowest places; " and with that, Morton went his elegant way, yawning behind his hand, as if to so much exert his intelligence wearied him.

For over nine years—ever since the death of Big Kennedy—I had kept the town in my hands, and nothing strong enough to shake my hold upon it. This must have its end. It was not in the chapter of chance that anyone's rule should be uninterrupted. Men turn themselves in bed, if for no reason than just to lie the other way: and so will your town turn on its couch of politics. Folk grow weary of a course or a conviction, and to rest themselves, they will put it aside and have another in its place. Then, after a bit, they return to the old.

In politics, these shifts, which are really made because the community would relax from some pose of policy and stretch itself in new directions, are ever given a pretense of morality as their excuse. There is a hysteria to arise from the crush and jostle of the great city. Men, in their crowded nervousness, will clamor for the new. This is also given the name of morals. And because I was aware how these conditions of restlessness and communal hysteria ever subsist, and like a magazine of powder ask but the match to fire them and explode into fragments whatever rule might at the time exist, I went sure that some day, somehow the machine would be overthrown. Also, I went equally certain how defeat would be only temporary, and that before all was done, the town would again come back to the machine.

You've seen a squall rumple and wrinkle and toss the bosom of a lake? If you had investigated, you would have learned how that storm-disturbance was wholly of the surface. It did not bite the depths below. When the gust had passed, the lake—whether for good or bad —re-settled to its usual, equal state. Now the natural conditions of New York are machine conditions. Wherefore, I realized, as I've written, that no gust of reformation could either trouble it deeply or last for long, and that the moment it had passed, the machine must at once succeed to the situation.

However, when the Reverend Bronson left me, vowing insurrection, I had no fears of the sort immediate. The times were not hysterical, nor ripe for change. I would re-carry the city; the Reverend Bronson—if his strength were to last that long—with those moralists he enlisted, might defeat me on some other distant day. But for the election at hand I was safe by every sign.

As I pored over the possibilities, I could discern no present argument in his favor. He himself might be morally sure of machine protection for those men of Barclay Street. But to the public he could offer no practical proof. Should he tell the ruin of young Van Flange, no one would pay peculiar heed. Such tales were of the frequent. Nor would the fate of young Van Flange, who had employed his name and his fortune solely as the bed-plates of an endless dissipation, evoke a sympathy. Indeed those who knew him best—those who had seen him then, and who saw him now at his Mulberry Traction desk, industrious, sober, respectable in a hall-bedroom way on his narrow nine hundred a year, did not scruple to declare that his so-called ruin was his regeneration, and that those card-criminals who took his money had but worked marvels for his good. No; I could not smell defeat in the contest coming down. I was safe for the next election; and the eyes of no politician, let me tell you, are strong enough to see further than the ballot just ahead. On these facts and their deductions, while I would have preferred peace between the Reverend Bronson and the machine, and might have conceded not a little to preserve it, I based no present fears of that earnest gentleman, nor of any fires of politics he might kindle.

And I would have come through as I forejudged, had it not been for that element of the unlooked-for to enter

into the best arranged equation, and which this time
fought against me. There came marching down upon
me a sudden procession of blood in a sort of red lockstep
of death. In it was carried away that boy of my door,
Melting Moses, and I may say that his going clouded
my eye. Gothecore went also; but I felt no sorrow for
the death of that ignobility in blue, since it was the rock
of his murderous, coarse brutality on which I split. There
was a third to die, an innocent and a stranger; however, I
might better give the story of it by beginning with a
different strand.

In that day when the Reverend Bronson and Inspector
McCue worked for the condemnation of those bandits of
Barclay Street, there was one whom they proposed as a
witness when a case should be called in court. This man
had been a waiter in the restaurant which robbed young
Van Flange, and in whose pillage Gothecore himself was
said to have had his share.

After Inspector McCue was put away in the Bronx,
and the Reverend Bronson made to give up his direct
war upon the dens, this would-be witness was arrested
and cast into a cell of the station where Gothecore held
sway. The Reverend Bronson declared that the arrested
one had been seized by order of Gothecore, and for revenge. Gothecore, ignorant, cruel, rapacious, violent,
and with never a glimmer of innate fineness to teach him
those external decencies which go between man and man

as courtesy, gave by his conduct a deal of plausibility to the charge.

" Get out of my station! " cried Gothecore, with a rain of oath upon oath; " get out, or I'll have you chucked out! " This was when the Reverend Bronson demanded the charge on which the former waiter was held. " Do a sneak! " roared Gothecore, as the Reverend Bronson stood in silent indignation. " I'll have no pulpit-thumper doggin' me! You show your mug in here ag'in, an' you'll get th' next cell to that hash-slingin' stoolpigeon of yours. You can bet your life, I aint called Clean Sweep Bill for fun! "

As though this were not enough, there arrived in its wake another bit of news that made me, who was on the threshold of my campaign to retain the town, bite my lip and dig my palms with the anger it unloosed within me. By way of added fuel to flames already high, that once waiter, but the day before prisoner to Gothecore, must be picked up dead in the streets, head club-battered to a pulp.

Who murdered the man?

Half the town said Gothecore.

For myself, I do not care to dwell upon that poor man's butchery, and my veins run fire to only think of it. There arises the less call for elaboration, since within hours—for it was the night of that very day on which the murdered man was found—the life was stricken from

the heart of Gothecore. He, too, was gone; and Melting
Moses had gone with him. By his own choice, this last,
as I have cause to know.

"I'll do him before I'm through!" sobbed Melting
Moses, as he was held back from Gothecore on the occa-
sion when he would have gone foaming for his throat;
"I'll get him, if I have to go wit' him!"

It was the Chief of Police who brought me word. I
had sent for him with a purpose of charges against
Gothecore, preliminary to his dismissal from the force.
Aside from my liking for the Reverend Bronson, and the
resentment I felt for the outrage put upon him, Gothecore must go as a defensive move of politics.

The Chief's eye, when he arrived, popped and stared
with a fishy horror, and for all the coolness of the early
morning his brow showed clammy and damp. I was in
too hot a hurry to either notice or remark on these
phenomena; I reeled off my commands before the visitor
could find a chair.

"You're too late, Gov'nor," returned the Chief,
munching uneasily, his fat jowls working. "For once
in a way, you've gone to leeward of the lighthouse."

"What do you mean?" said I.

Then he told the story; and how Gothecore and Melting Moses were taken from the river not four hours
before.

"It was a fire in th' box factory," said the Chief;

" that factory 'buttin' on th' docks. Gothecore goes down from his station. The night's as dark as the inside of a cow. He's jimmin' along th' edge of th' wharf, an' no one noticin' in particular. Then of a sudden, there's an oath an' a big splash.

" ' Man overboard!' yells some guy.

" The man overboard is Gothecore. Two or three coves come chasin' up to lend a hand.

" ' Some duck jumps after him to save him,' says this party who yells ' overboard!' ' First one, an' then t'other, hits th' water. They oughter be some'ers about.'

" That second party in th' river was Melting Moses. An' say! Gov'nor, he didn't go after Gothecore to save him; not he! Melting Moses had shoved Gothecore in; an' seein' him swimmin' hard, an' likely to get ashore, he goes after him to cinch th' play. I'll tell you one thing: he cinches it. He piles himself on Gothecore's back, an' then he crooks his right arm about Gothecore's neck—the reg'lar garotte hug! an' enough to choke th' life out by itself. That aint th' worst." Here the Chief's voice sunk to a whisper. " Melting Moses had his teeth buried in Gothecore's throat. Did you ever unlock a bulldog from his hold? Well, it was easy money compared to unhookin' Melting Moses from Gothecore. Sure! both was dead as mackerels when they got 'em out; they're on th' ice right now. Oh, well!" concluded the Chief; " I told Gothecore his finish more'n once. ' Don't rough people around

316 THE BOSS

so, Bill,' I'd say; ' you'll dig up more snakes than you
can kill.' But he wouldn't listen; he was all for th'
strong-arm, an' th' knock-about! It's a bad system.
Nothin's lost by bein' smooth, Gov'nor; nothin's lost by
bein' smooth!" and the Chief sighed lugubriously; after
which he mopped his forehead and looked pensively from
the window.

Your river sailor, on the blackest night, will feel the
tide for its ebb or flow by putting his hand in the water.
In a manner of speaking, I could now as plainly feel the
popular current setting against the machine. It was
like a strong flood, and with my experience of the town
and its tempers I knew that we were lost. That murdered man who might have been a witness, and the violence done to the Reverend Bronson, were arguments in
everybody's mouth.

And so the storm fell; the machine was swept away as
by a flood. There was no sleight of the ballot that might
have saved the day; our money proved no defense. The
people fell upon Tammany and crushed it, and the town
went from under my hand.

Morton had seen disaster on its way.

"And, really! I don't half like it," observed that
lounging king of traction. "It will cost me a round
fifty thousand dollars, don't y' know! Of course, I shall
give Tammany the usual fifty thousand, if only for the
memory of old days. But, by Jove! there's those other

chaps.   Now they're going to win, in the language of
our departed friend, Mr. Kennedy, I'll have to ' sweeten '
them.   It's a deuced bore contributing to both parties,
but this time I can't avoid it—really!" and Morton
stared feebly into space, as though the situation held
him helpless with its perplexities.

There is one worth-while matter to be the offspring of
defeat.   A beaten man may tell the names of his friends.
On the day after I scored a victory, my ante-rooms had
been thronged.   Following that disaster to the machine,
just chronicled, I sat as much alone as though Fourteenth Street were the center of a pathless waste.

However, I was not to be wholly deserted.   It was in
the first shadows of the evening, when a soiled bit of
paper doing crumpled duty as a card was brought me.
I glanced at it indifferently.   I had nothing to give;
why should anyone seek me?   There was no name, but
my interest flared up at this line of identification:

" The Man of the Knife! "

CHAPTER XXIII

THE WEDDING OF BLOSSOM

GRAY, weather-worn, beaten of years, there in the door was my Sicilian! I observed, as he took a seat, how he limped, with one leg drawn and distorted. I had him in and gave him a chair.

My Sicilian and I sat looking one upon the other. It was well-nigh the full quarter of a century since I'd clapped eyes on him. And to me the thing marvelous was that I did not hate him. What a procession of disasters, and he to be its origin, was represented in that little weazened man, with his dark skin, monkey face, and eyes to shine like beads! That heart-breaking trial for murder; the death of Apple Cheek; Blossom and the mark of the rope;—all from him! He was the reef upon which my life had been cast away! These thoughts ran in my head like a mill-race; and yet, I felt only a friendly warmth as though he were some good poor friend of long ago.

My Sicilian's story was soon told. He had fallen into the hold of a vessel and broken his leg. It was mended in so bad a fashion that he must now be tied to the shore with it, and never sail again. Could I find him work?—

something, even a little, by which he might have food and shelter? He put this in a manner indescribably plaintive.

Then I took a thought full of the whimsical. I would see how far a beaten Chief of Tammany Hall might command. There were countless small berths about the public offices and courts, where a man might take a meager salary, perhaps five hundred dollars a year, for a no greater service than throwing up a window or arranging the papers on a desk. These were within the appointment of what judges or officers prevailed in the departments or courtrooms to which they belonged. I would offer my Sicilian for one.

And I had a plan. I knew what should be the fate of the fallen. I had met defeat; also, personally, I had been the target of every flinging slander which the enemy might invent. It was a time when men would fear my friendship as much as on another day they had feared my power. I was an Ishmael of politics. The timid and the time-serving would shrink away from me.

There might, however, be found one who possessed the courage and the gratitude, someone whom I had made and who remembered it, to take my orders. I decided to search for such a man. Likewise (and this was my plan) I resolved—for I knew better than most folk how the town would be in my hands again—to make that one mayor when a time should serve.

" Come with me," said I. " You shall have a berth; and I've nothing now to do but seek for it."

There was a somber comicality to the situation which came close to making me laugh—I, the late dictator, abroad begging a five-hundred-dollar place!

Twenty men I went to; and if I had been a leper I could not have filled them with a broader terror. One and all they would do nothing. These fools thought my downfall permanent; they owed everything to me, but forgot it on my day of loss. They were of the flock of that Frenchman who was grateful only for favors to come.· Tarred with the Tammany stick as much as was I, myself, each had turned white in a night, and must mimic mugwumpery, when now the machine was overborne. Many were those whom I marked for slaughter that day; and I may tell you that in a later hour, one and all, I knocked them on the head.

Now in the finish of it, I discovered one of a gallant fidelity, and who was brave above mugwump threat. He was a judge; and, withal, a man indomitably honest. But as it is with many bred of the machine, his instinct was blindly military. Like Old Mike, he regarded politics as another name for war. To the last, he would execute my orders without demur.

With this judge, I left my Sicilian to dust tables and chairs for forty dollars a month. It was the wealth of Dives to the poor broken sailorman, and he thanked me with tears on his face. In a secret, lock-fast compartment of my memory I put away the name of that judge. He should be made first in the town for that one day's work.

My late defeat meant, so far as my private matters were involved, nothing more serious than a jolt to my self-esteem. Nor hardly that, since I did not blame myself for the loss of the election. It was the fortune of battle; and because I had seen it on its way, that shaft of regret to pierce me was not sharpened of surprise.

My fortunes were rolling fat with at least three millions of dollars, for I had not held the town a decade to neglect my own good. If it had been Big Kennedy, now, he would have owned fourfold as much. But I was lavish of habit; besides being no such soul of business thrift as was my old captain. Three millions should carry me to the end of the journey, however, even though I took no more; there would arise no money-worry to bark at me. The loss of the town might thin the flanks of my sub-leaders of Tammany, but the famine could not touch me.

While young Van Flange had been the reason of a deal that was unhappy in my destinies, I had never met the boy. Now I was to see him. Morton sent him to me on an errand of business; he found me in my own house just as dinner was done. I was amiably struck with the look of him. He was tall and broad of shoulder, for he had been an athlete in his college and tugged at an oar in the boat.

My eye felt pleased with young Van Flange from the beginning; he was as graceful as an elm, and with a princely set of the head which to my mind told the story of good blood. His manner, as he met me, became the sublimation of deference, and I could discover in his air a tacit flattery that was as positive, even while as impalpable, as a perfume. In his attitude, and in all he did and said, one might observe the aristocrat. The high strain of him showed as plain as a page of print, and over all a clean delicacy that reminded one of a thoroughbred colt.

While we were together, Anne and Blossom came into the room. This last was a kind of office-place I had at home, where the two often visited with me in the evening.

It was strange, the color that painted itself in the shy face of Blossom. I thought, too, that young Van Flange's interest stood a bit on tiptoe. It flashed over me in a moment:

" Suppose they were to love and wed? "

The question, self-put, discovered nothing rebellious in my breast. I would abhor myself as a matchmaker between a boy and a girl; and yet, if I did not help events, at least, I wouldn't interrupt them. If it were to please Blossom to have him for a husband: why then, God bless the girl, and make her day a fair one!

THE WEDDING OF BLOSSOM

Anne, who was quicker than I, must have read the new glow in Blossom's face and the new shine in her eyes. But her own face seemed as friendly as though the picture gave her no pang, and it reassured me mightily to find it so.

Young Van Flange made no tiresome stay of it on this evening. But he came again, and still again; and once or twice we had him in to dinner. Our table appeared to be more complete when he was there; it served to bring an evenness and a balance, like a ship in trim. Finally he was in and out of the house as free as one of the family.

For the earliest time in life, a quiet brightness shone on Blossom that was as the sun through mists. As for myself, delight in young Van Flange crept upon me like a habit; nor was it made less when I saw how he had a fancy for my girl, and that it might turn to wedding bells. The thought gave a whiter prospect of hope for Blossom; also it fostered my own peace, since my happiness hung utterly by her.

One day I put the question of young Van Flange to Morton.

"Really, now!" said Morton, "I should like him vastly if he had a stronger under jaw, don't y' know. These fellows with chins like cats' are a beastly lot in the long run."

"But his habits are now good," I urged. "And he is industrious, is he not?"

"Of course, the puppy works," responded Morton; "that is, if you're to call pottering at a desk by such a respectable term. As for his habits, they are the habits of a captive. He's prisoner to his poverty. Gad! one can't be so deucedly pernicious, don't y' know, on nine hundred a year." Then, with a burst of eagerness: "I know what you would be thinking. But I say, old chap, you mustn't bank on his blood. Good on both sides, it may be; but the blend is bad. Two very reputable drugs may be combined to make a poison, don't y' know!"

There the matter stuck; for I would not tell Morton of any feeling my girl might have for young Van Flange. However, Morton's view in no wise changed my own; I considered that with the best of motives he might still suffer from some warping prejudice.

There arose a consideration, however, and one I could not look in the face. There was that dread birthmark! —the mark of the rope! At last I brought up the topic of my fears with Anne.

"Will he not loathe her?" said I. "Will his love not change to hate when he knows?"

"Did your love change?" Anne asked.

"But that is not the same."

"Be at peace, then," returned Anne, taking my hand in hers and pressing it. "I have told him. Nor shall I forget the nobleness of his reply: 'I love Blossom,' said he; 'I love her for her heart.'"

When I remember these things, I cannot account for the infatuation of us two—Anne and myself. The blackest villain of earth imposed himself upon us as a saint! And I had had my warning. I should have known that he who broke a mother's heart would break a wife's.

Now when the forces of reform governed the town, affairs went badly for that superlative tribe, and each day offered additional claim for the return of the machine. Government is not meant to be a shepherd of morals. Its primal purposes are of the physical, being no more than to safeguard property and person. That is the theory; more strongly still must it become the practice if one would avoid the enmity of men. He whose morals are looked after by the powers that rule, grows impatient, and in the end, vindictive. No mouth likes the bit; a guardian is never loved. The reform folk made that error against which Old Mike warned Big Kennedy: They got between the public and its beer.

The situation, thus phrased, called for neither intrigue nor labor on my own part. I had but to stay in my chair, and " reform " itself would drive the people into Tammany's arms.

In those days I had but scanty glimpses of the Reverend Bronson. However, he now and then would visit me, and when he did, I think I read in his troubled brow the fear of machine success next time. Morton was there on one occasion when the Reverend Bronson came in. They were well known to one another, these two; also, they were friends as much as men might be whose lives and aims went wide apart.

"Now the trouble," observed Morton, as the two discussed that backward popularity of the present rule, "lies in this: Your purist of politics is never practical. He walks the air; and for a principle, he fixes his eyes on a star. Besides," concluded Morton, tapping the Reverend Bronson's hand with that invaluable eyeglass, "you make a pet, at the expense of statutes more important, of some beggarly little law like the law against gambling."

"My dear sir," exclaimed the Reverend Bronson, "surely you do not defend gambling."

"I defend nothing," said Morton; "it's too beastly tiresome, don't y' know. But, really, the public is no fool; and with a stock-ticker and a bucket shop on every corner, you will hardly excite folk to madness over roulette and policy."

"The policy shops stretch forth their sordid palms for the pennies of the very poor," said the Reverend Bronson earnestly.

"But, my boy," retorted Morton, his drooping inanity gaining a color, "government should be concerned no more about the poor man's penny than the rich man's pound. However, if it be a reason, why not suppress the barrooms? Gad! what more than your doggery reaches for the pennies of the poor?"

"There is truth in what you say," consented the Reverend Bronson regretfully. "Still, I count for but one as an axman in this wilderness of evil; I can fell but one tree at a time. I will tell you this, however: At the gates of you rich ones must lie the blame for most of the immoralities of the town. You are guilty of two wrongs: You are not benevolent; and you set a bad moral example."

"Really!" replied Morton, "I, myself, think the rich a deuced bad lot; in fact, I hold them to be quite as bad as the poor, don't y' know. But you speak of benevolence—alms-giving, and that sort of thing. Now I'm against benevolence. There is an immorality in alms just in proportion as there's a morality to labor. Folk work only because they lack money. Now you give a man ten dollars and the beggar will stop work."

"Let me hear," observed the Reverend Bronson, amused if not convinced, "what your remedy for the town's bad morals would be."

"Work!" replied Morton, with quite a flash of animation. "I'd make every fellow work—rich and poor alike. I'd invent fardels for the idle. The only difference between the rich and the poor is a difference of cooks and tailors—really! Idleness, don't y' know, is everywhere and among all classes the certain seed of vice."

" You would have difficulty, I fear," remarked the Reverend Bronson, " in convincing your gilded fellows of the virtuous propriety of labor."

" I wouldn't convince them, old chap, I'd club them to it. It is a mistake you dominies make, that you are all for persuading when you should be for driving. Gad! you should never coax where you can drive," and Morton smiled vacantly.

" You would deal with men as you do with swine? "

" What should be more appropriate? Think of the points of resemblance. Both are obstinate, voracious, complaining, cowardly, ungrateful, selfish, cruel! One should ever deal with a man on a pig basis. Persuasion is useless, compliment a waste. You might make a bouquet for him—orchids and violets—and, gad! he would eat it, thinking it a cabbage. But note the pleasing, screaming, scurrying difference when you smite him with a brick. Your man and your hog were born knowing all about a brick."

" The rich do a deal of harm," remarked the Reverend Bronson thoughtfully. " Their squanderings, and the brazen spectacle thereof, should be enough of themselves to unhinge the morals of mankind. Think on their selfish vulgar aggressions! I've seen a lake, once the open joy of thousands, bought and fenced to be a play space for one rich man; I've looked on while a village where hundreds lived and loved and had their pleasant

being, died and disappeared to give one rich man room;
in the brag and bluster of his millions, I've beheld a rich
man rearing a shelter for his crazy brain and body, and
borne witness while he bought lumber yards and planing
mills and stone quarries and brick concerns and lime
kilns with a pretense of hastening his building.   It is all
a disquieting example to the poor man looking on.
Such folk, dollar-loose and dollar-mad, frame disgrace
for money, and make the better sentiment of better men
fair loathe the name of dollar.   And yet it is but a sickness, I suppose; a sort of rickets of riches—a Saint Vitus
dance of vast wealth!   Such go far, however, to bear
out your parallel of the swine; and at the best, they but
pile exaggeration on imitation and drink perfumed draff
from trough of gold."

The Reverend Bronson as he gave us this walked up
and down the floor as more than once I'd seen him do when
moved.   Nor did he particularly address himself to
either myself or Morton until the close, when he turned to
that latter personage.   Pausing in his walk, the Reverend
Bronson contemplated Morton at some length; and then,
as if his thoughts on money had taken another path, and
shaking his finger in the manner of one who preferred an
indictment, he said:

" Cato, the Censor, declared: ' It is difficult to save
that city from ruin where a fish sells for more than an ox.'
By the bad practices of your vulgar rich, that, to-day,

is a description of New York. Still, from the public
standpoint, I should not call the luxury it tells of, the
worst effect of wealth, nor the riches which indulge in
such luxury the most baleful riches. There be those
other busy black-flag millions which maraud a people.
They cut their way through bars and bolts of government with the saws and files and acids of their evil influence—an influence whose expression is ever, and simply, bribes. I speak of those millions that purchase the
passage of one law or the downfall of another, and which
buy the people's officers like cattle to their will. But even
as I reproach those criminal millions, I marvel at their
blindness. Cannot such wealth see that in its treasons
—for treason it does as much as any Arnold—it but
undermines itself? Who should need strength and
probity in government, and the shelter of them, more
than Money? And yet in its rapacity without eyes, it
must ever be using the criminal avarice of officials to pick
the stones and mortar from the honest foundations of the
state!"

The Reverend Bronson resumed his walking up and
down. Morton, the imperturbable, lighted a cigarette
and puffed bland puffs as though he in no fashion felt
himself described. Not at all would he honor the notion
that the reverend rhetorician was talking either of him
or at him, in his condemnation of those pirate millions.

"I should feel alarmed for my country," continued the Reverend Bronson, coming back to his chair, "if I did not remember that New York is not the nation, and how a sentiment here is never the sentiment there. The country at large has still its ideals; New York, I fear, has nothing save its appetites."

"To shift discussion," said Morton lightly, "a discussion that would seem academic rather than practical, and coming to the City and what you call its appetites, let me suggest this: Much of that trouble of which you speak arises by faults of politics as the latter science is practiced by the parties. Take yourself and our silent friend." Here Morton indicated me: "Take the two parties you represent. Neither was ever known to propose an onward step. Each of you has for his sole issue the villainies of the other fellow; the whole of your cry is the iniquity of the opposition; it is really! I'll give both of you this for a warning. The future is to see the man who, leaving a past to bury a past, will cry 'Public Ownership!' or some equally engaging slogan. Gad! old chap, with that, the rabble will follow him as the rats followed the pied piper of Hamelin. The moralist and the grafter will both be left, don't y' know!" Morton here returned into that vapidity from which, for the moment, he had shaken himself free. "Gad!" he concluded, "you will never know what a passion to own things gnaws at your peasant in his blouse

and wooden shoes until some prophetic beggar shouts
' Public Ownership!' you won't, really!"

" Sticking to what you term the practical," said the
Reverend Bronson, " tell me wherein our reform administration has weakened itself."

" As I've observed," responded Morton, " you pick out
a law and make a pet of it, to the neglect of criminal
matters more important. It is your fad—your vanity
of party, to do this. Also, it is your heel of Achilles, and
through it will come your death-blow." Then, as if
weary of the serious, Morton went off at a lively tangent:
" Someone—a very good person, too, I think, although
I've mislaid his name—observed: ' Oh, that mine enemy
would write a book!' Now I should make it: ' Oh, that
mine enemy would own a fad!' Given a fellow's fad,
I've got him. Once upon a time, when I had a measure
of great railway moment—really! one of those measures
of black-flag millions, don't y' know!—pending before
the legislature at Albany, I ran into a gentleman whose
name was De Vallier. Most surprising creature, this
De Vallier! Disgustingly honest, too; but above all, as
proud as a Spanish Hidalgo of his name. Said his
ancestors were nobles of France under the Grand Monarch, and that sort of thing. Gad! it was his fad—this
name! And the bitterness wherewith he opposed my measure was positively shameful. Really, if the floor of the
Assembly—the chap was in the Assembly, don't y' know

—were left unguarded for a moment, De Vallier would occupy it, and call everybody but himself a venal rogue of bribes.   There was never anything more shocking!

"But I hit upon an expedient.   If I could but touch his fad—if I might but reach that name of De Vallier, I would have him on the hip.   So with that, don't y' know, I had a bill introduced to change the fellow's name to Dummeldinger.   I did, 'pon my honor!   The Assembly adopted it gladly.   The Senate was about to do the same, when the horrified De Vallier threw himself at my feet. He would die if he were called Dummeldinger!

"The poor fellow's grief affected me very much; my sympathies are easily excited—they are, really!   And Dummeldinger was such a beastly name!   I couldn't withstand De Vallier's pleadings.   I caused the bill changing his name to be withdrawn, and in the fervor of his gratitude, De Vallier voted for that railway measure. It was my kindness that won him; in his relief to escape 'Dummeldinger,' De Vallier was ready to die for me."

It was evening, and in the younger hours I had pulled my chair before the blaze, and was thinking on Apple Cheek, and how I would give the last I owned of money and power to have her by me.   This was no uncommon train; I've seen few days since she died that did not fill my memory with her image.

Outside raged a threshing storm of snow that was like

a threat for bitterness, and it made the sticks in the fire-place snap and sparkle in a kind of stout defiance, as though inviting it to do its worst.

In the next room were Anne and Blossom, and with them young Van Flange. I could hear the murmur of their voices, and at intervals a little laugh from him.

An hour went by; the door between opened, and young Van Flange, halting a bit with hesitation that was not without charm, stepped into my presence. He spoke with grace and courage, however, when once he was launched, and told me his love and asked for Blossom. Then my girl came, and pressed her face to mine. Anne, too, was there, like a blessing and a hope.

They were married:—my girl and young Van Flange. Morton came to my aid; and I must confess that it was he, with young Van Flange, who helped us to bridesmaids and ushers, and what others belong with weddings in their carrying out. I had none upon whom I might call when now I needed wares of such fine sort; while Blossom, for her part, living her frightened life of seclusion, was as devoid of acquaintances or friends among the fashionables as any abbess might have been.

The street was thronged with people when we drove up, and inside the church was such a jam of roses and folk as I had never beheld. Wide was the curious interest in the daughter of Tammany's Chief; and Blossom must have felt it, for her hand fluttered like a bird on my arm as, with organ crashing a wedding march, I led her up the aisle. At the altar rail were the bishop and three priests. And so, I gave my girl away.

When the ceremony was done, we all went back to my house—Blossom's house, since I had put it in her name— for I would have it that they must live with me. I was not to be cheated of my girl; she should not be lost out of my arms because she had found a husband's. It wrought a mighty peace for me, this wedding, showing as it did so sure of happiness to Blossom. Nor will I say it did not feed my pride. Was it a slight thing that the blood of the Clonmel smith should unite itself with a strain, old and proud and blue beyond any in the town? We made one family of it; and when we were settled, my heart filled up with a feeling more akin to content than any that had dwelt there for many a sore day.

CHAPTER XXIV

HOW VAN FLANGE WENT INTO STOCKS

IT was by the suggestion of young Van Flange himself that he became a broker. His argument I think was sound; he had been bred to no profession, and the floor of the Exchange, if he would have a trade, was all that was left him. No one could be of mark or consequence in New York who might not write himself master of millions. Morton himself said that; and with commerce narrowing to a huddle of mammoth corporations, how should anyone look forward to the conquest of millions save through those avenues of chance which Wall Street alone provided? The Stock Exchange was all that remained; and with that, I bought young Van Flange a seat therein, and equipped him for a brokerage career. I harbored no misgivings of his success; no one could look upon his clean, handsome outlines and maintain a doubt.

Those were our happiest days—Blossom's and mine. In her name, I split my fortune in two, and gave young Van Flange a million and a half wherewith to arm his hands for the fray of stocks. Even now, as I look backward through the darkness, I still think it a million and a half well spent. For throughout those slender months of sunshine, Blossom went to and fro about me, radiating a subdued warmth of joy that was like the silent glow of a lamp. Yes, that money served its end. It made Blossom happy, and it will do me good while I live to think how that was so.

Morton, when I called young Van Flange from his Mulberry desk to send him into Wall Street, was filled with distrust of the scheme.

" You should have him stay with Mulberry," said he. " If he do no good, at least he will do no harm, and that, don't y' know, is a business record far above the average. Besides, he's safer; he is, really! "

This I did not like from Morton. He himself was a famous man of stocks, and had piled millions upon millions in a pyramid of speculation. Did he claim for himself a monopoly of stock intelligence? Van Flange was as well taught of books as was he, and came of a better family. Was it that he arrogated to his own head a superiority of wit for finding his way about in those channels of stock value? I said something of this sort to Morton.

" Believe me, old chap," said he, laying his slim hand on my shoulder, " believe me, I had nothing on my mind beyond your own safety, and the safety of that cub of yours. And I think you will agree that I have exhibited a knowledge of what winds and currents and rocks might interrupt or wreck one in his voyages after stocks."

"Admitting all you say," I replied, " it does not follow that another may not know or learn to know as much."

"But Wall Street is such a quicksand," he persisted. "Gad! it swallows nine of every ten who set foot in it. And to deduce safety for another, because I am and have been safe, might troll you into error. You should consider my peculiar case. I was born with beak and claw for the game. Like the fish-hawk, I can hover above the stream of stocks, and swoop in and out, taking my quarry where it swims. And then, remember my arrangements. I have an agent at the elbow of every opportunity. I have made the world my spy, since I pay the highest price for information. If a word be said in a cabinet, I hear it; if a decision of court is to be handed down, I know it; if any of our great forces or monarchs of the street so much as move a finger, I see it. And yet, with all I know, and all I see, and all I hear, and all my nets and snares as complicated as the works of a watch, added to a native genius, the best I may do is win four times in seven. In Wall Street, a man meets with not alone the foreseeable, but the unforeseeable; he does, really! He is like a man in a tempest, and may be struck dead by some cloud-leveled bolt while you and he stand talking, don't y' know!"

Morton fell a long day's journey short of convincing me that Wall Street was a theater of peril for young Van Flange. Moreover, the boy said true; it offered the one way open to his feet. Thus reasoning, and led by my love for my girl and my delight to think how she was happy, I did all I might to further the ambitions of young Van Flange, and embark him as a trader of stocks. He took office rooms in Broad Street; and on the one or two occasions when I set foot in them, I was flattered as well as amazed by the array of clerks and stock-tickers, blackboards, and tall baskets, which met my untaught gaze. The scene seemed to buzz and vibrate with prosperity, and the air was vital of those riches which it promised.

It is scarce required that I say I paid not the least attention to young Van Flange and his business affairs. I possessed no stock knowledge, being as darkened touching Wall Street as any Hottentot. More than that, my time was taken up with Tammany Hall. The flow of general feeling continued to favor a return of the machine, for the public was becoming more and sorely irked of a misfit " reform " that was too tight in one place while too loose in another. There stood no doubt of it; I had only to wait and maintain my own lines in order, and the town would be my own again. It would yet lie in my lap like a goose in the lap of a Dutch woman; and I to feather-line my personal nest with its plumage to what soft extent I would. For all that, I must watch lynx-like my own forces, guarding against schism, keeping my people together solidly for the battle that was to be won.

Much and frequently, I discussed the situation with Morton. With his traction operations, he had an interest almost as deep as my own. He was, too, the one man on whose wisdom of politics I had been educated to rely. When it became a question of votes and how to get them, I had yet to meet Morton going wrong.

"You should have an issue," said Morton. "You should not have two, for the public is like a dog, don't y' know, and can chase no more than just one rabbit at a time. But one you should have—something you could point to and promise for the future. As affairs stand— and gad! it has been that way since I have had a memory —you and the opposition will go into the campaign like a pair of beldame scolds, railing at one another. Politics has become a contest of who can throw the most mud. Really, the town is beastly tired of both of you—it is, 'pon my word!"

"Now what issue would you offer?"

"Do you recall what I told our friend Bronson? Public Ownership should be the great card. Go in for the ownership by the town of street railways, water works, gas plants, and that sort of thing, don't y' know, and the rabble will trample on itself to vote your ticket."

" And do you shout ' Municipal Ownership ! '—you with a street railway to lose? "

" But I wouldn't lose it. I'm not talking of anything but an issue. It would be a deuced bore, if Public Ownership actually were to happen. Besides, for me to lose my road would be the worst possible form! No, I'm not so insane as that. But it doesn't mean, because you make Public Ownership an issue, that you must bring it about. There are always ways to dodge, don't y' know. And the people won't care; the patient beggars have been taught to expect it. An issue is like the bell-ringing before an auction; it is only meant to call a crowd. Once the auction begins, no one remembers the bell-ringing; they don't, really! "

" To simply shout ' Public Ownership!'" said I, " would hardly stir the depths. We would have to get down to something practical—something definite."

" It was the point I was approaching. Really! what should be better now than to plainly propose—since the route is unoccupied, and offers a field of cheapest experiment—a street railway with a loop around Washington Square, and then out Fifth Avenue to One Hundred and Tenth Street, next west on One Hundred and Tenth Street to Seventh Avenue, and lastly north on Seventh Avenue until you strike the Harlem River at the One Hundred and Fifty-fifth Street bridge? "

" What a howl would go up from Fifth Avenue!"
said I.

" If it were so, what then?   You are not to be injured
by silk-stocking clamor.   For each cry against you from
the aristocrats, twenty of the peasantry would come crying to your back; don't y' know!   Patrician opposition,
old chap, means ever plebeian support, and you should do
all you may, with wedge and maul of policy, to split the
log along those lines.   Gad!" concluded Morton, burst-
ing suddenly into self-compliments; " I don't recall when
I was so beastly sagacious before—really!"

" Now I fail to go with you," I returned.   " I have
for long believed that the strongest force with which the
organization had to contend, was its own lack of fashion.
If Tammany had a handful or two of that purple and fine
linen with which you think it so wise to quarrel, it might
rub some of the mud off itself, and have quieter if not
fairer treatment from a press, ever ready to truckle to
the town's nobility.   Should we win next time, it is already in my plans to establish a club in the very heart of
Fifth Avenue.   I shall attract thither all the folk of
elegant fashion I can, so that, thereafter, should one snap
a kodak on the machine, the foreground of the picture
will contain a respectable exhibition of lofty names.   I
want, rather, to get Tammany out of the gutter, than
arrange for its perpetual stay therein."

" Old chap," said Morton, glorying through his eyeglass, "I think I shall try a cigarette after that. I need it to resettle my nerves; I do, really. Why, my dear boy! do you suppose that Tammany can be anything other than that unwashed black sheep it is? We shall make bishops of burglars when that day dawns. The thing's wildly impossible, don't y' know! Besides, your machine would die. Feed Tammany Hall on any diet of an aristocracy, and you will unhinge its stomach; you will, 'pon my faith!"

"You shall see a Tammany club in fashion's center, none the less."

"Then you don't like ' Public Ownership? ' " observed Morton, after a pause, the while twirling his eyeglass. "Why don't you then go in for cutting the City off from the State, and making a separate State of it? You could say that we suffer from hayseed tyranny, and all that. Really! it's the truth, don't y' know; and besides, we City fellows would gulp it down like spring water."

"The City delegation in Albany," said I, "is too small to put through such a bill. The Cornfields would be a unit to smother it."

"Not so sure about the Cornfields!" cried Morton. "Of course it would take money. That provided, think of the wires you could pull. Here are a half-dozen railroads, with their claws and teeth in the country and their tails in town. Each of them, don't y' know, as part of its equipment, owns a little herd of rustic members. You could step on the railroad tail with the feet of your fifty city departments, and torture it into giving you its hayseed marionettes for this scheme of a new State. 'Pon my word! old chap, it could be brought about; it could, really!"

" I fear," said I banteringly, " that after all you are no better than a harebrained theorist. I confess that your plans are too grand for my commonplace powers of execution. I shall have to plod on with those mossgrown methods which have served us in the past."

It would seem as though I had had Death to be my neighbor from the beginning, for his black shadow was in constant play about me. One day he would take a victim from out my very arms; again he would grimly step between me and another as we sat in talk. Nor did doctors do much good or any; and I have thought that all I shall ask, when my own time comes, is a nurse to lift me in and out of bed, and for the rest of it, why! let me die.

It was Anne to leave me now, and her death befell like lightning from an open sky. Anne was never of your robust women; I should not have said, however, that she was frail, since she was always about, taking the whole weight of the house to herself, and, as I found when she was gone, furnishing the major portion of its cheerfulness. That was what misled me, doubtless; a brave smile shone ever on her face like sunlight, and served to put me off from any thought of sickness for her.

It was her heart, they said; but no such slowness in striking as when Big Kennedy died. Anne had been abroad for a walk in the early cool of the evening. When she returned, and without removing her street gear, she sank into a chair in the hall.

" What ails ye, mem? " asked the old Galway wife that had been nurse to Blossom, and who undid the door to Anne; " what's the matter of your pale face? "

" An' then," cried the crone, when she gave me the sorry tale of it, " she answered wit' a sob. An' next her poor head fell back on the chair, and she was by."

Both young Van Flange and I were away from the house at the time of it; he about his business, which kept him often, and long, into the night; and I in the smothering midst of my politics. When I was brought home, they had laid Anne's body on her bed. At the foot on a rug crouched the old nurse, rocking herself forward and back, wailing like a banshee. Blossom, whose cheek was whitened with the horror of our loss, crept to my side and stood close, clutching my hand as in those old terror-ridden baby days when unseen demons glowered from the room-corners. It was no good sight for Blossom, and I led her away, the old Galway crone at the bed's foot keening her barbarous mourning after us far down the hall.

Blossom was all that remained with me now. And yet, she would be enough, I thought, as I held her, child-fashion, in my arms that night to comfort her, if only I might keep her happy.

Young Van Flange worked at his trade of stocks like a horse. He was into it early and late, sometimes staying from home all night. I took pride to think how much more wisely than Morton I had judged the boy.

Those night absences, when he did not come in until three of the morning, and on occasion not at all, gave me no concern. My own business of Tammany was quite as apt to hold me; for there are events that must be dealt with in the immediate, like shooting a bird on the wing. A multitude of such were upon me constantly, and there was no moment of the day or night that I could say beforehand would not be claimed by them. When this was my own case, it turned nothing difficult to understand how the exigencies of stocks might be as peremptory.

One matter to promote a growing fund of confidence in young Van Flange was his sobriety. The story ran—and, in truth, his own mother had told it—of his drunkenness, when a boy fresh out of his books, and during those Barclay Street days when he went throwing his patrimony to the vultures. That was by and done with; he had somehow gotten by the bottle. Never but once did he show the flush of liquor, and that fell out when he had been to a college dinner. I had always understood how it was the custom to retire drunk from such festivals, wherefore that particular inebriety gave me scant uneasiness. One should not expect a roaring boy about town to turn deacon in a day.

Blossom was, as I've said, by nature shy and secret, and never one to relate her joys or griefs. While she and he were under the same roof with me, I had no word from her as to her life with young Van Flange, and whether it went bright, or was blurred of differences. Nor do I believe that in those days there came aught to harrow her, unless it were the feeling that young Van Flange showed less the lover and more like folk of fifty than she might have wished.

Once and again, indeed, I caught on her face a passing shade; but her eyes cleared when I looked at her, and she would come and put her arms about me, and by that I could not help but see how her marriage had flowered life's path for her. This thought of itself would set off a tune in my heart like the songs of birds; and I have it the more sharply upon my memory, because it was the one deep happiness I knew. The shadows I trapped as they crossed the brow of Blossom, I laid to a thought that young Van Flange carried too heavy a load of work. It might break him in his health; and the fear had warrant in hollow eyes and a thin sallowness of face, which piled age upon him, and made him resemble twice his years.

Towards me, the pose of young Van Flange was that

one of repectful deference which had marked him from the start. Sometimes I was struck by the notion that he was afraid of me; not with any particularity of alarm, but as a woman might fear a mastiff, arguing peril from latent ferocities and a savagery of strength.

Still, he in no wise ran away; one is not to understand that; on the contrary he would pass hours in my society, explaining his speculations and showing those figures which were the record of his profits. I was glad to listen, too; for while I did not always grasp a meaning, being stock-dull as I've explained, what he said of " bull " and " bear " and " short " and " long," had the smell of combat about it, and held me enthralled like a romance.

There were instances when he suggested speculations, and now and then as high as one thousand shares. I never failed to humor him, for I thought a negative might smack of lack of confidence—a thing I would not think of, if only for love of Blossom. I must say that my belief in young Van Flange was augmented by these deals, which turned unflaggingly, though never largely, to my credit.

It was when I stood waist-deep in what arrangements were preliminary to my battle for the town, now drawing near and nearer, that young Van Flange approached me concerning Blackberry Traction.

" Father," said he—for he called me " father," and

the name was pleasant to my ear—" father, if you will, we may make millions of dollars like turning hand or head."

Then he gave me a long story of the friendship he had scraped together with the president of Blackberry—he of the Hebrew cast and clutch, whom I once met and disappointed over franchises.

" Of course," said young Van Flange, " while he is the president of Blackberry, he has no sentimental feelings concerning the fortunes of the company. He is as sharp to make money as either you or I. The truth is this: While the stock is quoted fairly high, Blackberry in fact is in a bad way. It is like a house of cards, and a kick would collapse it into ruins. The president, because we are such intimates, gave me the whole truth of Blackberry. Swearing me to secrecy, he, as it were, lighted a lantern, and led me into the darkest corners. He showed me the books. Blackberry is on the threshold of a crash. The dividends coming due will not be paid. It is behind in its interest; and the directors will be driven to declare an immense issue of bonds. Blackberry stock will fall below twenty; a receiver will have the road within the year. To my mind, the situation is ready for a coup. We have but to sell and keep selling, to take in what millions we will."

There was further talk, and all to similar purpose. Also, I recalled the ease with which Morton and I,

aforetime, took four millions between us out of Blackberry.

"Now I think," said I, in the finish of it, "that
Blackberry is my gold mine by the word of Fate itself.
Those we are to make will not be the first riches I've
had from it."

Except the house we stood in, I owned no real estate;
nor yet that, since it was Blossom's, being her marriage
gift from me. From the first I had felt an aversion for
houses and lots. I was of no stomach to collect rents,
squabble with tenants over repairs, or race to magis-
trates for eviction. This last I should say was the Irish
in my arteries, for landlords had hectored my ancestors
like horseflies. My wealth was all in stocks and bonds;
nor would I listen to anything else. Morton had his own
whimsical explanation for this:

"There be those among us," said he, "who are
nomads by instinct—a sort of white Arab, don't y' know.
Not intending offense—for, gad! there are reasons why
I desire to keep you good-natured—every congenital
criminal is of that sort; he is, really! Such folk instinctively look forward to migration or flight. They
want nothing they can't pack up and depart with in a
night, and would no more take a deed to land than a dose
of arsenic. It's you who are of those migratory people.
That's why you abhor real estate. Fact, old chap!
you're a born nomad; and it's in your blood to be

ever ready to strike camp, inspan your teams, and trek."

Morton furnished these valuable theories when he was investing my money for me. Having no belief in my own investment wisdom, I imposed the task upon his good nature. One day he brought me my complete possessions in a wonderful sheaf of securities. They were edged, each and all, with gold, since Morton would accept no less.

"There you are, my boy," said he, "and everything as clean as running water, don't y' know. Really, I didn't think you could be trusted, if it came on to blow a panic, so I've bought for you only stuff that can protect itself."

When young Van Flange made his Blackberry suggestions, I should say I had sixteen hundred thousand dollars worth of these bonds and stocks—mostly the former—in my steel box. I may only guess concerning it, for I could not reckon so huge a sum to the precise farthing. It was all in the same house with us; I kept it in a safe I'd fitted into the walls, and which was so devised as to laugh at either a burglar or a fire. I gave young Van Flange the key of that interior compartment which held these securities; the general combination he already possessed.

"There you'll find more than a million and a half," said I, "and that, with what you have, should make three millions. How much Blackberry can you sell now?"

" We ought to sell one hundred and fifty thousand shares. A drop of eighty points, and it will go that far, would bring us in twelve millions."

" Do what you think best," said I. " And, mind you: No word to Morton."

" Now I was about tó suggest that," said young Van Flange.

Morton should not know what was on my slate for Blackberry. Trust him? yes; and with every hope I had. But it was my vanity to make this move without him. I would open his eyes to it, that young Van Flange, if not so old a sailor as himself, was none the less his equal at charting a course and navigating speculation across that sea of stocks, about the treacherous dangers whereof it had pleased him so often to patronize me.

CHAPTER XXV

PROFIT AND LOSS; MAINLY THE LATTER

SINCE time began, no man, not even a king, has been better obeyed in his mandates, than was I while Chief of Tammany Hall. From high to low, from the leader of a district to the last mean straggler in the ranks, one and all, they pulled and hauled or ran and climbed like sailors in a gale, at the glance of my eye or the toss of my finger. More often than once, I have paused in wonder over this blind submission, and asked myself the reason. Particularly, since I laid down my chiefship, the query has come upon my tongue while I remembered old days, to consider how successes might have been more richly improved or defeats, in their disasters, at least partially avoided.

Nor could I give myself the answer. I had no close friendships among my men; none of them was my confidant beyond what came to be demanded of the business in our hands. On the contrary, there existed a gulf between me and those about me, and while I was civil—for I am not the man, and never was, of wordy violences—I can call myself nothing more.

If anything, I should say my people of politics feared

353

me, and that a sort of sweating terror was the spur to send them flying when I gave an order. There was respect, too; and in some cases a kind of love like a dog's love, and which is rather the homage paid by weakness to strength, or that sentiment offered of the vine to the oak that supports its clamberings.

Why my men should stand in awe of me, I cannot tell. Certainly, I was mindful of their rights; and, with the final admonitions of Big Kennedy in my ears, I avoided favoritisms and dealt out justice from an even hand. True, I could be stern when occasion invited, and was swift to destroy that one whose powers did not match his duty, or who for a bribe would betray, or for an ambition would oppose, my plan.

No; after Big Kennedy's death, I could name you none save Morton whose advice I cared for, or towards whom I leaned in any thought of confidence. Some have said that this distance, which I maintained between me and my underlings, was the secret of my strength. It may have been; and if it were I take no credit, since I expressed nothing save a loneliness of disposition, and could not have borne myself otherwise had I made the attempt. Not that I regretted it. That dumb concession of themselves to me, by my folk of Tammany, would play no little part in pulling down a victory in the great conflict wherein we were about to engage.

Tammany Hall was never more sharply organized. I

worked over the business like an artist over an etching. Discipline was brought to a pitch never before known. My district leaders were the pick of the covey, and every one, for force and talents of executive kind, fit to lead a brigade into battle. Under these were the captains of election precincts; and a rank below the latter came the block captains—one for each city block. Thus were made up those wheels within wheels which, taken together, completed the machine. They fitted one with the other, block captains with precinct captains, the latter with district leaders, and these last with myself; and all like the wheels and springs and ratchets and regulators of a clock; one sure, too, when wound and oiled and started, to strike the hours and announce the time of day in local politics with a nicety that owned no precedent.

There would be a quartette of tickets; I could see that fact of four corners in its approach, long months before the conventions. Besides the two regular parties, and the mugwump-independents—which tribe, like the poor, we have always with us—the laborites would try again. These had not come to the field in any force since that giant uprising when we beat them down with the reputable old gentleman. Nor did I fear them now. My trained senses told me, as with thumb on wrist I counted the public pulse, how those clans of labor were not so formidable by three-fourths as on that other day a decade and more before.

Of those three camps of politics set over against us, that one to be the strongest was the party of reform. This knowledge swelled my stock of courage, already mounting high. If it were no more than to rout the administration now worrying the withers of the town, why, then! the machine was safe to win.

There arose another sign. As the days ran on, rich and frequent, first from one big corporation and then another—and these do not give until they believe—the contributions of money came rolling along. They would buy our favor in advance of victory. These donations followed each other like billows upon a beach, and each larger than the one before, which showed how the wind of general confidence was rising in our favor. It was not, therefore, my view alone; but, by this light of money to our cause, I could see how the common opinion had begun to gather head that the machine was to take the town again.

This latter is often a decisive point, and one to give victory of itself. The average of intelligence and integrity in this city of New York is lower than any in the land. There are here, in proportion to a vote, more people whose sole principle is the bandwagon, than in any other town between the oceans. These " sliders," who go hither and yon, and attach themselves to this standard or ally themselves with that one, as the eye of their fancy is caught and taught by some fluttering

signal of the hour to pick the winning side, are enough
of themselves to decide a contest. Wherefore, to promote this advertisement among creatures of chameleon
politics, of an approaching triumph for the machine, and
it being possible because of those contributed thousands
coming so early into my chests, I began furnishing funds
to my leaders and setting them to the work of their
regions weeks before the nearest of our enemies had begun to think on his ticket.

There was another argument for putting out this
money. The noses of my people had been withheld from
the cribs of office for hungry months upon months. The
money would arouse an appetite and give their teeth an
edge. I looked for fine work, too, since the leanest
wolves are ever foremost in the hunt.

Emphatically did I lay it upon my leaders that, man
for man, they must count their districts. They must tell
over each voter as a churchman tells his beads. They
must give me a true story of the situation, and I promised grief to him who brought me mistaken word. I will
say in their compliment that, by the reports of my leaders
on the day before the poll, I counted the machine majority exact within four hundred votes; and that, I may tell
you, with four tickets in the conflict, and a whole count
which was measured by hundreds of thousands, is no light
affair. I mention it to evidence the hair-line perfection
to which the methods of the machine had been brought.

More than one leader reported within five votes of his majority, and none went fifty votes astray.

You think we overdid ourselves to the point ridiculous, in this breathless solicitude of preparation? Man! the wealth of twenty Ophirs hung upon the hazard. I was in no mood to lose, if skill and sleepless forethought, and every intrigue born of money, might serve to bring success.

Morton—that best of prophets!—believed in the star of the machine.

" This time," said he, " I shall miss the agony of contributing to the other fellows, don't y' know. It will be quite a relief—really! I must say, old chap, that I like the mugwump less and less the more I see of him. He's so deucedly respectable, for one thing! Gad! there are times when a mugwump carries respectability to a height absolutely incompatible with human existence. Besides, he is forever walking a crack and calling it a principle. I get tired of a chalkline morality. It's all such deuced rot; it bores me to death; it does, really! One begins to appreciate the amiable, tolerant virtues of easy, old-shoe vice."

Morton, worn with this long harangue, was moved to recruit his moody energies with the inevitable cigarette. He puffed recuperative puffs for a space, and then he began :

"What an angelic ass is this city of New York!

Why! it doesn't know as much as a horse! Any ignorant teamster of politics can harness it, and haul with it, and head it what way he will. I say, old chap, what are the round-number expenses of the town a year?"

" About one hundred and twenty-five millions."

" One hundred and twenty-five millions—really! Do you happen to know the aggregate annual profits of those divers private companies that control and sell us our water, and lighting, and telephone, and telegraph, and traction services?—saying nothing of ferries, and paving, and all that? It's over one hundred and fifty millions a year, don't y' know! More than enough to run the town without a splinter of tax—really! That's why I exclaim in rapture over the public's accommodating imbecility. Now, if a private individual were to manage his affairs so much like a howling idiot, his heirs would clap him in a padded cell, and serve the beggar right."

" I think, however," said I, " that you have been one to profit by those same idiocies of the town."

" Millions, my boy, millions! And I'm going in for more, don't y' know. There are a half-dozen delicious things I have my eye on. Gad! I shall have my hand on them, the moment you take control."

" I make you welcome in advance," said I. " Give me but the town again, and you shall pick and choose."

In season, I handed my slate of names to the nominating committee to be handed by them to the convention,

At the head, for the post of mayor, was written the name of that bold judge who, in the presence of my enemies and on a day when I was down, had given my Sicilian countenance. Such folk are the choice material of the machine. Their characters invite the public; while, for their courage, and that trick to be military and go with closed eyes to the execution of an order, the machine can rely upon them through black and white. My judge when mayor would accept my word for the last appointment and the last contract in his power, and think it duty.

And who shall say that he would err? It was the law of the machine; he was the man of the machine; for the public, which accepted him, he was the machine. It is the machine that offers for every office on the list; the ticket is but the manner or, if you please, the mask. Nor is this secret. Who shall complain then, or fasten him with charges, when my judge, made mayor, infers a public's instruction to regard himself as the vizier of the machine? —its hand and voice for the town's government?

It stood the day before the polls, and having advantage of the usual lull I was resting myself at home. Held fast by the hooks of politics, I for weeks had not seen young Van Flange, and had gotten only glimpses of Blossom. While lounging by my fire—for the day was raw, with a wind off the Sound that smelled of winter— young Van Flange drove to the door in a brougham.

That a brisk broker should visit his house at an hour when the floor of the Exchange was tossing with speculation, would be the thing not looked for; but I was too much in a fog of politics, and too ignorant of stocks besides, to make the observation. Indeed, I was glad to see the boy, greeting him with a trifle more warmth than common.

Now I thought he gave me his hand with a kind of shiver of reluctance. This made me consider. Plainly, he was not at ease as we sat together. Covering him with the tail of my eye, I could note how his face carried a look, at once timid and malignant.

I could not read the meaning, and remained silent a while with the mere riddle of it. Was he ill? The lean yellowness of his cheek, and the dark about the hollow eyes, were a hint that way, to which the broken stoop of the shoulders gave added currency.

Young Van Flange continued silent; not, however, in a way to promise sullenness, but as though his feelings were a gag to him. At last I thought, with a word of my own, to break the ice.

"How do you get on with your Blackberry?" said I.

It was not that I cared or had the business on the back of my mind; I was too much buried in my campaign for that; but Blackberry, with young Van Flange, was the one natural topic to propose.

As I gave him the name of it, he started with the sudden nervousness of a cat. I caught the hissing intake of his breath, as though a knife pierced him. What was wrong? I had not looked at the reported quotations, such things being as Greek to me. Had he lost those millions? I could have borne it if he had; the better, perhaps, since I was sure in my soul that within two days I would have the town in hand, and I did not think to find my old paths so overgrown but what I'd make shift to pick my way to a second fortune.

I was on the hinge of saying so, when he got possession of himself. Even at that he spoke lamely, and with a tongue that fumbled for words.

" Oh, Blackberry!" cried he. Then, after a gulping pause: " That twist will work through all right. It has gone a trifle slow, because, by incredible exertions, the road did pay its dividends. But it's no more than a matter of weeks when it will come tumbling."

This, in the beginning, was rambled off with stops and halts, but in the wind-up it went glibly enough.

What next I would have said, I cannot tell; nothing of moment, one may be sure, for my mind was running on other things than Blackberry up or down. It was at this point, however, when we were interrupted. A message arrived that asked my presence at headquarters.

As I was about to depart, Blossom came into the room.

I had no more than time for a hurried kiss, for the need set forth in the note pulled at me like horses.

"Bar accidents," said I, as I stood in the door, " to-morrow night we'll celebrate a victory."

Within a block of my gate, I recalled how I had left certain papers I required lying on the table. I went back in some hustle of speed, for time was pinching as to that question of political detail which tugged for attention.

As I stepped into the hallway, I caught the tone of young Van Flange and did not like the pitch of it.   Blossom and he were in the room to the left, and only a door between us.

In a strange bristle of temper, I stood still to hear. Would the scoundrel dare harshness with my girl?   The very surmise turned me savage to the bone!

Young Van Flange was speaking of those two hundred thousand dollars in bonds with which, by word of Big Kennedy, I had endowed Blossom in a day of baby-hood. When she could understand, I had laid it solemnly upon her never to part with them. Under any stress, they would insure her against want; they must never be given up. And Blossom had promised.

These bonds were in a steel casket of their own, and Blossom had the key. As I listened, young Van Flange was demanding they be given to him; Blossom was pleading with him, and quoting my com-

mands. My girl was sobbing, too, for the villain urged
the business roughly. I could not fit my ear to every
word, since their tones for the most were dulled to a murmur by the door. In the end, with a lift of the voice, I
heard him say:

"For what else should I marry you except money?
Is one of my blood to link himself with the daughter of
the town's great thief, and call it love? The daughter of
a murderer, too!" he exclaimed, and ripping out an oath.
"A murderer, yes! You have the red proof about your
throat! Because your father escaped hanging by the
laws of men, heaven's law is hanging you!"

As I threw wide the door, Blossom staggered and fell
to the floor. I thought for the furious blink of the moment, that he had struck her. How much stronger is hate
than love! My dominant impulse was to avenge Blossom
rather than to save her. I stood in the door in a white
flame of wrath that was like the utter anger of a tiger.
I saw him bleach and shrink beneath his sallowness.

As I came towards him, he held up his hands after the
way of a boxing school. That ferocious strength, like a
gorilla's, still abode with me. I brushed away his guard
as one might put aside a trailing vine. In a flash I had
him, hip and shoulder. My fingers sunk into the flesh
like things of steel; he squeaked and struggled as does
the rabbit when crunched up by the hound.

With a swing and a heave that would have torn out a

tree by its roots, I lifted him from his feet. The next moment I hurled him from me. He crashed against the casing of the door; then he slipped to the floor as though struck by death itself.

Moved of the one blunt purpose of destruction, I made forward to seize him again. For a miracle of luck, I was withstood by one of the servants who rushed in.

"Think, master; think what you do!" he cried.

In a sort of whirl I looked about me. I could see how the old Galway nurse was bending over Blossom, crying on her for her "Heart's dearie!" My poor girl was lying along the rug like some tempest-broken flower. The stout old wife caught her up and bore her off in her arms.

The picture of my girl's white face set me ablaze again. I turned the very torch of rage!

"Be wise, master!" cried that one who had restrained me before. "Think of what you do!"

The man's hand on my wrist, and the earnest voice of him, brought me to myself. A vast calm took me, as a storm in its double fury beats flat the surface of the sea. I turned my back and walked to the window.

"Have him away, then!" cried I. "Have him out of my sight, or I'll tear him to rags and ribbons where he lies!"

CHAPTER XXVI

THE VICTOR AND THE SPOILS

FOR all the cry and call of politics, and folk to see me whom I would not see, that night, and throughout the following day—and even though the latter were one of election Fate to decide for the town's mastery—I never stirred from Blossom's side. She, poor child! was as one desolate, dazed with the blow that had been dealt her. She lay on her pillow, silent, and with the stricken face that told of the heart-blight fallen upon her.

Nor was I in much more enviable case, although gifted of a rougher strength to meet the shock. Indeed, I was taught by a despair that preyed upon me, how young Van Flange had grown to be the keystone of my arch of single hope, now fallen to the ground. Blossom's happiness had been my happiness, and when her breast was pierced, my own brightness of life began to bleed away. Darkness took me in the folds of it as in a shroud; I would have found the grave kinder, but I must remain to be what prop and stay I might to Blossom.

While I sat by my girl's bed, there was all the time a peril that kept plucking at my sleeve in a way of warn-

ing. My nature is of an inveterate kind that, once afire
and set to angry burning, goes on and on in ever increasing flames like a creature of tow, and with me helpless to
smother or so much as half subdue the conflagration. I
was so aware of myself in that dangerous behalf that it
would press upon me as a conviction, even while I held my
girl's hand and looked into her vacant eye, robbed of
a last ray of any peace to come, that young Van Flange
must never stray within my grasp. It would bring down his
destruction ; it would mean red hands for me and nothing
short of murder.   And, so, while I waited by Blossom's
side, and to blot out the black chance of it, I sent word
for Inspector McCue.

The servants, on that day of awful misery, conveyed
young Van Flange from the room.   When he had been
revived, and his injuries dressed—for his head bled from
a gash made by the door, and his shoulder had been
dislocated—he was carried from the house by the
brougham that brought him, and which still waited at the
gate.   No one about me owned word of his whereabouts.
It was required that he be found, not more for his sake
than my own, and his destinies disposed of beyond my
reach.

It was to this task I would set Inspector McCue.   For
once in a way, my call was for an honest officer. I would
have Inspector McCue discover young Van Flange, and
caution him out of town.   I cared not where he went, so

that he traveled beyond the touch of my fingers, already itching for the caitiff neck of him.

Nor did I think young Van Flange would resist the advice of Inspector McCue. He had reasons for flight other than those I would furnish. The very papers, shouted in the streets to tell how I had re-taken the town at the polls, told also of the failure of the brokerage house of Van Flange; and that young Van Flange, himself, was a defaulter and his arrest being sought by clients on a charge of embezzling the funds which had been intrusted to his charge. The man was a fugitive from justice; he lay within the menace of a prison; he would make no demur now when word and money were given him to take himself away.

When Inspector McCue arrived, I greeted him with face of granite. He should have no hint of my agony. I went bluntly to the core of the employ; to dwell upon the business would be nothing friendly to my taste.

" You know young Van Flange? " Inspector McCue gave a nod of assent.

" And you can locate him? "

" The proposition is so easy it's a pushover."

" Find him, then, and send him out of the town; and for a reason, should he ask one, you may say that I shall slay him should we meet."

Inspector McCue looked at me curiously. He elevated his brow, but in the end he said nothing, whether of inquiry or remark. Without a reply he took himself away. My face, at the kindliest, was never one to speak of confidences or invite a question, and I may suppose the expression of it, as I dealt with Inspector McCue, to have been more than commonly repellent.

There abode another with whom I wanted word; that one was Morton; for hard by forty years he had not once failed me in a strait. I would ask him the story of those Blackberry stocks. A glance into my steel box had showed me the bottom as bare as winter boughs. The last scrap was gone; and no more than the house that covered us, and those two hundred thousand dollars in bonds that were Blossom's, to be left of all our fortune.

My temper was not one to mourn for any loss of money; and yet in this instance I would have those steps that led to my destruction set forth to me. If it were the president of Blackberry Traction who had taken my money, I meditated reprisal. Not that I fell into any heat of hatred against him; he but did to me what Morton and I a few years further back had portioned out to him. For all that, I was coldly resolved to have my own again. I intended no stock shifts; I would not seek Wall Street for my revenge. I knew a sharper method and a surer. It might glisten less with elegance, but it would prove more secure. But first, I would have the word of Morton.

That glass of exquisite fashion and mold of proper

form, albeit something grizzled, and like myself a trifle
dimmed of time, tendered his congratulations upon my
re-conquest of the town. I drew him straight to my
affair of Blackberry.

"Really, old chap," said Morton, the while plaintively
disapproving of me through those eyeglasses, so official
in his case, "really, old chap, you walked into a trap, and
one a child should have seen. That Blackberry fellow
had the market rigged, don't y' know. I could have
saved you, but, my boy, I didn't dare. You've such a
beastly temper when anyone saves you. Besides, it isn't
good form to wander into the stock deals of a gentleman,
and begin to tell him what he's about; it isn't, really."

"But what did this Blackberry individual do?" I
persisted.

"Why, he let you into a corner, don't y' know! He
had been quietly buying Blackberry for months. He
had the whole stock of the road in his safe; and you, in
the most innocent way imaginable, sold thousands of
shares. Now when you sell a stock, you must buy; you
must, really! And there was no one from whom to buy
save our sagacious friend. Gad! as the business stood,
old chap, he might have had the coat off your back!"
And Morton glared in horror over the disgrace of the
situation.

While I took no more than a glimmer of Morton's
meaning, two things were made clear. The Blackberry

president had stripped me of my millions; and he had laid a snare to get them.

" Was young Van Flange in the intrigue? "

" Not in the beginning, at least. There was no need, don't y' know. His hand was already into your money up to the elbow."

" What do you intend by saying that young Van Flange was not in the affair in the beginning? "

" The fact is, old chap, one or two things occurred that led me to think that young Van Flange discovered the trap after he'd sold some eight or ten thousand shares. There was a halt, don't y' know, in his operations. Then later he went on and sold you into bankruptcy. I took it from young Van Flange's manner that the Blackberry fellow might have had some secret hold upon him, and either threatened him, or promised him, or perhaps both, to get him to go forward with his sales; I did, really. Young Van Flange didn't, in the last of it, conduct himself like a free moral or, I should say, immoral agent."

" I can't account for it," said I, falling into thought; " I cannot see how young Van Flange could have been betrayed into the folly you describe."

" Why then," said Morton, a bit wearily, " I have but to say over what you've heard from me before. Young Van Flange was in no sort that man of gifts you held him to be; now really, he wasn't, don't y' know! Anyone might have hoodwinked him. Besides, he didn't keep up with the markets. While I think it beastly bad form to go talking against a chap when he's absent, the truth is, the weak-faced beggar went much more to Barclay than to Wall Street. However, that is only hearsay; I didn't follow young Van Flange to Barclay Street nor meet him across a faro layout by way of verification."

Morton was right; and I was to hear a worse tale, and that from Inspector McCue.

"Would have been here before," said Inspector McCue when he came to report, "but I wanted to see our party aboard ship, and outside Sandy Hook light, so that I might report the job cleaned up."

Then clearing his throat, and stating everything in the present tense, after the police manner, Inspector McCue went on.

"When you ask me can I locate our party, I says to myself, 'Sure thing!' and I'll put you on to why. Our party is a dope fiend; it's a horse to a hen at that very time he can be turned up in some Chink joint."

"Opium?" I asked in astonishment. I had never harbored the thought.

"Why, sure! That's the reason he shows so sallow about the gills, and with eyes like holes burnt in a blanket. When he lets up on the bottle, he shifts to hop."

"Go on," said I.

" Now," continued Inspector McCue, " I thought I
knew the joint in which to find our party.   One evenin',
three or four years ago, when the Reverend Bronson and
I are lookin' up those Barclay Street crooks, I see our
party steerin' into Mott Street.   I goes after him, and
comes upon him in a joint where he's hittin' the pipe.
The munk who runs it has just brought him a layout,
and is cookin' the pill for him when I shoves in.

" Now when our party is in present trouble, I puts it
to myself, that he's sure to be goin' against the pipe.
It would be his idea of gettin' cheerful, see !   So I chases
for the Mott Street hang-out, and there's our party sure
enough, laid out on a mat, and a roll of cotton batting
under his head for a pillow.   He's in the skies, so my
plan for a talk right then is all off.   The air of the
place is that thick with hop it would have turned the
point of a knife, but I stays and plays my string out
until he can listen and talk.

" When our party's head is again on halfway
straight, and he isn't such a dizzy Willie, I puts it to
him that he'd better do a skulk.

" ' You're wanted,' says I, ' an' as near as I make the
size-up, you'll take about five spaces if you're brought to
trial.   You'd better chase ; and by way of the Horn, at
that.   If you go cross-lots, you might get the collar on
a hot wire from headquarters, and be taken off the train.'

" Our party nearly throws a faint when I says ' em-

bezzlement.' It's the first tip he'd had, for I don't think
he's been made wise to so much as a word since he leaves
here. It put the scare into him for fair; he was ready to
do anything I say.

" ' Only,' says he, ' I don't know what money I've got.
And I'm too dippy to find out.'

" With that, I go through him. It's in his trousers
pocket I springs a plant—fifteen hundred dollars, about.

" ' Here's dough enough and over,' says I; and in six
hours after, he's aboard ship.

" She don't get her lines off until this morning,
though; but I stays by, for I'm out to see him safe beyond the Hook."

" What more do you know of young Van Flange? " I
asked. " Did you learn anything about his business
habits? "

" From the time you start him with those offices in
Broad Street, our party's business habits are hop and
faro bank. The offices are there; the clerks and the blackboards and the stock tickers and the tape baskets are
there; but our party, more'n to butt in about three times a
week and leave some crazy orders to sell Blackberry Traction, is never there. He's either in Mott Street, and a
Chink cookin' hop for him; or he's in Barclay Street with
those Indians, and they handin' him out every sort of
brace from an ' end-squeeze ' or a ' balance-top,' where
they give him two cards at a clatter, to a ' snake ' box,

where they kindly lets him deal, but do him just the same. Our party lose over a half-million in that Barclay Street deadfall during the past year."

" I must, then," said I, and I felt the irony of it, " have been indirectly contributing to the riches of our friend, the Chief of Police, since you once told me he was a principal owner of the Barclay Street place."

Inspector McCue shrugged his shoulders professionally, and made no response. Then I questioned him as to the charge of embezzlement; for I had not owned the heart to read the story in the press.

" It's that Blackberry push," replied Inspector McCue, " and I don't think it's on the level at that. It looks like the Blackberry president—and, by the way, I've talked with the duffer, and took in all he would tell— made a play to get the drop on our party. And although the trick was put up, I think he landed it. He charges now that our party is a welcher, and gets away with a bunch of bonds—hocked 'em or something like that— which this Blackberry guy gives him to stick in as margins on some deal. As I say, I think it's a put-up job. That Blackberry duck—who is quite a flossy form of stock student and a long shot from a slouch—has some game up his sleeve. He wanted things rigged so's he could put the clamps on our party, and make him do as he says, and pinch him whenever it gets to be a case of must. So he finally gets our party where he can't holler. I makes a move to find out the inside story; but the Black-berry sport is a thought too swift, and he won't fall to my game. I gives it to him dead that he braced our party, and asks him, Why? At that he hands me the frozen face, springs a chest, and says he's insulted.

"But the end of it is this: Our party is now headed for Frisco. When he comes ashore, the cops out there will pick him up and keep a tab on him; we can always touch the wire for his story down to date. Whenever you say the word, I can get a line on him."

"Bring me no tales of him!" I cried. "I would free myself of every memory of the scoundrel!"

That, then, was the story—a story of gambling and opium! It was these that must account for the sallow face, stooped shoulders, hollow eyes, and nights away from home. And the man of Blackberry, from whom Morton and I took millions, had found in the situation his opportunity. He laid his plans and had those mil-lions back. Also, it was I, as it had been others, to now suffer by Barclay Street.

"And now," observed Inspector McCue, his hand on the door, but turning with a look at once inquisitive and wistful—the latter, like the anxious manner of a good dog who asks word to go upon his hunting—"and now, I suppose, you'll be willin' to let me pull that outfit in Barclay Street. I've got 'em dead to rights!" The last hopefully.

" If it be a question," said I, " of where a man shall lose his money, for my own part, I have no preference as to whether he is robbed in Barclay Street or robbed in Wall. We shall let the Barclay Street den alone, if you please. The organization has its alliances. These alliances cannot be disturbed without weakening the organization. I would not make the order when it was prayed for by the mother of young Van Flange, and she died with the prayer on her lips. I shall not make it now when it is I who am the sufferer. It must be Tammany before all; on no slighter terms can Tammany be preserved."

Inspector McCue made no return to this, and went his way in silence. It was a change, however, from that other hour when I had been with him as cold and secret as a vault. He felt the flattery of my present confidence, and it colored him with complacency as he took his leave.

Roundly, it would be two months after the election before Tammany took charge of the town. The eight weeks to intervene I put in over that list of officers to be named by me through the mayor and the various chiefs of the departments. These places—and they were by no means a stinted letter, being well-nigh thirty thousand— must be apportioned among the districts, each leader having his just share.

While I wrought at these details of patronage, setting a man's name to a place, and all with fine nicety of discrimination to prevent jealousies and a thought that this or that one of my wardogs had been wronged, a plan was perfecting itself in my mind. The thought of Blossom was ever uppermost. What should I do to save the remainder of her life in peace? If she were not to be wholly happy, still I would buckler her as far as lay with me against the more aggressive darts of grief. There is such a word as placid, and, though one be fated to dwell with lasting sorrow, one would prefer it as the mark of one's condition to others of tumultuous violence. There lies a choice, and one will make it, even among torments. How could I conquer serenity for Blossom?— how should I go about it to invest what further years were hers with the restful blessings of peace? That was now the problem of my life, and at last I thought it solved.

My decision was made to deal with the town throughout the next régime as with a gold mine. I would work it night and day, sparing neither conscience nor sleep; I would have from it what utmost bulk of treasure I might during the coming administration of the town's affairs. The game lay in my palm; I would think on myself and nothing but myself; justice and right were to be cast aside; the sufferings of others should be no more to me than mine had been to them. I would squeeze the situation like a sponge, and for its last drop. Then laying down my guiding

staff as Chief, I would carry Blossom, and those riches
I had heaped together, to regions, far away and new,
where only the arch of gentle skies should bend above her
days! She should have tranquillity! she should find rest!
That was my plan, my hope; I kept it buried in my
breast, breathed of it to no man, not even the kindly
Morton, and set myself with all of that ferocious industry which was so much the badge of my nature to its
carrying forth.   Four years; and then, with the gold of
a Monte Cristo, I would take Blossom and go seeking that
repose which I believed must surely wait for us somewhere beneath the sun!

While I was engaged about those preliminaries demanded of me if the machine were to begin its four-
years' reign on even terms of comfort, Morton was often
at my shoulder with a point or a suggestion. I was glad
to have him with me; for his advice in a fog of difficulty
such as mine, was what chart and lighthouse are to
mariners.

One afternoon while Morton and I were trying to hit
upon some man of education to take second place and
supplement the ignorance of one whom the equities of
politics appointed to be the head of a rich but difficult
department, the Reverend Bronson came in.

We three—the Reverend Bronson, Morton, and myself—were older now than on days we could remember,
and each showed the sere and yellow of his years.   But

we liked each other well; and, although in no sort similar in either purpose or bent, I think time had made us nearer friends than might have chanced with many who were more alike.

On this occasion, while I engaged myself with lists of names and lists of offices, weighing out the spoils, Morton and the Reverend Bronson debated the last campaign, and what in its conclusion it offered for the future.

"I shall try to be the optimist," said the Reverend Bronson at last, tossing up a brave manner. "Since the dying administration was not so good as I hoped for, I trust the one to be born will not be so bad as I fear. And, as I gather light by experience, I begin to blame officials less and the public more. I suspect how a whole people may play the hypocrite as much as any single man; nor am I sure that, for all its clamors, a New York public really desires those white conditions of purity over which it protests so much."

"Really!" returned Morton, who had furnished ear of double interest to the Reverend Bronson's words, "it is an error, don't y' know, to give any people a rule they don't desire. A government should always match a public. What do you suppose would become of them if one were to suddenly organize a negro tribe of darkest Africa into a republic? Why, under such loose rule as ours, the poor savage beggars would gnaw each other

like dogs—they would, really! It would be as depressing a solecism as a Scotchman among the stained
glasses, the frescoes, and the Madonnas of a Spanish
cathedral; or a Don worshiping within the four bare
walls and roof of a Highland kirk. Whatever New
York may pretend, it will always be found in possession
of that sort of government, whether for virtue or for
vice, whereof it secretly approves." And Morton surveyed the good dominie through that historic eyeglass as
though pleased with what he'd said.

"But is it not humiliating?" asked the Reverend
Bronson. "If what you say be true, does it not make
for your discouragement?"

"No more than does the vulgar fact of dogs and
horses, don't y' know! Really, I take life as it is, and
think only to be amused I remark on men, and upon
their conditions of the moral, the mental, and the
physical!—on the indomitable courage of restoration
as against the ceaseless industry of decay!—on the high
and the low, the good and the bad, the weak and the
strong, the right and the wrong, the top and the bottom,
the past and the future, the white and the black, and all
those other things that are not!—and I laugh at all.
There is but one thing real, one thing true, one thing
important, one thing at which I never laugh!—and that
is the present. But really!" concluded Morton, recur-
ring to affectations which for the moment had been for-

got, " I'm never discouraged, don't y' know! I shall
never permit myself an interest deep enough for that;
it wouldn't be good form. Even those beastly low
standards which obtain, as you say, in New York do not
discourage me. No, I'm never discouraged—really!"

" You do as much as any, by your indifference, to per-
petuate those standards," remarked the Reverend Bronson in a way of mournful severity.

" My dear old chap," returned Morton, growing
sprightly as the other displayed solemnity, " I take, as I
tell you, conditions as I find them, don't y' know! And
wherefore no? It's all nature: it's the hog to its wallow,
the eagle to its crag;—it is, really! Now an eagle in a
mud-wallow, or a hog perching on a crag, would be
deuced bad form! You see that yourself, you must—
'really!" and our philosopher glowered sweetly.

" I shall never know," said the Reverend Bronson,
with a half-laugh, " when to have you seriously. I cannot but wish, however, that the town had better luck about
its City Hall."

" Really, I don't know, don't y' know!" This deep
observation Morton flourished off in a profound muse.
" As I've said, the town will get what's coming to it, because it will always get what it wants. It always has—
really! And speaking of ' reform ' as we employ the
term in politics: The town, in honesty, never desires it;
and that's why somebody must forever attend on ' re-

form ' to keep it from falling on its blundering nose and
knees by holding it up by the tail.   There are people
who'll take anything you give them, even though it be a
coat of tar and feathers, and thank you for it, too,—the
grateful beggars!   New York resembles these.   Some
chap comes along, and offers New York ' reform.'   Being
without ' reform ' at the time, and made suddenly and
sorrowfully mindful of its condition, it accepts the gift
just as a drunkard takes a pledge.   Like the drunkard,
however, New York is apt to return to its old ways—it
is, really ! "

"One thing," said the Reverend Bronson as he arose
to go, and laying his hand on my shoulder, "since the
Boss of Tammany, in a day of the machine, is the whole
government and the source of it, I mean to come here
often and work upon our friend in favor of a clean
town."

"And you will be welcome, Doctor, let me say ! " I
returned.

"Now I think," said Morton meditatively, when the
Reverend Bronson had departed, "precisely as I told
our excellent friend.   A rule should ever fit a people;
and it ever does.   A king is as naturally the blossom of the peasantry he grows on as is a sunflower
natural to that coarse stem that supports its royal nod-
dings, don't y' know.   A tyranny, a despotism, a mon-
archy, or a republic is ever that flower of government

natural to the public upon which it grows. Really!—
Why not? Wherein lurks the injustice or the incon-
sistency of such a theory? What good is there to lie
hidden in a misfit? Should Providence waste a
man's government on a community of dogs? A dog public should have dog government:—a kick and a kennel,
a chain to clank and a bone to gnaw!"

With this last fragment of wisdom, the cynical Morton went also his way, leaving me alone to chop up the
town—as a hunter chops up the carcass of a deer among
his hounds—into steak and collop to feed my hungry
followers.

However much politics might engage me, I still possessed those hundred eyes of Argus wherewith to watch
my girl. When again about me she had no word for
what was past. And on my side, never once did I put
to her the name of young Van Flange. He was as much
unmentioned by us as though he had not been. I think
that this was the wiser course. What might either Blossom or I have said to mend our shattered hopes?

Still, I went not without some favor of events. There
came a support to my courage; the more welcome, since
the latter was often at its ebb. It was a strangest thing
at that! While Blossom moved with leaden step, and
would have impressed herself upon one as weak and wanting sparkle, she none the less began to gather the color
of health. Her cheeks, before of the pallor of snow,

wore a flush like the promise of life. Her face gained rounder fullness, while her eyes opened upon one with a kind of wide brilliancy, that gave a look of gayety. It was like a blessing! Nor could I forbear, as I witnessed it, the dream of a better strength for my girl than it had been her luck to know; and that thought would set me to my task of money-getting with ever a quicker ardor.

Still, as I've said, there was the side to baffle. For all those roses and eyes like stars, Blossom's breath was broken and short, and a little trip upstairs or down exhausted her to the verge of pain. To mend her breathing after one of these small household expeditions, she must find a chair, or even lie on a couch. All this in its turn would have set my fears to a runaway if it had not been for that fine glow in her cheeks to each time restore me to my faith.

When I put the question born of my uneasiness, Blossom declared herself quite well, nor would she give me any sicklier word. In the end my fears would go back to their slumbers, and I again bend myself wholly to that task of gold.

Good or bad, to do this was when all was said the part of complete wisdom. There could be nothing now save my plan of millions and a final pilgrimage in quest of peace. That was our single chance; and at it, in a kind of savage silence, night and day I stormed as though warring with walls and battlements.

CHAPTER XXVII

GOLD CAME, AND DEATH STEPPED IN

NOW, when I went about refurnishing my steel box with new millions, I turned cautious as a fox. I considered concealment, and would hide my trail and walk in all the running water that I might. For one matter, I was sick and sore with the attacks made upon me by the papers, which grew in malignant violence as the days wore on, and as though it were a point of rivalry between them which should have the black honor of hating me the most. I preferred to court those type-cudgelings as little as stood possible, and still bring me to my ends.

The better to cover myself, and because the mere work of it would be too weary a charge for one head and that head ignorant of figures, I called into my service a cunning trio who were, one and all, born children of the machine. These three owned thorough training as husbandmen of politics, and were ones to mow even the fence corners. That profit of the game which escaped them must indeed be sly, and lie deep and close besides. Also, they were of the invaluable brood that has no tongue, and any one of the triangle would have been broken upon the wheel without a syllable of confession disgracing his lips.

These inveterate ones, who would be now as my hand in gathering together that wealth which I anticipated, were known in circles wherein they moved and had their dingy being, as Sing Sing Jacob, Puffy the Merchant, and Paddy the Priest. Paddy the Priest wore a look of sanctity, and it was this impression of holiness to confer upon him his title. It might have been more consistent with those virtues of rapine dominant of his nature, had he been hailed Paddy the Pirate, instead. Of Sing Sing Jacob, I should say, that he had not served in prison. His name was given him because, while he was never granted the privilege of stripes and irons, he often earned the same. In what manner or at what font Puffy the Merchant received baptism, I never learned. That he came fit for my purpose would find sufficient indication in a complaining compliment which Paddy the Priest once paid him, and who said in description of Puffy's devious genius, that if one were to drive a nail through his head it would come forth a corkscrew.

These men were to be my personal lieutenants, and collect my gold for me. And since they would pillage me with as scanty a scruple as though I were the foe himself, I must hit upon a device for invoking them to honesty in my affairs. It was then I remembered the parting words

of Big Kennedy.   I would set one against the others;
hating each other, they would watch; and each would be
sharp with warning in my ear should either of his fellows
seek to fill a purse at my expense.

To sow discord among my three offered no difficulties;
I had but to say to one what the others told of him, and
his ire was on permanent end.   It was thus I separated
them; and since I gave each his special domain of effort,
while they worked near enough to one another to maintain
a watch, they were not so thrown together as to bring
down among them open war.

It will be required that I set forth in half-detail those
various municipal fields and meadows that I laid out in
my time, and from which the machine was to garner its
harvest.   You will note then, you who are innocent of
politics in its practical expressions and rewards, how the
town stood to me as does his plowlands to a farmer, and
offered as various a list of crops to careful tillage.   Take
for example the knee-deep clover of the tax department.
Each year there was made a whole valuation of personal
property of say roundly nine billions of dollars.   This
etsimate, within a dozen weeks of its making, would be
reduced to fewer than one billion, on the word of individuals who made the law-required oaths.   No, it need
not have been so reduced; but the reduction ever occurred
since the machine instructed its tax officers to act on the
oath so furnished, and that without question.

That personage in tax peril was never put to fret in obtaining one to make the oath. If he himself lacked hardihood and hesitated at perjury, why then, the town abounded in folk of a daring easy veracity. Of all that was said and written, of that time, in any New York day, full ninety-five per cent. was falsehood or mistake. Among the members of a community, so affluent of error and mendacity, one would not long go seeking a witness who was ready, for shining reasons, to take whatever oath might be demanded. And thus it befell that the affidavits were ever made, and a reduction of eight billions and more, in the assessed valuation of personal property, came annually to be awarded. With a tax levy of, say, two per cent. I leave you to fix the total of those millions saved to ones assessed, and also to consider how far their gratitude might be expected to inure to the yellow welfare of the machine—the machine that makes no gift of either its forbearance or its help!

Speaking in particular of the town, and what opportunities of riches swung open to the machine, one should know at the start how the whole annual expense of the community was roughly one hundred and twenty-five millions. Of these millions twenty went for salaries to officials; forty were devoted to the purchase of supplies asked for by the public needs; while the balance, sixty-five millions, represented contracts for paving and building and similar construction whatnot, which the town was bound to execute in its affairs.

Against those twenty millions of salaries, the machine levied an annual private five per cent. Two-thirds of the million to arise therefrom, found their direct way to district leaders; the other one-third was paid into the general coffer. Also there were county officers, such as judges, clerks of court, a sheriff and his deputies: and these, likewise, were compelled from their incomes to a yearly generosity of not fewer than five per cent.

Of those forty millions which were the measure for supplies, one-fifth under the guise of " commissions " went to the machine; while of the sixty-five millions, which represented the yearly contracts in payments made thereon, the machine came better off with, at the leanest of estimates, full forty per cent. of the whole.

Now I have set forth to you those direct returns which arose from the sure and fixed expenses of the town. Beyond that, and pushing for the furthest ounce of tallow, I inaugurated a novelty. I organized a guaranty company which made what bonds the law demanded from officials; and from men with contracts, and those others who furnished the town's supplies. The annual charge of the company for this act of warranty was two per cent. on the sum guaranteed; and since the aggregate thus carried came to about one hundred millions, the intake from such sources—being for the most part profit in the fingers of the machine—was annually a fair two millions. There were other rills to flow a revenue, and which were related to those money well-springs registered above, but they count too many and too small for mention here, albeit the round returns from them might make a poor man stare.

Of those other bottom-lands of profit which bent a nodding harvest to the sickle of the machine, let me make a rough enumeration. The returns—a bit sordid, these!—from poolrooms, faro banks and disorderly resorts and whereon the monthly charge imposed for each ran all the way from fifty to two thousand dollars, clinked into the yearly till, four millions. The grog shops, whereof at that time there was a staggering host of such in New York City of-the-many-sins! met each a draft of twenty monthly dollars. Then one should count " campaign contributions." Of great companies who sued for favor there were, at a lowest census, five who sent as tribute from twenty to fifty thousand dollars each. Also there existed of smaller concerns and private persons, full one thousand who yielded over all a no less sum than one million. Next came the police, with appointment charges which began with a patrolman at four hundred dollars, and soared to twenty thousand when the matter was the making of a captain.

Here I shall close my recapitulation of former treasure for the machine; I am driven to warn you, however, that

the half has not been told.   Still, if you will but let your
imagination have its head, remembering how the machine
gives nothing away, and fails not to exert its pressures
with every chance afforded it, you may supply what
other chapters belong with the great history of graft.

When one considers a Tammany profit, one will per-
force be driven to the question: What be the expenses of
the machine?   The common cost of an election should
pause in the neighborhood of three hundred thousand
dollars.   Should peril crowd, and an imported vote be
called for by the dangers of the day, the cost might carry
vastly higher.   No campaign, however, in the very nature of the enterprise and its possibilities of expense, can
consume a greater fund than eight hundred thousand.
That sum, subtracted from the income of the machine as
taken from those sundry sources I've related, will show
what in my time remained for distribution among my
followers.

And now that brings one abreast the subject of
riches to the Boss himself.   One of the world's
humorists puts into the mouth of a character the
query: What does a king get?   The answer would be
no whit less difficult had he asked: What does a Boss
get?   One may take it, however, that the latter gets
the lion's share.   Long ago I said that the wealth of
Ophir hung on the hazard of the town's election.   You
have now some slant as to how far my words should be

regarded as hyperbole. Nor must I omit how the machine's delegation in a legislature, or the little flock it
sends to nibble on the slopes of Congress, is each in the
hand of the Boss to do with as he will, and it may go
without a record that the opportunities so provided are
neither neglected nor underpriced.

There you have the money story of Tammany
in the bowels of the town. Those easy-chair econ-
omists who, over their morning coffee and waffles,
engage themselves for purity, will at this point
give honest rage the rein. Had I no sense of public duty? Was the last spark of any honesty burned
out within my bosom?   Was nothing left but dead
embers to be a conscience to me? The Reverend Bronson—and I had a deep respect for that gentleman—put
those questions in his time.

"Bear in mind," said he when, after that last election,
I again had the town in my grasp, "bear in mind the
welfare and the wishes of the public, and use your power
consistently therewith."

"Now, why?" said I. "The public of which you tell
me lies in two pieces, the minority and the majority. It is
to the latter's welfare—the good of the machine—I shall
address myself. Be sure, my acts will gain the plaudits
of my own people, while I have only to go the road you
speak of to be made the target of their anger. As to
the minority—those who have vilified me, and who still

would crush me if they but had the strength—why, then, as Morton says, I owe them no more than William owed the Saxons when after Hastings he had them under his feet."

When the new administration was in easy swing, and I had time to look about me, I bethought me of Blackberry and those three millions taken from the weakness and the wickedness of young Van Flange. I would have those millions back or know the secret of it.

With a nod here and a hand-toss there—for the shrug of my shoulders or the lift of my brows had grown to have a definition among my people—I brewed tempests for Blackberry. The park department discovered it in a trespass; the health board gave it notice of the non-sanitary condition of its cars; the street commissioner badgered it with processes because of violations of laws and ordinances; the coroner, who commonly wore a gag, gave daily news of what folk were killed or maimed through the wantonness of Blackberry; while my corporation counsel bestirred himself as to whether or no, for this neglect or that invasion of public right, the Blackberry charter might not be revoked.

In the face of these, the president of Blackberry—he of the Hebrew cast and clutch—stood sullenly to his guns. He would not yield; he would not pay the price of peace; he would not return those millions, although he knew well the argument which was the ground-work of his griefs.

The storm I unchained beat sorely, but he made no white-flag signs. I admired his fortitude, while I multiplied my war.

It was Morton who pointed to that final feather which broke the camel's back.

" Really, old chap," observed Morton, that immortal eyeglass on nose and languid hands outspread, " really, you haven't played your trumps, don't y' know."

" What then? " cried I, for my heart was growing hot.

" You recall my saying to our friend Bronson that, when I had a chap against me whom I couldn't buy, I felt about to discover his fad or his fear—I was speaking about changing a beggar's name, and all that, don't y' know? "

" Yes," said I, " it all comes back."

" Exactly," continued Morton. " Now the fear that keeps a street-railway company awake nights is its fear of a strike. There, my dear boy, you have your weapon. Convey the information to those Black-berry employees, that you think they get too little money and work too long a day. Let them understand how, should they strike, your police will not repress them in any crimes they see fit to commit. Really, I think I've hit upon a splendid idea! Those hirelings will go upon the warpath, don't y' know! And a strike is such a beastly thing!—such a deuced bore! It is, really! "

Within the fortnight every Blackberry wheel was stopped, and every employee rioting in the streets. Cars were sacked; what men offered for work were harried, and made to fly for very skins and bones. Meanwhile, the police stood afar off with virgin batons, innocent of interference.

Four days of this, and those four millions were paid into my hand; the Blackberry president had yielded, and my triumph was complete. With that, my constabulary remembered law and order, and, descending upon the turbulent, calmed them with their clubs. The strike ended; again were the gongs of an unharassed Blackberry heard in the land.

And now I draw near the sorrowful, desperate end— the end at once of my labors and my latest hope. I had held the town since the last battle for well-nigh three and one-half years. Throughout this space affairs political preserved themselves as rippleless as a looking-glass, and nothing to ruffle with an adverse wind. Those henchmen—my boys of the belt, as it were—Sing Sing Jacob, Puffy the Merchant, and Paddy the Priest, went working like good retrievers at their task of bringing daily money to my feet.

Nor was I compelled to appear as one interested in the profits of the town's farming, and this of itself was comfort, since it served to keep me aloof from any mire of those methods that were employed.

It is wonderful how a vile source for a dollar will in no wise daunt a man, so that he be not made to pick it from the direct mud himself. If but one hand intervene between his own and that gutter which gave it up, both his conscience and his sensibilities are satisfied to receive it. Of all sophists, self-interest is the sophist surest of disciples; it will carry conviction triumphant against what fact or what deduction may come to stand in the way, and, with the last of it, " The smell of all money is sweet."

But while it was isles of spice and summer seas with my politics, matters at home went ever darker with increasing threat. Blossom became weaker and still more weak, and wholly from a difficulty in her breathing. If she were to have had but her breath, her health would have been fair enough; and that I say by word of the physician who was there to attend her, and who was a gray deacon of his guild.

" It is her breathing," said he; " otherwise her health is good for any call she might make upon it."

It was the more strange to one looking on; for all this time while Blossom was made to creep from one room to another, and, for the most part, to lie panting upon a couch, her cheeks were round and red as peaches, and her eyes grew in size and brightness like stars when the night is dark.

" Would you have her sent away? " I asked of the

physician. " Say but the place; I will take her there myself."

" She is as well here," said he. Then, as his brows knotted with the problem of it: " This is an unusual case; so unusual, indeed, that during forty years of practice I have never known its fellow. However, it is no question of climate, and she will be as well where she is. The better; since she has no breath with which to stand a journey."

While I said nothing to this, I made up my mind to have done with politics and take Blossom away. It would, at the worst, mean escape from scenes where we had met with so much misery. That my present rule of the town owned still six months of life before another battle, did not move me. I would give up my leadership and retire at once. It would lose me half a year of gold-heaping, but what should that concern? What mattered a handful of riches, more or less, as against the shoreless relief of seclusion, and Blossom in new scenes of quiet peace? The very newness would take up her thoughts; and with nothing about to recall what had been, or to whisper the name of that villain who hurt her heart to the death, she might have even the good fortune to forget. My decision was made, and I went quietly forward to bring my politics to a close.

It became no question of weeks nor even days; I convened my district leaders, and with the few words de-

manded of the time, returned them my chiefship and
stepped down and out. Politics and I had parted; the
machine and I were done.

At that, I cannot think I saw regret over my going
in any of the faces which stared up at me. There was a
formal sorrow of words; but the great expression to
to seize upon each was that of selfish eagerness. I, with
my lion's share of whatever prey was taken, would be no
more; it was the thought of each that with such the free
condition he would be like to find some special fatness not
before his own.

Well! what else should I have looked for?—I, who had
done only justice by them, why should I be loved?   Let
them exult; they have subserved my purpose and fulfilled
my turn.   I was retiring with the wealth of kings:—I,
who am an ignorant man, and the son of an Irish smith!
If my money had been put into gold it would have asked
the strength of eighty teams, with a full ton of gold to a
team, to have hauled it out of town—a solid procession
of riches an easy half-mile in length! No Alexander,
no Cæsar, no Napoleon in his swelling day of conquest,
could have made the boast! I was master of every saf-
fron inch of forty millions!

That evening I sat by Blossom's couch and told her of
my plans. I made but the poor picture of it, for I have
meager power of words, and am fettered with an imagination of no wings. Still, she smiled up at me as though

with pleasure—for her want of breath was so urgent she could not speak aloud, but only whisper a syllable now and then—and, after a while, I kissed her, and left her with the physician and nurse for the night.

It was during the first hours of the morning when I awoke in a sweat of horror, as if something of masterful menace were in the room. With a chill in my blood like the touch of ice, I thought of Blossom; and with that I began to huddle on my clothes to go to her.

The physician met me at Blossom's door. He held me back with a gentle hand on my breast.

" Don't go in!" he said.

That hand, light as a woman's, withstood me like a wall. I drew back and sought a chair in the library—a chair of Blossom's, it was—and sat glooming into the darkness in a wonder of fear.

What wits I possess have broad feet, and are not easily to be staggered. That night, however, they swayed and rocked like drunken men, under the pressure of some evil apprehension of I knew not what. I suppose now I feared death for Blossom, and that my thoughts lacked courage to look the surmise in the face.

An hour went by, and I still in the darkened room. I wanted no lights. It was as though I were a fugitive, and sought in the simple darkness a refuge and a place wherein to hide myself. Death was in the house, robbing me of all I loved; I knew that, and yet I felt no stab of agony, but instead a fashion of dumb numbness like a paralysis.

In a vague way, this lack of sharp sensation worked upon my amazement. I remember that, in explanation of it, I recalled one of Morton's tales about a traveler whom a lion seized as he sat at his campfire; and how, while the lion crunched him in his jaws and dragged him to a distance, he still had no feel of pain, but—as I had then—only a numbness and fog of nerves.

While this went running in my head, I heard the rattle of someone at the street door, and was aware, I don't know how, that another physician had come. A moment later my ear overtook whisperings in the hall just beyond my own door.

Moved of an instinct that might have prompted some threatened animal to spy out what danger overhung him, I went, cat-foot, to the door and listened. It was the two physicians in talk.

"The girl is dead," I heard one say.

"What malady?" asked the other.

"And there's the marvel of it!" cries the first. "No malady at all, as I'm a doctor! She died of suffocation. The case is without a parallel. Indubitably, it was that birthmark—that mark as of a rope upon her neck. Like the grip of destiny itself, the mark has been growing and tightening about her throat since ever she lay in her cradle, until now she dies of it. A most remarkable case!"

It is precisely as though she were hanged—the congested eye, the discolored face, the swollen tongue, aye! and about her throat, the very mark of the rope!"

Blossom dead! my girl dead! Apple Cheek, Anne, Blossom, all gone, and I to be left alone! Alone! The word echoed in the hollows of my empty heart as in a cavern! There came a blur, and then a fearful whirling; that gorilla strength was as the strength of children; my slow knees began to cripple down! That was the last I can recall; I fell as if struck by a giant's mallet, and all was black.

CHAPTER XXVIII

BEING THE EPILOGUE

WHAT should there be more? My house stands upon a hill; waving, sighing trees are ranked about it, while to the eastward I have the shimmering stretches of the river beneath my feet. From a wooden seat between two beeches, I may see the fog-loom born of the dust and smoke of the city far away. At night, when clouds lie thick and low, the red reflection of the city's million lamps breaks on the sky as though a fire raged.

It is upon my seat between the beeches that I spend my days. Men would call my life a stagnant one; I care not, since I find it peace. I have neither hopes nor fears nor pains nor joys; there come no exaltations, no depressions; within me is a serenity—a kind of silence like the heart of nature.

At that I have no dimness; I roll and rock for hours on the dead swells of old days, while old faces and old scenes toss to and fro like seaweed with the tides of my memory. I am prey to no regrets, to no ambitions; my times own neither currents nor winds; I have outlived importance and the liking for it; and all those little noises that keep the world awake, I never hear.

My Sicilian, with his earrings and his crimson head-wear of silk, is with me; for he could not have lived had I left him in town, being no more able to help himself than a ship ashore. Here he is busy and happy over nothing. He has whittled for himself a trio of little boats, and he sails them on the pond at the lawn's foot. One of these he has named the Democrat, while the others are the Republican and the Mugwump. He sails them against each other; and I think that by some marine sleight he gives the Democrat the best of it, since it ever wins, which is not true of politics. My Sicilian has just limped up the hill with a story of how, in the last race, the Republican and the Mugwump ran into one another and capsized, while the Democrat finished bravely.

Save for my Sicilian, and a flock of sable ravens that by their tameness and a confident self-sufficiency have made themselves part of the household, I pass the day between my beeches undisturbed. The ravens are grown so proud with safety that, when I am walking, they often hold the path against me, picking about for the grains my Sicilian scatters, keeping upon me the while a truculent eye that is half cautious, half defiant. In the spring I watch these ravens throughout their nest-building, they living for the most part in the trees about my house. I've known them to be baffled during a whole two days, when winds were blowing and the swaying of the branches prevented their labors.

Now and then I have a visit from Morton and the Reverend Bronson. The pair are as they were, only more age-worn and of a grayer lock. They were with me the other day; Morton as faultless of garb as ever, and with eyeglass as much employed, the Reverend Bronson as anxious as in the old time for the betterment of humanity. The spirit of unselfishness never flags in that good man's breast, although Morton is in constant bicker with him concerning the futility of his work.

" The fault isn't in you, old chap," said Morton, when last they were with me; " it isn't, really. But humanity in the mass is such a beastly dullard, don't y' know, that to do anything in its favor is casting pearls before swine."

" Why, then," responded the Reverend Bronson with a smile, " if I were you, I should help mankind for the good it gave me, without once thinking on the object of my generosity."

" But," returned Morton, " I take no personal joy from helping people. Gad! it wearies me. Man is such a perverse beggar; he's ever wrong end to in his affairs. The entire race is like a horse turned round in its stall, and with its tail in the fodder stands shouting for hay. If men, in what you call their troubles, would but face the other way about, nine times in ten they'd be all right.   They wouldn't need help— really ! "

" And if what you say be true," observed the Reverend Bronson, who was as fond of argument as was Morton, " then you have outlined your duty.   You say folk are turned wrong in their affairs.   Then you should help them to turn right."

" Really now," said Morton, imitating concern, " I wouldn't for the world have such sentiments escape to the ears of my club, don't y' know, for it's beastly bad form to even entertain them, but I lay the trouble you seek to relieve, old chap, to that humbug we call civilization; I do, 'pon my word ! "

" Do you cry out against civilization? "

" Gad ! why not?   I say it is an artifice, a mere deceit. Take ourselves : what has it done for any of us?   Here is our friend "—Morton dropped his hand upon my shoulder—" who, taking advantage of what was offered of our civilization, came to be so far victorious as to have the town for his kickball.   He was a dictator; his word was law among three millions—really !   To-day he has riches, and could pave his grounds with gold.   He was these things, and had these things, from the hand of civilization; and now, at the end, he sits in the center of sadness waiting for death.   Consider my own case : I, too, at the close of my juice-drained days, am waiting for death; only, unlike our friend, I play the cynic and while I wait I laugh."

" I was never much to laugh," I interjected.

" The more strange, too, don't y' know," continued Morton, " since you are aware of life and the mockery of it, as much as I.   I may take it that I came crying into this world, for such I understand to be the beastly practice of the human young.   Had I understood the empty jest of it, I should have laughed; I should, really! "

" Now with what do you charge civilization? " asked the Reverend Bronson.

" It has made me rich, and I complain of that.   The load of my millions begins to bend my back.   A decent, wholesome savagery would have presented no such burdens."

" And do you uplift savagery? "

" I don't wonder you're shocked, old chap, for from our civilized standpoint savagery is such deuced bad form.   But you should consider; you should, really! Gad! you know that civilized city where we dwell; you know its civilized millions, fretting like maggots, as many as four thousand in a block; you know the good and the evil ground of those civilized mills!   Wherein lieth a triumph over the red savage who abode upon the spot three centuries ago?   Who has liberty as had that savage?   He owned laws and respected them; he had his tribe, and was a patriot fit to talk with William Tell.

He fought his foe like a Richard of England, and loved his friend like a Jonathan. He paid neither homage to power nor taxes to men, and his privileges were as wide as the world's rim. His franchises of fagot, vert, and venison had never a limit; he might kill a deer a day and burn a cord of wood to its cookery. As for his religion: the test of religion is death; and your savage met death with a fortitude, and what is fortitude but faith, which it would bother Christians to parallel. It may be said that he lived a happier life, saw more of freedom, and was more his own man, than any you are to meet in Broadway."

Morton, beneath his fluff of cynicism, was a deal in earnest. The Reverend Bronson took advantage of it to say:

"Here, as you tell us, are we three, and all at the end of the journey. Here is that one who strove for power: here is that one who strove for wealth; here is that one who strove to help his fellow man. I give you the question: Brushing civilization and savagery aside as just no more than terms to mark some shadowy difference, I ask you: Who of the three lives most content?—for it is he who was right."

"By the way!" said Morton, turning to me, as they were about to depart, and producing a scrap of newspaper, "this is what a scientist writes concerning you. The beggar must have paid you a call, don't y' know.

At first, I thought it a beastly rude thing to put in print; but, gad! the more I dwell upon it, the more honorable it becomes. This is what he says of you:

" ' There was a look in his eye such as might burn in the eye of an old wolf that has crept away in solitude to die. As I gazed, there swept down upon me an astounding conviction. I felt that I was in the presence of the oldest thing in the world—a thing more ancient than the Sphinx or aged pyramids. This once Boss, silent and passive and white and old, and waiting for the digging of his grave, is what breeders call a " throw-back "—a throw-back, not of the generations, but of the ages. In what should arm him for a war of life against life, he is a creature of utter cunning, utter courage, utter strength. He is a troglodyte; he is that original one who lived with the cave bear, the mastodon, the saber-toothed tiger, and the Irish elk.' "

They went away, the Reverend Bronson and Morton, leaving me alone on my bench between the beeeches, while the black ravens picked and strutted about my feet, and my Sicilian on the lake at the lawn's foot matching his little ships for another race.

THE END